THE
FOXES
OF
FIRSTDARK

GARRY KILWORTH

DOUBLEDAY   New York • London • Toronto • Sydney • Auckland

THE
FOXES
OF
FIRSTDARK

PUBLISHED BY DOUBLEDAY
a division of Bantam Doubleday Dell Publishing Group, Inc.
666 Fifth Avenue, New York, New York 10103

DOUBLEDAY and the portrayal of an anchor with a dolphin
are trademarks of Doubleday,
a division of Bantam Doubleday Dell Publishing Group, Inc.

Library of Congress Cataloging-in-Publication Data

Kilworth, Garry.
    The foxes of Firstdark / by Garry Kilworth.—1st ed.
        p.   cm.
    1. Foxes—Fiction.   I. Title.
PR6061.I39F69   1990
823′.914—dc20   89-17129
                                                CIP

ISBN 0-385-26427-5

TO SANDY AND ANDREA

ACKNOWLEDGMENTS

My thanks to Peter A. Gerrard's *Nature Through the Seasons* (Midas Books), Stephen Harris's *Urban Foxes* (Whittet Books), Brian Vesey-Fitzgerald's *Town Fox, Country Fox* (Andre Deutsch Ltd.); and finally and most especially to David Macdonald for his inspirational work *Running with the Fox* (Unwin Hyman Ltd.). Any deviation from normal fox behavior in this novel is the result of creative license taken by me, and not the fault of the nonfictional works acknowledged here.

Author's Note: Fox "language" involves sounds, movements, gestures, poises, scents, and probably other aspects not in this list; but for the purposes of this novel, fox language is English (except for a few words which have special meaning only to foxes). Other human languages are used for the various groups of creatures found between these pages, merely in order to differentiate between species. Words specific to foxes, such as *gerflan* (land forbidden to most humans, e.g., railway embankments), are apparent in the text; but the following names of the main winds may be useful to the reader at the outset:

Ransheen:	Winter winds
Scresheen:	March winds
Switter:	Spring breezes
Frashoon:	Summer winds
Melloon:	Autumn winds

CONTENTS

PART ONE

THE
FOXES
OF
FIRSTDARK

Through the jungle very softly flits
   a shadow and a sigh—
He is Fear, O Little Hunter, he is
   Fear!

—From "The Song of the Little Hunter," by
   RUDYARD KIPLING

ONE

Trinity Wood stood on a rise above a tidal river which wound its way over coastal flatlands. Its fox-spirits could tell you that it was an ancient knoll, its rocky ground untouched by the farmers who had closed around it since wolves had roamed the area. It was a dense place, grown to weakness in its center where spindly oaks and blackthorns fought each other for light and space. Moving outward, away from its heart, there were small glades that encouraged bluebells and ferns, ground ivy and tussocks of grass, and the occasional solitary cuckoo pint. Among its inhabitants were wood pigeons, badgers, grey squirrels, and foxes.

O-ha had not been born there, but had moved there shortly after the dispersal period, when cubs leave their parents.

O-ha had found an old earth in the clay bank just inside the tree line. She had freshened it a little by scraping out the tunnel and chamber, but like most foxes she was not fussy about the state of her home. The main priorities were that it remained warm and dry. It was simply a place of safety where a fox could sleep, hopefully without disturbance. Although she liked simple clean lines and might admire the earth for this reason, she was an untidy creature and any housecleaning consisted of tossing rubbish just outside the entrance. Even that chore was done with an impatient sigh, as if she were wasting her time with trivial unimportant matters while the world awaited great things from her. She was not unusual in these traits. Though personal cleanliness is important to foxes, the idea that one should spend time keeping the home tidy is dismissed with contempt.

The entrance to the earth was almond-shaped and around its roof arch was the strong protective root of a benign-looking oak tree. The oak had one of those sturdy squat trunks that brought its lowest branches close to the ground. On days when even the slightest breeze was blowing, the movement of the shadows from these boughs produced a camouflage effect which helped to disguise the earth's entrance. This, coupled with the way the exposed root twisted over and around the hole, giving it an overhang, meant that any unknowing observer would have to be at eye level with the opening to realize that there was a hole there at all. The tangle of roots breaking the surface all around the matronly oak would serve even further to confuse any enemy out searching for the homes of foxes.

To the other side of the earth's entrance, beyond the star mosses that formed a padded area running eastward, was an alder that dripped bright berries in the autumn. The cool forbidding shade of the oak kept this lesser tree, with its arthritic limbs, from encroaching on a space where it was unwelcome. Nailed to its trunk, however, was the remnant of a barbed wire fence, which O-ha found to be a very effective back scratcher in the warm weather when her fleas became too active.

Since O-ha was an intelligent-looking vixen, with a glossy coat that varied between rust-red and grey, depending on the light, she had been courted by at least three dog foxes. She chose a male her own age, a fox with humor in his eyes and a way of cocking his head to one side that turned her legs to willow wands.

"I admire you above all other vixens," A-ran told her. "You're bright, alert and . . . oh, dozens of other things. It would take too long to tell you all the reasons why you make me dizzy with excitement every time I see you."

When she gave him her decision, they were knee-deep in autumn leaves, and he showered her with them in his joy. The sky was alive that day with rushing clouds that swept shadows across the land and produced an ethereal half-light full of ever-changing shades. They went out onto the windblown grasslands under this strange sky. There, they seemed isolated. His eyes danced with wild unusual pigments, reflecting the strange radiance that surrounded them.

She gave herself a dozen practical reasons why he was the best mate for her, dismissing his claim that she was a romantic. In the warm damp grass, they tumbled and nipped each other, finding excitement in touching even though it was not a time for serious mating. They learned the intimate details of each other's bodies—the scratchscars on O-ha's nose, the small V that had been clipped from A-ran's right ear, both the result of hunting play with siblings. She thought the small white patch on his flank unusually attractive, and he remarked on the sleekness of her muzzlehair. They found other things upon which to comment, almost always favorably.

A-ran changed his name to A-ho to reflect her family name as was traditional among foxes. It was a heady time for both of them. They were young enough for the most ordinary experiences to be great new discoveries. Their parents, they told each other, were all right in their way, but somehow lacked the clear thinking and reasoned judgement that they themselves possessed.

"I suppose they were quite well thought of in their day," said A-ho, generously, "but that was ages ago. The world's quite a different place from what it was half a dozen seasons ago. The hunting issue, for example . . ."

And O-ha would lie beside him in their earth, adding her observed opinions as if they were the only ones an intelligent fox could possibly contemplate. Occasionally, in the darkness, she would lick his nose, or he would rest his head against her slim shoulder. They were entirely comfortable in each other's company, to the exclusion of the rest of the world.

"Do you love the smell of pine needles?" she might say.

"Pine needles? Wonderful aroma. I'd go out of my way to get a good whiff of pine needles—and sap."

"Oh yes, the sap too . . ."

And they would both marvel at their compatibility, how they both liked the same things, disliked the same things, how startlingly lucky it was that they had each found someone who liked the scent of pine needles, ". . . *especially* in springtime."

"Undoubtedly *the* most effective time for sniffing pines."

Were there ever two foxes more suited to each other in the whole history of the world? Was there ever a pair whose opinions on life matched each other's so sharply, so precisely? Was there ever a more intelligent vixen, or a wiser dog fox, given that they were still quite young and willing to learn? Never, they agreed.

"Of course," said A-ho, "I would not be so immodest as to say such things to anyone else but you."

"Oh no," agreed O-ha, "these observations are for our ears only."

That autumn was a magical time for the two new mates. There were golden scents to the air and hunting was good. They lived almost constantly in each other's company, though when the colder weather came and Ransheen cut through the grasses, it was necessary for one or the other of them to go out alone sometimes.

It was midwinter and the air was still, clean, and sharp.

A-ho had been keeping close to her side for many days and his rising excitement was indicated by the way he carried his tail: high, like a bushy pennant. O-ha was keenly aware of her mate and was sometimes irritated by him as he persistently brushed against her, leaving her hardly enough room in the earth to move a paw. His

bright eyes never left her, and though he might be the handsomest dog fox in the known world she felt she could not draw a breath without A-ho being there to watch and assist her. She felt that the atmosphere was claustrophobic and tense. She too was aware of a stirring of excitement in her body, but there were limits to her patience; and once, before she was anywhere near ready for him, he had even tried to mount her and she had had to snap at his flank, making him back away in disappointment.

However, today her body felt warm and sweet, and she was aware that she was putting out a fragrance that turned the brightness in his eyes to a hot fire. She waited as he shadowed her every move, his body language full of curves, soft displays.

Suddenly she rose to her feet and went to the exit leading from the earth; she licked her nose, went through the rituals to test the wind for danger, then slipped outside. As always there were a thousand scents vying for her attention, which her brain filtered automatically, so that the important ones received priority. A thousand scents, most of which were too subtle or too weak for a human to detect.

Although it was cold, the sun shone down with winter hardness through the trees of Trinity Wood. O-ha found a patch of grass and stood there, letting the weak rays warm her fur. A-ho was right behind her.

After a few moments he came up beside her and touched her flank with his forepaw. She could feel him trembling and an electric shiver went through her body. A-ho nuzzled her, under her chin. She could feel his hot breath on her throat and his tongue wiped a swath through her soft fur. She made a sound in the back of her mouth.

He was rubbing against her now, licking and nuzzling, running his paws over her back. She liked it. She closed her eyes and enjoyed the rippling sensation that traveled through her limbs and torso. That was nice. He was nice. Opening her eyes again, she looked at him. He was strong, proud, and magnificent. His fur was fluffed and clean, his dark ears erect. His firm jaw was the most handsome thing about him. No other vixen had a dog fox like hers, such a wonderful mate. She nipped him sharply, to demonstrate her affection. How

lucky she was to be the center of his attention. It was obvious to her that the whole world might collapse at that moment, and A-ho would not notice. He could see only her and he blazed like a high fire on the grass; warming her with the red flames of his coat, he was ready to burn deep inside her body.

Suddenly he was behind her, and the skies turned crimson and the grass began to crackle beneath her. She let out a short yelp: he crooned, once, and after a few seconds it was over, but it felt good and sweet and there was a taste in her mouth like windfalls coated with honey, which lingered for some time afterward.

After a while, the world righted itself and she was able to look at her mate again. She studied his long pointed muzzle, the black-tipped ears, the russet coat. He seemed happy. He lay on the damp grass, his narrow, foxy eyes drinking in her form, and his tongue lolling out.

"Put your tongue in," she said.

"Why?"

"Because . . ." She looked around, wondering if they had been observed. Not that she was worried about others witnessing a very natural act—they would not be interested anyway—but her curiosity was back, now that it was over.

A-ho let out a triple bark, and then a loud scream, before giving her his cocked-head look which he knew always endeared him to her.

"All right, tell the world," she said. "If you feel it's necessary. Personally, I don't. They can all see what a tremendously virile fellow you are."

"It's traditional," he remarked casually.

"Is it," she said, flatly. "I wonder who started that tradition? Some poor dog fox who had only just learned to play 'wind in the trees' with his new mate, I suppose?"

He needed no second teasing and was back with her again within a few moments.

Over the next three days they made love on several occasions and each time it was as good as the last: not better, but certainly as good. The sky changed color many times. The air seemed to have *promises*

hanging in it like the lanterns of fruit that had hung in the autumn trees, filling the world with heady scents.

Yet Melloon had long since departed, leaving bare damp trees, dark with fungi, and bushes without berries to blood their branches. Sodden leaves covered the floor of Trinity Wood, and there was great competition for meat amongst the predators: the owls, the hawks, the weasels. Three quarters of O-ha's diet consisted of meat. She had to be sharp. There were birds about, in the winter, and on days when the ground was soft there were earthworms to be had. She would also steal winter cabbage from the *havnot*, the farmlands around Trinity Wood. And shortly after the mating season was over, she found a fence full of *gubbins*, the fox word for animals killed and left by humans. These were old crows and stoats hung on fence wire. She cached some around the area, marked the locations, then took one home to A-ho. He thanked her by licking her ear. Now that the mating was over, there was no strain in the relationship. They could touch and be touched without any thick syrupy feelings interfering with their affection for one another.

Inside her there were changes taking place, which were pleasant. She looked forward to warmer weather and to Switter, the spring breezes. Many of the meadows around Trinity Wood were still *old grasslands*, and birds such as the partridge were still able to find the sawfly larvae and leatherjackets, which fed only on certain plants and without which they could not survive. There were still hedgerows and ditches, necessary to birds, mammals, and reptiles. The hedge-less landscapes and sterilized new grasslands were moving in, but had not yet overtaken the area around Trinity Wood.

The wood itself was an old-world mixture of coniferous and deciduous trees—yew, cedar, juniper, oak, beech, alder—and not one of the manmade silent forests of sitka spruce, where pine needles suffocate any undergrowth and the insects necessary to animal life are discouraged from moving in. Silent—utterly, unerringly silent. In the new pine forests the shadow was heavy and forbidding, the neat rows of trees so close together that a rabbit could not squeeze between them. In Trinity Wood, the shade was light, and the arrangement of the various trees was satisfyingly untidy.

Of course, O-ha and the other animals of Trinity Wood took all this for granted, even though itinerant beasts brought warnings of an outside world that was being reshaped to suit the comfort and needs of those ugly bipeds whose hairless, featherless bodies were draped with loose-fitting cloth, and who showed their teeth even when they were not angry.

Not in our time, they said to themselves and to each other. *The woodlands and fields will not change in my lifetime.*

True, said the widgeon, whistling on the wind.

And in a voice like two pebbles being struck together, the stonechat agreed.

The shrew, the grasshopper, the bark beetle, the fox, the squirrel, the gregarious rooks and solitary crows, the shellducks that nest in old rabbit-holes along the ditches, the adder, the smooth snake, the magpies who form mysterious ad hoc parliaments in open fields in which to conspire and discuss revolution, the winter balls of ants in hollow logs, the treecreeper, the nightjar, the hare and the rabbit, the badgers, the robin that sings for eleven months of the year and falls to silence in August, the coots floating in rafts on the river . . .

. . . they all sang the same song:

Not in our time.

So O-ha and the other creatures of Trinity Wood and the surrounding countryside did not concern themselves with the warnings brought in by outsiders. They confined their interests to the changing seasons; to the subtleties and vagaries of the winds that carried the scents and sounds necessary for everyday living; and to avoiding contact with humans. The wood mice, surrounded by predators, had enough to worry about without thinking of future catastrophes that might never come to pass. The swifts and swallows were too busy gathering insects over stagnant pools. The moorhens stuck their heads under leaves when such dreadful thoughts entered their minds, believing they were totally hidden from the world, but soon forgot why they were doing it and went out into the pond to feed again.

Life was already quite fraught enough, without having to heed something about which they could do nothing. O-ha's main anxieties concerned getting enough food for herself and her unborn cubs and evading the hunt.

One night she rose from her bed, leaving A-ho fast asleep, and staggered outside. She felt sleepy and failed to observe the rituals of leaving-the-earth—something she was normally *never* careless about.

Above the wood was a hunter's moon, whose light over the scene filled it with shadows. The shadows moved and danced as if they were alive.

O-ha set off across the *hav*, the uncultivated land, feeling quite strange. It was as if she were not herself, but some other vixen moving across the moonlit landscape of the slope below Trinity Wood. All around her were the sounds of other creatures in the grasses, going about their nightly business. Then suddenly, all went still. There was the smell of danger in the air.

The mooning note of a huntsman's horn floated over the fields.

O-ha's heart picked up the sound before her brain did and she was already moving rapidly through the thickets of blackthorn before she was conscious of what she had to do. Her feet kept getting tangled in the network of shadows, though, hindering her progress. She wished there was no moon, no hunter's moon, for the human beasts to see by. Yet they had their hounds and horses to see for them, to sniff her out and run her down.

The human barks grew louder and she could hear the thudding of horses' hooves on the turf. The hounds were screaming at each other, urging each other on. Shadows grew like brambles around her, catching her coat, holding her back. It was as if the black shadows of the briars had sided with man and were acting like snares and traps to slow her down, cage her, until the hounds caught up with her.

She ran until her heart was bursting. On the top of a ridge, in the full light of the hunter's moon, the hounds caught up with her and fell on her. She screamed for mercy as canine teeth crunched her bones and tore her joints apart. The pain was incredible as pieces of flesh were ripped from her live twisting body and her blood splattered the faces of her killers.

The eyes of the hounds were bright with bloodlust, and their faces changed as their jaws cracked her bones, stripped her coat from her flesh; they changed into white human faces, the lips curled back and that ugly barking, which only humans made, coming from their throats . . . "HA-HA-HA-HA-HA-HA . . ." relentless. Dogs with human heads, with coats and caps, dogs insane with the pleasure of tearing a living creature to pieces. Human heads with dogs' bodies, ugly with the excitement of death and its younger brother, pain. All the while she cried for mercy, for herself and her unborn cubs, but there were none to listen. All ears were deaf, except to the sounds of the kill.

Then, strangely, she was outside her body, and looking on. And she saw that it was not herself in the center of those frenzied human hounds, but A-ho, her mate. She screamed at them to stop, to leave him alone. She could see his body contorting in agony and his eyes pleading for her help. Yet she could do nothing but watch him being torn to death.

And when he was dead, one of the riders with a human body and dog's head lifted him up and bit off his tail, wiping the bloody end over his face. "HA-HA-HA-HA-HA!"

Then, as he dangled there from the human hand, a wasted empty skin with no tail, the head flopping this way and that, she could see that it was not A-ho, it was not herself, it was just another fox, only another fox, anonymous, unknown. It was another fox—but not *just* another fox, it was *the* fox, it was *all* foxes. It was her, it was A-ho, it was her grown cubs. It was her mother, her father, her kin and kind.

She woke up in her earth, A-ho beside her saying, "What's the matter? Are you having the nightmare?" and she realized she had been whining in her sleep. Her noise, her twitching body, had awakened him.

She nuzzled into him.

"Yes, it was the nightmare."

It was the bad dream of all foxes, the chase over the landscapes of the mind, and the gory end that was never an end because it would come again, and again. . . .

TWO

The winds are gods. Without them, survival would become a nightmare. They carry the scents and sounds necessary to fox awareness of all things: danger, food, rain, love, trees, earth, landscape—all things. Each individual wind is a deity with a secret name, to be whispered by the rocks and trees, to be written on the surface of the rivers and lakes. More important than the sun or the moon, the wind is the breath of life. Somewhere, seasons out of time, is a mythical land known as *Heff*, where a shapeless form breathes through a series of hollow tree-trunks full of holes of different sizes. This is the palace of the winds.

The time was Ransheen, the white wind, when darkness grew

like horns pressing deeply into the ends of the day. Soft things had become brittle and the landscape had taken on sharp edges. Ransheen brought with her a belly full of flints, and lungs that burned.

It was night and O-ha prepared with unhurried precision for the ritual of leaving-the-earth: an elaborate procedure that tested for dangers outside and ensured the secrecy of the earth's location. A-ho was already out there, somewhere, looking for water and food.

She licked her nose and poked it out into the cold path of Ransheen, getting her strength and direction. A thousand scents were out there, each one instantly recognizable. The smells of men and dogs were absent, however, and after some time O-ha was satisfied that it was safe and gradually emerged from the earth, to stand outside.

The world was a block of stone with a frozen heart. After the foxes' mating, the real winter had set in, almost as if their coming together had been a signal for the ice to advance. Around O-ha the trees of Trinity Wood were sighing in the moonlight. She moved her head from side to side, slowly, testing the odors that Ransheen carried in her unseen hands, the sounds that she bore.

Then the swift dash to put ground between herself and the earth, through the edge of the thicket and out into the *hav*, the open heathland.

There was a hunter's moon above, throwing its pale light over the landscape. When O-ha was a cub her mother had told her that the moon was the detached soul of the sun. That in the beginning, not long after the world was formed, there had been no night or day: worldshapers like the great fox A-O, and the wolf Sen-Sen, moved through the *Firstdark* using scent and sound, and had no need of light. This was at the time before humans came out of the sea-of-chaos. However, the giant *Groff*, sent by humans to prepare the world for their invasion, had been instructed to provide light for the humans to hunt by. He plunged his hand deep into the earth and came up with a ball of fire. He called this molten ball *the sun*, but when he tossed it up into the sky he threw it so hard that its soul became detached from its body. This ghost of the sun was called *the*

moon, and followed a similar but separate path in its circuit of the world.

The wolf and fox knew that the reason *Groff* was providing the bright light of day was to enable men to more easily find and kill them, and so they tried to destroy the giant. But *Groff* could not be hurt, since he was made of nothing but *belief*, and the only way he could be destroyed was for men to doubt their faith in his existence.

O-ha used the ancestral highway from Trinity Wood to Packhorse Field. Other fox and badger byways crisscrossed this main artery, but she ignored those, for none of them led to water, her present objective.

Her tread was delicate, and from time to time she paused to look over her shoulder, not to see but to listen, for like all her kind she was unable to focus on a stationary object for more than a few seconds. She passed by a cottage, using the ditch at the end of its long garden as cover. She could smell the iron fence-posts and the steel wires that ran between them. Her ears picked up the sound of the clock ticking in the bedroom of the house. Somewhere, out on the road that ran by the cottage—perhaps half a mile distant—a man was walking. His scent came to her on the back of Ransheen.

She lay in the dank ditch, watching the cottage for a while with her body tuned to the night. All remained still. It was wise to just wait sometimes, if for no other reason than that some faint distant sound had disturbed her mental attitude. Or perhaps nothing at all, nothing that could be seen, smelled, or heard. Perhaps just a feeling? Survival did not depend upon knowing everything, but on following instinct. If the feeling said "stay," then she stayed. Her thirst could wait. Unlike humans, O-ha did not invent reasons for continuing her normal activity. There were no chores that could not wait. She was quite willing to do nothing, be nothing, for as long as her mental state remained unsettled.

Eventually she resumed her journey to the pond.

O-ha was a very conventional fox, and even as she walked she carried out certain rituals. There was one set of these that was rarely referred to or spoken of in any society, even between pairs, though it was carried out religiously on all occasions: the *marking*. Almost subconsciously, O-ha marked certain areas of the highway with her urine, so that if A-ho came by that way, he would know she had recently been there.

As she walked along the ancestral highway O-ha felt the frosted grasses brushing her legs and she thought wistfully of Melloon, the autumn wind, and of the fruits and mushrooms that had since gone.

At one of the fox byways she heard a familiar tread, as delicate as her own, and smelled an odor that always sent a shiver of delight down her spine. She waited, poised, and soon another red fox came out of the tall white grasses.

"A-ho," she said. "I didn't hear you leave the earth. Why didn't you wake me?"

A-ho stopped, and scratched his muscled body with the fluidity of a cat.

"You were sleeping too soundly. Seemed a shame to disturb you." He flicked his head. "Been down to the orchard, looking for rats, but all the windfalls have gone. Nothing to get them from their holes. What about you?"

"Just going down to the pond."

"Well, you be careful—in your condition . . ."

She was three weeks pregnant now and a warm glow was in her belly.

"I'll be all right."

"Be careful," repeated A-ho, and then he was gone, his dark coat moving along the ancestral path, toward their earth.

O-ha continued her trek through the moonlight. In the distance a tawny owl hooted, Ransheen carrying the sound over the fields.

The man she had smelled earlier, out on the road, had now cut across the fields and was walking toward the animal highway. She could hear the crunch of his boots on the hard ground. The lumps of frozen soil were hampering his progress. Occasionally he lost his footing and barked softly.

O-ha slipped into the grasses and lay still, waiting for the man to pass. His direction crossed her path, and among all the scents he carried around him in a cloud was that of a shotgun. Although there was darkness to protect her, and the man appeared to be ill in the way that men she encountered in the early hours were often ill, she did not want him to fire the weapon. There were noises and smells associated with guns that were reminiscent of storms, of thunder and lightning and trees blasted into black charred stumps. It was always difficult to think, to keep a clear head, under such circumstances. It did not matter that one did not get hit; the shock as the weapon exploded and the pungent smell that followed, these were enough to turn a fox's head, to make a fox do something stupid.

The man came within a few feet of her, smelling strongly of smoke. His tread was unsteady, with much stumbling, and once he fell over and lay still for a few moments. His shotgun clattered against a stone and O-ha held her breath, expecting it to belch flame, to tear a ragged hole in the night's stillness. Nothing happened—no fire, no noise.

The man gulped at the frozen air, his breath snorting through his nostrils. He growled softly and heaved himself to his feet. Then he swayed forward, as if searching the ground. O-ha heard him pick up the shotgun and then bark harshly at the moon. His head began weaving about as he regained his stance. He slapped at his clothes, yapped again, then continued his meandering over the fields.

O-ha's encounters with humans were not infrequent, though it was rare for them to be aware of the meeting. Humans had the sharp eyes of predators who could not rely on smelling their prey, but they had lost the instinct that went with such vision. Many times she had held her breath, thinking that a human was aware of her, only to have the intruder pass by. She had decided that most humans were preoccupied creatures, whose anxious minds were on things that were outside the considerations of a fox. Why else would solitary men wear such strange expressions, walk around with eyes fixed on some point far beyond their range of vision, smell constantly of one kind of fear or another? And when there was more than one of them, they were usually so busy barking at each other that the world could turn upside down and they would not notice. As for killing, humans sometimes killed not for territorial reasons, nor for food, but for reasons that foxes had never been able to understand. There were times when humans made a great spectacle of killing foxes, and there were times when they did it slyly, secretly, while no one was watching.

O-ha was no stranger to death, even to slaughter. She and A-ho had once entered a chicken coop and slaughtered the whole population. For several minutes she had been able to see nothing but a hazy red cloud before her eyes, and her heart seemed to move to her head, pounding there. Her coat had overheated and she just snapped at anything that moved. This was not a bloodlust. This was good husbandry. Afterward the pair of them had carried away and cached as many chickens as they could before the farmer arrived on the scene.

O-ha understood about killing, even in large numbers, so she did not think humans *unnatural*, only unreachable.

She came to the pond and found there was a sheet of ice covering its surface. It shone frostily at her. She tested its strength with her paw. It remained firm, and she knew she would have to lick away at the edge. First, she muttered the ritual chants. "Water, preserver of life, body of A-O the first fox of *Firstdark*, cleanse my spirit. . . ." Then, while her senses remained tuned to the world around her, she licked steadily at the ice until she was satisfied. Never for a moment did she relax. She had to be constantly on the alert, for the one sound that spelled discord, for the one smell that meant danger. To survive, a fox must be invisible, a thread of cotton on the wind, and must know all things at once.

In the center of the pond, beyond the stiff reeds, was a small island. On this isolated piece of land stood a house-shaped coop which O-ha knew contained sleeping ducks. Well, they wouldn't be sleeping for long! She cocked her ear in the direction of the farmhouse, swimming out there somewhere in the darkness. She could smell humans—hear them breathing in their earth. She was not alarmed. There was no tension in the air.

She stared at the hut again for a few seconds before it swirled mistily before her eyes. The dark side of her soul slid forward and she walked out onto the pond, the ice crackling around her feet. Farmers

believed they were protecting the ducks by putting them on their little islands, but a fox is a superb swimmer. And, of course, they forgot that the ice provided a flat path for any predator.

In the middle of the pond, O-ha stopped and looked down. There was something under the misty ice, a shapeless shadow, that stared up at her. She shivered, but was unable to move for a few moments. The thing would not let her. It held her gaze, locked by its own. It was a thing from a time not now. A distant form, unable to reach her because it was too far ahead, or she was too far behind, but it promised a meeting. The promise was in its stare.

It let her go and she hurried on.

Once she was on the island the ducks began to stir, sensing her presence. She padded softly all around the coop, checking for the slightest crack or chink that might mean a loose board. She could hear them talking to one another in their own language as she checked the roof, investigating each part of it thoroughly. Not one square inch escaped her attention; she was methodical, her hunger honing her senses to a keen edge. A dark, red cloud was in her head, covering her eyes, filling her nostrils, and an urgent desire burned from deep within her belly to the tip of her tongue.

Just let me find a split in the boards, to get my nose inside, she thought, *and the rest of me will follow*.

Her mouth was awash with saliva. Her brain was alive with bloodflies. Her breath was as sharp as the edge of a blade of grass.

The ducks began to get alarmed and started to kick up a din, but still O-ha did not worry. She had an ear on the humans, her nose to the wind. And the old farm dog, Gip, was in his last few months on this world. He was sixty seasons old. His hearing had all but gone, and his sense of smell was tuned only to canned meat.

She made a long and painstaking examination of the coop. She worried the bolt on the door for some time, knowing that this thing was somehow connected with sealing the entrance to the coop, but was unable to understand how it worked. Eventually she abandoned the enterprise.

"You get away tonight," she whispered, the red cloud lifting. "I'll be back. Sometime the bolt will be forgotten, or a rotten plank left too long before replacement—then we'll see."

One of the ducks farted, but whether this was in fright, or intended as an insulting reply, O-ha could not tell. Domesticated creatures were strange, having given their souls to man, and therefore difficult for a wild creature to understand.

There was a sudden sound from the farmhouse. Something in its upper regions crashed against a wall and a human began barking into the night. O-ha flattened herself against the coop, wondering whether to dash into the fields or to stay where she was and wait for something more positive to happen. She would have to cross the thinnish ice carefully—not panic and run blindly—or she might go through it and quickly drown in the freezing water below. A beam of light came from the house, striking the coop. It swept around the island, missing her by a hair.

She waited, her heart pattering in her breast, for the sound of the gun that might send her to the Perfect Here—that place after death for foxes of a proper nature who were well regarded by their friends, respected by their enemies, hated by none that were not hated themselves.

Even when the sound did not come she stayed frozen to the ground, waiting. Her breath formed misty blossoms in the night air, which drifted away over the frostfire. Somewhere a mouse shrieked, probably pinned by the talons of an owl. A cloud dropped over the moon.

THREE

She lay in the shadow of the coop until the furor inside had ceased and the activity in the house had quieted. It was a cold night and no doubt the farmer was reluctant to leave his warm bed and venture out. Were it summertime O-ha might have been running against the gun.

Finally, she got up and walked back across the ice. She felt stark and vulnerable in the moonlight, and even more so when the ducks—on hearing movement outside—started complaining again. Gip was moving restlessly in his kennel. O-ha's mother, O-fille, had known Gip well in seasons gone by, and had told O-ha stories of being chased from the farm by the sheepdog. Gip had not been a killer, though, even in his prime.

"There was one time," O-fille had said to the circle of cubs, of whom O-ha was one, "when Gip had been left unchained and chased me from some rabbit hutches, just outside the kitchen door. I had just about gnawed through the leather hinges when he came hurtling around the corner and saw me.

"Of course, I was away like a cat with its tail on fire"—the cubs had laughed at this image—"with Gip close behind. He was young and nippy in those days, and broad at the shoulder. Like a fool I ran into the barn, where some men were working, and found myself being chased round in a circle with the farm laborers barking at us.

"Eventually Gip cornered me and advanced slowly toward me. The workmen were yipping in excitement by this time.

"Gip said, 'They're telling me to kill you!' He was angry with me for putting him in a position where expectations were high. At that moment I realized he was not a killer. I could see it in his face, in his stance. But under the eyes of his masters he had to do something to me. I tried to make a dash for it, but he caught me by the fleshy part of my throat. He tossed me into the air like a bundle of hay, over his shoulder.

"I hit the ground near the open doorway and was on my feet in an instant, and running for the *havnot*. Gip was not far behind me, shouting, 'Don't come back, vixen! You've had your warning. I won't be so lenient next time.'

"I did go back, of course. We have to, don't we? But I never pushed Gip too far. . . ." There were some farm dogs—efficient, firm, no-nonsense—who did their jobs effectively, without spilling unnecessary blood. Then there were those hounds, which of course included foxhounds, who would go out of their way to taste blood.

Now O-ha followed the frosted path beyond the ice, and was able to slip away across the *havnot* until she reached the relative safety of the open *hav*.

Her foray had taken a long time and dawn was beginning to creep across the fields. O-ha found a byway in the grass, following it

toward the sun. When she had traveled about two hundred yards, she stopped and sniffed the air.

Meat! She could smell the heady scent of meat.

Her senses flamed as the perfume swam to her nostrils on the back of Ransheen. She turned from the byway into untracked country, a place where the brambles wrestled with bryony, and tall thickets of blackthorn sprouted from the cropped grass. A stoat, having changed its name and color for the winter months to become the ermine, hissed and spat at her as she passed its labyrinth of tunnels. She was not hungry enough to tackle the ferocious little beast, and anyway, there was a promise on the wind. She had now identified the smell: rabbit. O-ha knew of a warren nearby, but it was a wounded or freshly dead creature that was sending out this signal. It was necessary to be wary, for this fact left many open questions.

She came to a wire fence stretching across the *hav*, beyond which some cows were grazing on frosted grass. Large as these creatures were, she knew them to be gentle and to offer no threat. Nevertheless she hesitated before going under the wire into the *havnot*, sniffing for a stronger scent of steel gin traps. She was not so stupid as to rush blindly into an area she did not know well.

Once she was satisfied, she slipped under the wire quickly, walking fast but still with great caution. She rarely ever broke into a trot, and ran only in emergency situations. Her mother had taught her that a cool head was more useful than hot feet.

Eventually she came to a covert of blackthorn, riddled with rabbit runs. At the entrance to one of these lay a rabbit. It was still. All around its throat was a line of blood.

Another of man's traps had caught the creature: a wire snare that strangled its victims to death. The more the rabbit had struggled, the tighter had grown the wire loop, and finally the creature had throttled itself. O-ha could see where the base of a blackthorn had been stripped of bark, as the rabbit had thrashed out with its hind legs.

O-ha licked her nose, sensitizing it, and tested Ransheen. Then she moved forward slowly, her muzzle close to the ground. The first thing she did was to pass her shadow over the rabbit twice, in the ritual cleansing of carrion. Then she gripped the freshly dead rabbit in her jaws and tried to pull it away from the wire, but as expected, it held fast. Even jerking it from side to side did not release the meat.

Realizing that it was impossible to free the meal from its trap, she satisfied herself by gnawing its underside and feeding on the soft organs beneath. Her snout buried itself inside the rabbit as she fed, and her belly welcomed the warm food.

When she had been feeding for some time, a sound came to her from the far side of the covert. Since her nostrils were still clouded with the smell of the rabbit's organs and blood, she could catch no scent. She stiffened, flattening herself to the ground. One thing she did know: it was not the tread of a human. It was too light and soft—a four-footed creature. A small dog, badger, or fox.

She was not afraid of badgers, even though they were more powerful creatures than foxes, but dogs were another matter. Her breath quickened as she swiftly assessed the avenues of escape.

Suddenly, a screech from above distracted her: a magpie had landed on the blackthorn. It strutted arrogantly along a branch, making too much noise for its size; then it became a blur of black and white as it stopped still and O-ha lost focus. Then the scent of fox, *old* fox, filled her nostrils. A grizzled dog fox came around the blackthorn, licking its grey muzzle. The rest of its coat was dark—darker than O-ha's—and its head looked too large for its body.

O-ha said, "A-magyr! You startled me."

The old dog fox eyed her belligerently. A-magyr had once been a *rangfar*: one of those itinerant foxes that wander the countryside, the gypsies of the fox world. Although he had now settled in the district, it was said he still had nothing but contempt for *ords*, the foxes that never move more than a mile from their parish.

"Startled?" he growled. "Foxes shouldn't be *startled*. They should have their wits constantly about them. They should know the time ahead as well as the time past." He shouldered her out of the way. "Now push off. I like the look of that rabbit."

Since A-magyr was well known for his own carelessness, this rebuke was a little unjustified. He was renowned for having once strolled down the middle of the local village street in broad daylight, unimpressed by the humans who stopped to goggle at him. Only when a vehicle honked its horn at him, had he deigned to acknowledge the presence of the humans, and slipped down an alley. He was a very big fox, larger than most, and it would have to be a brave town dog that took him on.

"Come on, shove off," he snapped, as she hovered by his shoulder.

O-ha considered the situation. She had eaten most of the soft meat and breast. Only the head and legs remained untouched. But this was *her* rabbit. She had intended to cache some of it and tell A-ho of its whereabouts. A-magyr was robbing her of her find, and he knew it.

She flattened her body against the ground in front of him, her ears against her head and her hind legs as taut as springs.

A-magyr looked up, almost lazily. His eyes narrowed.

"What?" he said. "Try me, would you? Go away, vixen, before you get hurt. You know how many foxes I've thrashed?"

"Tell me afterward," she snapped, irritated by his dog-fox boasting. If they did fight, there was a possibility of serious injury, even death, if it went that far. Her heart was pounding a little as A-magyr took up a stance in front of her. Then, just in time, she remembered.

She began to back away.

A-magyr's head came up and he affected an arrogant pose.

"Ah, thought better of it? Good for you. I hate fighting females—they're unpredictable. They hate losing, and they *always* lose against me."

This little speech made her bristle with frustration. She dearly wanted to make him roll over in submission, but she was concerned for her unborn cubs. It was wrong to put them at risk. If she stayed she might injure them, and A-magyr had little to lose.

"Be careful of my cubs," she said.

He paused to eye her haughtily.

"Pregnant, eh? Couldn't care less."

"Hope it chokes you," she said. "Of course you wouldn't know

anything about cubs, would you? Was there ever an O-magyr in your life? They say no vixen would ever live with such a . . ."

She stopped when he turned to face her.

"Watch your mouth, *ord*," he said. "Don't think those cubs will prevent me teaching you a lesson. Respect your elders."

The magpie glided to the ground now and strutted a few yards away.

"Respect your elders," it mimicked in a high, rasping voice. *"Ich glaube, ja."*

O-ha bared her teeth.

"And you can shut up," she said.

A-magyr crossed his shadow back and forth over the meat, the way O-ha had done, and then began to chew a hind leg. She watched him for a short while as he chewed the meat that was so precious during Ransheen, and then she strolled away at a leisurely pace.

He called out to her, with his mouth full, "Hunt on today. Heard the hounds this morning. Look to your tail, vixen."

A hunt!

A cold shiver went down her spine. She ought to thank A-magyr for the warning, but she wondered whether he was lying or not. It might be his idea of a joke, to watch her running back to her earth while he finished the rabbit. She sniffed the air instead. The trouble was, she was thirsty again after the meal, and she had not managed to get a great deal of liquid from the pond ice. The river was too far away. She considered other watering places.

O-ha carried within her an ancient knowledge of all the water-holes, soaks, and hiding places in her parish. Most of this topographical knowledge was passed between generations—from mother to cubs—but some of it was retained through racial memory from the time of *Firstdark*, when the world had been formed. Foxes had been on the earth longer than many animals, certainly longer than those upstart humans, and had witnessed the birth of the Long Hot Wind, Cle-am, that had shaped the world into its basic form. During *Firstdark*, foxes had fought great battles with other creatures much larger than themselves, and the ancestors of O-ha had triumphed. Those first heroes and heroines still lived on as the fox-spirits of the *hav*, and from time to time they appeared before distressed foxes to offer information and advice. You could not summon them, but they came to the spiritually oppressed when they felt their presence was deserved. They were especially active after some betrayal or treachery in which dogs were involved, since these cousins of the fox were now bound with humans in an effort to exterminate the foxes in the way they had done the wolves.

Survival, in any parish, depended upon the knowledge passed down from *Firstdark*, which was held in songs and chants.

The mystery and magic of *Firstdark* were locked in fox memory. O-ha knew all the tracks, all the fox highways and byways, all the soaks and waterholes in the district. Walking through the tall grasses, now glistening with the melting frost, she made her way to a depression a quarter of a mile from Trinity Wood, where water was often held in the natural cup of a rock. Facing south, the rock was one of the first objects struck by the morning sun and it was possible that there might be meltwater in the hollow. Once she had drunk, she intended to go back to her earth.

She stepped out with a determined stride. As she traveled along a ditch beneath a mossy bank, Ransheen brought a warning to her from up-wind. She stiffened. Almost immediately, she heard the terrible sound of the hunting horn and the distant yelling of dogs.

"Up! Up! Get the red devils up!" the hounds were shouting in that dog dialect of theirs.

The mob was abroad.

O-ha was alarmed, but did not panic. The hunt was still a long way off. She could not even smell the horses yet. She could hear their hooves drumming against the hard turf, but they were still at a canter. No gallop had begun, which meant they had not picked up a scent.

Look to your tail, vixen, A-magyr had said.

She intended to do so, for the sake of her cubs as well as herself.

She crossed from the bank to some trees, still walking in the shadows. A fox does not have the stamina nor the speed to beat foxhounds in an open race across country. The dogs were faster, stronger. They were able to run long after a fox's heart had burst, or

its legs had collapsed underneath it. Given such odds in favor of the pursuer, it was surprising that so many foxes escaped the pack. The reason they often got away was because they relied on wile, and guile, rather than on speed. Foxhounds were fast, but often not very bright. They stopped to verify every nuance in a scent before running on, sometimes blindly in the wrong direction. They paused at points where byways crossed, finding the mixtures of old scents and new scents confusing. Also, foxes are much more agile than dogs, and can leap fences, walk along the edges of planks with perfect balance, squeeze through holes, use the odors of external things such as cars to disguise their trails. O-ha had ten times more resourcefulness than any hunting hound.

Just as she was about to enter a covert, there was a barking from down-wind. A human on foot! He had seen her and was yapping excitedly to attract the distant riders. She saw the man, now running toward her, wave his stick and point in her direction.

"Damn you," she snapped, irritably.

Then she caught a whiff of his odor, between the safety of her earth and herself.

"The *hav*," she thought, heading out into open country, into the gorse and bracken. She tried to remember where she had last seen recently ploughed land, where her trail might be lost amongst the furrows, and then remembered it was winter: most of the fields had been turned a long time past.

"I'm not thinking straight," she muttered to herself.

Like the sound of a bloodthirsty beast itself, a nightmarish, many-legged monster with a hundred sharp-toothed mouths, the horn was louder, and nearer.

FOUR

The cries of the hounds filled the air, punctuated by the sound of the hunting horn and the baying of the huntsmen.

O-ha's heart was racing now as she zigzagged over the *hav*, hoping to find some hiding place where the hounds could not get at her. She had never witnessed the end of a hunt, but she had heard the tales from those who had. She knew the dogs would rip her to pieces and that her tail would be cut from her coat, to be wiped over the face of some human new to the gory business, smearing it with blood. It was one of those human rituals that went back to the time the two-legged beasts came out of the sea-of-chaos: a ritual they had brought with them from the other side. O-ha was not the first fox to wonder what kind of creature this was, this creature that used the reeking, smoking blood of another animal for ornamental pleasure; what kind of creature this was that decorated itself in the symbolic color of pain.

She reached a ditch by a road and immediately used it like a tunnel, hoping that the icy bottom would not hold her scent for long. There were heavy shadows in the trench, which hopefully would dilute her scent and weaken it to a point where it was hardly recognizable from the other creature smells, ditches being busy places. Smaller mammals scattered out of her way as she traveled along, none of them jeering, not even those who might one day end their lives in a fox's stomach. Fear was abroad, and they caught it from her as she swept past them. It got into their nostrils and choked their brains, so that they found themselves scurrying away to holes or nests in an effort to rid themselves of the foul smell that created such panic.

O-ha left the ditch at one end just as the hounds were milling around at the other, trying to pick up her scent at the point she had entered. She waited for a few seconds, gathering her breath. O-ha was terribly thirsty now and she knew that if she did not get a drink soon, her strength would rapidly ebb. If only she had been patient at the pond! Then she heard the hounds tumbling along the hedgerow, and she knew her ruse had not worked. Once again, she took to her paws.

Instead of crossing the field adjacent to the ditch, she traveled down the center of the road for part of the way. Her instinct told her to do the unpredictable thing. Behind her, the hounds still shouted: "This way! This way! We've almost got the devil." The riders were thundering alongside the road, knowing that the road's hard surface would damage their horses' legs with the jarring. It slowed them a little.

A car came around the bend, and its driver, on seeing O-ha, skidded to a stop. O-ha hesitated for a few moments. Her encounters with cars were limited. She knew them to be dangerous, because foxes, hedgehogs, rabbits, and even birds had been struck and killed by these machines. The smells associated with them were unpleasant. However, she knew from her experience with tractors that the fumes clouding them were able to mask an animal's scent.

The driver of the car was a female human and she was staring at O-ha with a strange expression on her face. O-ha made a swift decision, and jumped up onto the bonnet of the car, up again across the roof, and down to the roadway on the other side. She caught a glimpse of a startled face during the operation, but smelled nothing except car fumes. They would help to scatter her own odors over the landscape.

She continued along the middle of the road and a little later was rewarded for her courage. The sound of confused voices reached her ears, as the hounds milled around the car. The vehicle itself was trying to edge forward now and force a passage through the dogs, one or two of which had better noses than the others and were attempting to clamber up onto the bonnet, their claws skidding on the paintwork. Another car came from the opposite direction and became entangled with the hounds. Then the riders caught up with the pack and the car drivers began sounding their horns. O-ha gained valuable minutes of rest as dogs, horses, people, and machines tried to extract themselves from each other. The humans howled and the hounds cursed, shouting obscenities at the cars and their occupants and swearing at the horses who threatened to trample them. The horses themselves, having difficulty in keeping their footing on the slippery road surface, flung a few oaths into the melée in a language rich in expletives. O-ha was not entirely familiar with *Equidae*, but she had been the target of enough horse curses to recognize stronger forms of the word "dung."

The hunting horn was sounded, the dogs urged onward with human barks and whips. Soon they were in full pursuit again.

O-ha came to a roadside cottage, leaped up onto the fence, and, with remarkable poise, traveled along it to the gate from which she jumped down into the garden. There was a stone birdbath shaped like a church font in the middle of the small lawn. O-ha smelled the water and jumped up to balance precariously on the edge of the bowl. As she drank, quickly, the birdbath rocked under her weight.

Sparrows shouting insults at her from the eves of the cottage. A human was doing something in the corner of the garden and had not even noticed her, but from around a corner of the house came a small dog, which immediately shouted: "Ha, fox! Ha, fox!"

The birdbath came crashing down and the human figure, wearing a hat and gloves, dropped its trowel in fright. It turned and barked, its eyes round, as it backed away toward the cottage door.

O-ha bared her teeth at the mutt and then leaped the fence with an agility that had the dog looking vexed and angry.

"Stupid beast," the fox muttered to herself. The water had given her new heart and energy, but now the hunt was very near. The dogs would surely clamor in and around the garden for a while, and hopefully the human in the house would detain the riders with vocal abuse, but O-ha could not hope for more than a few moments of delay.

A sudden noise behind her told her that she had been spotted by a huntsman who had unwittingly overtaken the pack, and the hounds were screaming now in a frenzy of excitement.

Too close, she thought, panting, as her heart hammered in her breast. They're getting too close. I'm going to be caught. Oh, A-ho! Oh, my poor cubs. How am I going to throw the huntsmen off now?

She made a circuit, crossing the road again, and set off over the fields. She ran and ran until her heart was bursting within her, and her brain jangled. There was a thought in her head that she could lead the hounds on to where she had left A-magyr. He would have gone, but the remains of the rabbit would still be there. It might delay them long enough to enable her to get back to her earth.

She reached the field of cows and ran in and out of the animals, hoping their presence would help in throwing the hounds off her scent, but the lead hound was only a dozen yards behind her now. He was calling in a voice short of breath, "I'm here, I'm here! Don't look back, fox. You're about to die. I am Breaker, lead hound of the hunt. Breaker will run you to a standstill. Breaker will tear your throat, spill your fox-blood. Breaker, Breaker, Breaker . . ."

The other hounds took up his cry behind him, screaming,

"Breaker, Breaker, Breaker—follow him close—follow him close. The kill is only a nose away."

Waste your breath, she thought, but the misery and terror of death was on her, and she had to fight the pain in her body to force it onward. While she still ran, there was hope. Many a fox had escaped in the nick of time, at the last moment, through some fortuitous action.

The cows began running this way and that, slowing the riders but not the dogs. The dogs were still there, right at her heels. She found a thicket of blackthorn and hurled herself into it, not caring about the sharp spikes that tore her coat. Out the other side, and into another patch. At the end of the field was an encampment of travelers' caravans. She ran right through the center, narrowly missing a lurcher dog, as lean as herself, as it slept by an open fire. It jumped to its feet and was about to give chase when it was bowled over by the impetuous Breaker, who seemed to care nothing for gypsies or their animals.

The travelers themselves cheered the fox on through the encampment and even made an effort to prevent the hounds from following, until the huntsmen came up and began barking at their fellow humans, and flailing at them with riding crops. One or two fights broke out, but Breaker was still on O-ha's tail and she knew that most of the other hounds would follow his determined lead.

She reached the edge of a copse, and just as she entered she heard a voice she knew well.

"Quick, up onto that branch. I'll take over."

It was A-ho, her mate.

She needed little encouragement. She leapt from the ground, up into the tree, and balanced there against the trunk.

A-ho showed himself briefly to Breaker, who came crashing into the undergrowth, and then the brave dog fox was away.

"Don't worry," he called, "I'm as fresh as a daisy. I'll get rid of this one, and then see you at the earth!"

Oh, run, run, she thought, gasping for breath and hardly able to maintain her position on the branch. Several of the hounds began milling around the base of the tree, looking up at her, but on hearing

Breaker's full-blooded, throaty cries, they continued the chase. The hatted and coated riders swept by, urging any slow hounds onward, unaware that the quarry had changed and that a relay had taken place. Soon the sounds of the hunt drifted into the distance and she was able to think a little more clearly.

To say that she was concerned was to understate the fact. She was terrified, but not now for herself—for A-ho, her mate. Although his voice had been full of bravado when he told her to jump into the tree, she had smelled his fear-sweat, and she knew he would be in the same turmoil of fear that she had just been in herself. She felt an agony of apprehension for him, but she told herself he was no fool. If anyone could outwit the hounds, it was A-ho. He was a clever fox among clever foxes. He knew the tricks, knew the parish. He would have some idea in mind of how to rid himself of Breaker and the hounds, and he would carry that out no matter how frightened he was. She told herself all this as she waited for the tiredness to abate from her limbs, so that she could be on her way back to the earth.

Some time later, she jumped to the ground and padded to the top of the rise beyond the copse. She sniffed Ransheen for any scent of the hunt, but there was nothing. No sounds fell on her ears either, and she was beginning to feel something of relief that the nightmare was over. A-ho had said he would see her back at the earth, and she began to make her way across the *hav* toward Trinity Wood. Around her, the world had returned to normal as if there had never been a horde of savage creatures on horseback, sweeping across the countryside like the barbarians they were, intent on gorging their lust for blood.

As she approached the wood, there were warnings on the wind. She moved slowly and deliberately, until she could hear certain sounds: clinks of metal on stones. She went no further. There were humans around her earth, with digging implements. Sometimes, before or during a hunt, they filled in the earth to stop foxes from returning to relative safety. She imagined that was what was going on at that moment.

"Do your worst," she said. "A-ho and I will dig another earth." She remembered it was winter and that the ground was hard. "Or find an empty one," she added. The home was not important. The home was just a hole in the ground and could be abandoned without regret. Winter *was* a difficult time to find another earth, but there were two of them to search.

She went back to the tall grasses, where she could lay and be aware of the people digging, without being seen herself. Although her poor eyesight did not permit her to observe the activity in detail, she could use her other senses to tell her what was going on.

After a while she realized that the digging was going on too long for the men to be filling in the earth. Besides that, they were hacking away on the spot itself, and she could smell fresh clay. With a start she came to the conclusion that they were not filling the hole, but digging it out. The only reason they would bother to do that was if they believed there was a fox inside.

Her mouth went dry at the thought that A-ho might be in the earth. Could he have returned so quickly? She realized with a sickening feeling that it was possible. Still, that did not mean he was in there. The men could have found the earth and *assumed* it had a fox inside. They were not the most intelligent of creatures and would work at something like this on little or no evidence, simply because they had nothing else to do.

Suddenly the chinking of metal against flint ceased, there was a moment of quiet, and then a great howl of delight went up from the men. O-ha stood up, careless of being seen, and witnessed A-ho being dragged from the remains of the earth by his tail. He dangled on the end of a strong-looking arm, trying to turn and bite at the wrist. She could smell the fear in him.

Oh, A-ho! The odor of his terror almost drove her crazy. She ran back and forth in the grasses, knowing she was helpless to give him any kind of support. There was a vague thought that if she could get to the man who held him, A-ho might have a chance, but it was against her nature, the nature of a wild thing, to launch a direct frontal attack on a human. Were she cornered, she might fling herself forward in desperation, but now the instinct to run away was powerful. It was all she could do to remain within listening distance. Her frustration, the misery she experienced in being so close to

A-ho's tormentors, was overwhelming. Finally she could stand it no longer and began to run. In her frenzy, she was not sure which direction to take, but in any case a sound went up from A-ho that stopped her in her tracks again. She saw one of the men raise a spade above his head and swing downward. Immediately afterward there was another, more horrifying sound. It could have been a metal blade striking turf, except that O-ha knew it was not. No more sounds came from her mate after that. She smelled blood and slunk away, bile rising to her throat.

She spent the rest of the day in a daze of disbelief. Her rational thoughts were blanked by a buzzing in her brain, which did not allow her to sort through the events she had witnessed in order to come to a conclusion. The idea that A-ho was dead was such a terrible one that unconsciously she put up a great resistance toward it. She had seen sights, heard sounds, smelled odors, but fitting them together and using them to reach a conclusion was not possible for her at that point in time. For the rest of the day she lay in the grass, resting and getting her strength back to normal. She chewed at frozen grassroots to while away the time and satisfy a growing hunger. The rabbit seemed so long in the past, it might have been a week ago.

When evening came, she returned to Trinity Wood. There was neither a scent nor a sound of human activity, and she walked up to her earth.

It was a scene of devastation. The tunnel had been torn open, the soil scattered in all directions. Clods of frozen turf lay amongst the dried leaves of last autumn, and a gaping hole was in the place of the narrow entrance. There was a brown stain on the scarred root of the oak.

A hard cold lump formed in O-ha's stomach. At last there was an acceptance of what had happened. Grief flooded through her.

"A-ho!" she called, frantically.

The wind soughed through the trees.

"A-ho—please answer me. Please don't play jokes."

Two pigeons left the edge of the wood, noisily.

"A-ho, A-ho . . ."

She called and called, knowing then that she would never receive an answer. The men had executed her mate. They had not even left his body, but had carried it off somewhere for their own purposes.

Then she had the wild thought that maybe he had escaped, wriggled out of their grasp. Perhaps he was hiding somewhere, waiting for her to return? The blood on the ground meant nothing. It could have been any creature's blood. Maybe A-ho was out looking for her, thinking that she had not returned because she had herself been caught?

"It's all right," she called, out into the darkness, "I'm alive. They didn't get me."

She lay down and waited. It was no use running all over the country. One of them had to stay put, while the other found her.

All through the long night she waited, the hope barely alive in her breast. When the twilight of dawn came, she had lapsed into despair, knowing that he was gone. A lone hawk flew over the wood and then descended, but never reached the ground. It stooped several times over the slope where O-ha lay, but it seemed that the world and the bird of prey were flung apart each time they tried to come together. There was a force on the land, repelling the hawk's attempts.

As a red sky began to emerge above, a fox came to O-ha from out of its half-light: an insubstantial fox with a pure, white flame hovering a few inches above its head. The flame did not flicker, but burned steadily. An eternal flame.

The fox-spirit paused by Trinity Wood, and then continued its journey.

O-ha climbed wearily, morosely, to her feet and followed it, across the fields, to the manor house beyond the farm. There, hanging by the neck from a piece of wire, was the shredded body of her mate A-ho. He swayed gently in Ransheen's unseen hands. They had left him on a corral fence, like a piece of *gubbins*, to warn all foxes that the gamekeepers of the manor house were people to be reckoned with.

"The hunt—he evaded the hunt. He was a clever fox, my A-ho," said O-ha to the fox-spirit.

Vacant eyes were turned on the vixen.

"Yes, he evaded the hunt. I think you are aware of what happened. He was seen by some stableboys, returning to your earth, and they dug him up, killed him with spades. They brought him here, threw him to the hounds."

"And his tail?"

"They took that first. They have a word for it. A *brush*. It's their word, not ours."

O-ha stared at her mate, at the ragged fur that used to lie beside her own, full of warmth, full of vitality. Now it was an empty thing, full of holes, covered in black, dried blood. Glazed empty orbs, more vacant than those of the fox-spirit, were in the place of those hot bright eyes she was used to seeing as they looked into her own. It was not A-ho. Nevertheless, she asked the fox-spirit, "Does he have to stay there?"

"Can you get him down?"

"I don't think so. He's tied too tightly."

"Neither can I. We are made only of mist and light, of dreams and visions, of songs and memory—I have no power over physical matters. You understand? I am the fox-spirit that leads the living to the dead. Another will come to guide your mate to the Perfect Here."

O-ha watched as the cloud of mist scattered before her eyes, and the flame, the bright white flame, drifted away over the grasses.

O-ha then began the ritual for which she had been led to A-ho's corpse by the fox-spirit. She chanted sacred and secret rhymes, while at the same time she traced symbols on the ground around the hanging body. To anyone but a fox these marks would be incomprehensible scratches in the dirt, but to *vulpinae* they represented the four main winds: Ransheen, the winter wind; Melloon, the autumn; Frashoon, the summer; and the most erratic and unpredictable, the wind-from-all-ways, the outsider, the crazy wildwind Scresheen, who came during the month of birth and created turmoil amongst the trees. After this the ground was marked in a special way, which to humans would be nothing but an offensive smell. Then O-ha walked from the three corners of the trinity *toward* the body of her mate, but from Scresheen's corner she walked *away* from the carcass and kept walking, drawing the unpredictable one away from the corpse; this was to allow the remaining trinity to attract the fox-spirits to her mate's soul, and so carry it to the Perfect Here, the fox heaven where no human spirits reside, and the *Unremembered Fear* does not exist. The Perfect Here is the fox's own parish, with all its familiar woods and fields, coverts and streams, grasslands and hummocks, but in the otherworld beyond death. A safe, mystical shadow of a beloved landscape, without the terrors found in the world of the living.

A-ho was at peace, but she was alone.

She took one last backward look at her erstwhile mate, and then made her way back to Trinity Wood, pausing only to savage some winter cabbages in a field on her way. Outside the wood, she took stock of her situation. She had no earth to go to and no mate to help her find another. She was homeless. All she had left was herself, and her cubs.

"It isn't enough," she said fiercely, the pall of grief for her mate heavy on her spirit. Then the fear for her cubs came through. "I have to have somewhere to rear my cubs."

She first went looking for the mystic fox, A-konkon, famous for his wisdom. It was her hope that he could offer some practical advice on finding a new earth in the middle of winter. Instead, when she found him—which was not easy for he had no permanent home in the wood—he gave her a lecture on the spiritual joy of death.

"A-ho has undergone a release," said A-konkon. "He's quite happy where he is."

"I know he's gone to a nice place," she said. "A better place than this—but I still feel terrible. *He* might be happy, but I feel bad. I don't understand why. I mean, if the land beyond death is a happy place, why *do* I feel so bad?"

A-konkon folded his paws over one another and looked her directly in the eyes.

"Grief is a complex thing," he said. "We do not grieve because someone is dead, but because they are no longer alive. They have left us."

"You mean, it's selfish?"

"It has selfish elements, certainly, but there are all sorts of other emotions entangled with bereavement. We might feel guilty because we treated them badly at some time, or because we feel responsible for their death. . . ."

She saw a lot of truth in this last statement.

". . . the fact is, we can't reach them any more, to talk to them about it, so these things are difficult to work through. The important thing is not to idealize A-ho. He was not a perfect fox—he had good and bad in him, like all of us. He made mistakes, he had his faults."

O-ha wanted to argue with this, but wisely kept her tongue.

"What I'm trying to tell you is that although we believe A-ho has gone to a better land, we still have to work through this storm of emotions within us, to resolve them slowly, so we can be free to get on with life."

"Believe?" she contested hotly. "I *know* he's gone to a better place. I saw the fox-spirit, remember."

"*You* saw, no one else. Think. If we believe in something strongly enough—which we all do about the Perfect Here—then isn't it possible that our brains, fevered by emotion, might produce what we want to know?"

"You mean, I had an hallucination?" She was getting very angry with A-konkon.

"It's possible. Anything's possible. The Perfect Here is possible. What it is not is a *certainty*."

"Thank you," she said, coldly, "for your *help*."

"You're entirely welcome—I shan't expect payment for a couple of months, but once the weather turns and the hunting gets better . . ."

Before she left she again asked A-konkon if he could offer some advice about finding a new earth, but he shrugged that question off impatiently.

"Material needs are not my concern. I can help your soul, your mind, but not your body. You must do that for yourself. Personally, I think an earth is an unnecessary luxury."

Nevertheless, unsatisfactory as her talk with A-konkon had

appeared to be, she felt a little more fortified. He had angered her to a certain extent with his useless words, and there is nothing like anger to oust other less welcome emotions. *He* might not need an earth, but in her condition, she certainly did. Later, it came to her that A-konkon might have said what he said on purpose, in order to redirect her anger. It had raised her out of her apathy and got her to think about searching for a new home.

She decided he was a very wise fox, after all. His methods were so subtle they had almost escaped her.

It was at this time that she began composing a song in her head to her departed mate. Once she had all the lines in her head, she could sing it to the wind and it would be in the world forever, as permanent as a mountain. The wind would re-sing it for her, in the reeds on the marshes, in the branches of the trees, around the corners of buildings.

The first line was: *You came and went, like a season never.*

However, it *was* painfully slow and difficult to complete such an enormous task, and O-ha saw the impossibility of abandoning herself to this creative work while she was searching for a home, thinking about her cubs, and generally coping with the ache of bereavement. Strangely enough, grief did not help her in her efforts at composition. It intruded, got in the way of those old feelings, those old ways remembered from the life she had enjoyed with A-ho. One of the reasons for this, she had to admit to herself, was a *tiny* icicle of resentment toward A-ho for abandoning her, for going away and leaving her behind. This cold spike of bitterness, she knew, was unreasonable and quite stupid, but she could not deny its presence in her. A-ho had not died on purpose and she felt terribly guilty for having such a grotesque emotion at such a time, but it would not go away.

FIVE

There was a storm, with rain coming down like lead shot and battering the saplings, forcing them into a position of genuflection. They bowed low, as if the weight of the heavy black bull-clouds was borne by their supple stems. Giant goat-gods fought in the heavens, their eyes flashing in terrible anger, their great skulls crashing together and shaking the skies. Through this driving rain, light, and noise, O-ha stumbled around, looking for a home. She was still too numb with the shock of her loss to be concerned by the weather, but it hampered her search.

For a whole day, O-ha searched Trinity Wood for any empty earth, or something that could be turned into a home for herself and her unborn cubs. She found an earth on the north side, but it turned out to be occupied by a *stoad*, an elderly fox whose age entitled her to a certain respect and esteem. A-magyr had hinted earlier that he was a *stoad*, but in fact he was far too active to fall into that category. This one was a testy vixen who did not want a young parent-to-be invading her earth. She screeched at O-ha, telling her to find some other place.

"Have you no heart?" said O-ha. "My mate has just been killed and our earth filled in. I need somewhere to stay, just for a while."

"No heart, whatsoever," snapped the *stoad*. "I lost it a long while ago, and I don't remember the last time I had a mate, so you won't get any sympathy out of me on that score. Dirty, messy creatures, dog foxes—wouldn't want one anyway," she muttered.

O-ha was too weary and dispirited to fight with the *stoad* and she left, to wander the woods again. By the time the moon was high, she had found a large oak and was curled up in a hollow between the half-exposed roots. It was cold and damp, however, and she knew that if she did not find shelter soon, she might put her unborn cubs in danger. The hard edge of winter was cutting into her like a blade. There was snow in the air and Ransheen had increased in force since the darkness had fallen.

One day, she thought to herself, we shall win some victories back over men and dogs.

In this way she kept her spirit warm, although her body remained frozen. The thought was, in fact, an idle one, since the damage was done and nothing could repair it. She was entitled to her wrath, but as with most creatures it would remain contained and not be transmuted into direct action against her enemy. O-ha would remember, and possibly never forgive, but to attempt to punish the perpetrator of the crime would do nothing to restore A-ho to her side and would probably result in her own death.

The following morning she shook a light fall of snow from her fur and staggered to the edge of the wood. There she dug as well as she could in the humus, looking for earthworms to eat. She found a rotten log that was full of dozing woodlice, which she devoured along with bits of sodden wood. Then she licked what moisture she could from the grasses, in the form of snow, before setting off again to search for a home.

The day seemed full of angles and sharp edges. The sky was a hard blue, with little relief. Even the sunlight seemed cold. Her body trembled as she wandered in the *hav* beyond the wood, along the ditches and hedgerows. Once she came across another pair of foxes, O-lan and A-lon, but they told her there was no room in their earth. The vixen was pregnant, like O-ha, and would soon be having a litter.

"We'd like to help," said O-lan, "but our earth is small. It's clay and you know how hard clay gets in the winter. You can't scrape out a hole big enough to store an acorn, let alone a place big enough for another fox. Sorry, but there it is."

As O-ha stumbled away, A-lon ran after her and she turned to face him.

"Listen," he said, "I've just remembered something. There's a colony of badgers on the south side of Trinity Wood—a large sett. Why don't you ask them if they'll take you in? It's a fairly common arrangement, you know, for badgers to share their homes with us. You'll probably be expected to contribute to their larder occasionally, but—well, you haven't got a lot of choice at the moment, have you?"

"You think they will?"

"You can ask. One of my brothers lives with badgers. He gets on all right with them . . . and I have a friend—"

"A-lon!" called his mate, probably a little worried about the length of time he was spending with this homeless vixen.

"Well—good luck," he said.

"Thanks—thanks very much. I'll give them a try if nothing else turns up."

She spent the rest of the day searching, occasionally grabbing a bite of this or that to keep her on her feet. She found some running water in a ditch. By the time evening came again, she was still in the same situation. Being near the south side of the wood, she searched for an entrance to the badgers' sett. There was a depression in the snow at the base of an elm; when she cleared this she found a hole. She went through it, down into the darkness, and then along a sixty-foot tunnel. The smell of badgers was strong in her nostrils and she could hear them moving about in adjacent chambers. While she was not afraid of badgers, she felt insecure in one of their tunnels. They were extremely powerful creatures who could certainly kill her if they wished. She was by no means sure of a welcome.

She came to a point where the tunnel opened up into a chamber and a voice cried, *"Feond oder freond?"* in harsh tones. Although it was completely dark in the sett, O-ha had a good mental picture of her surroundings from senses other than sight; these included an awareness factor which could not be named or even explained, but which animals who live underground have developed through countless millennia. She knew she was being confronted by a large, elderly male badger.

"Fox," she said, not understanding the guttural tongue of the badger. "I . . . I lost my earth. The humans destroyed it."

"Guman destroy? Ah, I speak some fox. You lost, eh?"

"No—I was wondering if . . . hoping that you had some room? A spare chamber? I have nowhere to live."

The badger grunted.

"Ah, no-home fox; eh? We got plenty room. You want stay, eh? I ask the others. You wait here. No move yet, see."

"I'll stay here," she replied, relieved.

There was a shuffling from the other side of the chamber and then silence. She waited for some time before there were sounds of the badger returning. By this time she was getting used to the unusual smells of a foreign earth, and had begun to feel more confident.

"Others say you stay—most say. You no bother us, eh? You keep yourself and no bother. I show you bed, top level."

"That's very kind . . ." she began to say, but the badger merely said gruffly, "Follow."

The badger took her up to the second level, to a chamber which felt quite roomy and which had dry bedding on the floor. First she marked the chamber under the disapproving eyes of the badger, then she regarded the dry grass and leaves. She was not used to a bed, having a fox's ascetic nature, but now she sank gratefully onto the warm leaves, her eyes closing almost as her head touched her paws. She heard the badger saying, "You go out through top hole. No come through my hole no more, see . . ." Then she was asleep.

On waking the next morning, she stretched out a paw to touch A-ho. She wondered, sleepily, why she could not hear or smell him. Then bewilderment followed, as she failed to recognize anything about the dark chamber in which she found herself.

"A-ho?" she whispered, a little afraid. Where was he? Out hunting perhaps, hoping to surprise her with a rabbit or some other kind of food? Where was the scent of his marks? Why did the earth not smell of his warm, musty fur? His sleep-odors?

Where was this place in which she found herself?

She searched the floor for her mate, still confused, and wondered whether she was still asleep and dreaming some horrible dream. If she could just speak with her mate, then she might be able to orientate herself.

Then, at last, she remembered the events of two days ago: the hunt, and the fox-spirit leading her to her mate's torn body. She remembered that A-ho had gone—would never return. The sense of loss was even more overwhelming than it had been during the previous day and night, as the full impact of his death now descended on her like a heavy coat, smothering her. Grief, the pain of the spirit, is worse than physical hurt, since it has no remedy outside time; and because no sufferer can see into the future to a point where the pain ceases, it is eternal. Such grief brings with it almost total internal collapse. The body walks around while the spirit lies still, in an agony of darkness and despair.

The previous day she had awakened in the wood and remembered that A-ho was gone, and this had immediately choked her spirit and caused her to acknowledge her pain; but this time, waking and *forgetting* he had gone, and *then* remembering was far worse. It was something she would do again many times, for seasons out of time, and it would never cease to cause her spiritual torment.

With heavy heart she found the tunnel and was about to go along

it when she recalled the badger's last words to her. She was not to use that way. There was a second, narrower exit on the far side of the chamber and she found that this led to the surface within thirty feet, without entering any other chambers. She went outside and visited A-ho's *sowander*, or holy place, just that once. Thereafter she never returned to that exact spot, since there was no comfort to be had in crossing the path of the dead. Also, it was a dangerous place. She had a duty to her unborn cubs now, and her responsibility to them was more important than her own feelings anyway.

During her confinement, O-ha tried to have as little as possible to do with the badgers, simply because they preferred it that way. If she met them in the tunnel, she nodded and said hello, but there was little communication necessary. One evening, however, just before she was due to leave the sett and search for food, the badger who had first spoken to her came to her chamber. His name was Gar.

"I come to say how you are?" he said, settling down.

"I'm fine," she said. "A little lonely, but . . ."

"Sure, sure. This is bad thing that happen to your mate. I understand this. *Guman*, huh!" He clicked his teeth to show what he thought of mankind. "We badger no bother this men. Once they send dog down here—small-middle dog. I bite him—ha!" Gar bared his ferocious-looking incisors.

O-ha was impressed.

"You fought a dog?"

"Ya. Fight him and send him run. We badger very strong animal. We badger, long, long history. We no bother this men, but they all the time try kill badger—some. Many *guman* not hurt badger, but some . . . they kill."

"Oh, we have a long history too, and they bother us all the time. I don't know why."

"You fox run fast, is why. They like run, *guman*—run, run, run, for no thing. Crazy animal, *guman*. Not all. Sometime they give us food, in the little field by house. Watch through window. Look, look, brock eat our food! What they think we do? Push it up nose?" He grunted, to show his contempt. "Gar not worry, though. Gar

strong in here," he said, indicating his chest. "Men can take old Gar body, but not his soul. Soul belong to no one but Gar."

She liked Gar. He seemed to have found the something that foxes talked about and believed existed only in the spirit world, beyond death.

"What you should do," said Gar, dreamily, "is go for long journey. Things happen on long journey. Great things. Make you see the world for sure. Big hill, deep valley, fast, fast river—see all these things. World is big place."

"I don't want to go on a journey. I like my own," she said. "Boring as that may sound, I like my own. This parish is large enough for me."

"I understand," said Gar. "Listen, I hear you fox can copy other animal—like sheep, or bird. This is true?"

O-ha said, "We can mimic other creatures, yes."

"Let me hear—you make bird sound."

O-ha obliged by chirruping.

"Ha. That sound like bird. Now sheep."

She bleated plaintively, like a lamb calling for its mother.

"Ha, good. I heard this was true."

"*Unlagu*," cried a voice, from one of the other chambers.

"What's the matter?" asked O-ha.

"Argh, no thing. She asked to be quiet—making noise not allowed, except for chatter-chatter, all time. Loud noise not allowed. Never mind. This is good, we talk. Find out about fox. You find out about badger. What you think, this *guman* not like fox because run fast, eh?"

"I think—well, I was told as a young cub that humans have never liked us because we kill chickens."

"What means is, fox kill chicken before *guman* kill chicken, is all. Everybody want eat chicken. *Forpan* people not like fox."

She had to confess that she agreed with what he said, but added that the situation was now well established and unchangeable.

"Anyway," said Gar, "they not *all* hate fox. No, no. I know fox live in *guman* place. They no kill him. Is only *guman* on horse—*guman* with gun—these hate fox."

"Those are the only kind I have met," said O-ha grimly.

"Whole world full of other kind. You go on long journey—you see other kind."

"I'd rather stay here," she repeated.

"*Eall ic waes mid sorgum gedrefed,*" said Gar incomprehensibly, obviously quoting some saying in his own language. "Sorrow, sorrow . . ." He sighed. "Well, I getting back now. Nice to talk. We do some more some time, eh?" She heard him get to his feet and shuffle out of the chamber, down the tunnel toward his own bed.

She slept after that, dreaming of humans, the secondary fear of foxes. Their primary terror was the *Unremembered Fear*, the Shadow-with-a-thousand-names, all of them forgotten; the White Mask, with its terrible white eyes and white jaws; about this, they never dreamed. It lurked somewhere beyond even the subconscious, deeper than dreams could reach, for its gruesome distorted features marred a face even the bravest of the brave could not visualize without traveling to the borders of madness. Long ago it had been pushed down into the back of the mind, where it could not be retrieved—not without showing its ugly visage in the land once again, and mercifully that had not happened for some time.

The next time O-ha saw Gar, however, he was as grumpy as he had been on their first meeting. She guessed that he was one of those animals who needed to be in the right mood for a conversation, and that such a mood came around very seldom.

One evening, when she was out hunting, she came across an old disused shed in a copse not far from a human dwelling. She checked around the rotten timbers for footprints or other recent signs that men had been there, and found nothing to arouse her fears. Inside the shed were some metal implements, all rusting away and joined to the shed walls by the lacy traps set by spiders for their prey. Tufts of grass were growing through the floorboards and a shelf hung down like a slide from under the glassless window. There was a blackbird's nest tucked high up in one corner: a good indication that the place was not frequented by humans.

It had been worrying O-ha for some time that she would be exposing her cubs to danger by having them in the badgers' sett.

Possibly the badgers would not harm them, but a fox likes complete security for her young and O-ha was no different from any other vixen. This shed might be a good place to have the cubs. The grass between the shed and the house, which stood at a distance of some three hundred yards, was high and had not been trampled. Perhaps some old humans lived in the house: people too frail to use their shed any longer? Whatever the reason, it seemed as if the hut had not been visited for a long time. Another thing in its favor was that the door was still secure. She could enter only through the small window. A dog would have great difficulty in following her through that high hole. Only squirrels, birds, and bats could enter, and she was not concerned about such creatures.

So she set her heart on using the small shed.

Until the time came, she would continue to live in the sett. It was convenient to be in a place where others could guard her stores of food, even if they did not realize they were doing it. Like all her kind, O-ha was a great horder, which made her an untidy creature to live with; but since the badgers left her to her own part of the complex, there was no one to complain. O-ha marked her chamber frequently. She scattered the feathers of birds, the inedible parts of vegetables, the bones of her prey, all over the chamber and outside around her personal entrance to the sett. She had heard some rumblings about this from some of the badgers, but though she promised herself to become tidier, she never put such promises into action. A fox has far more important things to think about than cleaning up around the place.

The days slid into weeks. Iron-grey skies were broken only by the occasional day of weak winter sunlight. There were no heavy snowfalls, but rain and sleet lashed down quite often and made life a little easier. The smaller creatures were often washed out of their homes and hunting was not as difficult as it might have been. The humans stayed inside their houses when rainstorms were sweeping across the land, and in any case, the ground was too wet to hold much of a scent.

One day, when Scresheen was screaming across the fields, blowing rubbish in all directions and snapping the branches from

trees; when the hares were doing silly things out in the fields, and weasels danced in front of stupefied rabbits before flying at their throats; when hawks dropped out of nowhere on unsuspecting mice—on such a day O-ha felt strange things happening inside her. She made the briefest goodbye call on Gar, telling him she was leaving.

"Where you going?" he asked, surprised.

"To see the world," she lied.

"Ha. Well, give it some kick from me," he said.

"I will," she said. "And thank you for the kindness. You took me in when I was at my wits' end."

"Pah. You look to them cubs, vixen. I see you someday. Gar see you when he nosing around that big old world, and you come back full of great things. Ha."

She left the sett with a few misgivings, but these were soon dispelled when she reached the small shed. There were no indications that anyone, dog or man, had been near it since she was there last. She jumped through the window and settled down on some old sacks in the corner, to give birth to her cubs.

It was a painful business.

SIX

Once upon a time there was no
hav or *havnot* for the windwalking foxes. There was no *face*, which is
the word for land covered by concrete, brick, or asphalt; and
consequently no *gerflan*, which is land not usually frequented by
humans, such as military ranges. For a long time after Cle-am, the
Long Hot Wind, shaped the world, the land was just the land,
consisting of earth and sky—and, after A-O, rivers and ponds as well.
The immediate descendants of the first heroes and heroines had no
need to give areas special names because the world was all one and
the same. In those days, when the world was still warm underfoot
and the rocks were living things that moved ponderously over the

landscape like giant snails, there were no humans. There were wolves, deer, tree martens, wildcats, but no men. There were forests then, stretching into infinity, and the universe was green from end to end, from top to bottom. Birds carried mouthfuls of seed—cow parsley, primrose, ragged robin, restharrow, vetch, coltsfoot, dandelion, tutsan—scattering them over the new soils. Then the first rains came, and the earth smelled good, the plants smelled green.

In the beginning, before the animals learned the effects of different fungi and herbs, they had to taste them all. Some became sick; some became addicts of hallucinogenic plants and wandered the world in a bemused state; some died. Gradually they learned the good and the bad. Foxglove and deadly nightshade were to be left well alone. Chives, wild horseradish, tansy, ground elder, chicory, were good. Mugwort and wormwood, bitter and pungent-smelling, were to be avoided. Amongst the fungi, parasol, chanterelle, cep, deceiver, wood blewitt, grisette, were good. Devil's boletus, yellow-stainer, fly agaric, death cap, destroying angel, were bad. Once the experiments were over, the plants identified according to use or non-use, the information then went into chants and songs, which were passed down through the generations. This was after the creatures of the earth had found their voices.

The first sound had come from a grasshopper, rubbing his legs together in delight, following a good meal. The noise stunned the rest of the animals and birds, since until that moment the world had been utterly silent. A blackbird found its voice and told the grasshopper to quiet down. A jackdaw yelled at the blackbird to watch the noise. A wolf told the jackdaw to mind its own business. Pretty soon, all the animals and birds were calling to one another, and many have not stopped since that time.

As the animals and birds found their voices and practiced with them, only the rocks and stones refused to add to the cacophonous choir. These solid members of the community were dense in more ways than one. In those early times even the mountains were as gentle as moths.

When the first humans arrived they frightened the timid rocks and stones so profoundly that they froze in their tracks and never

gain. The new two-legged animals began cutting down the
nd clearing the land, until it lay bare and cold under the
moonwatch. All other living things became their prey. The fox-
spirits roamed the land, creating *sowanders*, or holy places where the
ground had been soaked in the blood of martyrs—those foxes killed
not for food but simply because they wore red coats, walked on four
legs, and refused to capitulate like the dogs and cats. One by one
many other animals fell under the tyranny of man, some resisting,
some too timid to put up a fight. The horses fought and went down
early. Many of the pigs held out for a long time, in the remains of the
forests, but they too were overcome eventually. The wolves, cousins
of the foxes, refused to give ground and were largely exterminated.
The foxes themselves changed to meet the new circumstances: they
went underground and took to using the night, instead of the day.
They survived by wit and guile, by stealth and determination. They
became ghosts, fleeting wraiths that men caught sight of only out of
the corners of their eyes.

One of the reasons for the successful survival of the foxes was that
they elected no leaders to follow blindly into hopeless battles. There
were, and are, no king-foxes, or chief-foxes, or shamans, or tribal
elders. They did not form packs, like the wolves, or herds, like the
deer. They recognized no oligarchies or heads of any kind. Each dog
fox was his own leader, relying only on himself. No vixen followed
any instructions or orders from any other fox. They had no totems
or sacred stones, which could be used to trap them in certain places.
They had no organization to bind them to specific actions. They
remained as individuals, able to adapt to circumstances as external
changes took place. They did not howl at the moon, nor turn the sun
into a deity. Even the *sowanders* were merely places where a fox could
cross but not remain: in other words, areas in which it was forbidden
to stay, rather than places where they would gather, as the wolves
gathered around a sacred tree or overhang. There was no spot that
man could point to and say, "That's where the foxes gather—we can
wait there and ambush them." The foxes took notice of, but did not
worship, their ancestors, the fox-spirits of the *Firstdark*.

Since those early times foxes have managed to keep to their

solitary ways, living in small groups that meet with other groups only occasionally and never by design. They use many voices, from a cold bark to a banshee scream, to fool any listeners. They use the darkness as a cloak. They never rush or hurry, knowing that such feverish activity might be fine for other creatures, such as the shrew or the hare, but that for them a cool, clear hand and calculated movement are more likely to keep them alive.

All of this, O-ha was prepared to tell her cubs once they had grown to an age when they could understand. There were six in the litter and she licked them clean with an air of contentment. They were hers and she was prepared to defend them to the death. On the first day she had managed to catch a rat that came into the hut, but she now realized she had a grave problem. There was no dog fox to hunt for the family while she stayed and kept the young warm. At the bottom of the garden attached to the house, she found a sack of rotten potatoes that had been thrown onto a compost heap; but when these ran out she knew she had a problem facing her.

As it happened, she was seen by one of the house's occupants from a window, and to her surprise food was left for her about halfway down the garden. Gar had mentioned this strange behavior by some of the humans—how they would leave food for wild creatures and watch them eat it from behind their windows—and she could not believe her luck in having found such people. They did the same for the hedgehogs, which became alarmed by the presence of a fox and were constantly rolling into balls on O-ha's approach. Had she been starving she might have attempted to get at the creatures, but the humans' food was sufficient to sustain her and she knew from her days as a cub that hedgehogs were almost impenetrable. Certainly she had never yet met a fox who had managed to make a meal out of one of the prickly beasts.

When the cubs were eight days old, the food source suddenly disappeared. The house appeared empty and it seemed that the occupants had gone away temporarily. They had done so without realizing how much O-ha relied upon their generosity, possibly thinking that they were merely supplementing her diet rather than keeping her alive. She was bereft of support and had to wander further afield in order to keep herself fed and her milk flowing.

The next human dwelling, beyond the small cottage, was a great manor house where the man who led the foxhunts made his home. The cottage was in fact the gatehouse at the entrance to the long driveway that led to the manor itself. It was a house of many windows: a large, foursquare, cold-looking dwelling of grey stone blocks. The lawns around it were kept short and neat, with shrubs and evergreens placed at appropriate intervals and box-gardens enclosing rectangular concrete lilyponds. It was not a place that attracted foxes.

O-ha kept as far away from the manor as possible, in her short forays for food, but one night was attracted to a gazebo at the bottom of the lawn. Some human had been there during the day and had left bacon sandwiches balanced on the white woodwork of the hexagonal structure. She could smell the bacon from the safety of the unkempt grasses beyond the manor, and eventually climbed the ivy covering the red brick wall that encircled the estate. She made the short journey to where the food lay. Quickly, but without rushing, she went up the steps and hopped onto the rail next to the sandwiches. After a quick look around to see that she had not been observed, she snatched up the package and began to chew, grease-proof paper and all.

At that moment a shape came hurtling out of the darkness: a huge hound with a savage face. O-ha's instincts were ahead of her heart, and though afterward she felt the latter organ thumping in her chest, she was by that time on the roof of the gazebo and out of range of the hound's snapping jaws. Strangely enough, this giant beast from the Unplace—most definitely the largest dog she had ever seen in her life—was not shouting at her. Doubtless it did not want to attract human attention and have them spoil its fun. It tried to reach her by leaping high off the ground with its powerful hind legs, but when it was apparent that she was too high to get at, the dog lay on the grass and watched her through narrowed eyes. The great bone head lay on massive paws, waiting for her to make her move.

She said nothing and quickly assessed her chances of escape. They were almost negligible.

"You can look around all you want," said the hound. "You don't stand a chance. Sabre will break your neck, fox."

She shivered on hearing the rich timbre of this beast's voice, which was full of confidence.

"Why would you want to do that?" she asked, playing for time. "I mean, we're both canines—cousins, in fact—we speak the same language. The only small difference between us is . . ."

"That I live with men. That's more than a small difference, fox. I know what you think of dogs. We're the traitors, the weaklings, the pampered darlings, the *slaves*—you've got all sorts of names for us, haven't you? Well, let me tell you something. I would kill you even if you were another dog—another ridgeback hound—one of my own kind. I was trained to hunt lions in the hotlands beyond the sea. You know what a lion is, eh fox?"

Ridgeback? She had never heard of ridgebacks. She noticed a dark-brown ridge of hairs running counter to the normal, backswept hair of his tawny coat. This strip of coarse hairs growing the wrong way obviously gave the breed its name.

"No, I don't know any lions."

"You wouldn't, you ignorant bitch—"

"Vixen," she interrupted.

"I don't care what you call yourself, you're dead meat. I enjoy killing. It's my reason for living. It's what I'm here for—to kill. I'm not one of your namby-pamby foxhounds. I can snap a fence-post in two with these jaws. I'm one of the world's biggest breed of dogs and I recognize no such word as *compassion*. There's not a spark of cowardice in my body—only a need for blood. I have killed a human in my time, in that land I was telling you about . . . oh, you can look around while I'm talking. Don't think because I blow off at the mouth that I'm any less attentive. I'll bring you down within a few feet and rip your heart out . . ."

O-ha was beginning to get worried about her cubs. She had already left them too long and they would be cold and mewling for her warm belly-fur. Still she did not show any signs of frantic activity to this ridgeback. Instead, she sat on her haunches and began to scratch her ear with her hind leg, as if careless of his presence.

"I can stay up here all night," she said.

"And I can stay down here just as long. I could of course yell for assistance, bring the men out here, but I'm not going to. I want you for myself. They'll only shoot you. That's too quick, and it wouldn't satisfy this internal craving, now would it? You stay there all night. I'll stay here all night. We'll see who weakens first. I've tracked a lion over several days, without sleep. It's the thrill of the kill, you see. The thrill of the kill."

"I'm not one of these lions," she said. "You might be trained to catch those, but you're not trained to get foxes. We have our own ways of getting out of trouble."

"I've seen jackals and hyenas, pi-dogs as well. I know your kind. You're all the same, you skinny wild scavengers. You think you're clever, crafty, sly, but I know all the tricks, see? You can talk as much as you like. You're going to die, painfully, and that's that."

"No," she said, simply.

The baleful eyes were on hers.

"What do you mean—no?"

But she refused to answer; she lay on the roof of the gazebo, her heart in her mouth, awaiting the slightest chance. She was no good to her cubs dead, that was certain, yet her anxiety for them outweighed any personal concern for her own safety. Just a *chance*, that's all she wanted.

For a long while they just stared at each other, the night growing into itself. An owl came by, silently observed the scene, then left quickly. Gradually, the lights went out in different rooms of the house as the occupants settled down for the night. Finally the whole place was in darkness, save for one small room on the ground floor. This single light remained switched on well into the early hours of the morning. O-ha remarked on it, hoping to distract the hound, but Sabre refused to turn his head.

"My master," he said, "in his study. He's at his desk—be there until morning. Don't you worry about that, vixen."

Silence fell between them for a few minutes.

Then O-ha had an idea. She stood up, on the roof of the gazebo, and began screaming at the moon. Her voice went out, clear, cold, and ugly—her banshee shriek.

"Quiet," growled the hound. "That won't do you any good."

She continued to scream. Just as the hound was about to speak to her again, a human bark came from the direction of the house. The dog's instinct was to turn toward the call from his master and in that instant O-ha was down from the gazebo and racing for her life, zigzagging across the stretch of short grass between her and the undergrowth. The ridgeback was swift in following, and twice he almost had her in his jaws, but she evaded the large beast by leaping sideways. She hit the tall grasses and brambles, jumping over high objects that he had to race around, until they reached a wall. With supreme effort and agility she managed to spring to the top and down the other side. The dog could not follow. She heard him calling, in a voice cold with rage: "You haven't seen the last of me. I'll hunt you down, you skinny bitch. These jaws will crack your skull. . . ." The sounds faded into the distance, as she ran through the garden of the gatehouse to reach her precious cubs. One final leap and she was through the small window and inside the shed.

Two of the cubs were dead. When she nosed them over, they were cold to the touch. The others were barely alive. She set about trying to warm the living cubs, without pausing to take out the dead ones. Seconds were vital.

She had not long settled on her brood, when smells and sounds came to her that were unmistakable. The dog was leading his master to her hideout, following her scent from the grounds to the house. She snatched up a cub in her mouth and leapt through the window, just as the door was being forced open on its rusty hinges.

O-ha ran into the wood. She paused for a moment and looked back, hearing the hound call to her.

"We've got them, vixen, wherever you are out there! Can you hear me? My master has crushed them under his boots. He hates foxes just as much as I do. Can you hear me, vixen? Can you hear . . . ?"

An overwhelming despair arose within her.

The ridgeback had beaten her after all. The last cub had gone cold in her mouth. She could feel no pulse, no heartbeat against her jaws. Had she snatched up a dead one in her haste? Or had it died since leaving the hut? The dog could not have devised a more cruel punishment for entering his territory and escaping his wrath if he had sat for seasons, planning it.

Sabre was, without a doubt, on a leash and unable to follow her; otherwise he would have done so.

She laid the cub down and screeched:

"You killed my cubs, but you failed to catch me. Your stupidity, even for a lowlife dog, amazes me. I'll catch you sleeping one day and tear your throat out!"

She knew, of course, that such a threat was impossible, but it had its effect on the dog. She could hear the sounds of fury coming from the shed. O-ha picked up her dead cub and ran.

She returned to the badger colony two days later, prepared to make that place her home for the rest of her life. She was no longer interested in dog foxes, or litters, and her heart had hardened against life and all its highways and byways.

When she ran into Gar again, he said, "Ha! The little fox. How was it, the world?"

"It was a cruel, terrible place," she answered.

He nodded his head sagely.

"That so? That so? Some animals tell me this, but I think is it so? This can be cruel place *here*, if you look for cruel."

"I'm sorry to disappoint you," she replied.

"Not me," he said. "You disappoint *you*. When you go out again, you must look for different, not for same." He nodded at her breast. "In there is where eyes to see world, not in head. Next time you go, you look from inside."

"There won't be a next time," she answered, bitterly. "The world has taken all I ever had."

For quite some time she thought about committing *ranz-san*—tearing open her own stomach with her teeth—but something

held her back, some thought that such an act at that time would be regarded in *Heff* as wrong. So she did not resort to this last of fox actions, available to foxes caught in savage metal gins, or snares. It was not for foxes who were just tired of living. It was not for the weary in spirit, but for the sorely oppressed, the fox hemmed in by wire or trapped in a cage.

So, O-ha continued to live: a very difficult thing to do. She was not the first fox to ponder deeply on the nature of that strange emotion called *sadness*—on whether sadness entered the soul from the outside world, or was an inherent emotion that was in the fox from birth and merely triggered into a wakeful state by an external event.

Back at the manor house, another creature was swearing vengeance. The ridgeback, Sabre, was furious at the little fox for thwarting his attempts to kill her. *I'll remember that scent*, he thought. *I'll find that vixen again if it takes me a lifetime, and rip her from nose to tail. No one makes a fool of me and gets away with it. The dog will have its day.* Thus the vow was taken, the promise made, that would end in death for one of the two antagonists. Unfortunately for O-ha, she was not just another close encounter for the ridgeback. She had exposed the one weakness in his nature for which he hated himself—the deep-seated instinct to obey his master—and he could never let that pass. Hate for oneself is almost always transferred to some other creature, and in Sabre's case that creature was O-ha. For the rest of his life Sabre would be on the lookout for O-ha and her kind. In the hotlands beneath a fierce sun he had tracked lions; with his peers he had hunted down leopards and killed them; he had (at his master's instigation) attacked and torn the throat out of a fugitive black man trying to return to his homeland. To be outwitted by a small red-coated animal not much bigger than a cat was a terrible smear on his record as a hunter. Such an insult could not be forgotten.

PART TWO

ESCAPE FROM BEDLAM

SEVEN

The sign on Camio's cage said: AMERICAN RED FOX. The back of this board, which held more interest for him than the front, was gnawed at the corner, where he had cleaned his teeth on it through the wire mesh. Camio had a coat of rich, dark-red fur—almost chocolate—and he was, or had once been, bright-eyed and with a knowing look. He was a suburban creature, from a place with wide streets and houses with plenty of space around them. Most of the houses had had porches, under which a fox could hide, could sleep away the day in the shade, could make an earth—providing there were no children. (Human children, like foxes, enjoy the musty, spidery atmosphere of the twilight world below the floorboards.)

In that far-off place of his birth and upbringing, Camio had lived on the small creatures that were to be found under the houses, and on the food thrown away by humans. He was a scavenger, not recognizing any detriment in so being. There were those who believed hunting was a more noble way of obtaining food than was scavenging, but to most animals this was a load of nonsense. To survive was the prime objective, and if this could be achieved by making use of man's wasteful ways, then so much to the good.

Like many streetwise creatures, Camio was audacious and impudent with a cocky walk. He was aware that he did not know it all, but there was no reason why the rest of the world should be enlightened as to that fact. If he gave the impression that there was nothing he could not handle, nothing beyond his intellect, nothing to match his cunning and cleverness, then he saw no reason to interfere with this picture. His vixen, Roxina, had not shared the world's illusion with regard to her mate, but she allowed that he had certain features and aspects of his character possessed of charm and strength. She would have been proud of the way he conducted himself in the zoo, he thought: with quiet dignity and reserve.

He lay on the floor of his prison, while visitors to the zoo peered in at him or pointed their cameras and flashed bright lights into his eyes. He ignored them all. Let the monkeys show off and get all the attention: *he* was not going to demean himself by cavorting all over the place just to hear humans bark. He would get fed whatever he did, whether it was lazing around on the floor, or snapping at the faces that peered through the mesh. He considered himself lucky that he was not one of the more exotic creatures. Had he been a duckbilled platypus he might not be able to escape the foul air created by the visitors as they crowded around the cages. As it happened he was a fox, and not a very unusual one at that, so visitors to his cage were small in numbers and tended to stay only briefly.

A keeper went by, leading two Alsatian dogs on leashes. These were two of the animals that helped guard the zoo at night. Camio saw a chance for a little sport.

"Morning, minions," he drawled, "how's the great brotherhood of slaves today?"

One of the Alsatians jerked on its lead, snapping at him, "Keep your trap shut."

"Yes," said the other, "at least we're out here in the fresh air."

"Fresh air? With all those humans stinking the atmosphere? Some fresh. Some air. You can keep it, cousin."

"Don't call me *cousin*," said the first dog, "or I'll . . ." The rest of the sentence was choked off as the keeper tugged on the lead and barked at the dog.

"Convict," snapped the second dog.

"Look who's talking," replied Camio. "The one on the end of a chain! Catch me being dragged along with that thing wrapped around my neck. But then you poor saps haven't got much choice, have you? Your ancestors made sure of that, when they gave in meekly to the domination of man."

The dogs erupted into fury and were dragged away by their puzzled keeper, who barked at them in a high shrill voice, and pulled on their choker chains until they stopped fighting against them.

Camio scratched his ear in a show of contempt.

"German Shepherd hounds? Killers. They should be behind bars, not me. I never bothered a human in my life. . . ." He grumbled away to himself for the next hour, until his meal was delivered. The truth was, Camio was going a little crazy. The zoo around him was like an asylum for mentally disturbed animals. If they weren't crazy when they came in, it did not take long before most of them were.

In their wild state, the carnivores came into contact with the herbivores only when they were hungry and needed a kill. Their hunting modes came into operation then, and all the small chemical changes and mechanisms required for speed, agility, and single-minded sense of purpose, were triggered into action. The brain was honed to sharpness, the muscles were brought to peak, the senses were primed.

On the other hand, when the grazing animals smelled a hunter, their defense circuits were electrified. Their hearts pumped adrenalin, their minds flashed through possible escape routes, their senses sought the nuances in the wind.

In the zoo they found themselves living yards from each other, always scenting, seeing, hearing each other. Their bodily juices ran wild, sending waves of panic through the grazers, sending frenzy to the brains of the hunters. The leopard could scent the antelope, the lion, the wildebeest. They were all too close to each other to allow any respite. On their part, the deer could smell the cheetah, and the rabbit could see into the eagle's cage. It was madness, pure madness.

Prey could smell predator, hunter could smell quarry.

The rabbits spent their lives in perpetual panic, hearing the cry of the wolf, the bark of the fox, the shriek of the hawk. The deer could smell the scents of their deadly enemies—enemies with belly-ripping claws and terrible teeth—and went berserk occasionally under the cold eye of a caged lynx or python. A thousand animals were crammed into less than a square mile. A thousand animals, one half of which were going crazy trying to get at the other half, and that second half going insane with fear. And no one going anywhere, because the bars were too strong and the pits too deep. So they traveled around in circles, tying themselves into mental knots and eventually lapsing into vacant stupidity.

There were other ways to go insane, besides having your instincts constantly being tinkered with. You could literally die of boredom and apathy. You could lose your mind quite easily in a place where the scenery remained the same—four walls and a set of bars—and nothing happened from one day to the next. You could disappear into yourself in an area where three strides took you to the edge of your world and then, when you turned around, another three strides took you across it again.

Camio had not quite reached this state, but he was not far from it. A hopelessness was beginning to set in; a despair had opened beneath him like a giant black pit, and he was in danger of falling into it. Only a spark of his former self remained, a spark that he kept alive by baiting the Alsatians, or snapping at the visitors.

That night, after the visitors had gone and he was alone with a thousand other creatures, he paced the cage, grumbling to himself.

At one point in his turn he knocked against the cage door, which rattled loudly. For a moment this did not register, but after two more circuits of his cage he thought: *Something's not right.* The door to the cage did not rattle when fastened securely.

He went to it again and threw his body against it. It rattled once more and jiggered itself open, just half an inch, enough to get his nose behind.

Still Camio was not completely aware of what this meant. He had been locked up for so long, he was numbed into a state of acceptance.

Then he hooked a paw behind the metal edge of the door and it swung inward. The path to freedom was unblocked, the barrier gone, and he could slip away into the night. The keeper had forgotten to lock the cage door and the way was open. He needed no more convincing. In the next moment he was padding quietly between the cages of other animals, primed for danger, his tread wary. It was all coming back to him now: his strong sense of survival.

A wolf called to him as he passed, "Hey, cousin. Let me out."

Camio paused, but then said, "I'm sorry. I don't know how. I would if I could, but the way they work those locks is a mystery to me. You need fingers for such things. I'm sorry."

The wolf looked disappointed, but shrugged.

"That's all right, cousin." The canid's eyes took on a glazed look and she slipped back into her former state of hopelessness.

Camio continued to the inner wall of the zoo. Although he was out of his cage, he was far from free. There was a high wall around the zoo, beyond which was an empty area patrolled by dogs, and then finally a chain-link fence.

The Alsatians were in fact there to prevent people from entering the zoo and stealing rare creatures, rather than to stop animals from getting out. After all, a German Shepherd dog would not be able to prevent a lion from escaping. However, the Alsatians hated foxes and wolves so much, Camio knew they would not hesitate to attack him if they could catch him.

Camio stopped by the cage of a lion and peered in. A pair of baleful eyes met his own. In the dark shadows of the cage sat a great

tawny beast. A few strange words rumbled from the throat of this muscled character and despite his curiosity Camio hurried on. He had always found the lions awe-inspiring creatures from a distance, but up close they were chilling in their aspect. The bars of the cage looked positively flimsy compared with the powerful physique of the great cat, and Camio was not about to test the strength of either by hanging around where he was not wanted. The musty smell of the lion remained in his nostrils: even the odor seemed to be charged with lazy strength.

Finally, Camio saw a way to reach the top of the wall. He managed to get onto this barrier by running along the banked rock of the bear pit and up to the goat pinnacles above. There was a fence on top of this outcrop of rock, which took him three tries to leap. The last time, he managed to get over, but not without cutting his underside on the sharp wire. The wound was not deep, however, and certainly not bad enough to keep him from going on.

Even having made it to the far side of this wall, he was not yet out of the zoo. There was the chain-link fence to negotiate: the fence that kept the public out, and within which roamed the Alsatians. Camio warily entered this region, his nose to the wind, trying to get an indication of the dogs' whereabouts. When he was halfway across the concrete gap between the wall and the fence, he caught a warning on the night air. He paused, unsure whether to run for the fence, or to retreat into the shadows and hope that the noses of the domestic animals were not as good as his own.

While he hesitated, the two dogs he had baited that day came hurtling around the corner. They seemed in some state of excitement. Then Camio saw that there were seven or eight humans right by the fence, eating sweet-smelling cooked meat skewered on sticks. They were loud, noisy creatures, juveniles by the look of them. Camio slipped into the shadows of the goat pinnacles, where he watched and waited with a pounding heart.

The Alsatians threw themselves at the fence, shouting insanely at the group of young humans who at first backed off, startled. Then, when the juveniles saw that the dogs could not get at them, they began barking in raucous voices. They were flashy, gaudy creatures, covered in leather and chains, and as the dogs jumped and screamed, the humans kicked at the fence, driving the hounds into a frenzy. One of the female humans, with hair the color of several sunsets, kept teasing the Alsatians with a piece of meat, offering it to the dogs while knowing they could not get at it.

Eventually the juveniles tired of baiting the Alsatians and walked off, down the street. Still the German Shepherds foamed at the mouth, screaming after those ugly humans. Eventually they walked from the fence, grumbling to each other, and moved toward Camio's hiding place.

The fox held his breath. The smell of the spicy meat was still in the air, but if the dogs came any closer even *they* would not be able to miss his scent.

One of the Alsatians stopped to scratch behind his ear.

"Come on, come on," growled the other, moving off along the corridor between the wall and fence. He seemed anxious to do another circuit of the zoo, but his companion yawned.

"Wait a bit . . ." the scratching Alsatian paused for a moment, still on his haunches. He sniffed.

"Can you smell anything?" he said. "I could swear . . ."

"Can I smell anything?" said the other, the sentence dripping with sarcasm. "Only cooked steak, that's *all*."

"No, something . . . something . . ." the first Alsatian's head snapped up. "FOX. I can smell fox!"

"What?" The other turned, and began trotting back.

It was time for Camio to move.

He dashed forward out of the shadows, leaped over the Alsatian who had been scratching himself, and headed for the fence. The second dog came at his flank, but Camio managed, by halting and swerving, to avoid the snapping jaws.

The little fox hit the chain-link fence about halfway up, and his scrambling paws tried to obtain a purchase. He slipped. He fell on one of the dogs below, rolling off its back. There were canine teeth on his hind leg, trying to get a firm grip. He wrenched his leg free without the bone breaking. A second set of jaws went for his abdomen, but he rolled over a dozen times. They snipped like metallic incisors, catching only a few belly hairs.

Gasping for breath, Camio ran again for the fence. This time the two dogs came at him from different directions. He swerved and turned, and they crashed into one another. The fox saw his chance, and, running full circle, used their backs for a launching pad. He took off from their tangled bodies, gaining extra height. The dogs were furious when they realized they were being used to leapfrog the fox to his escape.

It was a supreme jump, worthy of a springbok antelope, and Camio's front paws caught the top of the fence. He hung there, suspended for a moment. He felt weak and drained, and almost fell backward. Below him the two dogs were jumping, snarling, and snapping at his hindquarters. He could feel their hot breath on his fur.

Having got this far he was determined he would either escape or die in the attempt. He was certainly not going back to that cage to wither away, his brain atrophying in his skull, and all sense of time and energy dissipating into the foul atmosphere of the lunatic asylum.

Employing the last of his reserves, he managed to scramble on top of the fence, revealing almost as much agility as a monkey. He fell to the ground on the other side, hurting his right forepaw, and the Alsatians hurled themselves at the chain-link fence in fury, their red mouths wide and their eyes blazing hatred. Camio was triumphant.

"You brainless brutes, you've let me get away. Maybe they'll put you in my cage, to take my place?" he said, but a weariness descended upon him, which did not allow for further comment on his part. For one thing he realized he was now in a street, with traffic roaring past and people hurrying along the pavements. He took to his paws, limping along at the edge of the street, hoping to find a place where there were fewer human beings.

He need not have worried overmuch. City people, especially those using the streets at the time Camio had jumped the fence, are notoriously blind. They have set purposes and walk with glazed eyes and determined tread from one place to the next. They like nothing to interfere with that purpose, and even a murder amongst their own kind has them faltering only when they cannot avoid it. Most of them, if they noticed him at all, took him for a stray dog and barely glanced at him. Those who did notice something unusual about him, or even recognized him as a fox, merely paused for a second in their stride before going on. They were not interested in anything but their destinations. A news vendor pointed to him and barked something, but it was not a sound of alarm, merely of curiosity. The news vendor had no doubt seen many foxes in and around the city where he worked, since there was quite a colony of the red-coated animals in the vicinity.

Having eaten earlier in the evening, Camio was not interested in the smells that issued from restaurants and cafés during his walk, and contented himself with making his way down to the river that ran through the center of the city. There he found a place under one of the bridges, where he could rest his injured leg and lick his belly wounds. He felt very pleased with himself. Now that he had escaped there was no possibility of going back again. He was out and he would stay out. Had he been a lion or a cheetah, they would have sent out hit squads to net him—or shoot him—never resting until he was caught. Had he been an eagle, the news broadcasts would be flashing his picture on the screen. Since he was a fox, and not at all dissimilar from several thousand other foxes in the city, they would quietly count his loss as unfortunate and set about getting some other poor creature to take his place in the cage. He was lucky. He was neither rare, nor valuable, nor dangerous to humans. He was just another fox.

Camio was not unused to city life. In his former homeland he had lived on the outskirts of a city, enjoying suburban surroundings. The traffic had not been as fierce as it was here, but he knew enough to stay off the road whenever possible; and he knew that one could live quite well on hamburgers and sausages thrown away by drunks with eyes stronger than their stomachs. He also knew that though the city was crammed with people, they were not as dangerous to him as humans out in the country, because if they did carry guns it was to shoot each other and not the foxes that robbed their trash cans. They did not ride you down on horseback in the city, or send highly trained packs of dogs to rip your guts out. There were dogs, but most of them were on leads and those that were not could be evaded very easily. The most dangerous thing about the city was the road and its traffic, which indeed accounted for many deaths amongst the shortsighted foxes. You took your chances with cars and trucks, however, and at least they were not malicious. They were not out to get you. If they killed you, it was an accident, and they never came up on the pavement to get you, or jumped a wall, or climbed a fence. They remained on that hard black river.

Camio stayed under the bridge the whole of that night, watching the riverboats slide by in the dark, glistening with bright berries of light. The air stank with the fumes of engines, but at least there was not a jaguar pacing up and down a few feet away, swearing under its breath that it was going to kill every living thing in existence once it got out. At least there was not some poor creature breaking down every five minutes and keeping him awake with pitiful cries for freedom. The air stank but it was a clean stink and could be borne. Camio added to the odors by marking the area under the bridge. He might be there for only a short time, but that was no reason not to define his squat for the benefit of passers-by.

Once, during the night, a lean feral cat came under the bridge (obviously ignoring the fox marks) looking for mice, and Camio snarled at it. For a few moments they eyed each other, each trying to burn its opponent with the sheer power of will, and then the cat pretended it had seen something beyond the bridge. Cats were like that. They would never admit to defeat, and certainly Camio had yet to meet a cat that was afraid of him. Cats, despite their size, had quite an array of weapons that they were not slow to use, and they were quick; he had to admire their speed. When you met one you had to face it out until it went away. If you happened to be sitting near a litter of feline kittens, however, your hide wasn't worth a damn.

No doubt he would run into a raccoon or coyote next: they were town dwellers too, these days. He had seen more and more of them enter the suburbs before he was taken away.

The next morning Camio's leg felt better. He tested it out by walking along the river bank and back again. The limp was still in evidence but most of the pain had gone. Within a day or so it would be forgotten completely.

Traffic had begun thundering over the bridge in earnest, and humans were clip-clopping in that cityhurry way of theirs, going everywhere and nowhere. Camio stayed where he was until midday, before venturing out again. The tide had ebbed and the river had retreated a little, so he went down onto the mud and chased a seagull, mostly for fun. There were bits of food in the mud, which could be got at with a minimum of fuss, keeping him interested until the evening. People on barges and boats could see him and gestured occasionally, but those on the streets above were at the wrong angle. He enjoyed a day of running around in freedom, getting strength back into his bad leg on the soft mud and generally having a fine time of it. By the time it got dark, he was ready for the streets again. There was a flurry of snow in the air, and though the city was warmer than the country, it could still be bitter if you were caught with an empty stomach. He followed his nose to a restaurant and went around to the alley at the back, where the waste bins were.

Each of the bins had a lid, fastened securely, so he had to wait in the shadows until someone came out. In the meantime, cats and rats slid in and out of the shadows, also intent on finding scraps. They took little notice of him. He might have taken a rat, if one came close enough, but there were easier pickings to be had if he was patient. At one point someone came out of the back of the restaurant and opened a bin, tossing stuff inside. The lid was thrown back on casually, the human being in a hurry to return to the kitchen. Camio went forward as soon as it was safe and nosed the lid off. It clattered to the floor and he leapt inside the bin, gobbling down the mess inside. Then he heard a barking and before he could escape, the lid was slammed back onto the bin again, and jammed tight. He pushed with his head, but it would not move. He contented himself with eating his fill for a while, but eventually realized he would have to wait until someone came out to put more scraps in the bin, before he could escape.

The humans came out all right: he heard them. But they went to other bins, leaving his alone. Once someone tried to open it, but the last person had obviously done a good job, because the top would not move. He was trapped inside until something else happened.

It was a long, tiresome wait. Camio used it to dream of better places, of his lost mate, of new freedoms and exciting times ahead.

EIGHT

Camio was awakened by the clatter of bins and the grinding sound of something mechanical. From within the bin the noises outside were terrifying and for a few seconds he tried to gnaw his way through his metal prison. Then the bin moved and the lid was raised. Camio sprang from a sitting position out into the day, narrowly missing a human face. There was a startled bark, and the bin was dropped. He did not wait to see the results of his sudden appearance, but raced away down the alley and over a fence at the end. He could hear yaps and barks behind him as he continued out into another street.

Without thinking, still being spurred on by a certain amount of panic, he walked out into the road. He felt something strike his shoulder with great force and he went spinning, head over foot, into the gutter. His mind whirled with dizziness and when he tried to get to his feet, he fell over again. Around him were the muted barks of humans and eventually he felt someone lifting him bodily. Although the hands were soft and gentle, and exuded a sweet perfume, he tried to bite them. Then he was aware of being placed on a soft surface and shortly afterward, a sensation of motion.

Gradually his senses came back to him and he was able to lift his head. He was in a small room with a human being. The human was facing the front, looking out through one of the windows that surrounded them. Beyond the window to Camio's left, the world was racing by in a blur of light and dark. This sensation brought back the giddy feeling, and he lay back again, feeling sick, his head on his paws. The human in front glanced back once or twice and Camio could see the black around the eyes and the red lips. From studying them in his zoo days, he knew this was the female of the species, since the human young were always more attached to the painted ones than to the ones with unpainted faces. He knew that females, providing they were not keepers, were often a soft touch. The females, and *very* occasionally the males, sometimes tried to disguise themselves by wearing the coats of other creatures, such as minks. This kind of human was unpredictable and Camio was glad to see that his female companion had adopted no such affectation.

Finally the motion ceased and the female turned right around in its seat to look at him. He snarled into the painted face, which went white with fear. The human opened a door and jumped out, closing it before Camio could follow. For the next few seconds he tore around the inside of his new prison, trying to find a way out, getting snagged on projections on the floor. When that failed, he went to one of the windows and was aware of someone other than the female looking in at him as if he were back in his cage. He recognized the human type, well known to him at the zoo, by the white coat. It was one of those that held you as if they knew what they were doing, and then stuck needles into you, or sprayed you with some foul-smelling thing, or forced hard pellets down your throat: a white torturer!

Got to get out of here, thought Camio, *before this one sends me to sleep!* They did that when they wanted to take you away somewhere—and he knew where he would be going: back to the zoo.

The white torturer was shaking his head at the female, who was gesturing now, and unbelievably the door was opened and the way left clear for him to escape. He did not run out immediately. He suspected some trap. Then he realized it was now or never, and hopped down onto the pavement to walk away in a dignified manner. No one chased him, and when he looked back the female was waving an arm at him.

"Weird, weird creatures," he said to himself. "First they capture you and carry you off . . ." he could see now that his "prison" had been a car, "and then they let you go." There was no fathoming such behavior and he did not try. He had long since given up trying to understand the behavior of humans. They were *all* unpredictable, fur coats or not.

He walked the length of the street and found an area with a tall boarded fence around it. There was a small gap in the boards, through which he squeezed his pliable body, and he found himself standing on the edge of a great square hole. Inside the hole and around the edge were huge mechanical devices, all lying idle. Not a human in sight. He heaved a sigh of relief. Time to gather his faculties and reassess his situation. He walked down an earth ramp into the hole itself, the bottom of which could not be seen from the surrounding houses.

There were puddles down there, one of which he drank from, satisfying an increasingly irritating thirst. Then he put his nose to the wind and scented a fellow fox: a female. Following the scent, he came across a vixen who was lying asleep on a pile of rags. She awoke when he nosed her.

"Hello," he said.

She opened one eye and replied, "Hello yourself. What do you want?"

He was taken aback for a moment, having expected a more friendly reply, but then he was a stranger in this place. It was up to him to make the overtures toward friendship. Of course the locals would be suspicious of uninvited foxes. "Nothing really—it's just that I haven't talked to another fox in a long while."

"You're wasting your time," she said in a bored tone. "Despite the funny accent, I'm not interested. Wrong time, wrong place."

He did not know what she meant at first, then realized she must have thought he wanted to mate.

"Hey, look—I just wanted to talk."

"Really?" she said, yawning. Camio noticed how ragged her coat was, and that she smelled a little of unlicked fur. Clearly she did not take care of herself as well as he thought foxes should. "And you woke me up for that?"

"I told you—I've been out of circulation. Humans trapped me a long while ago, took me on a long journey, then stuck me in a cage to be gawped at by them and their young. I haven't contacted another fox for . . . I don't know how long. What gives around here? Where are all the coyotes and raccoons? All I've seen so far are cats and dogs."

She was awake now, and looking at him strangely. Her bleary eyes took in the details of his appearance.

"Coy-*what*? Raccoons? I don't know *what* you're blabbering about. I came in here to get a rest, not go through some sort of interrogation. Go look for your raccoons somewhere else."

"I'm not looking for them—I just thought . . . look, what is this place? Why aren't there any humans in here?" He gestured with his nose at their surroundings. Clearly men were working to build something over the great square pit. In which case, where were they?

"Part-time *gerflan*," she said. "You don't get humans in here all the time. They leave the place empty at night and every seventh day for some reason. Don't ask me why, because on the other days the place is crawling with them, but it's a fact. Every seventh day—empty. This is it. Now can I have some peace?"

"*Gerflan*? That's a new one on me. I'm obviously a long way from home. Are there more places like this? More part-time *gerflans*?"

"Lots of them in this part of the city. Places where they put their cars on five days and almost empty on days six and seven. . . ." She

seemed to be enjoying the conversation, now that it appeared she was teaching a green fox about the ways and wiles of the city. "You from the country?" she asked. "You have a strange way of talking. I've never heard anyone talk like you. And your fur—it's darker than . . . you're not from around here, are you."

"Not exactly. As I said, I'm new to these parts."

"Not exactly," she mimicked his dialect. "How can you be *inexactly* from these parts?"

"I don't know. I mean, I know I'm not from here, but I'm not sure quite where I am from—in relation to this city."

"Well, don't get fooled by these holes the humans dig. They're not always what they seem. There are some which are *gerflans* for five days of the week and have humans in them on the sixth and seventh. Sounds confusing, eh? You have to be in the know, friend. You see, in holes like this they use big shovels and those machines, but in the five-day *gerflans* they use tiny shovels, no bigger than their hands, and in those pits they work very slowly, digging them out almost by the mouthful, and use little brushes to blow away the dirt from anything they find in the holes. Here, in places like this," she gestured expansively, "they just dig as much out as they can and don't worry about what they find in the holes. Far from being precious, the stuff they find here is just thrown away with the rest of the clay. Confusing, isn't it?"

"Yes, but interesting. How can you tell the different types of holes apart?"

"Well, mostly your one- or two-day *gerflan* is BIG—like this one. But your five-day *gerflan* can be a lot smaller, and broken up into several different-sized pits. Usually there's a lot of string and tape about on the second type, though you get *some* of that around here too. You just have to have a nose for it. You'll learn—or get a shovel around the backside—one or the other."

She rose lazily to her feet and went to one of the puddles for a drink, returning to his side a little later. For a while she stared at him, then said, "You got a mate?" He noticed that her mouth and teeth were stained yellow—not a dull shade, but vivid—and he wondered if she had been eating yellow-staining mushrooms, which he knew could sometimes be poisonous. Not always, but they were risky. Out of politeness, he remained silent on the subject. He would ask when he knew her better.

"Not at the moment," said Camio. He studied her carefully. She was meaty and middle-aged, and was losing her fur rapidly. That did not mean very much. He was not a cub himself and his own fur had begun to molt. By summer they would both be poor-looking specimens—along with the rest of the fox community.

"Neither have I. Last one ran off with a . . ." she swore. "He was pretty useless anyway. Tends to be a little bit like that in the *face*. I come from the country like you"—he was about to protest and then decided it would only confuse things more—"and there we used to find a mate and stick with them. Happens in the *face* too, of course, but since there's more foxes here, more opportunity to change partners, so relationships are not as stable. I like the look of you. . . ."

"Thanks," said Camio, feeling uncomfortable for some reason. This vixen was a little too sharp-featured and cynical for him. Maybe he was old-fashioned, but he preferred foxes that were less jaded. His own mate had escaped the net that had caught him, back home, but she had not been as knowing as this one. She had just been bright and alert.

"You going to hang around for a while?"

"For the day at least. I want to learn a little more about where I am and what the rules are."

"I know what you mean." She came up beside him and settled down so that they were touching. He was not offended, even that she was invading his body space more than was comfortable, and he stayed where he was. They lay like that for about two hours, each warming the other.

"You know," he said dreamily, as they lay there, "I once heard of a land where the trees are tall and wide at the top—not bushy, but flat, so they throw out a large area of shade. And the sky is big there—really big—and always blue. It rains, of course, but all the water comes down at once and fills the rivers until they rush in torrents over the land. Brown rivers, full of crocodiles and hippos . . ."

"Full of *what*?"

"Oh . . . creatures of that land. You don't get them here, except in the zoo. That's where I heard of this place, from the jackals. It's the Land of the Lions, and the air is full of mountains and dust, and there's hardly a human to be seen. It's a lazy land, touched by dreams, but there's excitement around every bush. The jackals said you could *smell* the excitement in the atmosphere . . . and no humans. Well, very, very few. Those that are there are only interested in the elephants and rhinos . . ."

"The *what*?"

"The . . . oh, never mind. You wouldn't understand unless you'd been where I have. And they all go mad. So would I if I'd been taken from such a wonderful place—a place where you can run and run and never reach a town or city. I'd like that, I think, though food's easier to get in areas where the humans collect like ants. . . ."

"The *face*," she said, breaking his reverie. "Talking of food, let's go get something to eat."

"Right," said Camio, realizing he was hungry again.

She walked languidly toward the hole in the fence, saying, "My name's O-tasso, by the way—what's yours?"

"Camio," he replied.

"A-camio?"

"No—just Camio."

She turned and looked at him closely.

"Funny name. Where did you say you were from?"

"The country," he said, not wanting to get into one of those confusing conversations again. "Now, where do we eat? I had a bad experience last night—got trapped in a bin. I don't want that to happen again."

She bared her teeth.

"No—stealing from bins is too easy," she said. "We'll have some fun, you and me. There's a place not far from here where humans collect hot food and carry it home. We'll go there. . . ."

She slipped out into the street and Camio followed her, his

stomach doing flip-flops at the thought of warm food. He preferred it to cold, but getting it was another thing. It cooled off very quickly in the bins. But then she had said they were not going to steal from bins . . .

He followed her through the near-deserted roads to a cobbled street with posts at each end. In the middle of this small street was a take-away restaurant, where humans did not stay to eat but carried their meal home with them. Camio knew of such places and they often had delicious hamburgers covered in sauce.

This place smelled a lot different from others he had known, though. The scents were sharp and spicy and the meals were carried out in shiny tin-foil containers. O-tasso motioned for him to crouch down, in the shadows of a shop doorway, and wait there. She did the same, her bright, keen eyes on the take-away door, directly opposite.

"Hot, hot, hot . . ." she kept muttering. "*De*-liciously *hot*."

"Are we going around the back?" he whispered after a while, but she glared at him, indicating that he should be quiet.

Behind the glass-fronted take-away restaurant Camio could see brown-skinned humans hard at work, the steam billowing around them like hot mist. The decor was dark-red cloth, with pictures of waterfalls on the walls. Of course, being a fox, Camio could not focus on these things for very long, especially the stationary ones, and he concentrated on the smells which were among the most exotic and pungent he had ever experienced. He could not imagine what was in those tin-foil boxes.

Still O-tasso waited, as couples and threesomes went into the take-away and came out laden with goods. Then finally a single human went in on its own, and O-tasso stiffened and seemed to make ready for something.

"Okay," she said, "this is it. I'll make the snatch and you act as decoy. When I say *now*, you follow me out, but take a different . . ." She stopped, because the man was leaving the restaurant.

"NOW!"

She flew forward with amazing speed, and instinctively Camio followed, though he had no idea what was going on.

As if she were mooncrazy, O-tasso ran straight at the human, leapt into the air, and snatched the package out of his hand with her teeth. Then she hurried away down the alley, leaving Camio running in her wake.

The human gave out a sharp bark and kicked at Camio, just catching his flank, but not hard enough to bowl him over. Then there was a short chase, as two other people came out of the restaurant and joined the man in trying to run down Camio. O-tasso was nowhere to be seen.

With his heart thumping in his throat, Camio wheeled around a corner and eventually managed to evade his pursuers. Then he retraced his earlier passage and got back to the boarded place with the hole behind it. A spicy aroma was in the air and Camio was sure every human for miles around would know exactly where to look for the stolen goods. Down below, in the pit, O-tasso was eating, wolfing down the contents of the box.

"Come on," she said, as he approached her, "I've left you half . . ."

This was not quite true. When he looked into the box he saw that only about three mouthfuls remained, but these he was determined to have since he had risked his life to get them. The vixen was obviously as mad as a weasel with a worm in its brain. There was nothing wrong with thieving food, but to steal directly out of the hands of humans was *insane*. There was no other word for it.

He took a mouthful of the yellow-juiced, greasy-looking slops in the bottom of the shiny box—and the next second felt his brains spurting through his ears and nostrils! HOT!

HOT! HOT! HOT!

Not only did it burn his sensitive mouth, throat, and gullet, but the stuff numbed his taste buds with an eloquence of spicy fire that had his eyeballs starting out of his head and water pouring from the sockets.

"HAAA!" he cried.

O-tasso nodded. "Wonderful, isn't it?"

Camio ran to the nearest puddle and drank a bellyful of water before returning, to find that she had finished off what was left in the bottom of the box.

"Sorry," she said, as if she had just noticed what she had done. "We'll go out to another one. This time you can make the snatch and I'll be the decoy. We make a good team, don't we?"

"What is that stuff?" he asked, huskily.

"Oh—food, you know. You have to get it fresh from their hands or it's not the same. The waste they throw out the back goes cold very quickly. This is the real thing. Hot, eh? I love it. Can't get enough. I won't eat anything else now. Mind you," she said reflectively, "it plays the devil with your guts, but you get used to that after a while. It's a matter of acquiring the taste and getting your gut to accept it—but once you've mastered it, there's nothing to equal it. I love it. It's the hot spices, you see."

Camio was beginning to see why her mate had gone off with another vixen. This one lived very dangerously, and was addicted to food that would burn through solid stone. He would not call himself a coward but if he did something brave there had to be a reward at the end of it, not a punishment.

"I think I've had enough," he said. "Ate very well last night. We'll go out again tomorrow, shall we?"

She looked disappointed, but settled down on the rags again.

"All right. Wake me up when the men come. Once they start those machines there's no rest for the wicked. You'll soon get used to life in the *face*, Camio, and I'll teach you all I know. When we have our first litter, you'll have to go out and get the food on your own, you know."

"Won't—well, ordinary food do?"

She looked shocked.

"Oh no! It has to be the real thing. Just think what strong cubs we'll raise. The real thing—or nothing."

"Right," he said. "The real thing."

Once she was asleep he slipped away quietly, thinking that city life was not quite as agreeable as life in the suburbs. He would have

to find a way of getting further out, on the edge of the city, where food was cooler and sweeter to the taste.

He trotted through the evening streets, occasionally coming across another fox or a cat, but very few humans. Apparently the city was especially different from the suburbs on this, the seventh day. In the suburbs humans were out on their lawns, washing their cars or weeding their gardens. In the suburbs there were dogs all over the place and people dressed up in white clothes and hats, walking along the sidewalks toward churches (which were safe, empty hiding places on most other days) or visiting other people's houses. It seemed that on the seventh day in the city everyone went underground, which was all right with Camio.

The thing to do, he mused, was to find another one of those *gerflans*. He liked the idea of places where humans came only infrequently and in small numbers. They had had such areas back home, of course, like the railroads, but foxes there did not have special words for such places. There was just *safe* and *unsafe*. '*Is it safe?*' was all a fox would ask of a raccoon or coyote. And it was the one question that all wild urban creatures were obliged to answer, regardless of feuds or traditional wars between species. You might battle to the death with the animal who posed the question, but *after* you had informed him or her that the area you were battling in was safe from human intervention.

"Funny world," he said to himself.

Competition for food did not seem to be so fierce here, either. Back home he would have been running into another animal every twenty yards, but then there seemed to have been more food available in the old country. True, he had seen a lot of feral cats in the city, ghosting by his vision, and pretty mean-looking characters they seemed, too. Some of them looked as though they had been mangled into a ball and then knocked roughly back into shape again. There were ears and eyes missing, and lumps of fur, and the ends of one or two tails. Yes, there were some tough individuals around.

He trotted on through the windswept streets, looking for a new home but feeling that perhaps the city was not the place for him. Feral cats warned him away from dank-smelling alleys with their cold, electric eyes. Other foxes glared at him when he entered parklands, hurrying him on with hard looks and the righteousness provided by home ground. Mangy-looking dogs threatened him with their diseases if not their teeth. The city was quite different from what he had expected.

NINE

Camio was not at all sure that the city was the place in which he wanted to spend the rest of his life. It seemed that survival in the busy streets was far more complicated than he had first imagined.

For the three days following his encounter with O-tasso he went hungry. His wanderings took him into parts of the city where food was either at a premium or not in evidence at all. On the first day he found himself in a disused dock, which was fine for avoiding the human race, but all other creatures had also vacated the area. Not even rats had remained on the stark, clean concrete. Here the waves still tugged on the leashes of tame, rusting ships, but the goods had long since ceased arriving and departing. On the second day he re-entered the area of tall, glassed buildings, also very clean, where men and women dashed from one doorway to another, looking as if they had been carved from obsidian. They seemed not to eat anything the whole day long. On the third day Camio was beginning to wish he had stayed with O-tasso, despite her penchant for pepper-hot food. He had walked into a poor district, where the humans had hardly enough to feed themselves, let alone itinerant foxes. He found small scraps in the garbage dumps, but nothing of significance. His stomach felt as if it had been turned inside out and dragged along the ground beneath him.

That evening, walking past prone bundles of rags that had humans inside them, he went down an alley and found the knob end of a moldy loaf of bread. He was halfway through chewing it when he was aware of the corpse of a fox lying at the end of the alley. Camio went up to it and sniffed around it. A glassy eye stared into his own. A strange feeling went through the live fox as he stepped around the dead one. He found it difficult to come to terms with the stiff meat that was not food. Had it been any other dead animal, he could have eaten it. But it was a fox, and though he was almost starving he could not bring himself to touch the corpse. There was a severity in the dead eye; a sternness around the dead mouth; a harshness in the dead face. Camio found he was looking at *himself*. He was just a puff of wind away from that poor creature on the alley floor. His lungs were full of air, the other fox's, empty—that was all; just a puff away. It worried him, coming face to face with his own mortality. Camio left the alley.

A few moments later, he was vomiting the crust. He knew the smell of the rat poison, once it had mixed with his stomach enzymes and he had brought it up again.

Later that night he stumbled across a railroad depot and met a friendly fox called A-lobo who, on seeing that he was starving, offered him some food from one of his caches. Camio was as grateful as any hungry animal could be, on finding such generosity in a strange land. He thanked the dog fox profusely, as he gobbled down the food.

A-lobo was a nervous, neurotic fox who had abandoned the streets for the relative safety of this *gerflan* that ran in long strips over the whole country. Of course, there were still vehicles to avoid, but you could hear them coming along the rails from a long way off: the metal vibrated and hummed before the thunderous arrival of a mighty machine. You learned, he told Camio, the busy times, when the tracks were in almost constant use, and the quiet times. There were mice and rats to be had, when there were no packets of sandwiches or half-eaten pies by the tracks, and though the scenery was a little boring, the smell of oil and grease made up for that.

"You *like* this stink?" Camio asked. They were lying on the bank beneath black cables that looped from post to post for as far as you could see.

"I adore it—ab-ab-absolutely adore it," stuttered A-lobo. He filled his lungs, through his nose, to prove it. "N-N-Not stink—a wonderful s-smell. And when they b-burn it in their fires—oh, sweet Perfect Here . . ."

A-lobo was not pretty to look at. He had once been struck by a train, and the left side of his face was badly scarred and he had lost an eye and an ear in the accident. He was very agreeable, though, and enjoyed, as O-tasso had done, teaching Camio all about the railroads (which he called "railways") and life near the depot.

"Switter is here—so spring isn't far away. G-G-Good to get rid of the cold w-weather."

"*Switter?*"

"You know. S-Small breezes."

"Oh."

Camio was beginning to wonder whether there were any normal foxes in this city he had to make his home. There was O-tasso, addicted to food that sent steam spurting out of your ears, and now A-lobo, who could not breathe clean air without longing for the stink of burning oil to satisfy some acquired craving.

A train thundered by, interrupting their conversation. Sunlight flashed on its many windows, which had a dazzling, mesmerizing effect on the foxes. It was true that at such times, an enemy could walk right up to them and grab them by the scruffs of their necks without them being aware of anyone. The noise was overpowering, the smell of diesel oil blotted out any other scents, and their eyes were fixed on those blinding panes of glass.

When it had gone, A-lobo asked Camio if he had ever played "the game."

"Game? I haven't played games since I was a cub. Foxes haven't got time for games, have they?"

"T-This game is a li-li-little different. You want to try it? It adds a b-bit of spice to life. Otherwise, it's the same boring old th-thing—eating and sleeping. There's got to be more to life than eating and sleeping, hasn't there?"

"Well, I suppose so—I don't really know. When I was in the zoo I used to think that there should be. Now there's a place where you do nothing else but eat and sleep. Out here, the excitement is in finding the food and a place to rest your head without fear of disturbance. Just staying alive is pretty exciting, isn't it?"

"N-No," said A-lobo bluntly. "It isn't." He twitched his head, nervously, as a group of humans passed by on the path running adjacent to the railway lines. Camio had been near railways before and he knew that humans never climbed the fence to get to the rails. Sometimes they walked along it, wearing bright jackets and doing things with tools to the tracks, but such visits were reasonably rare and you could always see them coming in time to hide in the long grass.

"What does this game consist of?"

A-lobo climbed to his feet and shook himself.

"Come on—I-I-I'll show you."

He walked leisurely down to the rails and Camio followed him, very curious now as to what was going to happen. A-lobo selected a spot in between the rails of one track, laying across the chunky gravel, his head on a wooden sleeper.

"Like this," he said.

Camio went and lay beside his new friend, wondering what they should be sniffing or listening for. Perhaps A-lobo knew of some kind of creature, a rat perhaps, that traveled underneath the rail, and he was waiting in ambush for such an animal?

"What are we waiting for?" he whispered, after they had been lying there for some time.

"Shhhh."

So Camio went quiet again. It was pleasant enough, between the rails, with the warm sun on their backs and the breezes passing overhead. He could almost drop off to sleep, except that a train might come along. He closed his eyes and dreamed of a land where there were no trains or cars, and where the mountains had white tips to them. The sun ran warm fingers through his russet coat until even his fleas were dozing. He remembered such a day, in the old land, when he had been with his mate by a stream that cut through the suburbs. The humans hardly went there any more, since most of the bank had been concreted and fenced off from the street and much of the water ran through underground tunnels. So there were fish to be had, in the shade of bridges and building overhangs: careless fish, that were easily snapped from the water when they rose to feed on the surface. He and his mate had eaten their fill and were sunning themselves on the concrete, with the trucks rumbling by creating pleasant vibrations. . . .

Camio woke with a start. The rails were rattling and jumping as if they were alive! There was a noise in the near distance, which grew louder by the second. Even the gravel was beginning to tremble as if it were hot and excited.

A train!

Camio jumped to his feet.

"Train coming!" he yelled.

As he leaped away he felt the slipstream of the monster blow him sideways, and the scream of its passage through the air stunned him with its volume. His brain jangled with the roar and rush of wind and sound, as he came down heavily on his side, striking the hard earth between the rails and the grass verge. Just inches away, the railway train still careened along the steel strips, its wheels singing a loud metallic death song that hurt Camio's ears and drove terror into his heart. He thought that it would never stop; that it would go on forever, or until he was completely insane. Never had he been so close to a train before, and he knew that if he had been just a moment later in jumping, there would not have been enough meat left from his corpse to satisfy a small carrion crow. Most of him would be plastered upon metal, a smudge of hair and blood. The machine was indeed a mighty beast that punched great volumes of air out of its way as it sped along, invincible, immortal, irresistible, and noisier than a thousand foxes screaming their banshee screams in unison.

Then the train was gone.

Still badly shaken, Camio staggered to his feet and looked around him. Poor A-lobo, he was sure, had not got away in time. Yes, there he was, lying between the tracks as still as death, his ragged, molting coat fluffed by *switter*, or whatever the spring breezes were called in this strange land. Poor A-lobo. How pathetic he looked, lying there on the sharp gravel, his nervous soul twitching its way through his mouth, finding the passage from this now useless body a slow, laborious task.

Suddenly, the corpse sat up! There was a dull gleam in A-lobo's eyes that reminded Camio of the time he had seen another fox eat an unusual, viridescent mushroom with a livid bloom on its canopy.

"You're—you're *alive*," said the amazed Camio. "But the train—it went right over you."

"Ahhh—that's—that's the game," replied A-lobo in a voice like honey trickling from a fractured beehive. "The *excitement*— wonderful, wasn't it? Every time I do it I say to myself, this is *it*, this is the day you die, A-lobo. Always, as the train thunders over you, it's metal hooks missing you by fractions, there's the feeling of *panic*, the almost irresistible urge to *run*. But you have to resist it—to run is death. To run is the end of all. So you lie there, enclosed by roaring metal, with spinning steel on both sides and a rushing river of steel above you, knowing if you move a muscle you will lose your head—lose it completely—you can almost picture your severed head bouncing along the gravel—your limp, squashed corpse being dragged along like a red rag. You lie there as still as stone, enduring the terrible noise, until the light returns and the sound recedes and you know you've done it again. You've beaten fear. You've met it face to face in mortal combat and you have won—won, won, won. The elation! I love it." His face had a faraway look on it: the same kind

of look that the jackal had had when telling Camio about the Land of the Lions.

During this speech A-lobo had not stuttered once and Camio noticed a confidence in the animal that had not been there before, that was absent for most of the time. Clearly "the game" did something for A-lobo, which helped him; but whatever it was, Camio did not need it. He could do without it quite well.

"You almost got me killed," he said, not without a little anger.

A-lobo looked surprised.

"Did I?"

"You should have told me—given me the choice," replied Camio. "I would like to have been given the choice."

"But you would have said *no*."

"Of course I would—it's madness . . ."

"And you would never have got to try it. You might have liked it, but unless you try it you can't find that out, can you?"

"I don't have to jump into a fire to know I'm going to burn."

A-lobo shook his head. "I've heard that sort of argument before. It's not the same thing." He paused, then asked tentatively, "D-Did you enjoy it?"

"*Enjoy* is not a word I would associate with my feelings for this game of yours. I jumped—the train almost hit me. No, this kind of foolishness is not for me."

A-lobo shrugged, nodding his one-eyed, one-eared head.

"Well, I'm sorry about that. My mate did the same thing, the first time she tried it. For a long while she just watched me do it, and then one day she tried it herself. She panicked though and jumped just before the train reached us, like you did."

"So, she must have told you the same thing I have."

"She didn't tell me anything. The train hit her. She's dead."

Camio was too shocked to say anything for the moment.

The pair of them spent the rest of the day looking for sandwiches along the line and for what A-lobo called *gubbins*. They found some, and this passed the time until evening. Some humans came along the line during the darkness, to light up the track with lamps; soon they had a fire going in a punctured oil drum, which filled the night with fumes that A-lobo gulped greedily down into his lungs. He was disinclined to move just because the humans were nearby, so Camio stayed with him, but remained cautious the whole time they were there.

Toward dawn, he said to A-lobo, "I think I want to get away from here—out of the city."

"L-Leave the *face*? Whatever for?" The stutter had returned.

"I'm not used to it. I think I want to get out a bit, onto the edge of this *face* of yours. How far is it, do you know? Could I walk it in a night?"

A-lobo shook his battered head.

"I don't know, but I think it's a l-long way—much further than you think. I've walked these r-r-rails all over, and I've never been where the buildings stop. Maybe you should think about st-staying?"

"No—I've made up my mind. I'm going as soon as I can."

"Th-Th-Then the only thing I can suggest is, you jump a train."

"Do what?"

"There are some t-trains with big open boxcars and no people in them. If I take you to the place where they stop for the night, you can get inside one and wait until it halts again, out of the ci-city. I knew a fox who did it all the time—went everywhere on trains. You can do it if you're not afraid. . . ."

"I'm not exactly happy about the idea, but I think it might work—providing I don't get caught."

"I think you'll be all right. Th-These men don't carry guns or anything. They m-m-might chase you a little way, but have you ever been caught by a man on foot?"

"No, I haven't."

"Well—there you are then."

That night A-lobo took him along to the depot, where trains were lying idle, waiting for the morning to arrive before moving off to places unknown. There was a faint hope in Camio's breast that he might find himself back in his own home, or perhaps the Land of the Lions, if the train went fast and far enough. It was only a very dim hope, though, because if he had learned one thing at the zoo, it was that the world is vast and that the chance of finding a single square mile on it, by accident, was a very remote possibility.

They found him a suitable boxcar, with straw in the corner for him to lie underneath, and then they said goodbye.

"Y-You think we'll see each other again?" asked A-lobo.

"It's doubtful, isn't it? Anyway, you'll be dead soon—knocked down by a train."

A-lobo shook his head firmly.

"No. Not that. Probably the mange, or someone coming up on my deaf side without me knowing. At l-least I'll go with the smell of the railways in my nostrils."

"If that's what you want . . ."

"Yes—I'm a railway fox. You—you're one of the strangest I've ever met—and one of the best. You talk funny and you say some peculiar things, but you're a good fox, Camio."

"Thanks. Keep your head down for me, A-lobo . . ."

And with those parting words, he leaped up into the car and buried himself beneath the sweet-smelling straw, ready for his journey into the unknown. He would have been lying to himself if he said that he was not afraid, but there was something of the excitement that A-lobo found in his "game" rushing around through his veins. It had to do with reaching out into the unknown. When he had been with his mate, in the old country, he had definitely been a *stayner*—but now that he had done some traveling, there was no reason not to become a *longtrekker*. The problem with that was, you never knew when you might end up in some bad part of the world, where foxes were run down by hunters in open-topped cars, carrying expensive guns that were difficult to miss with, even given that they had bleary-eyed idiots looking down the telescopic sights. Or even wander onto a fox farm, where you were kept in cages like at the zoo, and well fed, but where the inmates mysteriously "disappeared" from time to time even though they were in healthy, prime condition.

Perhaps, now that I'm more worldly, thought Camio, I will become a *longtrekker*, like my father?

He was thinking about it when they slid the doors shut, leaving him in darkness. After a while the train began to move off and

Camio, who did not like the sensation of motion, pressed his head against the wooden floor and hoped that this would not be the train that would separate A-lobo's soul from his body, even though that body was a little worn and wretched.

Not this train, he thought. I don't want it to carry A-lobo along as *gubbins*, to the suburbs. It would be a bad way for me to start a new life. Some other train, when he's old and grey and his bowels are giving him a bad time. This is *my* train.

PART THREE

THE COMING OF THE STRANGER

TEN

Spring had arrived on the back of Switter, the breeze-carrier, and there were births all around the badger sett: in the bushes, on the ground, under the earth. In the trees of Trinity Wood, eggs were cracking and blind heads, mouths open, emerged from the shells. The urgent cheeping of newborn birds mingled with the mewling of mammal young.

If O-ha had been a weaker fox she might have resented the coming of spring, but in fact she was happy to smell the apple and cherry blossoms, and did not mind the sounds of the young that filled the air. Her heart was still heavy, both for her mate and her cubs; but she contented herself with refreshing her memories of both, sitting once a day in the traditional pose of the mourner, her forelegs crossed and her tail straight out and flat against the ground. Gar realized that his friend was still grieving and came to visit her as often as his temperament would allow.

One evening, they were sitting in her chamber. Gar was remarking on the freshness of the world outside: how clear the streams were in the spring, and how good the soil smelled. Neither foxes nor badgers are much interested in the way the world decks itself out visually, with pretty blossoms, wildflowers, and greenery. It is not the garnish that interests them, but the clarity and the aromas that such dressings bring with them.

"You see the *gaers*—the "grass" you call it—how sweet is coming to the tongue at this time? Eh? No more *hagolian*, this hail, bang, bang, bang . . ."

"Yes, this is a good season. I like it very much," O-ha replied.

"So," Gar said, "you were telling me from this *halga gast*, this spirit-time of foxes—what you call it?"

"The *Firstdark*."

"Ya—that the thing. We badger have something like, when *Fruma-ac-Geolca*—this is first two badgers who live on world—they find each other and make love—come ten thousand badgers from this mating, all one time, half, half. Some badger not grow and these become weasel, otter, and stoat, who are cousins of Gar but not like by Gar . . . so, this *Firstdark* very like same badger story, I think?"

"It sounds like the same time. Our Great Ancestor is A-O, who was both male and female in one, and who gave birth to A-wan and O-won, before changing into a great lake of water. Because the land could not breathe under the water, it rose up from underneath to get to the air, and A-O was split into many parts, which are now our ponds and streams, our lakes and rivers. It is A-O we drink to cleanse our souls, and A-O who washes our coats to cleanse our bodies.

"A-wan and O-won were giants, left by their mother-father to fight for a place in the new world. They battled with the rocks and stones, who wanted to cover the ground so that they could prevent the trees from coming and casting shade, and could thereby sun themselves for eternity. A-wan gathered up in his mouth all the stones he could find, and spat them out into a great pile. O-won did the same with the rocks. Then they both turned their backs on the piles and sprayed them with earth, using their paws to dig. Soon the trees marched onto the land and covered the new hills, one of which we live on now; the other is on the far side of the river, beyond the marshes. . . ."

"I know it—I know it," said Gar. He seemed fascinated by the tale and so O-ha was encouraged to continue.

"Next, the two giant cubs fought with the wolves and—she was about to say "badgers" but changed her mind quickly—"dogs and other beasts, for a right to live in the world. There were many other terrible beasts at that time, put on the earth by the giant *Groff*, the secret agent of the humans, who were waiting for a chance to sneak into the world when the other animals were not looking. *Groff* took the clouds and fashioned them into false creatures called gryphons, senmurvs, dragons, chimeras—lots of strange forms—to confuse the foxes and the other real animals and to do battle with them. O-won found out, from a king-hound she'd trapped in her mouth, that these fabulous beasts were not real, so she swallowed stone that went molten in her belly and then she defecated the lava over *Groff's* false creatures. The stone cooled and solidified immediately, leaving the gryphons and dragons and other false beasts trapped inside a hard shell. When humans eventually managed to creep into the world, aided by the dogs and cats who formed paths for them from the sea-of-chaos, they took Groff's creations and put them on their gateposts and buildings as totems to warn away the rightful owners of the land they had stolen."

"Ha! I have seen this creatures, on gate at manor. And on church place. Yes, I wonder then how such ugly things came to be. So, now I understand. Of course," he puffed out his chest, "at same time badger was making great tunnels through earth, building places for rabbit, mole, and badger himselves. Funny thing," he said, pausing, "we badger sometimes eat rabbit, but sometimes live in same sett and not bother. . . ." He changed the subject. "But then I think, fox not live underground, eh?"

"No. In those days we lived out in the woodlands and grasslands,

and didn't have to come down here with the badgers and rabbits until men started to hunt us with dogs. We have lived underground for so long now we're used to it."

The pair of them continued to exchange stories about the beginnings of the world, until well into the night, after which O-ha went out to find food. She went into the *havnot*, chased and caught a rabbit, and satisfied her hunger.

When she was returning to the sett, just as the dawn rays were striking the topmost whips of a crack willow, turning them a yellow-red, a distant rumble made O-ha halt in her tracks. She was using the main highway from the farm to Trinity Wood, and the sound seemed to be coming from the direction of the village. However, it was much nearer than the houses and its exact location was probably somewhere on the road between the village and the manor house.

She licked her nose and tested Switter, but the breeze was too light to carry scents from very far away. The sound was of heavy machines, bigger and louder than tractors or any of the other farm equipment, though it might possibly be a group of combine harvesters. But why a group? And in this season? She did not understand it. Something was happening in her parish that was out of the ordinary.

Had it been later in the year, during Melloon and shortly before the dispersal of cubs, then she might have put the noise down to vehicles en route to the manor house. Autumn was the time when the humans came out to encircle known coverts, cracking whips and hallooing to create a panic amongst the foxes. The juveniles caught out on their own, without their parents, were the most likely victims. Mature foxes, versed in these invasions, usually managed to evade the hunters by slipping away, despite the noise. Foxes born that year, however, were unused to such a row, and the less knowledgeable among them, those unable to keep their heads, often made stupid rushes at the ring of men and were shot down within yards.

This was not Melloon, though, and the noise was louder than cars or even cross-country vehicles made. She decided to investigate.

She took one of the byways across the *hav* to a network of

drystone walls that enclosed the *havnot* in that area. She traveled along the top of these walls and reached the remains of an old windmill of which only the stone tower remained. She climbed fallen stones as agilely as a cat, finding paw-holds in the crumbling crevices of the stonework, where the mortar had turned to dust. At the top, she looked out toward the noise.

Her poor eyesight defeated her, though, because she was looking directly into the morning sun, and could see only a haze of light sparkling on some objects in the distance. Just as she was about to go down, a jay landed on the far side of the tower, well away from her. It eyed her suspiciously.

She said to the jay, "You know what's going on over there?"

"*Bitte?*" said the jay. "*Ich verstehe nicht.*"

"The noise—that over there—the machines . . ."

The jay refused to glance behind itself, but said, "*Maschine—oh, ja—maschine.*"

"What? What are they? What?"

"*Was? Oh, fur ausgraben.*"

Then the bird flew off, still keeping a wary eye on this fox that asked so many questions. O-ha saw the flash of blue on its wing as it dipped down and disappeared near the place where the shiny vehicles were rumbling along. The *Corvidae*—the jays, magpies, rooks, crows, jackdaws, ravens—appeared to be a sinister lot, full of intrigue, but they knew what was going on and they were harmless enough. The birds to watch were the gulls—now *there* was a vicious lot of villains and thieves! The bird world had a saying: *I'd rather trust a housecat than a seagull.* Seagulls would steal the food out of your mouth, or the young out of your nest.

Ausgraben? What did that mean? Well, there was only one way in which she might find out. She climbed back down the tower and went straight back to the sett, to find Gar. She tracked him down in his chamber and he was not pleased to see her, but this time she was not going to be put off by his gruff manner until he deigned to see her. She said, "Do you know the language of the *Corvidae?*"

"What—eh?—oh, little. Crows, eh? What crows?"

"Look, this is important, Gar, or I wouldn't disturb you. There are some machines coming down the road—big ones by the sound of them—and a jay told me they are for owsgrabben, or something like that. What does it mean?"

"Owsgrabben, owsgrabben," he said, scratching his head in irritation; then, "Oh, you meaning *ausgraben*—what we badger do, and fox. It means to dig—to dig up land. Now, you go away like nice fox and let me be miserable, eh? Sometimes Gar enjoy being unhappy, like today." He did not mean that he liked being unhappy, exactly, but that he did not want company. He wanted to be alone. It probably came of living with others, a clan, which meant that privacy was at a premium.

"To *dig*? To dig up the ground? But they didn't sound like farm machines."

"No? Then maybe to make road, eh? Dig road, or make house?"

"Houses?" A cold shiver went through her. "You mean, they're going to put some *face* around here? There were a lot of machines—they wouldn't have all those for one house. I don't like this, Gar. I don't like it at all."

"No? But what you going to do, eh?" He sounded irritable. "You can do nothing—nothing is what you can do. The humans build house, they build house. Who can stop them? Maybe they only build one? Maybe only new road, no house? Anyway, they not come here, in the wood. Too much work, chop, chop down tree. They maybe put up new farm—old one falling down anyway. You see—no worries. Now, Gar will be unhappy. . . ."

But, as subsequent events proved, it was to be more than just a farm. Over the next few weeks the machines were all over the landscape, their noises loud enough to wake the beetles buried deep in the bark of trees, their lights bright enough at night to bring a second daytime to the world. They chugged and hummed, they clattered and scraped. Flints saw the light of day for the first time and clumps of chalk appeared like the backs of giant white fish swimming through the clay. Soon a pattern of roadways began to form around Trinity Wood, marked off by posts and string, with colored tags hanging from the loops.

Flattened against the ground, in the cool shade at the edge of her covert, O-ha felt the tremors drumming through the clay and wondered why the earth did not scream out in agony as its green skin was flayed open to reveal the raw brown flesh beneath. She watched great steel-toothed jaws biting into the ground, coming up with huge gobbets of clay which were then spat onto an ugly, gathering mound. Deep, musty wounds were everywhere: open sores covered the backs of the slopes. The machines were like brittle, giant predators, tearing apart a live creature. Heavy shovel-nosed, jerky brutes crushed the bushes and shrubs to pulp; they charged the spinneys and herded the trees before them, until they cracked and splintered like old bones, ending in a heap of skeletal remains that were finally burned. At night, O-ha lay and watched the fires crackling and flaring, lighting up the wasteland that had once been tall with grasses, wildflowers, and shrubs; that had been populated by myriads of electric insects, policed by thousands of busy voles, shrews, and mice, and patrolled by hundreds of birds of many varieties.

This destruction of the living landscape was carried out with a swiftness that astounded the vixen, who clung to her own patch of grass, bracken, and trees, afraid that it might be destroyed in a day: that she might wake one evening to find her homeplace bared to the dark, churned clay with not a blade of grass remaining.

And everywhere, the smells of men and machines, the sounds of destruction.

There were men all over the place, gesturing, digging, grunting. It was almost impossible to avoid being seen, especially as the lights never went out, but to O-ha's surprise these new men seemed quite delighted by the sight of her. Whenever she got caught out, slinking past their little encampments, the men—without rising from their seats or putting down their steaming drinks—would point to her and exclaim, and their barking had none of the usual animosity or bloodlust in it.

Still, it was a troubled time for her and for the badgers. Each day they expected an invasion of the woodland, which never came. O-lan and A-lon had to move out of their earth in the ditch beyond Trinity Wood, but they made themselves another by digging out O-ha's old

earth, and re-establishing it: something she had been intending to do herself, now that the ground was soft and easily moved. Some of the animals that lived on what used to be the *hav* prepared to evacuate the area and set out on expeditions, looking for new pastures (the rabbits did this, and a few others), some of the animals moved into Trinity Wood. The new concentration of animals in the ten acres of woodland had everyone confused for some time, and tripping over each others' tails. Some fights occurred over territorial rights, which resulted either in the shrinking of an animal's hunting zone, or the expulsion of the newcomer. Occasionally the immigrant would get the better of a longstanding resident; but that was seldom, since the established members of the wood felt they had right on their side and thus fought to keep their ground with a ferocity that could not often be matched by newcomers hoping to settle there. It was easier for the latter to move on. Though there were some larders that were fuller than usual, in the carnivore and omnivore camps, there were no deaths as a result of territorial disputes.

By midsummer, and Frashoon, most of the battles had been fought and settled, and there was only the activity around the wood to worry about.

"Things will change," remarked Gar. "Ya, things will change round here."

"Will you and the other badgers move on?" asked O-ha.

"We wait—we wait to see what happen. I think we stay for a while. What about you?"

"I have nowhere else to go. I must make the best of it. It must be nice at times like these to have others to talk things over with."

She surprised herself by getting used to the new face of the landscape fairly quickly. Many points of reference had changed, but although there were new landmarks to learn, it did not take very long before these were in her head. One thing was certain: there were now plenty of earthworms to be had.

This new landscape played havoc with the ancestral highways and byways, of course. The fact that the humans were building themselves new roads did not mean the animals were prepared to alter their ancestral highways. On one of her walks, O-ha found that a new road had been built that cut one of the animal highways in half. She did not hesitate to cross it, even though vehicles were now moving along it. Her highway had been there for thousands of seasons. Why should she change direction simply because humans had decided to lay *face* across the country?

Another time, she came across a wall that had sprung up overnight. At its base, glaring up at it, was a badger. Again, the wall had been built right across an animal pathway. The badger could have gone round it, since the wall extended only a few feet beyond the highway, but the animal stubbornly refused to do so. Instead, it sat there swearing oaths in its gravelly voice, calling down all kinds of terrible events on the heads of those humans who had had the audacity to block its path.

When she discussed it with Gar one evening, the elderly badger nodded thoughtfully and said, "If we go round things every time *guman* build it, we would change highways every day. Best to ignore. Some seasons go by, then all things change again. One day we get our highways back."

One night, when most of the workmen had gone home, leaving only one or two night watchmen, O-ha went down the slope to inspect the diggings. There were deep trenches everywhere, the red clay sliced away to form smooth subsurface walls. She tested the bricks, sand, and bags of cement with her nose. She walked away from them, unimpressed. However, she did at one point find a pile of wood shavings where the carpenters had been at work inside an unfinished house. O-ha pushed her nose into these, and inhaled deeply. The heady scent of sawdust made her brain revolve in a delicious way, but some toadstools had once done it better. She rolled in the shavings, getting them caught in her coat. They fell away from her like snowflakes. Later, she patrolled high up on the scaffolding, looking down on the world. It was easy. Finally, she marked several of the empty rooms in the house, tore open a black bag with her teeth and scattered the contents around the floor, and rolled a bottle with her nose. Then she went home, feeling she knew all about what was going on, down below. The *face* was neither the most fearsome nor the most wonderful place in the world.

Despite the invasion of the countryside, and the displacement of millions of insects, thousands of mammals, and hundreds of birds, life in Trinity Wood tried to move into summer much the same as always. The froghoppers left their "cuckoo spit" on the hedges that remained intact; the woodbine and the honeysuckle drugged the moths with their heady perfumes; in amongst the many different kinds of grasses of the *havnot*—timothy grass, Italian rye, quaking grass, cocksfoot, fescue—grew the common herbs like yarrow, ribwort, plantain, dandelion, and chicory, whose seeds had blown into the wild from fields cultivated by man. Ferocious and aggressive mother shrews led their strings of babies through tunnels in the grass, each one holding onto the tail of the next with the smallest, at the end, being dragged and bumped along as the mother hurried from one place to the next. Hawker dragonflies patrolled the ponds, and buzzards circled the fields and woods, both levels of flying predator having awesome weapons at their disposal. Otters cruised the rivers and inlets of the wetlands; coypu busily dug up the beets and bulbs planted by the humans, for whom these rats with South American ancestry had no regard whatsoever. Kingfishers flashed like blue darts along the banks of streams, and crested newts put color amongst the roots of water lillies.

Life and death went on in the old ways, in those places where the ground remained untouched by the digging machines; but gradually the process of stripping the land forced more and more creatures to abandon the area for other places, which they often failed to reach alive. Soon the population of Trinity Wood and its surroundings was a fraction of what it had been the previous summer. Many species would never be seen again in that part of the world.

Three nights after visiting the building site, O-ha had a dream. It was a dream in which fear rattled in her throat, and her legs were weak with terror.

She dreamed she was in a bright place and struggling to walk. Suddenly, black bars . . .

ELEVEN

A hot summer sun lay heavy on the fields, like a huge invisible weight pressing evenly on the land. Flies buzzed over ditches whose marrow was dry and brittle. Animals, going about their business, constantly blew hot air through their nostrils to rid themselves of the feeling that there were cobwebs in there. The earth was parched and as crisp as old reeds.

Over the dusty stretch of *hav* between the site under construction and the manor house, came a red fox, a fox that appeared just a little different from the others living in the area: a dark fox with a jaunty step and a head held high. He walked across the land below Trinity Wood as if he knew the whole earth intimately and no place was

strange to him, no place was not home. Those animals that had any interest at all in the coming of this new fox could have been forgiven for thinking that he was a *rangfar*, an itinerant fox. However, if they had bothered to study him closely they would have seen that he stared about him keenly, gathering impressions, as if looking for something. He was in fact seeking a place to stay, to remain, to become part of. Camio was not a *rangfar*—or in his own idiom, *longtrekker*—by choice, but by circumstance. In his heart he was a fox who wanted to make his mark on a square mile of land and say, "This is my parish. Here I shall live, and die."

Camio passed by the large manor house, which was outside an area being devastated by men in shirtsleeves and hard hats. There was a set of wrought iron gates at the beginning of the driveway to this country mansion, behind which paced a dog as large as a tiger. Camio stopped and regarded this beast, the like of which he had not seen even in the zoo. He was terribly impressed. It was a giant among dogs, and on seeing Camio its jaws slavered and a sound came rumbling up from the depths of a hard-looking, muscle-ridged belly. The American Red Fox decided that he had seen enough and slipped away into the hedgerow before the monster threw itself at the gates, bursting them. Camio decided that such a dog could swallow him whole.

A hound from the dark side of the moon, he thought. There was no sense in antagonizing such an enormous beast. Camio was no coward, but a fox is only a fraction bigger than a house cat in body size and only about two pounds heavier. In comparison, an Alsatian dog is twice a fox's height, while a St. Bernard weighs fourteen times more. The hound behind the gates was an Alsatian and a St. Bernard rolled into one. For Camio to face such a monster would have been like a cat meeting with a lion. A fox, after all, is no taller than a daffodil. He slipped through the workmen, as they toiled on the grounds surrounding the wood, and entered the coolness of a covert on the north side. No sooner was he within the woodland's shade than he encountered another dog fox, an elderly one, who barred his way. Camio sighed, inwardly. He knew from experience that he was trespassing, because he could smell the dog fox's marks from where he stood, and he knew he was going to have to either turn around or fight. Normally he would have respected another fox's area, but he wanted only to pass through unmolested—the code of right-of-passage—and he had come a long, hot way. He was tired and irritable, and consequently feeling stubborn.

They regarded each other for some time, before Camio broke the silence.

"Is there a problem?" he asked.

"There might be," said the other. "It depends on where you think you're going."

Camio said, "You have a name, I presume—mine is Camio."

"They call me A-magyr. I'm the toughest fox in the parish, and one of the oldest—though don't get the idea that my strength is ebbing, I'm as strong and hard as any you're likely to meet."

Though grizzled, he did indeed look like a gritty, mean character, and Camio decided that he might prove a nasty opponent in a fight. But another fox was a different proposition from the hound he had slipped away from, and he did not like to be told where to go or what to do by one of his own kind. He certainly was not going to lie on his back with his paws in the air in some act of submission, just because this local dog fox wanted to add another victory to his list.

"So," said Camio, "you want to stand here all day, or are you going to let me pass? I'm reasonably patient, but I've come a long way and I need a place to rest."

"What's wrong with where you're standing?" asked A-magyr.

"What's wrong with it is *I* didn't choose it. You did, and while I'm a peaceful type of fox, I like to pick my own bed."

A-magyr narrowed his eyes.

"No one has spoken to me like that in a long time. I've torn the tails off bulldogs and walked away unmolested. I could chew you and spit you out . . ."

Camio shrugged, and then crouched, ready to spring.

"Right, let's see you do it, A-mouthy—I'm ready if you are. I came into this wood seeking nothing but friendship—something I got from the city foxes without asking—but if I have to fight to get it here, I will."

A-magyr made a rush at him, but he leaped neatly aside, turning in the air so that he faced his opponent again.

"That's a clever trick," snapped A-magyr, "but it won't work twice. . . ." He made another dash. This time Camio jumped to one side, still keeping his head toward his combatant, and managing to nip A-magyr on the haunch as he passed. A look of disbelief and pain crossed A-magyr's face.

"I've killed foxes who . . ." A-magyr started to say, but Camio interrupted him.

"Swallow it," he said, "the time for talking is over. You do too much of that."

A-magyr bristled, sinking low into his legs, so that his body arched downward and his look of menace increased. He did indeed look like a formidable opponent, with his head low and horizontal, his teeth bared, his ears flat against his skull, and his eyes burning ferociously at Camio. Camio stared back and this time he was pacing, more with his hind legs than his forelegs, so that although he was constantly on the move, he remained on virtually the same spot the whole while. Every so often he would snap at the air, just in front of A-magyr's face, daring the old dog fox to make another move.

"I'll tear you . . ." began A-magyr, but this time he did not need Camio to tell him to shut up—he knew he had lost a small advantage, just by opening his mouth. It had not been necessary for Camio to say anything. He had forced his opponent to fall back on words, twice, and had thus won the first psychological victory. A-magyr had allowed himself to be beaten into oral defense. While they faced each other they constantly calculated the moves that each might make, and what counter-moves would be required to obtain the upper position. *If I do this, he will do that, or that, and then I will do this and this, and he might come back with that, and so I will . . .* The positions, the actions, the reactions, the leaps, the folds, the hits, the whip-fast strikes, the runs, the sidesteps; the raking claws, the snapping jaws. These convoluted thoughts and images, few of them conscious, incessantly revolved inside each fox's head, until one fox became unsure and his lack of confidence showed in his eyes. The other then went in immediately for the kill.

Inside a split second, Camio was astride his opponent who was then on his back, paws in the air, staring at the savage face that looked down into his eyes. Camio's teeth were bared back to the gum as they hovered over the neck of this adversary. A-magyr slowly turned his head away, exposing his throat. Now both his jugular and belly were open for the teeth to tear, should Camio wish to take advantage of his superior position.

However, he did not go for A-magyr's throat. Foxes do occasionally fight to the death, but more often, once they have gained the upper hand, they allow a retreat to take place. A-magyr had been broken, which was for him perhaps worse than death. His spirit had been crushed within him. He was lost in his shame, and the fact that they both knew this was enough. The battle was over. The loser slunk away, tail between his legs. This is not to say that there would be no more fights between them, but A-magyr would need to have a very good reason for attempting the same thing twice. With Camio, at least, his confidence had been shattered, and a great psychological advantage lay with the newcomer.

Camio heaved a sigh of relief, thinking that if all rural foxes were like A-magyr he was going to have a hard time establishing himself. Certainly Camio was not going to leave without giving the area a good try. He was weary of the city and the so-called "suburbs" which seemed as dense and limitless as the city itself. He was also sick of trains and traveling. It was time to put his pawprint on a piece of clay and say, "I'm not moving from here!"

Camio entered the depths of the wood and found a place to lie in the half-exposed roots of an old oak. He sank wearily to the ground and there he rested until the evening.

He woke as a sun the color of drying blood threw dark lanes through the woodlands. There were blue clouds of midges hanging above the woodland floor. He climbed to his feet and drank some murky water from a hollow in a rotten tree. He opened the bark with his teeth and found bugs beneath, which he ate quickly. Above him, pigeons were settling for the night and sparrows peppered their favorite plane trees, creating a disturbance with their clamor. He cleaned some of the dust from his coat, and then decided to explore the remainder of the woodland.

He found a fox's earth at one point, but the occupants were out and he did not wish to violate a home without being invited. As he was leaving the spot, on the edge of the wood, a vixen came out of the trees and took a brief look up into the night sky, before noticing he was there. Camio studied this female of the species. She was, he decided, a mature but attractive creature—very attractive—and he found himself walking toward her, wondering what to say. For once in his life he felt tongue-tied, and though he felt like howling or barking at the moon, his conversation seemed buried somewhere at the back of his throat.

The vixen glanced at him and then made to leave the place.

"Wait," said Camio, quickly. "Could we—talk?"

She stopped, but remained on all fours as if still prepared to leave within the moment.

"Talk?" she said. "About what?"

"Well, I'm a stranger around here . . ."

"I know that."

". . . and I wondered if you could give me some information, about the lie of the land, that sort of thing. I recently escaped from a zoo and I'm . . . I'm a little lost."

"A zoo? I don't know what a 'zoo' is."

"It's a place where they lock animals in cages—like chickens, you know?—so that humans can come and look at them without being bitten. Not a very pleasant place, if you happen to be caged in it rather than visiting. However, I got out, and here I am."

"What's all this got to do with me?" She seemed very haughty and superior, and for the first time in his life Camio was suddenly concerned about his antecedents. It had never occurred to him before that there might be something inferior in coming from a background of suburban foxes, who had discarded their cultural origins as being less important than learning who filled the trash cans outside the restaurants and on what day.

"Well, nothing I suppose . . ." a flash of inspiration came to

him, ". . . unless you have a regard for hospitality? I'm a strange fox in a strange land, and I need help. Is that to do with you?"

She looked a little contrite at this, but still the impatience showed on her face.

"If you could be more specific, I'll try to direct you to wherever you're going. I can hardly help you if you don't tell me your problem."

Before he could stop himself, he threw all caution away and plunged in headfirst. It came out all in a rush, the words tumbling over each other like torrents of white water, and even before he had finished he could see by the coldness in her eyes that he had made a terrible mistake. He had been too rash, too impetuous.

"I need a home, and a vixen to share that home, I've been alone too long, maybe I'm not easy to live with, I don't know, but I'm tired of wandering, I want to settle down, have a family, be a father-fox with a mate again. . . . I know how this must sound, since we don't know each other, but I'm not a fox to hold back my feelings. I saw you with the dying sunlight behind you and you looked so—so beautiful. Such a fiery red and—beautiful." He plunged into desperation as her look formed droplets of ice in the air between them. "You have such *delicate* lines. Your scent is like a drug to me—it makes my head spin. And your voice! A thousand nightingales . . ."

"You want to be a father-fox, *again*?" The haughty look was redoubled. "The trouble with you *rangfars*"—

"We *what*?"

—"you travelers, or whatever you like to call yourselves—you think you can walk into a parish, *stroll* into a strange covert, and make up to any female that takes your fancy. No doubt you have dozens of so-called mates over the whole country, all panting away for the devil-may-care dog fox that calls when he feels like, *when* he's in the vicinity. Well, let me tell you that I am one vixen who is proud to be an *ord*, one of those you secretly find very boring and just want to give a quick once-over before going back on the road again. No, I do not find you attractive, whatever-your-name-is—I assume you've actually *got* a name—and I don't wish to share my home or my life with someone who just walks out of nowhere and will no

doubt go back there twice as fast, once the business has been done. Don't bother to say good night."

She turned abruptly on her heels and began to walk off, when he shouted, "Camio."

She turned again, as if he had yelled a common insult.

"What?" she said.

"My name—it's Camio—and I think that's one of the most magnificent speeches I've ever heard. I'm just sorry I had to be at the sharp end of it. Listen, I'm not a *rangfar* or whatever you call it—we say *longtrekker* back home—I'm just an ordinary fox in extraordinary circumstances. I didn't ask to go on the road—it was thrust upon me. I was captured, drugged, and put in a cage. I don't know where my home is, but believe me if I did I would go there in an instant. No one likes to have to start again. Fact is, I *don't* know where it is and I don't think I've got a bat's-eyes' chance of finding it again. The world is too big. I've tried city life. It doesn't suit me. So I came out here, on the train, and here I'm going to stay. I've already had a run-in with one of your local foxes, someone called A-magyr, and I had to thrash him to enter the wood. Now I get the treatment from a vixen—a very hoity-toity vixen, I might add, who thinks she's better than me but who hasn't seen anything of the world, or done half of what I've done. Well, let me tell you, madam—I've had better welcomes from a cage full of monkeys. And I'll find my way around here without your help."

"Monkeys?" she said, in a small voice.

"Man-like creatures, with a little more sense than the hairless ones—though not *much* more," he added, recalling their empty chatter and their willingness to imitate human actions.

"Where did you get a name like 'Camio'?"

"I told you, I'm not from around here."

"But so far as I know, foxes all over the country take a letter from A-O, depending on their sex."

"Then I don't come from this country. Don't ask me how I got here, because I don't know. Some say we were flown through the air, inside a man-made bird called an airplane, but I'm not sure that's true so I don't repeat it."

"And you fought A-magyr?"

"Fought and *beat* A-magyr—his own mouth beat him, that is. I think he prefers to rant and rave rather than fight, but one usually leads to the other where I come from."

She regarded him for a little while longer as they stood several yards apart in the gloaming. Her attitude was less superior than it had been before but she still maintained a certain poise, a kind of affected pose that had invisible walls around it, so that he could not approach her without feeling he was desecrating holy ground, or violating some sacred trust. He did not understand why this should be so, but it was, and he knew he wanted her very badly. This high-minded, proud vixen with an obviously impeccable lineage stretching back to the most noble of all foxes, Menxito—he wanted to call her his own. He wanted her beside him while he slept; he wanted her with him while he hunted; he wanted . . . her.

His mind was in a turmoil of passion, which he kept under control with difficulty. He knew they could not mate: it was not her time. But the very thought of it—the thought that when her time came, it might be him—sent his brain into a spin.

"What do you want to know?" she asked, her tone softer.

"I've said—do you have a mate?"

"No, and I've no wish for one. My mate was killed by the hounds, some time ago. You may want to start again—Camio—but I've no wish to. I intend to enter my old age as an unattached female *stoad.*"

He thrilled to hear her say his name, but answered in a steady voice, "I'm sorry—about your mate. It wasn't that big bastard down at the great house? I saw him as I came by." Secretly he was glad she had no mate, not daring to believe his good luck, and he could not be sorry for the death of somebody he had never known. He felt a little guilty, too, for having such selfish thoughts.

Her back bristled, but she said, "No, not Sabre. He has other things to answer for. Now, I must . . ."

She turned again, and walked away into the wood. Camio watched her go, then did a little dance on the grass in the moonlight. *No mate. She has no mate!* He kept telling himself this, over and over again. He stared down the slope from the wood, into the surrounding area. And what have we here? A town being built, by the looks of it. A new town. Well, well. A nice suburban area, with new houses and new restaurants. A lovely vixen without a mate. A local bully he had thrashed, and so established himself. He was on top of the world. How could anything be better? And if this snooty vixen did not like him now, because she had lived the country life, close to natural things, in a green environment full of apples and pears and the scent of bryony—if this madam of the woodlands, with her high nose and dainty step, and her rows of ancestors steeped in good breeding—if she would not take notice of him *now*, she would do so soon. He was a fox who knew how to survive in the streets, amongst the bricks and mortar, the fast vehicles, the baby carriages and roller skates, the many boots and high-heeled shoes, the iron grids, the sewers, the vacant lots, the alleys, the rooftops—yes, the rooftops, where the foxes glided from one building to the next, unseen by those in the street. He knew that man-made jungle, its ways, whys, and wherefores. The city fox and the kestrel hawk—they knew the *face*, and how to stay alive within its walls. She might know where to find a tree fungus, but she would not know that mushrooms and toadstools grow in the cracks of shaded buildings, or at the base of gravestones, or under wrecked cars at the breaker's yards. She could climb a tree, but could she climb a garage, or walk the length of a gutter some thirty feet off the ground?

I've got a chance, he told himself. I've got a chance to make this place my home.

TWELVE

Gar and O-ha were sitting outside the sett, amid the wildflowers on the edge of Trinity Wood, lazing in the hot noonday summer sunshine. Gar was watching a bee making crazy flight patterns in the air, flying from bloom to bloom, but taking the longest possible route between each. It was one of those days when foxes emptied their heads of care and allowed Frashoon to ruffle their coats with warm fingers; days when they dreamed of their own *sowander*, where their spirits would rest forever amongst the grasses of the Perfect Here. It was one of those days when the minds of badgers turned to philosophy and invention.

O-ha had learned that badgers were wonderful creatures for

thinking up great sayings, great truths, by which others could live their lives—but that the badgers themselves forgot them the moment the mood passed. Badgers were also marvelous inventors of the most delicate, intricate devices, but never got around to producing any of them; this was either because their paws were inadequate for the task, or, most likely, because once they had invented it in their minds, they lost interest, since that was where the fun was—in the *inventing*, not in the making.

O-ha had not much patience with this side of the badgers. They appeared to be the most impractical of creatures: dreamers and storytellers, whose great minds were of little use because they had neither the tools—the hands of man—nor the determination to carry their schemes through to conclusions that resulted in something tangible. She said this to Gar.

"Ha," he said, "you fox are *wintrum geong*—young in winters." He watched the crazy bee through narrowed eyes. "Importance of dreams is not in *using*—importance is in *having*. You think dreams must mean something real, that fantasy bad for the soul. All wrong, all wrong. Fantasy just as important as reality. Reality is feeding body—finding food for keep alive. Fantasy feeds *spirit*. Soul need food same as body, and dreams, philosophies, stories, *creations*, all food for spirit, see?" There were some scratches in the dust, where earlier he had tried to show her an invention he had just thought up for getting honey out of hives without disturbing the bees. To O-ha they were incomprehensible marks on the earth, which might have been useful if she could grasp the practical use behind the idea, but since she could not she had dismissed them as worthless. He pointed to the scratches.

"Here is wonderful idea, full of sticks that move against each other, vines that pull, forked twigs that push, stones that swing—but it is wonderful because it *swefna cyst*—how say? best of dreams. I see it all, up here," he said, nodding his head, "how it work, push, pull, swing, honey in paw, bees all happy. It fill me with delight, to see this pictures in my head—my mind all golden with dream. If I try to *make*," he snorted, "it become something else. No longer dream, but something of world. Inside is best. Once come *outside* then something lost to spirit. Something gain for body, but something lost for spirit."

"But how useful it would be."

"Useful, yes, but badger not care for useful unless *absolutely necessary* for life to go on. Badger not want to lose dream—*syllicre* dream—just for sake of useful. See?"

She sighed. "No, I'm afraid I don't, but it doesn't matter. You are what you are—I'm different. I don't suppose we can change one another. I wish I could invent things. I would build something to catch those hounds—Breaker and Sabre—and then . . ."

"Then you would be sorry. *Faehoe*—no good, this *vengeance*."

"That's easy for you to say, Gar, but I have a dream too. My dream is full of blood and satisfaction."

The badger shook his big head.

"I think that is nightmare, not dream. Blood and satisfaction not go together well, not well at all."

He went back to studying the bee, which was going berserk amongst the blooms, seeming to prefer certain colors to others. Blue was a favorite.

Out of the trees, further down the wood, came another fox. It was O-lan, one of the "perfect pair." O-ha called them that because they seemed never to argue or fight over trivial things, seemed absolutely happy in each other's company, never crossed each other in talk, and professed to live in bliss. The *boring* perfect couple, she thought to herself, rather maliciously.

Gar was muttering away to himself in a contented fashion as O-lan approached, treading daintily through the wood-edge grasses. Gar's eyes were still fixed on the bee when O-lan absently snapped it out of the air and swallowed it.

Gar's head jerked up.

"Eh? Ahhhhh! What you do? You *eat* my inspiration! Ah! Fox! Uncultured fox. Destroyer of dreams. You eat him. You eat up my dream-bearer!"

He climbed to his feet looking absolutely disgusted and went toward the entrance to the sett. O-ha called after him, but he shook

his head. "Your friend is crush my philosophy. I go home. I go where animal is not all the time eating, thinking of belly. I go . . ."

He disappeared down the hole. O-lan was looking distressed and said helplessly, "What did I do?"

O-ha shook her head.

"He told you—you ate his dream-bearer. He was using the bee to do something inside his head—I don't know what, but it was important to him. Never mind, you couldn't have known."

O-lan flopped down beside her.

"Well, I'm sorry I upset him. You'll tell him that, won't you? I don't like upsetting anyone."

"I know—I know."

There was a long period of silence, but O-ha knew that the other vixen had not come to merely pass the time of day. She suspected that a favor was about to be asked: O-lan's expression was one of disinterest, and that always made O-ha suspicious.

"Well?" she said at last, unable to contain her impatience. "What have you come to talk about?"

O-lan turned an innocent-looking face on her acquaintance.

"Why," she said, wide-eyed, "I just thought to come for a chat. You know how much I like chatting with you, O-ha. How are you getting along? Isn't it time you moved out of that badgers' sett and into your own earth again? It can't be good for you, living with those grumpy creatures—they're always in a bad temper—well, not in a bad temper, but sullen, you know?"

"They are in fact very nice animals—placid and self-contained. They just *look* dour, that's all."

"Really?" O-lan flicked an ear. "Well, you know them better than anyone, I suppose. Just *look* at that *hav*," she said, directing O-ha's attention to the devastation of the land around the wood. "All our fine fields, the heath, all gone."

There were now half-built houses below, and streets were beginning to form networks in the churned clay and mud. It seemed that the builders were determined to get some people into the new town before the winter arrived. They worked night and day to that effect. Trinity Wood had so far not been touched, but there were rumors that it would be drastically pruned, when the time came. The new fox, Camio, was telling others that it seemed as if the wood were destined to become a park—a place where humans would walk their dogs and put up devices for their young to play on—and, he said, it would be landscaped. Trees would be cut down and areas cleared, but if his experience was anything to go by, a lot of the old wood might remain untouched. Humans liked to think they had a wild wood in the middle of their town: somewhere they could go to find a little natural life.

"I would like to think they would make it a nature reserve, where only those humans that want to watch the animals from a distance through glasses would be allowed to go, but unfortunately, I don't think that will happen. Camio says the wood is too central, and anyway, hooligans would ignore any signs that told them to keep out of the wood . . ." said O-lan.

This Camio seemed a bit of a know-it-all to O-ha, and she was inclined to treat the hearsay (she had not spoken to the animal herself since that night he had accosted her on the edge of the wood) as dubious information, not to be taken at face value. He probably *thought* he knew what he was talking about, she decided generously, but there was every reason to suppose he was mistaken. No one had approached Trinity Wood, and she had never heard of a garden—for that was what a park seemed to be—that was for the use of all. Gardens were private things, attached to individual houses. No, this impertinent new fox had got it all wrong and was afraid to admit it. She hated boastful animals, and it seemed that Camio was so full of himself he got carried away.

"Yes, it's very sad," replied O-ha. "We're losing our ancestral highways, our hideouts, and many of our soaks and waterholes. You can't walk through brick walls. There are new ones, of course, but they aren't the same, are they?"

O-lan nodded.

"Still, it's *very* exciting. All that hustle and bustle going on down there—and Camio says that when it's finished, it'll be easier to get food than in the countryside. They waste so much, those humans. It won't be like the farmers, or the country people, who use their scraps on the pigs and chickens, or are too poor to throw away anything. These humans are quite different. They're all as rich as those in the manor house, but not as mean."

"Camio, Camio, doesn't anyone talk about anything else these days?" snapped O-ha. "I'm sick of hearing that fox's name—and he doesn't know *everything*. He just thinks he does."

O-lan's eyes opened wider in surprise.

"No, he doesn't know everything, and he doesn't pretend to, O-ha. He's just giving us the benefit of his experience. He's lived in a town, after all . . ."

"So he says," sniffed O-ha.

"And there's no reason to suppose he's not telling the truth, is there? My goodness, O-ha, you have got a down on him, haven't you? And he speaks nothing but good of you."

"Does he?" she said quickly, suppressing a flicker of feeling deep inside her breast.

"Yes, he does—and I think you would do well to take notice of that. You've been too long on your own. . . ."

O-ha acknowledged an ironic thought.

"Oh, I understand. We're matchmaking, are we, O-lan? Getting poor O-ha, the pitiful, lonely vixen, a new mate? Well, I don't need one, thank you. I do very well on my own. I *like* living on my own. It's less troublesome and I'm fond of not having any responsibilities. All right?"

"Yes, of course. *We* know we don't need dog foxes to fulfill us—I'm not suggesting that we do. A vixen can manage very well by herself. But what about cubs, O-ha. Look at my cubs. Don't you want a family? It's delightful . . ."

"I'm sure it is," snapped O-ha, "but I've no time for such things. I'm not interested in dog foxes, cubs, or anything else."

O-lan rose to her feet, looking sad.

"Oh, well, you know your own mind best. I'd better get back to my litter. I've been teaching them how to hunt. They're doing very well, but they're getting lazy. I must say this *face* has got into everyone's lives. My cubs are saying they'll have no need to hunt, once the town is there. They'll just pick things up in the streets. I must admit I don't like the idea that hunt-and-search skills will not need to be taught—I think we should keep the old ways as long as possible, don't you?"

"I couldn't agree more," said O-ha. "These new foxes, they're impressive, but they don't realize the harm they're doing. They don't realize we have a history, a culture behind us, which is thousands of seasons old. They're a bad influence on us. Hunting skills will always be needed. Searching for fungi, wildroots, vegetables—this will always be necessary too. I for one am not going to let such things drift away from me."

O-lan blinked.

"Oh, I don't think *Camio* is saying that, O-ha. He is as good a hunter as anyone I've seen, and he certainly doesn't advocate that we ignore all our old ways, our skills. It's the cubs—they're getting unmanageable, that's all. When they reach a certain age, they think we can't teach them anything. They know it all, already."

"I still think that there are bad influences around, which need to be curbed," O-ha said.

"If you say so."

With that, O-lan left her to herself.

The day following this conversation, there was a hunt. When O-ha heard the horn, the hallooing, the shouts of the hounds, she froze in her chamber. Gar went to the entrance of the sett and poked his nose out, and came down later with the news that there had been great battles on the land outside. Other humans had come to interfere with the hunt by spraying things on the ground to confuse the hounds, and by generally causing consternation amongst the riders. Some of the huntsmen beat the interferers with riding whips, and then the workmen on the roads around the wood helped the newcomers turn back the riders. It seemed they were angry with the huntsmen riding into the building sites and knocking down their makeshift fences.

"Oh, what *onmedlan*," he cried, becoming more excited than she had ever seen him before. "Such happenings! Such anger! I never saw such glorious things. And the dogs—they ran this way, that way, sniffing, screaming in frustration. I saw them—they shake their head

like this"—and he gave a furious demonstration of a hound that had sniffed something unpleasant—"and run around like this," he said as he raced around the inside of the chamber. "It was good to see this. You should see this happenings, O-ha."

She lifted her head from her paws.

"I—I was afraid. Poor A-ho—it was as if it were happening all over again. I was afraid."

Gar became tender, realizing that she had rerun her old ordeal in her head while the horn had been sounding and the shouts had been ringing through the countryside.

"Oh, ya. I see. Well, never mind. I have report to you the things I see, and this is true. I think we get no more hunts in this place now. Maybe the workmen burn down the manor—that would make nice bonfire, eh?"

"Fire is never good, you know that, Gar."

He nodded his great head.

"Ya, yes, is true. One of my silly dreams."

He left her then. Later she went up to the surface, to look around. The workmen below were preparing to leave for the night, locking up their site sheds and leaving their great machines silent. Why hadn't they used those machines in battling with the riders? O-ha wondered. But then humans had their rules too, when dealing with one another. They were not without a vestige of culture.

The moon came out, a hazy light in the heavens, and O-ha made her way to the farm, picking her way carefully between the digging machines that smelled strongly of steel. Gip had died early that summer and a new dog had taken his place. She had not yet met this new hound, and did not particularly want to. However, as she approached the farmhouse, she was aware of him sitting outside of his kennel, a chain attached to his collar. His pose was a forlorn one. He looked miserable and dejected, and despite her hatred for dogs, she felt sorry for him. She could not imagine anything worse than being restricted to a few square feet of ground, a prisoner on a chain. Then she recalled that Camio had been in a similar position. How had he stood it? She would have killed herself—ritual suicide, *ranz-san*—rather than submit to such terrible treatment. He must

have had a high survival instinct. There was a saying that "foxes know no tomorrows." It was the present, always, that counted.

She crouched by one of the barns and stared at the dog, whose large mournful head looked up at the moon. He seemed familiar.

Suddenly the hound smelled her, and lifted his head. O-ha prepared to flee, thinking that his yelling would have the farmer running out with a gun, but the dog did not cry out. Instead, he called softly, "Is that a fox out there?"

Without thinking, she replied, "Yes."

"Ah." He placed his head on his paws with a sigh.

O-ha was desperately curious.

"Why don't you yell for your master?" she asked. "I'm up to no good, you know. I've come to steal chickens."

"Get on with it then. I'll start yelling once you attack the chickens, if I feel like it. Right now I'm of two minds."

She was amazed at this talk.

"But you're a farm dog. You're supposed to protect the place."

He snorted then, through his cavernous nostrils.

"Farm dog? I'm no farm dog. I'm a hound—a hunting hound. I've run down more foxes than you've caught chickens. I've broken them—broken their necks—"

"Breaker!" she breathed.

His head came up again.

"Yes—that's my name. How do you know my name, fox? Famous, is it? Famous among foxes, eh?"

"You killed my mate," she snapped, "toward the end of winter. There was a hunt. You chased me along a road, to the wood, then my mate took over and you killed him."

"Not me. I've not caught a fox for a long time. That's why I'm here, in this place," he said and looked around him in disgust. "This is my punishment, to be trussed up here, chained. My usefulness as a hunting hound was questioned. I was given a trial, and here I am—talking to foxes from the end of a chain. You must be feeling good, seeing me like this, when I was once a hero of the pack, a hound looked up to by all. It must make you feel good."

She remembered, then, that A-ho had not been caught by the

pack, but dug out of the earth by stableboys, *then* thrown to the hounds once he was dead.

"No, I don't feel good. I still hate you, but I don't like seeing any animal chained. You could tell them I'm here . . ."

He made a grimace.

"Let them find out for themselves. Only, don't go near the chickens or the ducks, or I'll have to make some sort of row. I suppose I still have a little honor left in my bones. It might not be much, but it's there. And don't come near me. I'm a trained killer. I'll have your neck . . ."

"I know," she said.

She drifted around the farm, finding some *gubbins* hanging on the corral fence at the back. The cows watched her with round eyes as she crossed her shadow twice over the *gubbins* and then ripped it from its wire. The cows said nothing, their mouths busy the whole time, chewing, chewing. She thought they were very silly creatures, but there was little point in saying so.

When she had performed the ritual chants and drunk from the pond, she returned to the sett. She fulfilled the requirements of entering-the-earth, for even though this was a sett, she was a conventional creature and did not like to deviate from the proper procedures necessary to fox security. The badgers were having a gathering when she arrived, and she listened to their strange language, their old, old tongue, before dropping off to sleep.

When she woke she went through that terrible routine of thinking A-ho was still alive, but came to her senses sooner than she used to. It was probably meeting Breaker that was responsible for her slipping back into old habits.

She left the sett, and for the first time since his death she visited the *sowander* of her old mate. She passed through the spot several times, imbibing the spirit of the place, which gave her a tremulous feeling in her heart. She told herself she was there to pay her respects to A-ho, but buried beneath that acknowledged reason was a subconscious desire to obtain his approval for something—for someone. The face she put to the world was strong and unyielding, but inside she was very lonely. The badgers were kind and she was especially fond of Gar, but they were no replacement for a mate.

So the messages went out from her heart, to her erstwhile mate, while she hoped for some guidance from him: some sign that might tell her whether he approved or not of what she wanted to happen in the near future.

Nothing happened. It is the living who must make the decisions concerning their own lives. She went home desperately disappointed, but refusing to admit it to herself.

"A-ho knows how I feel," she told herself. "That's the only important thing."

The dream came again. Fear and the chase. She dreamed she was in a bright place and struggling to walk. Suddenly, black bars fell across the ground. They were like . . .

THIRTEEN

The summer ended and Melloon was sweeping across the landscape like a grand shaggy fox. The river began to gather more scarlet hues upon its surface during twilight, and ripe fruit and nuts fell to the earth. Around Trinity Wood the town was taking shape and the first occupants were moving into completed dwellings, though many roads were still unfinished and dozens of houses were still empty shells, some without roofing. The evacuation of the animals had continued throughout the warm months. Some animals were determined not to recognize the human invasion, or to ignore it as long as possible. Prominent among these was A-konkon, visionary, mystic among foxes.

He had been born "A-kon" on the far side of the river, in the crypt of a church, the spire of which could be seen from the wood, piercing the sky on the other side of the valley. Often, when the river mists curled up from the water, it was the only thing that could be seen on the distant ridge. The repetitive syllable was added to his name when he was three months old and his mother realized that he had special powers. It was said that A-konkon was able to recognize as many colors as humans themselves could, the result of laying as a cub beneath the great stained-glass window that arched over the church altar, where he soaked up the brilliant hues projected by the sun onto the stone floor. During his cubhood he had also imbibed much that was sacred to humankind, listening from the crypt below the altar while their religious services went on overhead, and falling into a trance under the murmurings and organ music that came from above.

After his parents had left their breeding earth, in the church, A-konkon still returned to ponder over the symbol of the cross, to listen to the choir filling the church with its howling and baying, and to wander amongst the gravestones. His presence was tolerated by the humans whose church it was and who had certainly known of his mother's breeding earth and yet had not interfered with it. The ancient stones of the old building whispered secrets to the fox, and the buttresses, the beams, the organ pipes confirmed these clandestine utterances. They were secrets that could not be fully understood by an animal unversed in the ways of men, but some gleanings of intelligence did fall on the consciousness of the mystic fox. There was a strange bright light—a shaft that penetrated from above, carrying a message for him and imprinting itself in colors on the floor of the church.

"There is something that is denied us," he told other foxes, "because man does not believe we have a spirit, a soul. I cannot tell you what it is—there is not one animal in the whole world who understands humans or their language—but I know it is important and we are excluded from it. But A-O was not the first, that much I can tell you."

Such heresy was not popular amongst the common foxes.

A-konkon was considered mad, and for many seasons was regarded as an outcast, to be shunned and abused. Treatment such as this did not make him contrite, and he continued to preach obscure and recondite theories about a superior Being under whose judgement all would eventually fall. A-konkon believed utterly in the purity of the soil and all things that sprang from it—except the works of man. These, he said, were a blasphemy, false in the eyes of nature.

"A fox's life should be based on the doctrine of asceticism," he told those who would listen. "A fox should practice frugality and austerity, and learn to do without such bodily comforts as warmth, food, and shelter. A fox should deny himself material things. . . ."

This was one aspect of his preaching that many foxes understood and agreed with, but not to the extent A-konkon required. He told them that they should sleep in the open, even during the most inclement weather, and never, *ever* soil their bodies with the food of humans.

"The impurities in such foul waste will stain your souls and the fox-spirits of the eternal landscapes cannot accept into their number such blemished creatures. You will be denied access to those grasslands and coverts of the world beyond death, the Perfect Here, and be left to wander—deaf, blind, and without a sense of smell—the muddy wastelands of the Unplace. Foxes of the Earth, go forth and gather seeds from the wind in your coats. Let the burrs from the bushes tangle your fur. Collect twigs in the beautiful rust of your brow, the white of your bib, and know you are nature's children. You are the salt in the wound of man, because you have not kneeled before him. You are the clay that he has been unable to mold. Your face on the landscape is man's failure to subdue all to his way. Your tail flying above the grass tells man that he has never gained complete control. You are nature's blessed creatures, full and happy. You are the personification of autumn, you are the spirit of fire manifest. Go forth and roll in the wet clays, the saltings of your homelands. Let the mud of the ancients cling to your fur, dry on your jowls, and know that you are *foxes*."

If nothing else, A-konkon gave his disciples and followers an image of themselves that they had not had since the time the little foxes stole the grapes. He told them they were not sly, sneaking creatures who had to slink over the world, but proud, keen hunters who could outwit even the most intelligent of all animals: the name-caller, man.

The fox-mystic was also a herbalist who prescribed remedies for fox maladies and advocated the eating of herbs as clarifiers, purgatives, and energizers. This, too, the other foxes understood, but not to the extent to which A-konkon took them. His depth of knowledge was awesome, even alarming if one started to wonder where he had acquired it. For example, he prescribed St. John's wort to banish bad moods, hemp as an aid to visions of the future, vervain to locate lost souls. Some foxes considered such uses of herbs to be close to the dark side of the moon.

On the other hand, much sensible advice came from the lips of A-konkon. He told his disciples and others willing to listen, "Be in harmony with your body, be in tune with your environment, reject stress and a negative outlook. View yourself and the world through positive senses. Hate is destructive to your spirit. Guilt undermines your efforts to become a better fox. . . ."

However, except when being visited by an itinerant disciple, A-konkon slept in the snow and ice alone, and was despised for his rejection of the easy pickings to be found in and around human habitations. When others challenged him with one very real objection to his teachings—that weaker foxes might die when exposed to Ransheen's savage breath for days on end—he replied that death was not a state to be kept at bay for the sake of life, that it should be accepted as a reward. Death was not a failure of the body and soul, but a victory over life.

Despite this personal belief, A-konkon would help ailing foxes when he could, proving to be a very able physician, albeit his patients were often quite afraid of him. Sick foxes would reluctantly go to him when all else failed, to be told, "Go out and eat the fangs of the toothwort plant" or "Eat some thyme, sweet cicely, and tansy, in equal proportions." If a fox was having bad dreams, A-konkon might suggest placing a yarrow in the earth to drive away any bad spirits that lurked there, but he was just as likely to order the fox to sleep

in the open for a full month. "Wouldn't some jack-by-the-hedge do the trick?" one vixen asked hopefully, when told to stop nursing one of her cubs that was showing signs of summer lethargy. She balked at the idea of sending out her favorite cub to hunt for itself. "Vixen," he replied, "you can give your young feverfew, foxglove, hyssop, or anything you like, including jack-by-the-hedge, but don't come to me when it doesn't work. I've given you my remedy." "But," she said—quite reasonably, she thought—"you told O-lan . . ." A-konkon gave her one of his withering stares. "All foxes are different," he said, "and so the cures for the same problems are different in each case. Your cub has darker ears than O-lan's cub and therefore I prescribe a milkless period, not jack-by-the-hedge. Do you understand me now?" The vixen replied hastily that if this was the case, of course, she understood perfectly.

"Now," said A-konkon, "for your own problems—worms in the belly and flatulence—chew alchoof, dock, and samphire until the cud has the consistency of pond scumweed, then . . ."

Camio was talking to A-lon about A-konkon, one morning just after the rain had ceased and the smells of the earth wound themselves around tree trunks.

"I admire him," said Camio, "but I can't agree with him about "human obscenity." There are humans and humans, some good, some bad. Likewise their influences, and they're animals too—they are entitled to live in the world."

"Live, yes," replied A-lon, "but not claim most of it for themselves—even areas they don't use. And you must admit, some of that food they throw away does terrible things to the gut."

"Only if you're not used to it."

At that moment, a vixen walked out of the trees, on her way back to her home. Camio's legs went a little shaky, but since he was sitting he was not too worried about it.

"Hello," he called. "How are you?"

O-ha looked up, though she had obviously smelled and heard the other two foxes from some way off. She followed her nose and came up beside them.

"I'm very well—thank you for asking."

"We—we were just talking about A-konkon, weren't we, A-lon? About his ideas . . ."

"Oh," she said, "you wouldn't agree with him, of course, coming as you do from another land."

Camio did not see what that had to do with his beliefs, but he did not want to antagonize her, so he said, "Well, there are aspects I don't think are particularly relevant to our situation."

"What about dogs?" she asked. "A-konkon maintains that dogs are no longer true animals, that every vestige of purity has been drained from them and that they have become something other than real creatures, something apart from nature—unnatural beings."

"Bit strong, I would have thought," said A-lon, bravely.

O-ha said, "Oh, you think so? Well I know one hound that isn't natural. . . ."

"Sabre," said Camio, "the ridgeback at the manor house."

O-ha drew herself up.

"Yes, *Sabre*, and if my mate were alive he would have found some way to repay that particular beast for the death of our cubs—he would have—"

A-lon interrupted with, "Oh, come on, O-ha, A-ho would have done no such thing, and well you know it. What can a fox do against such a creature?"

Camio said quietly, "He killed your cubs?"

"He didn't actually kill them, but he was responsible for their death, and I'm sorry there's not a fox around with enough courage to put an end to him. We all know our strength is limited, but there have been foxes with enough art to get around that drawback. Clever foxes . . ."

"Like your A-ho?" said Camio.

"I think so."

Camio seemed to slip into a reverie at that point. He stared out across the fields, looking toward some distant place which could not be seen. O-ha wondered whether the new fox was remembering something about his old land, whether he was feeling homesick. She suddenly felt guilty for baiting him, but she could not seem to help herself. Why she should feel angry with this dog fox who had wandered into her life, she was at a loss to explain to herself. She did her best to avoid him, turning away if she saw him approaching, because of an awkwardness she felt deep within herself whenever she had to speak to him.

He turned to her now. "If someone were to destroy this beast for you, no doubt you'd be eternally grateful?"

"Of course," said O-ha, stiffly.

"I see," said Camio. He looked rather grim. She wondered if she had gone too far this time, and was about to retract much of what she had said, when he spoke again.

"Well, you two, I'd better be on my way. I'll see you soon."

With that he walked down the slope toward the river, which sparkled in the morning sunlight.

For a while there was silence between A-lon and O-ha. All that could be heard was the crickets in the wet grasses, and the birds yelling at each other in the treetops. Suddenly A-lon said, "I think that was the most despicable thing you've ever done, O-ha. I used to like you—admire you, for the way you conducted yourself after the death of your mate—but that was really low."

O-ha looked at him in surprise. She had never heard anything so heated come out of A-lon before, and she did not know what to say for a moment. She had no idea what he was talking about.

Finally she said, "I'm sorry, I don't understand."

There was condemnation in A-lon's features.

"You don't understand? Let me enlighten you then. You've just sent a good dog fox to his death. I can tell you that he's probably on his way down to the manor now, to attempt the impossible—to try to kill Sabre. And all to satisfy this bloodlust of yours, which you insist on keeping hot in your mouth like stale breath. I don't want to have any more to do with you."

O-ha faltered. "He—he wouldn't do that?"

"Why not? It's the only hope you've ever given him. I've seen vixens plant themselves in his path and he's ignored them, keeping this ember alive within himself, a small glow of hope that one day you'll change your mind and accept him for what he is. Your bitterness will be his death, though."

She felt, amid the confusion whirling in her brain, a terrible fear. She did not understand what A-lon was talking about. Why should Camio want her to "accept him"? Surely all this was nonsense on A-lon's part? Yet the dog fox before her looked deadly serious.

"I still don't know what you're talking about," she said. "I can see I've upset you, but—oh, I suppose I went a little too far, but he—he *annoys* me so much. He won't go down to Sabre. Why should he?"

A-lon shook his head impatiently.

"You *still* haven't got it, have you? You're not trying to tell me that Camio hasn't asked you to become his mate."

O-ha shuffled, uncomfortably.

"Well, yes, but I expect he's asked every available vixen within the vicinity at some time or another. He's that type of fox. You can see from just looking at him that he makes up to females at the least opportunity. One can't take flatterers seriously."

"Sometimes you exasperate me beyond reason, O-ha. I'm glad you're not *my* mate. Let me tell you something about this Camio. To my certain knowledge he hasn't even once "made up" to another vixen in the region. All he ever talks about is you. In fact he's quite boring about you. And let anyone try to say a word against you—let them try to tell him you're not worth the effort—and he looks them coldly in the eye and says, 'I must have been mistaken. Excuse me,' and walks away. You have the feeling at such times that he's holding himself in check, a hairsbreadth away from attacking."

"*You* told him I wasn't worth the effort?" she said, indignantly.

"No, but I now agree with the fox that did. Because of Camio's feelings for you he has gone to fight Sabre, and as good as he is the fox will not win, *can't* win. We know that."

A chill went along O-ha's spine. Surely Camio admired her only in the way he admired all vixens? Was it possible that he found her so attractive that he would . . . that he would *die* for her? Foxes didn't do such things.

Then she remembered A-ho's sacrifice, and she knew that she herself would have sacrificed her own life for her cubs, if that would

have saved them. This was serious. She had done a very silly thing. If Camio was besotted, not so much with her of course but with the thought of having a mate, and if he foolishly believed *she* would make his ideal partner, well, it was possible he might do something stupid.

"We must stop him, A-lon. We must stop him."

"Too late for that. He's gone. I couldn't catch him, and neither could you. I hope you're satisfied."

With that, the dog fox walked away, toward his own earth, leaving O-ha feeling wretched and miserable. Of course, she told herself, she knew what she had been doing—trying to make Camio feel small—and she had gone too far. That he should take her words seriously, she had not intended. A-lon was right, it had been a terrible thing to do. Her mind had been twisted by all that hatred, which might now lead to the death of a fox she . . . she did not particularly think a great deal of . . . but oh yes she did, it was time to stop lying to herself. She admired him greatly. He had been through terrible adversity and had survived—not only survived, but managed to remain a balanced, considerate, kind creature. A little undereducated perhaps, and rough around the edges, too persistent in his pursuit of her, but nevertheless—"Oh, no!" she cried, "what have I done?"

There was only one thing to do. She had to go to the manor house and either stop Camio from doing something foolish, or help in the enterprise, if it had already started and could not be halted. She set off at a fast pace in the direction taken by Camio.

Camio, in the meantime, had gone not to the manor, but to seek out A-konkon. He wanted to speak to this prophet among foxes, to try to understand the vixen he wanted so much. If he could not receive any insight into her complex attitude toward him, he would abandon all attempts to reach her and would instead spend his time mooning around the landscape looking for something easier to understand, like the meaning of life.

Why, for instance, was she trying to bait him? He could not think she was serious about asking *any* fox to go down and fight a dog like Sabre. It was like asking a hedgehog to attack a wolf. In an act of open confrontation the odds were impossible. Yet she had thrown this challenge down at his feet. He wanted to understand *why* she treated him this way.

"You come to me asking for information I cannot give," A-konkon said to Camio. "One animal can never fully understand another, unless he or she has a duplicate personality of the other and goes through exactly the same experiences at the same time of the season, at the same age . . . I could go on, but you must by now see it is impossible. We are all different—we react differently to various circumstances. Basically, we all *seem* the same, but though our differences may be subtle, those subtleties become as insurmountable as the sun itself. We can *try* but we cannot hope for success."

"That's a pretty bleak picture," said Camio, despondently.

"It is indeed, but a true one. My advice to you is to become celibate—a state in which I have kept myself since birth. Unions soil the soul . . ."

"But there would be no new foxes, no cubs born, if everyone felt like that."

"You talk as if procreation and continuation of the species is a necessary thing. The world will still be here when we've gone. It isn't necessary for a single fox to inhabit the earth to ensure that the sun rises in the morning, or to keep water in the rivers, or to bring rain from the sky."

Camio did not agree with this but there was something about A-konkon which deflected argument.

A-konkon filled the silence.

"To me, the most noble creature on the whole earth is the snake—the adder is closer to the soil than any other beast . . ."

"Except the worm," interrupted Camio, without being able to help himself.

A-konkon gave him a bland stare.

"Except the worm, which is not a true animal . . ."

"Or the mole," said Camio.

"The *mole*," spat A-konkon, "to the *infamy* of its kind, insists on burrowing through gardens desecrated by humankind, as does the *worm*," he added, as if he just realized this fact. "Only the snake remains aloof and for this reason it is hated and feared by humans . . ."

"And because its bite is poisonous," said Camio.

"That too," replied A-konkon, after another long stare, "but that is its defense against the poisonous nature of man. The *nagas*, the snake, has its spiritual homelands under the earth, or beneath the waters of rivers and seas. These the serpents keep holy by denying access to humans or any of their minions, such as the dogs. Such a place is rich in pure thought, and the snake-spirits there are dedicated to the expiation of the evil wrought here on the surface of the world. Ever since man split the tongue of the snake by planting sharp grasses where the serpents lick the dew, *nagas* has kept distant from him and managed to remain pure in spirit. Of all the animals only the physical form of the serpent is eternal. *Nagas* alone shall inherit the earth, because he has maintained the proper spiritual distance between himself and the poisonous odor of humankind— the stink of people whose houses and machines breathe foul gases into the air, whose waste pollutes the waters of A-O, and whose bark wounds the ears of all those who have to suffer its sound."

"I once knew a keeper that I quite liked," said Camio, reflectively. "She never tried to stroke me, and when I rubbed against her leg, she allowed me to do so. She had one of the softest barks I have ever heard—quite pleasant to the ear—and despite my snapping at her on several occasions, she showed nothing but kindness to me."

"Did she open your cage and point the way to freedom?"

"No, but I've heard there are those that do."

A-konkon sighed deeply, and stared into Camio's eyes until the American Red Fox felt himself going dizzy.

"I'm afraid you are lost to me, Camio," said A-konkon. "You've been tarnished by your experiences in the world of men. I can do nothing to save you . . ." he said, pausing as a glazed look came over his features, ". . . just as you can do nothing to save the vixen, O-ha."

Camio jerked upright.

"What do you mean by that?"

"Eh?" A-konkon's voice was far away, as if he were somewhere in the back of his own mind, unable to come forward to speak consciously to the other fox.

"What do you mean?" shouted Camio. "Where is she?"

"She is walking into the jaws of death," cried A-konkon. "The slavering jaws of death." His eyes seemed to focus once more. "I saw her just before you came to visit me. She was heading toward the manor house, and she exuded an odor of fear and apprehension. I think she has gone . . . gone . . ."

Camio jumped to his feet.

"Damn your red hair, why didn't you tell me before!"

He left the mystic to his mutterings and ran at full speed toward the place where O-ha had gone.

FOURTEEN

There was a strong scent of humans at the manor house, and O-ha skirted the lawn, using the shrubbery directly in front of the building. She entered an area of low, squared hedges not much higher than herself, planted in rectangles. There were stone figures of humans here and there: the guardians of the property. These were surrounded by rose bushes and other cultivated plants. Set back from the house was a lily pond with concrete stepping stones. Some of the individual bushes had been cut into the shapes of animals: there was a cockerel, a peacock, and a dolphin. None of the bushes was shaped like a fox.

Several pieces of white furniture had been set out on the lawn between this garden area and two big glass-paneled doors, which now stood open. The growling of humans could be heard coming from within the house. Sabre was nowhere to be seen. Neither was Camio, and O-ha began to wonder whether A-lon might have been wrong about the dog fox's intention to settle her score for her with the ridgeback. She was just about to sneak away when there was movement at the doors, and humans spilled out onto the lawn. There was a strong smell of burning in the air, and smoke wafted from several of the humans' faces. O-ha wrinkled her nose as the stink of human sweat, mingled with the frightening odor of fire, reached her sensitive nostrils. She flattened herself against the ground.

The humans sat on the furniture, barking at one another, and the clinking of glass added further sounds to the confusion. They all appeared to be trying to communicate at once, seemingly none of them listening to anyone else; and that strange noise they made when they appeared to be happy, when their bodies rocked and jumped, floated over the shrubs to where O-ha lay. She sneaked a quick look at the scene, but no one was moving and her poor eyesight gave her only an impression of colors, predominantly white. Then another odor came to her, which made her heart patter faster in her breast.

Sabre was in amongst them, somewhere. His scent was one she would never forget, and she judged that he was not more than a short run away from her on the lawn. Then a head jerked up, its ears erect and its nose high, as if sniffing the wind. Yes, he was there, lying full length on the short grass, near one of the humans. From the signals he was putting out, both in smell and movement, she knew he was aware that something was not right in his world. He was now a domestic animal, but she remembered that he had once been a hunter and that his sense of smell would be good, for a dog. This was no pampered pet she was dealing with, but a killer with a nose for blood. He had caught a whiff of fox, and though he did not yet understand why, he would shortly begin investigating to either confirm or disprove his suspicions.

Inside, her initial panic subsided and gave way to the cool

reasoning of the fox in danger. She quickly assessed the situation and her chances of escape. She could run, now, before he really knew what was happening in his own back yard; or she could stay, creeping backward very, very slowly, hoping that the wind would not carry her scent to the suspicious animal. If she ran, there would be mayhem because the humans would surely catch sight of her and might also give chase. Was it possible that one of them had a gun? Unlikely. Their clothing had a different smell when they were out hunting, and though farmhands occasionally carried guns when they were not specifically out hunting—when they were driving the tractor, for instance—the kind of people who lived in or visited the manor house always wore special clothes when shooting things. Their voices were different at those times, too: they were not as loose, the barks coming out in a taut staccato rhythm.

So, no guns. The humans then could be discounted. Were there any other dogs? She could not smell any and certainly Sabre was not paying attention to anyone but himself. Good, only Sabre to deal with.

Only Sabre? She had got away from the ridgeback once, but could she hope to do it a second time? The wall at the bottom of the garden was a good long run. He would overtake her before she even covered a quarter of the distance, and even if she took him by surprise it was extremely doubtful she would get halfway there without getting her back broken.

So she had to stay where she was and hope the breeze remained constantly in her direction, keeping her down-wind of her adversary. In order to keep herself calm, to contain any odor of fear, she began running through the names of all the grasses in her head—cocksfoot, fescue, timothy, rye, wild oat, black, couch, tor, quaking, tufted hair, false-brome, wood millet, marram, cord . . . There were more. When she had finished those she began on the wildflowers, then the trees, and all the while she kept her nose keen and her ears sharp for any signs that Sabre was coming in her direction.

For some time the human sounds continued unabated: especially the rattle of stoneware, the tinkle of metal on glass. Then something began, further out on the lawn. Some sticks were pushed into the ground and the humans began throwing a leather ball and hitting it with a flat piece of willow. O-ha had seen this kind of activity before, and knew how engrossed humans became in such things. Sabre, too, would have his attention taken up by this game. Dogs had lived with humans for so long that they enjoyed the same sort of games and would race after sticks or balls thrown into the air. Foxes played too, of course, but their activities were centered around developing their hunting skills.

Sure enough, Sabre went out to try to join the game, running after the ball, but one of the humans barked orders at him and he had to return to the same spot as before. During this time O-ha managed to back away, putting several more shrubs between her and the hound. Once more she was amazed at the size and speed of the ridgeback. He was a giant among dogs.

The sound of the ball being struck, and the excited barks of the humans, continued for a while. Then something alarming happened. A cat came creeping around the corner of the house, her eye on a thrush that was passing the time of day hollering at the clouds from a windowsill. At first she was intent on the thrush, but it saw her and flew away, leaving her to lick her paw as if she had no thought of birds in her mind anyway. Then she saw O-ha, crouched behind a bush. Her fur went up and the usual hissing, spitting face was presented to the vixen.

"Get lost," said O-ha, as softly as she could. "I'm not interested in you."

"*Cambrioleur!*" cried the cat. "*Allez vite!*"

The two of them sat and regarded each other with mutual hostility, before the cat finally found its legs and marched off toward Sabre. For a moment O-ha's heart was in her mouth, but when the cat reached the dog she pranced past him, not forgetting to spit in his face and show her claws. Sabre took no notice of her. They obviously shared the same household, tolerating each other's presence, but there seemed to be no love lost between the two of them. O-ha had seen cats smaller than this one scratch the noses of large dogs and get away clean, and she had a healthy respect for the feline members of the animal world, whether they were domesticated or not. Cats had never fully capitulated anyway, and used humans rather than the other way around.

The wind began to make tentative changes in direction, and once again the dog got a whiff of the fox and puzzled over this. His head went up; first it jerked one way, then the other. O-ha wondered what was happening. Sabre was on his feet, his head whipping backward and forward as if he were not sure in which direction lay his quarry. The master barked at him, but the dog refused to obey. It came trotting toward the shrubbery, its eyes narrowed, then stopped and went the other way toward a flower bed.

Then O-ha realized what was happening. She had now caught a scent of fox herself, and knew that Camio was in the flower bed, on the far side of the lawn. Sabre was confused. O-ha knew it was time for her to flee.

She came out of the shrubs running, and headed straight for the game in progress on the middle of the lawn. Camio had seen her break and went at the same time, running parallel to her.

"Go, vixen, go!" he yelled. "Head for the humans. Confound the dog."

"Exactly what I was doing," she snapped through clenched teeth. She ran right through the middle of the players, who barked and howled at her, some of them mesmerized and others looking for objects to throw.

A club was swung by one of the humans in white, missing her head by a fraction, and she ran between him and the three sticks. She felt the wind of it. Then a boot struck her side, but not hard enough to put her off course. A quick glance told her the dog was almost on her. His teeth were bared to the gums and his eyes were demonic. His determination was evident in the way he remained silent, intent only on running down his prey.

Camio came rushing in at the ridgeback from the side, distracting him so that he turned his head for an instant. There was indecision in the way he weaved between the foxes, trying to make up his mind which one to go for.

At that moment the sky overhead suddenly went black, as if there were an eclipse of the sun, except that the air became full of sound.

The clamor was appalling and even the foxes, in danger of being caught, looked up for an instant. A noisy, dark sheet was moving over the sky. The dog, unused to such a strange phenomenon, looked for too long, and stumbled. The two foxes were quick to take advantage of the situation, increased their speed and reached the wall almost together. The dog recovered, but was still unsure about which one to attack. Finally he decided on Camio, who was closer. The American Red was at the foot of an oak, however, and within a moment was up in its branches and jumping for the wall. He ran along the top in the opposite direction from O-ha with the dog following him. Now the hound was screaming threats, but it knew it was beaten. O-ha took two leaps at the wall before she finally scrambled over the top and down to the other side. She ran out and on until she reached the building sites. There she waited for Camio.

When he arrived he began to remonstrate with her.

"What on earth made you go to the manor?" he said. "You were almost caught."

"I might ask you the same thing."

"I came to rescue *you*."

"Well, it wasn't necessary. I'm quite capable of looking after myself, thank you." She faltered. "I—I was told you had gone to the manor first."

"Now you know that's not true. I was with A-konkon when he informed me that he had seen you heading in that direction. I guessed you were going down to try to even the score with Sabre. It was a silly thing to do. You have to forget that hound. There's not a fox on earth that could kill such a creature. He's too big and fierce and he's not worth it."

She sniffed.

"Well, I couldn't expect *you* to fight my battles for me, that's obvious. It's a good job the geese arrived when they did."

"Me? Have a go at that beast? You must be mad. Next time you get such a crazy idea into your head, I suggest you go down to the pond at the farm and stick your head into the water—wash it clean of such thoughts. I've never heard of such an idiotic obsession . . ."

He continued in that vein until she could stand no more, and walked away toward the wood.

Overhead the geese, some twenty thousand of them, were rhonking away to each other in their own particular tongue, their wings creaking and filling the air with sound. They came down from the north every winter to spend the cold months on the mud flats of the estuary. This year they were, thankfully, unusually early. In fact they often did not arrive until well after the autumn. They darkened the sky with their numbers, as they realized the journey to the southern lands was over and thus began to break formation.

O-ha went to the top of the ridge and watched the large birds landing on the fields adjacent to the river. They were all talking to each other, milling around in their multitudes, the occasional head winding up above the crowd looking for a friend or relative missing since the flight began. "Has so-and-so made it?" they would be saying. "I saw her start out, but lost her when I took the lead. Oh, yes, there she is, with whatsisname!"

With tired wings, aching muscles, relieved hearts, they were all down there on the mud. Some of them would not have made it, of course—the sick and the lame, the elderly, those who had become dispirited and had dropped into the ocean. Then the stragglers coming down in twos and threes. They would be flying in for the next few hours, days perhaps, in large formations or small clutches, encouraging one another: "Come on, only another few wingbeats. Don't give up now—we're nearly there."

"You've—been—saying—that—since Godknowswhen . . ."

"And I'll keep saying it. We're *nearly* there. I mean it. I can see the coast. Look, look. *Not* down there—only water—"

"Endless—water—waves—white foam—death . . . I'm so tired—so tired. I can't—not another wingbeat . . . so—desperately tired."

"Never mind all that. Look at that dark smudge on the horizon. That's land, I tell you."

"Cloud—"

"No, *land*. Look how it sweeps around in a curve. And there's a landbird—see, see. Come on. We're there. We're there."

"Land? You're sure?"

"See how it grows out of the mist! Forget those damn waves. Forget everything but getting to that black strip of mud. Everyone will be there. Think about that. Everyone. We've made it," cries the optimist. "I told you we would."

"Probably get there now—yes—only to be eaten by a fox," says his pessimist friend.

O-ha watched the birds for a long time, wondering what it must be like to set out on such an arduous journey: what fortitude was required in such an enterprise. Yet it all seemed so silly to her. Why not stay where they were? Or, since the winters were obviously too harsh up there, why not stay down here in the south, once the journey had been made? But geese obviously had their own ideas about such things. Their own motivations. The urge to use their wings in some desperate adventure was obviously necessary to them. Geese. Who could fathom them?

Then she thought about Camio. He had saved her life and she could not bring herself to thank him. It was a problem. He was a problem to her.

Dog foxes, who could fathom them?

She went back to the sett, her earth, not forgetting the rituals of entering before going down. That night, under the moon, she left the sett and stole a chicken from the farm. Breaker was fast asleep during the whole operation and she could not help hoping that he would get into trouble for allowing the theft to take place. When she returned to her chamber she stripped the carcass there, scattering feathers everywhere. There were already small bones and other debris on the floor, and when Gar came down to see her he said, "Is a mess! How you live in such chaos?"

She looked around her, seeing the rubbish for the first time.

"Foxes are not very tidy creatures, I'm afraid."

Gar grunted. "You tell me? What is this? One new goose, fly in today?"

"No," she said, more sharply than she had intended. "No, it's not a goose, Gar. I wouldn't touch the geese."

He shrugged his back, asking for no explanations, but she could see he was puzzled by the reply. No doubt he was saying to himself, "Vixens—who could fathom them?"

Humiliation! If Sabre could have wept tears of frustration, the way humans frequently did, he would have done so at that moment. To have been outwitted by that vixen *once* was bad enough, but a second time . . . unthinkable. Yet, she had done it. It was almost as if she were deliberately mocking him. Why had she come to the manor? Why? To make him look ridiculous, of course. The walls that contained him were barriers that would have to be breached. He would get out one day—one day soon—and go looking for that vixen and her mate. They had been responsible for a beating, when Sabre had returned to the manor without so much as one of their pelts in his mouth.

The male guests at the house had taunted his master (he knew the whining note of such barks!) and Sabre, in turn, had received his thrashing for coming back without a kill. He knew that he deserved the stick his master had administered. He shared his master's feelings of shame at his ineptitude.

He would scour the countryside, the streets of the town, until he found that vixen. His spies had been out, the dogs that visited the house and had more freedom of the town, and had given him her name. *O-ha*, that was the vixen's name, wrested from a weasel close to death.

Sabre paced the wall around the estate, looking for a place to get over or under. He found a place where the mortar was crumbling and scratched at it with his claws. It fell away as dust.

There was a bark from the house. His master. He would have to go. But he would come back here, to this spot in the wall, and work on those bricks until there was a gap large enough to let him escape. Then he would go looking for this O-ha, this blight on his honor, and crush her skull in his jaws. It might take a season, perhaps more, to find her, but he would eventually taste her blood. Domesticated canines had suffered the jibes and jeers of wild creatures for too long, simply because of the relationship dogs had with humans. Most domesticated hounds were unfit for tracking down and killing wild animals, but Sabre was different. He felt deeply the wounds caused by fox words, just as he had felt those of the jackals, the hyenas, and other such creatures in the old land. It was time for dogs to reassert themselves and show their cousins that they had not been tamed beyond redemption: that there were hounds whose honor was unbesmirched.

Sabre had a pride in his ancestry that was unusual for this day and age. It was an old aristocrat's pride, in family, in kin, in kind. He could not bear the thought that he was being laughed at. There were those, even other dogs, who called him a relic of the past, an old colonial who held in esteem a culture that had all but died. Sabre saw no reason to let go of values that had been discarded by the weak.

He recalled being taught the "middle history" of dogs: a time when men and their hounds were much closer, in spirit as well as in body. In those days, hounds used to lie under the table when dining was in progress, and receive choice bones from the hands of their masters. And man and dog would hunt in the forests together, for the boar and the wolf.

Sabre wanted a return to those old times, when dogs were valued not for sentimental reasons, but because of their ability to track and hunt down such wild creatures. The land of his birth, where the lion and the elephant were struggling to survive, bore witness to those times. There were packs of stag hounds running through the streets and bush country: hounds that had been abandoned by their masters seasons out of time ago, and left to fend for themselves. It was to their credit that they were managing to survive and continue their line. They were noble hounds, from noble families, and yet they had not slipped into the beggary that might be expected of them.

So Sabre could not afford to let an insignificant creature like a fox, a vixen, bring ridicule upon his head. A dog with a mission as lofty as Sabre's could not "drink ditchwater," since he had to be held up as an example to all other hounds. He had to be the epitome of houndhood: noble, strong, chaste, able, revered, admired, unsullied, passionate in war, merciless, and above ridicule.

It was essential to kill the vixen.

PART FOUR

THE UNREMEMBERED FEAR

FIFTEEN

The time was Ransheen, and she blew through the streets of the new town finding fresh directions— being deflected down alleys, into courtyards, around squares. Although the buildings, many of them still unfinished, were new they had a period design. There were external beams on the more expensive buildings, and cobbled precincts in and around the central square. There was even a mock water pump and horse trough for the birds to drink from, though of course the foxes used it as well. The animals found the inhabitants to be generous. Saucers of bread and milk were left out for the hedgehogs (who would have preferred cat food), and the birds grew plump and lazy. Not many thought to feed the foxes, but then the red-coated ghosts were rarely seen. Their earths were dug in various places, some within a few feet of a human dwelling. One fox even had its earth in the utility room of a house that had a cat and a dog; it managed to evade the bumbling old Spaniel whenever it had to leave or enter its home. The fox used the cat flap to enter and leave the premises. The owners of the house knew it was there, of course, but tolerated its presence for reasons known only to themselves.

Another vixen lived in the boiler room of a school and managed to chew through a water pipe while cleaning her teeth. She sat at a safe distance, behind the central heating expansion tank, and had the audacity to wait and watch while the plumber fixed the damage. Instead of chasing her away, the school authorities had the pipes sheathed. It seemed that having a fox on the grounds was sometimes regarded as a status symbol amongst the human occupants.

Trinity Wood was indeed landscaped in places, and was modeled at the south end after certain city parklands, with devices for children to play on, and asphalt walks. Exotic trees and flowers were introduced into the traditional woodland, and the wild creatures therein were pushed into an even tighter area. A pond was dug and swans introduced into the neighborhood.

Luckily the sett was not interfered with, since the park authorities wanted to retain what wildlife still remained in the wood. Food, however, was a problem. Many of the hunting areas had disappeared, along with the highways and byways, and much was *face*. O-ha had to go down into the streets (where Camio now lived) to find food. There were bins to raid, and black plastic bags full of rubbish in certain streets on certain days. Under Camio's guidance she learned quickly where to go and at what time. Other animals did not fare as well, as they were unused to town life. Some of them went hungry.

Camio had said it would be easy, but he had reckoned without the great numbers of creatures that would be dependent on the town; without the fact that most of them did not have the skills necessary to live in the streets; and without the fact that the town itself was only partially built and would take some time to begin flourishing. It was the *next* generation of creatures who would find the life easy, when their numbers had settled to acceptable levels for the food available. Until that time, survival would continue to be difficult for those without sound knowledge of street life.

O-ha still maintained a rather aloof attitude toward the dog fox, but was gradually melting inside. They would walk together, through the pools of light thrown down by coruscating street lamps, discussing the differences in their cultural backgrounds.

"So you don't know about A-O," she asked him as they skirted the main square one evening, heading for a bin that stood outside a take-away that had closed for the night.

"It's not that I don't know—it's that I don't recognize she-he as the originator of the fox race. I was taught that Menxito was the first fox, also of dual sexuality I might add, so there's a common link there."

"But that's *wrong*—A-O . . ."

"Look, there's no right or wrong about it. It's just a fox by another name. Don't keep falling back on dogma."

"There's no need to bring dogs into it," she replied, knowing full well what he meant, but wanting to save face a little.

Suddenly, he turned to look at her intently.

"Isn't it about time we set up an earth together?" he said, bluntly.

"I don't know what you mean."

"You know very well what I mean. I want us to live together, have a litter. Your time isn't far away. Who are you waiting for? A-magyr?"

She sniffed.

"There no need to be insulting. No, of course I'm not waiting for him. I can't stand the animal. But that doesn't mean I'm going to fall over myself to get to *you*."

"Fall over yourself? That'll be the day. I wonder why you even bother to speak to me. Don't you like me?"

She stared at the ground.

"Of course I like you. But you're so different from me. We have different backgrounds. I'm—I'm still not sure about you."

"What's to be sure of? I'm a fox, you're a fox. The time for mating

is near. I've lived with a mate before—I told you. I shall never see her again and no doubt, if she's still alive, she's found another. There's no other vixen I want around here. You're the one I want."

"You can't have me just because you want me."

"I know that—that's why I'm asking. There are other vixens who would have me—"

She stiffened.

"Well you'd better go to one then, hadn't you . . ."

"—but none as good as you. I know we'd do well together. I'm not one of your promiscuous foxes. I won't leave you in the lurch once the cubs are born. How can I convince you of that?"

"If—if I came to you, it would have to be for always. I've lost one litter because there was no dog fox to feed me while I kept the cubs warm. I couldn't bear it, if it happened again."

His eyes were suddenly very bright and she warmed to him.

"Look," he said, "I respect your memory for A-ho, but he's dead and nothing can bring him back to life. I'm sure he was a good mate, none better, because I can't imagine you choosing anyone that wasn't . . ."

She made a snorting sound.

"There's a little bit of immodesty in there somewhere, since it's now clear that I've chosen you."

He looked hard at her, and then did a little dance around a lamp post, before saying, "You mean it? You will come to me?"

"Yes—just don't let me down."

"Wonderful! Let you down? Not in a million seasons. The winds will stop blowing before I did such a terrible thing. Now, we must choose a suitable earth. You must leave the sett, of course. The place I have at the moment isn't good enough. I live in the roof of a garage, but the fumes there—well, you wouldn't like it. Neither would the cubs. They must have good, clean air, and a certain amount of greenery. I've seen a house on the edge of—what do you call it—the *face*. It's not one of the new ones. There's an orchard at the back, which has been neglected. The female human that lives there is very old, and no one comes to do the garden. We could live under the shed at the bottom. How do you feel about that?"

"Sounds quite good."

"Yes, well don't go berserk with joy."

"I must see it first."

"We'll go tonight."

They rummaged in a bin, finding some waste food, and ate their fill before he took her to the place he had found. When she saw where it was, her heart turned over. It was the gatehouse to the manor where she had lost her previous litter. She said nothing of that to Camio, however, and showed delight in his choice of location. Since the time she had lived there, the house, garden, and shed had been surrounded and encroached on by the new town, and was now part of it. The manor house itself was near enough to concern O-ha, but Camio took her on a tour of the wall and showed her that Sabre's kingdom was completely enclosed and the barbarian was a prisoner of his own world. She reluctantly accepted this reassurance.

Life was good once again. There was a space beneath the shed, suitable for an earth. The trees in the orchard were a little mature, but would certainly show fruit the next summer. There were apples, pears, and greengages, laid out in rows a little too neat for his taste, but it suited her very well.

The next day she visited the sett for the last time before moving out. She found Gar in a grumpy mood, but when he heard she was leaving he stayed to talk to her.

"Ha, you go. It happen sometime, I suppose. I miss you fox *hearda*—most strong I miss you. We talk good together, eh? Well, you go—make nice little foxes—come see badger sometime with little fluffy foxes. We made good friends, ya? Good, good."

And with that he ambled away to his own chamber, a place she had not been inside since that first night in the sett, when she had been looking for a new home. He was a very private badger in many ways and though she had spent some time with the creature, she felt she hardly knew him at all. Apart from having to leave Gar, she was not sorry to move out of the sett. Badgers were noisy creatures, always chattering and snuffling with their rubbery noses in corners of the sett. There had been times when she had been close to shrieking at them to keep quiet, when she wanted to rest and they continually disturbed her. Still, that was behind her now. She was ready for a new life.

When she got back to the earth in the orchard, she spent some time sanctifying the new home with various rituals performed around the entrance and inside. Camio watched her, mystified by all the to-ing and fro-ing, the chanting, the squared spirals scratched in the dust. He started to complain, once, but she glared at him so hard he shut his mouth immediately. When it was all over, he said, "Is that it? Are we safe from mad spirits and tree ghosts?"

"You be careful what you say about tree ghosts," she replied, while marking the posts around the garden with her scent.

He looked astounded, probably because he had no doubt been guessing and was amazed to find he had hit on the right subject. Actually, he could not have been further from the truth, but she let him think he knew what he was talking about.

When they were settled in for their first rest together, side by side, she said sleepily, "You must change your name now, to A-ho."

"What?" he said as his head jerked up. "I'll do no such thing. A-ho was your old mate. My name is Camio."

"But it's traditional. The dog fox takes its name from the vixen, and since my name is O-ha, you have to be . . ."

"That's a stupid tradition. I've never heard of such a thing. I must admit I wondered why all the pairs around here had reflecting names, but I never thought . . . no, no. I won't do it."

"I suppose you expect me to change my name to reflect yours?"

"No such thing. You keep your own name and I'll keep mine. I see no reason to change either of them."

"But the other vixens—they won't know you're *my* fox."

"Good thing, too. Smacks of ownership—*my* fox, *your* fox. Look, I couldn't care less about the other vixens, or the dog foxes, or anyone but us. We know we belong to each other. We don't need signs to tell the world what we know in our hearts. I'm sorry to disappoint you—I know you like all this tradition, but I find it all a bit too tight—too constricting. I like things a little bit more loose than you do. I'm afraid it's something about me you'll have to put up with."

She got up and went back to the entrance to the earth.

"There—I knew it was a mistake. We *are* very different."

"But this is just a little thing."

"If it's so little, then why not do as I ask? After all, this is my country, not yours. You should go by the customs here, not try to import your own ways and change us."

He looked very hurt, and crossed his forepaws.

"A-ho, A-ho," he repeated to himself. "I'll never get used to it. It's not me at all. I don't feel like an A-ho—I feel like a Camio. A-ho—I'll be a stranger to myself. I won't know when I'm being called, or who this person is that foxes speak of. I'll have the ghost of another fox inside me." He looked into her eyes, which were glowing in the near darkness. "I'm *not* him, you know. You can't make me into him. If you try, it'll only bring us both grief. I'm me, Camio, the fox from another land. A-ho is dead and wandering the woodlands of the Perfect Here."

She suddenly saw the logic of his reasoning. When she called him, she would in unguarded moments be surprised that his voice was different from the voice of A-ho. She still dreamed of her previous mate, and those dreams would become confused with the reality of her present situation, if she could not clearly differentiate between what was and what is.

"You're right. A-ho is A-ho, you are not him. I'll call you A-camio."

"No, not even that. I'll be just Camio. You can be O-comia, if you like."

"I certainly *don't* like, thank you. It seems we're to share an earth without belonging to each other in the eyes of the world. So be it, if that's how it *must* be. I don't suppose it'll make any difference to the way we feel about each other. I don't know. To my knowledge, it's never been tried before. I suppose it's my strict upbringing that results in these qualms over what must appear to you to be silly issues. A-konkon will have a fit when he finds out—if you think *I'm* a traditionalist, wait until you meet him on the highway sometime and see what *he* has to say about such unorthodox pairings. Well, don't let's argue about it all day. Let's get some rest."

He seemed satisfied to leave it at that. They marked each other and then lay together, touching.

When her time came, she was surprised how good it was with a fox other than A-ho. Camio was just as sensitive and considerate to her needs, and spent a long time gently nipping her flanks with his teeth, and nuzzling her, encouraging the excitement within her to rise to a high pitch before the actual act, which after all lasted only seconds. During the third time they became so excited that they "locked," ending up back to back the way foxes and dogs sometimes do, and had to wait several hours until he was able to free himself. Still, apart from that incident—which wasn't so bad, since they were in a lonely place and unlikely to be disturbed—everything went well. Her fur got that electric buzz, the static crackling between them as they rubbed against each other. She went hot with passion when he brushed full length against her and had to bite him once or twice, just because the feeling overwhelmed her so much that only a physical action on her part would serve as a safety valve for such contained emotion. He yelped, and whispered that he wanted her more when she did such things.

When it was over, Camio let out a triple bark and a scream, and she thought: *Some things never change.* Then they lay contentedly side by side, touching just enough to know the other was there.

In the world around them, winter set in. Frost made the grasses crisp underfoot, and they had to pick out the ice from between their claws after spending any time outside the earth. Everything crackled with hardened moisture, and fern patterns appeared on the windows of the shed. The soil became solid and impossible to dig, so that earthworms could not be reached. Insects disappeared from the face of the world. Water was hard to find.

She taught him the rituals of leaving and entering the earth, which were (after all) she said, their insurance against discovery. If one spent time and patience going through the correct procedures, the safety factor was increased. He wanted to please her, and also to ensure that his future cubs had a home that was not likely to be attacked while they were too young to run, so he learned her ways.

Midwinter came, and with it heavy falls of snow. On occasion it was a matter of burrowing blindly through the cold white crystals, and finding their way by tunnels. It was a dangerous time, since their prints were all around the earth, but there was nothing they could do about it. Besides, being foxes, they left debris around and all over the place, on top of the snow.

One night, Camio left the earth only to come back a little while later without any food. His eyes were full of anxiety and O-ha knew that something terrible had happened.

"What is it?" she asked. "Tell me what it is?"

"Keep calm," he replied. "We have to get out—go away—as quickly as we can. There are men abroad—men with guns. They're all through the town, and out in the countryside too. They're shooting anything that moves, especially foxes."

Her heart felt leaden in her breast.

"Foxes—why foxes? Why us?"

"It was A-konkon, damn his soul to oblivion," said Camio with great feeling.

"A-konkon? But what could he possibly have done to bring the humans down on us like this?"

"We must get out—get you to a safe place, where the cubs—"

"*What did he do?*"

"He committed *ranz-san* in the main square—tore his own stomach out and died in front of a dozen people. They didn't understand—they're humans—how could they understand? He did it as a protest against the decadent life we were leading here, as he called it. Said it was time to re-establish old values. A *protest!*"

"But what was it they thought? Why are they up in arms against us?"

"They're frightened. As soon as A-lon told me what had happened I guessed. The humans are scared out of their wits—they're terrified—and when humans get like that, they'll destroy everything and anything. They're frightened for their young—and you know how *we* will do anything to protect our cubs."

"You still haven't told me—I still don't understand."

"The Shadow-with-a-thousand-names. The White Mask of Terror. *Now* do you understand? They think A-konkon died the death of the Foaming Mouth." There was the sound of shots outside, and humans barking into the night. Feet were running heavily through the streets. There was fear behind those sounds—not just ordinary fear but an insane terror of a disease that was transmitted by the bite of a dog, or fox, or human. "They're killing dogs out there, as well as foxes. Dogs, cats, everything."

"But . . ." she faltered, reaching deep down into her mind for the *Unremembered Fear*, deep down into the black well where it had been laid long ago by her ancestors, and finding something there that was ugly and devastatingly cruel. "But—we haven't had such a thing here for—for seasons out of time."

"Well, I've seen it—in the old country. It's *not* here. They only think it is—but that's enough. They'll kill and kill until there's nothing left to shoot. Or until reason returns to them once again. We can't wait. We have to go. At least they're not using dogs to hunt us down—they daren't. The dogs might get bitten and then they would have to shoot their pets. Come on—we must go."

She followed him to the entrance to the earth. For once she did not complain when he failed to observe the rituals.

SIXTEEN

The fox-spirits from the *First-dark*, who know all things, said there had not been so many men abroad with death on their minds since the infamous days of Herod and the mass murder of human babes. There were shadows moving across the land and the night was full of thunder and fire. There were desperate retreats across snowy wastes, screams pregnant with fear, miraculous escapes, and loud reports followed by intense silence. All the animals along the broad sweep of the coast caught the smell of terror and either froze or ran. Blood fell on the snow like warm red rain, and the land choked on its own fear.

And the fox-spirits knew that as much dread was in the pursuer as in the pursued, and that the hunters believed they were the hunted, and that the world moved in circles and spirals of madness. The stark, leafless trees were inadequate hiding places for those who had no knowledge at all of why this fear had erupted so suddenly; there were holes in the banks of the rivers and creeks where small mammals quaked and wondered if the end of the world had come to the living; and some animals, being frail, died of sheer fright without leaving their homes.

For Camio and O-ha, the flight from the *face* began with a hazardous journey through the streets. In the town it was Camio who took the lead. Each street corner was a potential death trap. There were men everywhere, in cars and on foot. The rust-colored foxes moved against a backdrop of red brick walls, and slipped down dark alleys, over the fences of gardens, across low rooftops. The hunters did not think to protect their own back yards; having once checked them, they believed them empty. Whether Camio was aware of this or not, his instinct took him along creosoted wickerwork panels, against which it was difficult to see a red-grey coat, especially if it was moving quickly and in darkness. The snow held their spoor, however, and they had to be away from the town before the morning light.

Whenever the smell of man was strong, or the sound of his boots crunched on the snow, they found a hiding place; sometimes it was in waste bins or sheds, or behind a stack of red clay plant-pots, or under a car—anywhere, especially if the space was small. Camio knew that humans often have a strange idea of a fox's size, thinking it to be as large as a medium-sized dog, whereas it is only a little larger than a cat and can squeeze into spaces that look too narrow to take a man's fist. Once, a pair of legs passed them only inches away from their noses.

They found a manhole cover off a sewer in the part of the town where building was still in progress, and went down and traveled along the pipes beneath. Even under the ground they could hear the reports of the guns, and boots thumping the snow-covered concrete above. There were other animals in the sewer pipes, quaking with fear, frozen to the spot. Camio ignored these creatures, who were mostly smaller mammals.

At one point O-ha said, "Why don't we stop here?"

"Because we'll have to go out for food sometime," he answered, "and they'll be waiting for us. You'll see. They won't stop tomorrow, or the next day. This thing will go on for at least a week or two. Even then—even if they somehow find out that A-konkon committed ritual suicide—humans seem to have remarkable powers of discovery, given time—even if that happens, there will always be doubt in those who are told. This needs a lot of time to drain from people's memories. We have to go somewhere and let that time pass."

Once they reached the point where they had to abandon the sewers, they made a mad dash across a building site. A shotgun opened up on them, but the user was inexperienced and did not allow for the kick. The lead pellets went high, shattering some ceramic pipes that were stacked and ready for installation in the new houses. Pieces of pottery rained down on the two foxes, but this only served to spur them on. The man who had fired at them howled to his companions, and then raced after the two foxes. At the same time, he was trying to reload his weapon. O-ha turned on the human when he got too close and even in the poor light she could see his face turn pale, as he skidded to a halt. There was more fumbling with the breech of the gun, and cartridges fell from the man's trembling fingers into the snow. As he bent to pick them up, the foxes continued their flight into the darkness.

They reached the edge of town, but the roads were full of vehicles, few of them moving. There were watchfires ringing the *face* and gun-carrying silhouettes could be seen moving in front of them, walking along the highways. Camio quickly realized these figures were here to keep foxes out, rather than to stop them from getting away, but they would shoot anyway if they saw something slinking through their lines.

There had been another time when foxes were killed out of fear rather than for sport, and the fox-spirits of the *Firstdark* remembered that era—the seasons when Matthew Hopkins, the Witchfinder General, swept across the land ordering hangings and drownings

wherever he wished to exercise his evil power. Foxes had died in those bad times, along with cats and dogs, all taken for familiars of people accused of witchcraft. They were crucified and hanged, in the manner of men, rather than shot. The fox-spirits recalled these seasons of darkness and likened them to this night.

It was O-ha's turn to find a path through the men. She used her nose, while running parallel to the line of fires, and finally came across some humans whose attention was on the bottle they had rather than on the night. The group was huddled around a fire in an oil drum and barked loudly, warming their hands. She and Camio crept past, low to the ground, their belly hairs touching the snow, on the side of the fire where the men were shoulder to shoulder and blocking the light from the white ground. She was sure they could hear the faint swish of fur against the snow, for it was as loud in her ears as dry rushes brushing against tree bark.

When the two foxes were almost out of the light of the fire, one of the men turned and stared in their direction. He growled to his companions. One of them shone a powerful light out onto the snow, the beam sweeping the ground just in front of the noses of the two runaways. The light-bearer stood up and began walking toward them, but another of the men coughed something and he stopped. After a few moments he went back to the fire and took a drink from the bottle that was being passed around. O-ha and Camio waited for a few moments before continuing their perilous journey.

Once they were past the men they had to go over plowed fields, the furrows rigid beneath the snow and difficult to negotiate when walking crossways to them. When they reached a ditch, they lay in the bottom for some time, gathering their strength again.

"I'm not sure this is the right way," she said to Camio. "I've never been this far from home before."

"It doesn't matter for the moment," he replied. "We're out of the town at least. Just think of the creatures in Trinity Wood—that's the first place the humans will have gone—and it's ringed by the town."

"Oh—Gar," she said.

"Gar—the 'perfect pair'—and the others . . ."

When morning came they were aware that they were being tracked, and set off again at a fast pace over the fields. They tried all the tricks: climbing trees and running along a branch, to jump off at the end, hoping to break the line of spoor; traveling along ice in ditches; balancing on the edges of fences. Still they could not shake off their pursuers. The men behind them were determined to get them, and it seemed that nothing would deter them. A farmhouse was circumnavigated with caution. Finally, they came to a railway track.

"Quick, they're not far behind," said Camio. "Up on the track."

O-ha followed him, wondering what he had in mind. She mimicked his actions, though she had never seen a railway line before. He ran along the steel rail for quite a distance, before dropping between the tracks and flattening himself against the gravel. O-ha copied him, lying close to his body.

Shortly afterward, the barks of men could be heard, and she was aware of some confusion amongst them. They had lost the trail at the point where the two foxes had climbed the embankment, and they were searching for the point where the spoor began again.

There was a loud report, which almost had O-ha bolting, and this was followed by a strong smell of cordite. One of the men had fired his gun, hoping to flush the foxes from their hideout. It had almost worked. Then the rails began vibrating and humming, and O-ha was almost beside herself with fright.

"Stay here," whispered Camio. "Don't move a muscle. You'll be all right, I promise. I know what I'm talking about. The train is coming—it'll pass over us. We won't be hurt. Stay, stay . . ." His voice was calm and gentle, with only a trace of apprehension behind it.

The vibrating increased to a rumble. A machine was hurtling down on them at tremendous speed and O-ha was convinced they were going to die. She could not understand why Camio did not bolt, at the last moment; but she trusted his judgment, waiting, waiting for a move from him before she went herself.

The noise was excruciating, hurting her ears. They were entombed in living steel that screamed all around them. The ground beneath her body jumped and the stones rattled and jostled each other around her head. She thought it would last forever: the sensation of being crushed, without any pressure on her body. Then it was over just as suddenly as it had begun, and all she was left with was a ringing in her ears and a heart that had gone on with the train, to travel the land at speeds she could not even imagine.

They lay there together for a long time, and finally she whispered, "Camio?"

There was no answer for a moment, and she began to wonder whether they were dead after all, when he said, "A little while longer."

Ransheen whistled over their bodies, lifting their fur, and when she was sure there was no scent of man, no sound of man, she lifted her head.

"I think we'd better be getting on. They've left. We must move sometime."

"I think you're right," said Camio. Then, "That was some experience, wasn't it? The train, I mean?"

She looked at him in surprise.

"You talk as if you've never done it before."

He flicked his head.

"I haven't—not quite. I almost did it once, but my courage failed me at the last moment. Nearly got killed. A city fox taught me that there was no problem, provided you keep your head down and remain quite still. I was worried for you. I prayed you wouldn't panic—you were very brave—extremely brave . . . that *was* your first time?"

"I've never been near a railway in my life. So," she said, not without a trace of condescension, "you actually jumped clear the first time *you* did it?"

"I'm afraid so. It's a horrible experience."

"Oh," she said, "I quite liked it." Then she added, generously, "I expect it was because you were with me. I had company that knew what was happening."

"I had company too, my first time, and I still panicked and ran. I don't think I have your courage."

He was so magnanimous in his praise that she felt guilty for lying to him.

She confessed, "I *was* scared."

"I expect you were—you'd be very foolish not to be—but the important thing is, you didn't let that fear rule your head. Come on, let's get out of here. Those hunters might be back. Which is the best way to go?"

"I think if we head toward the sun, following the tracks, we should reach the marshes of the estuary. Perhaps we can hide out there until all this has been forgotten?"

So the pair of them began walking, keeping their noses to the wind and their ears tuned for the sound of men. By midday they had reached a point where the ridge dropped down gently toward the creeks and saltflats of the estuary, and they left the railway. Several trains had passed them by, while they had been walking, and O-ha marveled that she had ever allowed one of them to hurtle over her prone body.

When they reached the flats of the wetlands, the tide was out, leaving only thin slivers of water running between the banks of the river and its inlets. Here were several square miles of marsh samphire, bladder wrack, and seablite, with long strips of mauve sea lavender whose flowers die in autumn but retain their color long beyond that season. Here, just below the water, was eel-grass, the only flowering subsea plant, and cruising through this was grey mullet. Here were hidden godwits, knots, and oystercatcher birds who never eat oysters. Here the sharp sound of the wading birds mingled with the deep rhonking of the Brent geese. Here was mud aplenty, embedded with shellfish and perforated by ragworms and roundworms. Here were gulls of several varieties, that robbed as well as scavenged or found their own food; and graceful dagger-faced herons that went out on lonely patrols at dawn looking for silver meals in shallow pools. These were the wastelands, the wetlands, the saltings, the marshes, where wrecks of rotting vessels appeared to be climbing from the sludge like grey-green corpses rising from their graves on the day of salvation.

The pair of foxes traveled along, hidden by the dikes that protected the land around the creeks. There were dozens of new smells out here, tangy and sharp, that took time to assess, classify, and store in their olfactory memories for future reference. They found a place to cross to an ancient wreck on an island of sea poa grass. The hulk was cold and damp, but in what used to be the cabin there was a space that seemed to remain clear of the water when the tide was in. This they decided to make their home for the winter months, which they knew would be hard and difficult to survive, but better than facing the *Unremembered Fear* now implanted in the minds of humankind.

The first time O-ha went out hunting she found a group of seagulls that refused to fly away when she caught one of their kind. It was a time when she had the urge to kill, wantonly, the way she and A-ho had done in that hen house so long ago. The red mist clouded her brain for an instant, and the unnatural situation of having prey that remained in her presence in large numbers, almost turned her head. But her experience of the last few days had somehow penetrated beyond that drive to kill for the sake of killing. Something akin to sympathy for the birds entered her emotions—a feeling that was strange to her, since her emotional mechanism was geared to survival, and survival meant obtaining food when and where it was available. She repressed the urge to run amok, and took only the quarry she had first caught. It was something she did not speak to Camio about later, because she could not explain it even to herself. She just knew that out there in the river mists, in the heron-grey dawn, something unusual had happened to her. She had found something far more important than a tangible enemy.

That winter, they suffered a great deal. When the tides came in, most of the boat was all but covered, leaving only a small space in the cabin for the two foxes to huddle in together and await the retreat of the water. The shellfish—the mussels and cockles that they cracked open with their strong jaws to get at the molluscs inside—did something to their constitutions that left them sore. The cold was far more bitter than it was in both the town and the wood they had left. Ransheen had nothing to stop her out on the flatlands and came across the marshes like a well-honed scythe, ready to cut down anything taller than a blade of grass. The alluvium of the estuary was always wet and stuck to their paws, freezing solid in the spaces between their pads, so that they had to spend much time digging it out with their teeth. There were dens of hibernating adders in holes in the grasses over the dikes; if disturbed, these vipers would have bitten, resulting in death. Sometimes single snakes lay sleeping on the snow on cold, sunny days, reluctant to move, and the foxes trod warily around them.

Each day was taken as it came, and visits by man were rare. When humans were abroad, the geese set up such a clamor that it was known for miles around, and the foxes were warned well in advance. O-ha would sit for hours on the deck of the hulk, watching the geese feed in the mud: bulky birds that shouldered each other out of the way for a scrap of food, and chased away gulls or oystercatchers that tried to enter the mass of immigrants who had come from the north like nordic raiders, to plunder their homelands. These rough, coarse birds who had traveled the airways above the waves were formidable creatures even to a fox, and no thought entered her head to ever attempt to make a meal of one of them. Every word they spoke sounded like a harsh obscenity to her, and though they gave her a wide berth, they swore and glared at her when she crossed the mud as if she were invading their private grounds and had no business to be there. They slopped around on large flat feet, occasionally unwinding their necks to have a look around as if contemplating some idea of breaking out of a boring feeding routine and going on an adventure. Then suddenly one would take to the air, followed by others, until the sky was full of them. As if by magic they became regimented creatures, each knowing his or her place in the squadron, and they flew low V-formation flypasts, rippling over stumps or other objects in their path as smoothly as a snake sliding over a log. This was in complete contrast to the knots, who traveled in huge flocks, wing-tip to wing-tip, turning sharply every few seconds to some unheard command.

O-ha and Camio learned to avoid the crazed creeks, with their sludge that could suck a fox down to an ugly death. They hunted on the network of raised areas that were sometimes islands at high tide. Come spring there would be eggs and elvers, spawn and spanworms aplenty. But until that time, the pair had to make do with what they could find under the mud, or flying above it.

SEVENTEEN

Although O-ha and Camio were not as well fed, or warm and dry, as they would have been out of the marshes, there was a certain feeling of security that came with being surrounded by mud and water, especially in the winter. No doubt during the summer months there were hunters with guns in the creeks, or fishermen at high tide, but there was something about the bleak, windswept saltings during the winter that filled human hearts with dread. There was a flat grey emptiness to the crazed landscape that seemed to speak of eternal vacancy, it was the sort of place that hell might really turn out to be. Mists slid like cold wraiths over the surface of the sludge, and the cries of the birds were the plaintive calls of lost souls doomed to a forever of lonely wanderings over wastelands drear. But at least the merciless winds and unerring drabness of the place ensured that humans kept their distance.

The two foxes lived on a day-to-day basis: just surviving the hours was ambition enough. The slime-slicked hulk, covered in algae and slipping gradually into the ooze, provided the barest of shelters. The creeks that surrounded them were sufficiently stocked with food of a kind the foxes were unused to but quickly developed a taste for. They occasionally caught an unlucky bird, but lived mostly on shellfish, crabs, shrimps, worms, and roots. O-ha missed, most of all, the succulent chanterelle fungus and wood blewitt that she loved, and the nests of tree insects found in the rotten logs of Trinity.

Once, out on the mud, she had an encounter with a creature she had never seen before, who left her pride damaged and her nose sore. She was picking her way carefully through poa grass, sniffing at holes that might have contained eels abandoned by the tide, when something gripped her sensitive snout. She pulled back from the mud, to find a creature like an elongated crab dangling from her face. After a few moments of painful struggle she managed to loosen the shellfish's grip and let it fall onto the mud.

It was a greyish-colored, plated thing with a long tail and two huge pairs of pincers out in front. Thereafter she left these creatures alone, making sure the mudholes were clear of them before investigating further.

One evening, after she had been out hunting, she returned to find the smell of dog clinging to the wind. The odor came from the direction of the dike, and for a while she crouched in the bladder wrack and waited for more scents and sounds to reach her.

The odor was persistent and there were no sights or sounds of movement from the tall grasses on the river wall, so she went back to the boat. She leapt up onto the sloping deck and then down through the hole into the dank interior of the hulk. Camio was there, asleep, and she woke him and asked if he could smell the enemy. He licked his nose and sniffed the air for a few moments, sorting through the many odors, and then confirmed her suspicions.

"Dog—most definitely. But what would an unaccompanied dog be doing out here in the marshes? Lost?"

"I suppose so," she replied. "There's no human scent, so it must be. Perhaps it's hurt—lying there injured? Do you think we need to worry?"

Camio shook his head and suggested they stay where they were for the rest of the night, just to be sure. She laid her head across his shoulders and tried to sleep, though she had difficulty doing so. During the night both animals were awakened by a whining from the dike: a pitiful sound that filled them with a feeling of despondency. Neither wished to investigate the source of this misery, however, since it might be a trap; and anyway, it was foolish to become involved in anything that smelled strongly of their worst enemy.

When morning came they saw a movement on the dike. It was indeed a dog and O-ha recognized him immediately: Breaker, the ex-hunting hound and now farm dog. He sounded as if he was in a sorry state. He looked half starved and misery seemed to have hammered his features flat. There was a mournful note to his wailing which would have had humans running to him with armfuls of sympathy, but the foxes were less inclined to sentiment of this sort. Camio, in fact, expressed a certain amount of contempt.

"What's he yelling like that for? If he's unhappy, why doesn't he *do* something?"

"He is, in his opinion," replied O-ha. "He's calling for help. That's doing something, as far as a hound is concerned."

Suddenly, Breaker seemed to see the boat for the first time, half hidden by reeds and partly submerged in the mud. He began to make his way toward it, sinking in the sludge up to his belly. Near the stream in the center of the creek, he almost disappeared completely, but managed with great effort to struggle onto a sunken piece of driftwood—the branch of an oak—and used this as a walkway beneath the silt. As he began to approach the boat, O-ha started to get alarmed.

"He's coming here," she whispered. "What are we going to do?"

Camio obviously did not know, but decided to find out before the dog actually reached them and got his paws onto a firm footing.

"Hey," he called. "You, dog. What do you want?"

Breaker paused in the act of climbing an overhanging bank, and looked at the boat. He would know by the dialect that it was a fox talking to him, but the only change in his scent was an odor of relief—as if he had found what he was looking for.

"Fox? I smelled you around here, a day ago. There's two of you—a vixen and a dog fox. I still have a good nose—still a good nose, even though they've thrown me away like a piece of trash. Look, I'm nearly done in. I'm hungry and tired. Need a place to rest. I'm coming into the boat."

"You are?" said O-ha, her instincts telling her to bolt.

"I'm coming into the boat, but I promise I won't attack you. You understand?" His loose-lipped mouth burbled out the words but that was a hunting hound's way, to burble and bluster through his words rather than speak them clearly. They used it as a kind of social badge: the sporting dog's dialect.

Camio snorted. "You promise you won't attack *us*? I think you've got it the wrong way around, my friend. You're in a very vulnerable position out there, on the soft mud, where we lighter foxes could dance rings around you. There are two of us, as you so rightly assess, and we're fit and strong. There's only one of you . . ."

Breaker had another go at the bank, slipping back down again, but at the same time saying, "You think you could take a *hunting hound*? No way. I've broken more foxes in half than you have hairs on your brush . . ."

"*Tail!*" shouted O-ha.

"What? Oh, very well, *tail* then. Anyway, you get the point?" he flapped with his mouth. "I'm a killer, a spine-snapper with a vicious streak. My jaws are deadly weapons. My teeth crunch bones to powder. I am savage, cruel, without mercy. I do not know what the word compassion means. I was two seasons old before I knew kill-the-fox was three words, and not one. I am the destroyer . . . the . . ." He slipped down the bank for the third time, clearly out of breath, all his strength gone. At that moment one of the foxes could have gone out and ripped his throat open, and he would have been able to do nothing about it. He was helplessly in the grip of the mud, and clearly almost starved.

"I—promise—won't—harm—you. . . ." he gasped. "Honor. Promise. Not hurt . . . you."

They watched him while he rested. Camio asked O-ha if she wanted to leave while the beast was recovering, but she said there was no wreck as good as the one they were sheltering in and it did not look as if Breaker could damage a soft-shelled crab in his condition, let alone a fox. So she remained, though not without all her nerve ends tingling as she kept a wary eye on the dog throughout. Her whole nature was against such close proximity with a dog, especially a hunting hound, and though Camio was used to other animals from his zoo days, she could see that he was uneasy too.

Finally, Breaker struggled to his feet and this time managed to crawl up the bank and into the bottom of the wreck. There he found some scraps of food that the foxes had cached, and chewed the salty pieces, swallowing them with obvious distaste.

"Muck," he kept muttering to himself. "Not a decent piece of meat amongst it."

"Listen to him," said Camio. "He scorns the fare of outlaws, but he doesn't ask whether it can be spared before he gobbles it down, does he? Maybe you can hunt for your own the next time?"

Breaker growled.

"You be careful what you say to me, or I'll have your skin, Reynard."

"We don't like that name," snarled O-ha.

"That so, you red-skinned savage? I'll have to remember not to say it then, won't I?—*Reynard*."

Camio responded by nipping the dog's nose with his sharp teeth.

"Hey!" said the hound, his eyes watering, "there's no need for that. If you're not careful I'll have to break your back for you. I'll overlook it this time . . ."

The exhausted dog licked the place where he had been bitten with such a feeble effort that the other two could see he was almost finished. His eyes told them that it was possible he would not live

through the day, and that despite all his brashness and bravado, he was as weak as a kitten with no promise of its mother's milk. Although Camio should have felt shame at taking such advantage of this weakness, albeit unknowingly, foxes have been hunted by dogs for so long, have been torn to pieces in so many orgies of bloodlust, so many frenzies of artificial hate, that it was difficult for Camio to see anything but a killer before his eyes, no matter in what condition.

O-ha said, "Let him alone, Camio. He can't do anything to us. We might as well go out and hunt, while the tide's still on the ebb. Come on."

While they were out hunting, it rained heavily, and they knew they would have drinking water that was not brackish waiting for them back at the boat. It happened that on that day they found three geese that had been shot by hunters—probably, it appeared, in mistake for foxes, dogs, or badgers, which told them the *Unremembered Fear* was still abroad—and left on the mud. They dragged one into the sea poa grass, caching it amongst the reeds, and then took one each back to the wreck. They did not sling the bodies of the geese over their backs and carry them with ease, as some humans believed they did, but pulled them by their necks across the mud.

When they got back to the boat, they found Breaker still alive and drinking rainwater, though the luster had gone from his eyes. He looked starved, his ribcage showing through his skin like a row of iron hoops. He viewed the geese hungrily as the two foxes tore away at them, eating their fill. When O-ha and Camio had swallowed all they needed, and had left the carcasses in the bottom of the boat, the dog approached the meat and began chewing. O-ha thought about protesting, but she was full and had little interest in the meat now so she said nothing, lying back and resting her head on Camio's rump. The dog fox uttered no protests either, and the hound ate his fill. Afterward the light behind his eyes seemed a little more alive. He found himself a beam on which to lie while the tide swirled into the hull, causing a small whirlpool to swill the feathers of the swallowed geese around in circles. What was left of the birds' corpses floated around in the brackish water.

O-ha's feelings over sharing her hideout with a fox hound

confused her. Each time she woke and smelled the dog's presence, a panic began in her breast that was difficult to suppress. She found the odor unpleasant and offensive, especially when it mingled with the scent of her Camio. When the dog moved, to make some noise associated with the bodily functions, like belching or breaking wind, she almost flew at him in rage. His very presence was an obscenity.

Yet when she was able to put these thoughts aside, when Ransheen blew through the holes in the hull and took the dog's scent away from her, she was able to view him with a more dispassionate eye. What she saw was a hound whose spirit was broken, whose body had betrayed him, who was too stubborn to admit that he was finished as a hunter. When he mumbled about past glories, which inevitably involved the killing of a fox, she found it invited her pity rather than her scorn. The dog's whole history involved someone who had, at the end, subjected him to a treacherous act. Breaker had placed his faith in a faithless master, had carried out that master's bidding, and when his body began to fail had been tossed aside like a used object. It made his whole existence a lie: a lie that he attempted to relive, painting false pictures for his listeners.

"My master regarded me, admired me, above all the hounds he had ever known. I was given the choicest cuts of meat, the best accommodations. I deserved it, of course—I *was* the best. My master cried the day I left the pack for the farm. But he knew I was a working dog and would not have been happy trailing around after the rest of the pack. And although guarding the farm was not anywhere near as exciting as hunting foxes, it was a very *important* job. Security, you know. Humans need to feel secure . . . they value me tremendously at the farm. . . ."

Had Breaker stuck with this story all the time they might eventually have believed him, but he did not. Sometimes he cursed his old master with savage oaths. Occasionally he spoke of his hatred for the farm and its occupants. And just once in a while he even swore at himself and mouthed contempt for his present condition, his place in dog society.

O-ha should have felt only contempt for Breaker, but instead there were times when he made her feel sad. Feeling this, in turn, made her angry with herself. Thus a confusing cycle of paradoxical emotions swirled around in her breast.

When darkness came one evening, Camio said to the dog, "What made you come out here? Did you get lost?" This time they got something close to the truth from him.

"Hounds like me don't get lost, Reynard," said the dog, now without malice in his voice. "I know this countryside backward. I could find my way home if the world were flooded with farmhouse soup. No, I escaped."

O-ha said, "Escaped? From what?"

"Oh, I got tired of that chain. You remember the chain, vixen? You're the fox that came to the farm one night—I never forget a scent. That damn chain. I'm a hunting hound, not a mongrel. I'm used to running free, with the wind in my coat and the scent of the earth in my nostrils . . . you foxes can understand that. I nearly went crazy at that farm, stuck on the end of a chain with seven paces of ground."

"I know," said Camio, sleepily. "I've been there—those seven paces, I know them well. We have walked the same short piece of the world, dog. We have endured the same long, bleak nightmare . . ."

Camio was becoming too erudite, and O-ha, who knew this side of him well, shushed him.

"So what happened?" she asked Breaker.

"So one night I slipped the collar—and I was free. I ran through the fields and woods, chased anything that moved, foxes included. Would have broken them if I could have caught them. That's me, Breaker, the lead hound of the hunt. Then in the morning, I went home. I never intended to stay away. I'm a dog—a loyal hound. To have remained away would have been a betrayal of all that I stand for. My masters are my masters. No question. I just wanted a little freedom."

"And?"

"And they were waiting for me with guns. They were going to shoot me. *Shoot me*, Breaker, the fox hound—blast me like a common wild animal."

"I see," said Camio. "They thought you might have come into contact with the *White Mask*? That's it, isn't it?"

"White Mask?—why mince words?—*rabies*. They were scared I'd caught rabies and they weren't taking any chances. After all I'd done for them. Protected their property, played with their children, hunted foxes for them . . ."

"They didn't trust you anymore," said Camio. "The faithful old Breaker had to die. He might have had a devil in him that would emerge while he played with the children, and that was unthinkable."

"Anyway, I could smell the fear in them. Their mouths were barking softly—'Come on, Breaker. Good boy, Breaker. Here, dog, here. Come and get the nice juicy bone we've got for you'—but the muscles in their faces were rigid, their eyes wild with terror. Oh, I was used to seeing guns, and they held them casually enough, under one arm, but the tenseness was there and they were ready to jump the weapons level and blow me to pieces once I got within range. I pretended to approach them in joy—you know, tongue lolling out, lazy rolling gait—but the closer I got the more agitated they became and finally one of the guns came up and I ran. I was well out of range. I felt the pellets lift the earth behind me, and then the shot sounded in my ears. Maybe they fired more than once, I don't know. I was gone by that time—over the fields and far away. Since then I've been wandering, avoiding them whenever they appeared. . . ."

O-ha became alarmed.

"You don't think they followed you here, do you?"

"Not a chance. They couldn't follow a . . . a . . ."

"An elephant?" suggested Camio, wanting to be helpful.

"A what? Anyway, humans are useless at tracking without dogs to help them—you know that, Reynard. Me? I could have found me easily enough, but those farm boys are blind. They can't smell a dead rat until it's ten days old. What's an elephant?"

"Big animal. Big as a house, and leaves tracks the size of dustbin lids on the ground."

"I never heard of such a beast," said Breaker.

"They come from the Land of the Lions," replied Camio.

"What's a lion?"

"Forget it," finished the fox. "I'm tired. It's time we all got some sleep. If you've any ideas about trying to reach us during the night, forget it. You'll drop into the freezing water and in your state, drown very quickly."

"I couldn't care less about either of you," said Breaker. "My pals aren't here to see me, and neither are my masters. It's not the kill, it's the thrill. Spectacle. The show. I couldn't care less about a pair of tatty-looking Reynards with no one to watch me break their backs. You can sleep in peace."

"Thanks for nothing," said Camio, and O-ha felt him snuggle up closer to her, to keep her from the night frost.

EIGHTEEN

In the Beginning—that time shared by all the canid mythology—and after the *Firstdark*, the wolves ruled the forests. They were swift to organize themselves into packs, with leaders called Strongones, and quickly parceled out areas of land for the separate packs. While the foxes were able to remain in these territories by virtue of their ability to ghost past the packs either singly or in small groups, the dogs were driven out onto the unsheltered plains, where the horses grazed in their herds. The dogs too, found security in forming into packs, but being weaker than wolves were unable to match them in battle. A resentment against the wolves built up amongst the dogs, as the wolves had the choice hunting grounds and kept the dog packs on the move. The dog packs, by necessity, had to become nomadic, fearing the sound of the Howling Master, which was the name given to the wolf of each pack who had the most resonant and far-carrying call, and who thus warned its fellows of any interlopers in their territory. The Howling Master would position himself on a high rock, where the breeze was strongest, and would keep his nose tuned for any intruders. When dog was scented, the high crooning note would go out over the forests and surrounding plains, and the wolves would gather and storm down on any unfortunate dog pack that was trying to wrest a meager existence from the treeless wastes.

So, despite the fact that overall there were far more dogs in the world than wolves, the latter had managed to gain supremacy over the former by virtue of their ability to create a stronger organization, at the heart of which was good communication between wolf packs and a clear understanding of their need to remain on good terms with one another.

Some time after the *Firstdark* the dogs, who were now close to starvation, set aside their individual differences and gathered on the great central plains to form a single mighty pack that would sweep the wolves from the forests and into the sea. In hound mythology, this was called the Season of the Dog, and it was their finest time outside the beginning of their pact with humans. All quarrels and arguments between separate packs were placed aside, and Skellion Broadjaw, the leader chosen to be king-hound in the coming battle, invented the saying that was to be their watchword during the struggle for supremacy over the wolf packs. The saying went thus: *I am against my brother dog, but my brother dog and I are against our cousin wolf.* In this way their petty jealousies, their rivalry against each other, could be contained without being dismissed. One of the reasons the wolves had been successful in driving out the dogs was because the wolf packs respected each other's territory, conducted discussions over their differences in dignity, and recognized a need to regard each other as equals. The dog packs, on the other hand, had squabbled continually, called each other unforgivable names, carried out despicable raids on neighboring packs, and generally built up an enmity between the various packs that no amount of negotiation and diplomacy could erase. Skellion Broadjaw realized that the individual feuds between his packs could not be put aside entirely, so a promise of a truce until the wolves were defeated, and then a settling of differences between themselves, was the best he could hope for. His recognition of this fact, and the allowance for it in his rallying cry, was a clever move on the part of a dog who knew that their only hope of survival lay in an all-dog policy.

During this time the foxes merely looked on and no doubt hoped that their two major rivals in hunting would wipe each other out.

At first the dogs were extremely successful. They swept across the countryside, driving the smaller wolf packs out onto the plains where the horses grazed. The horses were no friends of the wolves, who cut down their numbers by attacking stragglers, foals, and sick mares when the chance arose; thus the horses welcomed the opportunity of battering down these grey shapes being chased out of the forest, who then had to try to escape the horses' flailing hooves. This intervention by the horses was welcomed by the dogs, and Skellion Broadjaw was regarded by them as one of the greatest chiefs of all time.

The wolves were in a state of panic. Despite a good communications system, they were unable to gather in the right place at the right time. They suffered a terrible defeat at the Place of the Swamps, when they gathered together a mighty pack on the edge of the eastern wetlands. The scouting dog packs in the area had watched with some dismay while the wolves gathered, as Skellion Broadjaw and the main army were a two-day run from that place and the wolves outnumbered them ten to one. They sent a runner to Skellion Broadjaw, and prepared to try to hold off the wolves until the main army arrived. The wolves, aware that they were watched by only a few small dog packs from the ridge above the swamps, set about choosing leaders and organizing strategy and tactics, ignoring the presence of the dogs.

However, about noon on the second day the dogs noticed there was some confusion below. More wolf packs had arrived and had swelled the numbers to such an extent that they were jostling each other for room on the firm ground. The wolf leaders had thought that with the marshland on three sides of them, they would be protected at both flank and rear, and would need to worry only about their front. When the sun reached its peak a dog named Zerfuss trod on a thorn and let out a high-pitched cry of pain. In their excited state, most of the dogs on the ridge misinterpreted this yell as a command to charge, and began running full pelt down the slope toward the wolves. The geography of the landscape ensured that the dogs were channeled into a narrow dip between two spurs; and unable to control their speed on the steep slope, they hit the wolves in a solid wedge of bodies, driving the grey ones backward and to either side. Thousands of wolves found themselves floundering in the mire and sinking to their deaths. Those that remained fought bravely enough, but the psychological advantage was with the dogs, who overwhelmed individual wolves and bore them down while other wolves attempted a retreat across any firm ground the marshes had to offer.

It was a great victory for the dogs, and when Skellion Broadjaw arrived, there were celebrations in progress that he felt obliged to endorse. However, he was none too pleased that it had been Zerfuss, a relatively minor chief, who was responsible for the victory, and not himself. He was lavish in his outward praise toward the other dog, but secretly vowed that a settlement would come later, when the wars were over.

The final great battle was to take place on a promontory north of a wide river. Skellion Broadjaw's forces outnumbered the wolves this time, by almost twenty to one. The evening before the fight was to take place a messenger came from the wolf camp to offer single combat to a warrior of the dogs' choice. He explained that while the wolves were outnumbered, and would possibly lose the final battle, a great many dogs would die. The wolves had resolved that not one of them would leave the battlefield alive. Each wolf would fight to the death and would take several dogs with him. Shesta, the great wolf warrior-priestess, had therefore offered to fight any dog, and the winner of this single combat would carry the day. In this way much bloodshed could be avoided.

By this time the praise of his troops had gone to the head of

Skellion Broadjaw—they called him the Invincible One, the Dogday Warrior of Ten Lives, Hound Magnificent—and his vanity was so swelled that he believed no animal on earth could defeat him.

He informed the messenger, "Tell the bitch I'll meet her at One Tree Hill, at dawn tomorrow."

So, at the place of the single tree, Skellion Broadjaw met his death under the savage teeth of Shesta the warrior-priestess. She tore him from throat to groin and ate his heart before thousands of dismayed dogs and crooning wolves. The dogs immediately began accusing each other of all manner of failure, and were routed by the triumphant wolves who took advantage of their disarray. Had Skellion Broadjaw seen through this wolf ruse and stuck to his original plan, the dogs would without doubt have carried the day; however, he had chosen instead to place his advantage aside in favor of a chance at Immortal Legend. Had the dogs managed to rally and see the defeat of their leader in single combat for what it was— merely one death, which should not have affected the battle in any way—they would have defeated the grey hordes. In the end, they were beaten by their own character.

Skellion Broadjaw's body was dragged by the wolves into the forest and buried under the roots of an unnamed tree. To this day, when a dog sees a tree, he will piss on its trunk hoping to desecrate Skellion's monument, wherever it may be. He went down in dog legend as the Dog Whose Bowels Stink of Pride, which is a little harsh for an animal who made only one mistake, though it was the most crucial of all in the war against the wolves.

These battles had left the wolf population severely depleted, however, and against their better judgement they became allies with the boars of the forest, whose tusks took many a dog life. This was the time when the giant *Groff*, the agent of the humans, came down from the white-peaked mountains to gather allies himself, and to pave the way for the humans from the sea-of-chaos. At first he was unable to gather any recruits and made his fabulous beasts from the clouds. He tried to copy known animal forms, but the laws of nature did not allow for perfect imitation, and deviant shapes emerged from his modeling hands. When he tried to make a horse, the result was a unicorn. When he tried to copy the eagle, it developed a mammal's torso and became the griffin. In the end he just gave up imitation and produced one of the most terrifying of false creatures, the fire-breathing dragon. Dog mythology, which differs slightly from wolf and fox mythology, maintained that dogs were the creatures responsible for driving *Groff's* monstrosities into a lake of lava (of which several existed at that time), and that when the false creatures emerged from the molten rock, it cooled and solidified, leaving them as rigid forms.

This failure on the part of *Groff* did not deter the giant from his task of getting the humans into the land. The first real animals he won over for the humans were the cats, who saw an easy way of life ahead of them if these tool-handed creatures called men were allowed to establish themselves in the world. They told this agent of men that they would help him, provided they were allowed to retain a certain autonomy once the humans were in the land.

"We will work with man, but not under him," said the she-cat Callissimmini. "We will live with him and keep house with him, but there will be no question of a master-slave relationship. We own our own selves. Our souls belong to none but Ssassissellissi-the-She. We have nothing but contempt for all other creatures, and that includes you and your clients. I hope we understand one another?"

Groff accepted this proposal, but when he went to the dogs he told them that the cats had capitulated unconditionally, and the dogs were thus tricked into complete submission. To this day the dogs maintain they were misled by the cats.

So, under the guidance of cats and dogs, men came up from the ocean of darkness with spears and bows, and systematically began to hunt and kill the wolves and boars. The dogs rejoiced in victory at last, acting as trackers and scouts for the men, and leading them to their deadly enemies. The dogs were even willing to drag the machines of men over the snow, when horses could not serve. The horses themselves went down hard. They fought against the humans but eventually succumbed and were yoked to the plough and the cart, suffered the indignity of having men on their backs, and finally became as much a part of man's progress as dogs themselves.

• • •

O-ha and Camio had sat listening with interest to this discourse by the hound that shared their dwelling. However, they pointed out to Breaker that their own stories of the past, though tinged with a certain amount of similarity, differed from that of dog mythology. In fact, O-ha's version of how things began was considerably different from Camio's, and the two of them argued well into the night about the names of various fox heroes and heroines, and who was responsible for what, and where the winds came from.

In the end, Camio said, "It doesn't really matter whether this was that, or that was this—what is important are the similarities, not the differences. I know I was born a long way from here—how far is impossible for any of us to guess—yet the *same* tales of the world's beginning are told in that place. Yes, there's a difference of opinion as to names and places, but think of it! How much alike we all are."

Before he fell asleep, Camio asked O-ha in a tired voice, "What happened to your *Groff*?"

She replied, "As a reward for his services, the humans built him a palace of ice with many chambers and tunnels, on the peak of their highest mountain. Thousands of icicles decorated the spires and domes, the towers and buttresses, the bridges between high walkways, and all of this sparkled in the light. There were soft carpets of snow upon the floors, and a fast, cold stream ran through the Great Chamber at the center of the palace. The archway over the tall gate was studded with diamond-ice from the heart of a winter land, and beneath this ran secret passages to all points of the mountaintop. Finally, the great edifice was clothed in clouds so that no other creature could see the giant's home and covet it for itself.

"For a while it was thought that *Groff* lived there in blissful solitude, but as new generations of men came along he was forgotten. Since he was fashioned of nothing but men's belief, and they ceased to believe in him, he gradually disappeared. Perhaps he could have shown himself, and reawakened men's minds to his presence, but he chose not to and so he went the way of the mists and vapors of the marshland—he was blown gently into oblivion.

His ice palace is somewhere beneath the weight of many winters, but occasionally his spirit walks abroad, as the minds of men waver, and his footprints can be seen in the high snows."

Camio nodded, satisfied.

"More or less what happened to our *Agarth*."

With that he fell asleep, and O-ha followed his example not long afterward.

She dreamed. She dreamed she was in a bright place and struggling to walk. Suddenly, black bars fell across the ground. They were like the iron rods of a cage at the zoo, once described to her by Camio. Then she was . . .

NINETEEN

Oha felt like a ripe autumn plum, ready to split down the middle: there was a warmth, a mellowness in her spirit. She had not told Camio that she was pregnant but her condition was now obvious to both him and the hound. The dog fox had said nothing, waiting for her to open the subject. The problem was that she felt insecure once more, and wanted no one around at the birth. If she could have crept away and had the cubs and raised them in secret, then she would have done so. Since the death of her first litter, she trusted no one, not even the father of the cubs. It was not a feeling she *liked*; she even hated herself for harboring such disloyal misgivings toward her present mate, but she could not help herself.

She watched the Brent geese getting ready to fly back to the land where they spent their summers, far in the north. Their exodus would begin in a few days. They waddled around, calling to one another, preparing themselves mentally for the long flight ahead that would be bound to cost a few lives. Once again she wondered why they bothered, but could come up with nothing more satisfactory than a restlessness of spirit. O-ha did not deny that she felt a similar sort of urge to fly off into the sunset, but she had neither the courage nor, of course, the physical equipment necessary. She could *walk*, though. There was nothing stopping her from becoming a *rangfar*. Nothing except . . . except that she would have to go out into the unknown and leave her homeland behind. It was a good dream, but the birds obviously had something more, some psychological advantage over her.

Just the same, she realized it was time to leave the marshes and go back to the town. The hunters and fishermen would soon be swarming over the marshland. She said to Camio, "We must leave this place soon."

"I understand," he replied. He was obviously waiting for something further from her, but she turned away from him. She was thinking of A-ho—of his gentle passion for her, of his sacrifice—and at that moment it did not seem right that Camio was the father of her cubs. It seemed *unfair*—a word that practical foxes like her rarely used—unfair that her former mate should be robbed of his right to immortality through his young. He had died without seeing or knowing his cubs, and they had not lived to carry his line forward.

When A-ho had died she had tried to make a song for him, to sing to the wind. It had been impossible at the time, for various reasons. Now she felt able to compose something. It took a great deal of mental energy, and left her feeling limp and exhausted each night, but eventually her creation was completed. One evening when Camio was out hunting, and the hound (who had clung tenaciously to life, and was now growing stronger on the leftovers of the foxes—not that he was grateful, or that they expected any gratitude) was fast asleep, she sang her song for A-ho:

> *"You came and went*
> *like a season never*
> *seen again, taking your*
> *scents and sounds.*
>
> *What are these you leave*
> *behind? These strange*
> *sad flowers that bloom*
> *in my breast?*
>
> *Who are those singers*
> *of haunting songs*
> *I hear in places*
> *where we walked?*
>
> *If these are memory-dreams,*
> *why are their shadows*
> *stronger than sunlight? their*
> *echoes louder than the sound?"*

She sang the song softly, to the moon, hoping that wherever her former mate was, in the Perfect Here, his spirit would receive the words and he would know that he had not been forgotten. After all, the same winds that blew in this world blew there also, and they would carry the song to him.

Breaker stirred and she knew that he had not been asleep. She was angry with herself for not going out, on her own, to some lonely place to sing the song, for she realized she had been singing it close to the ears of one who had some responsibility in the death of her lost mate. However, Breaker said nothing about what he had heard; instead he muttered, "You'll be leaving here soon."

"Yes," she replied, "soon."

"We can all go back now. They'll have found out that there was no rabies. That fox you told me about—A-konkon—they'll know by now that he did not die of the *White Mask*."

"I suppose so."

"I'm a lot stronger now," Breaker said. "I think I can make it back to the farm."

"Good. You can be there to kill more foxes, when they raid the farm for chickens."

"It's what I'm there for—to protect the place. Chickens want to live too."

She accepted the admonishment.

"I suppose so."

Breaker said, "Don't come to the farm any more. If *you* come, either of you, I won't be able to do my job."

It was the closest he ever came to thanking her for keeping him alive. He was telling her that she would be safe if she ever encountered him again. That he would not attack her, or Camio, if they crossed his path. Secretly, she was astounded by this confession. A dog, a hunting hound, had made a pact with two foxes.

Camio returned a little later and they talked about going back to the town, or at least looking for some dry place. She agreed that they should set off before dawn.

So in the early hours they swam across the river. The tide was at its height and the current locked against itself, so there was little danger. They went across country to the railway embankment and followed it to the point where the *havnot* lay between them and the *face*. There was no suitable place for an earth on the farmland, so eventually they entered the town and began a search.

There were the beginnings of a scrap-yard on the edge of town where already there were several wrecks of cars and other items discarded by the newcomers to the town. Presumably having settled into their new, modern houses, they were now setting about replacing their old appliances. The town had not been established long enough for the yard to have crushing machines, and the rusted vehicles had been stripped of useful parts, leaving only the shells. It seemed a safe enough place for the time. Camio and O-ha chose a suitable wrecked car in which to set up their home. They marked the territory together, setting boundaries that seemed reasonable, considering they were in the *face*.

"If we find too many humans coming here," said Camio, "I'll look for somewhere else."

"That's fine," she said. Then, "Camio—I—feel very strange at the moment. Old memories keep interfering with what's happening now. . . . I'm sorry if—I can't explain it."

He looked away from her.

"Well, we'll see how things go. When are the cubs due?"

It was the first time her pregnancy had been mentioned between them, and she felt guilty that it had turned out to be Camio who spoke of the forthcoming birth first.

"Soon."

"I won't let you down, you know. If you're thinking that I'll go out one day and not come back, you're wrong. I *like* the idea that I've got responsibilities. I told you I wanted cubs by you. It's not as if it's my first litter."

Her guilt almost crushed her on hearing these words. He was such a thoughtful mate. Why couldn't she have the same feelings for him as she had had for A-ho? It was so stupid, dreaming about what might have been, when a good life lay ahead of her. She wanted to be fair to Camio, to give him all she had to offer, but there was still something—something undefinable—holding her back, preventing her from opening herself to him completely.

"It's—it's not that *exactly*," she said.

"No? Well, whatever it is, you can rely on me. I know you think I'm some kind of adventurer who breezed into town and might very well breeze out again, but I'm not. I *am* reliable and I'll prove that to you over the course of time. Only death will keep me from you and the cubs now—"

"Don't *say* that." She suddenly had visions of his mangled body lying in a road somewhere, or hanging over a fence, torn and bloody. That he might be killed before the cubs were born filled her with panic. It was possible. Of course it was possible. But she did not want to think about such things or be reminded that they might happen. And she suddenly realized, too, that it was not just the cubs—it was *him*. She did not want to lose *him*. He was part of her now. They were linked by their cubs: those little lumps that squirmed around in her body, making her feel warm and motherly. She licked his ear, making him wriggle.

"Don't talk about death while I have our life within me. I'll be all right, I promise. Vixens get funny dreams when they're having cubs. Things are happening inside them and their feelings get churned up—lots of odd emotions—I'm not really me at the moment. I'm feeling too protective toward the litter and I'm afraid I look on everything and anything as a threat to them."

"Even me?" He looked surprised and desperately hurt.

"Perhaps. I don't know. I told you, I'm not really myself. The changes inside me are ruling my spirit, putting dark suspicions where there should be none, filling me with mistrust. I—I want to meet you at the place where you are—where you stand ready to receive me—but it's not possible for me now because I don't own myself. The fact that I do *want* to meet you in that halfway place has to be enough at the moment. Will you be patient with me?"

"Of course I'll be patient." He still sounded upset and his scent was strange. She could smell the hurt in his spirit. "I knew something was wrong. I thought it was this *rangfar* business. I know when you met me you thought I was some kind of wandering rogue. But . . ."

She sighed. "You don't understand. But that's not surprising. I don't understand myself. We'll just have to put up with it until my body goes back to normal." She realized how selfish she was being, trying to foster old feelings and keeping everything tight around herself, as if Camio were an intruder rather than the father of her cubs. He was entitled to his share of the anticipatory joy. "Camio? Don't look so *hurt*—I want to lick your face all over when you look like that."

His eyes narrowed.

"Well, that doesn't sound like a bad idea, but I've got to go out and get food for us. Don't run away. I'll be back before noon."

With that he left her.

She felt dreadful for some time after he had gone, but then the men who owned the scrap-yard came and began clattering around on the edge of the heap. The car the foxes had chosen as an earth was in the center, under a pile of other scrap, so she felt quite safe. There were only small tunnels through the jagged metal, which no man could crawl along—even supposing men did such things, which they did not.

Camio came back later with some cold scraps of meat wrapped in paper and a half-full carton of yogurt. She could see he had had difficulty in carrying the items, and expressed her appreciation.

"The curdled milk stuff is for you," he said, "and the cubs."

Scresheen came, screaming through the torn metal and whistling insane tunes along the open ends of pipes. One night when Camio came back to the earth, she told him he could not enter. He had to remain outside until she called him. He began pacing up and down the tunnels waiting for the moment when he was allowed to enter the earth again. There was a full moon that night and he spent the time pretending he could see shapes crossing it. Then he listened to the mice scampering in amongst the rusty bales of chicken wire, where he could not get at them. Then he sniffed the air for bats. Once he tried coughing a little tune to himself, but then he thought he might be disturbing her and so he went on to other pastimes again.

The cubs were born in the early hours of that morning: four little mewling blind and deaf blobs. All except one were covered in short black fur. O-ha cleaned them, and then settled them in the warm cavity of her belly-fur. Camio, once he was allowed back in the earth, sat by, looking on with a kind of wonderment in his features. He said nothing: just let her get on with what she had to do. It may have been that he wanted to assist in some way, but she would brook no interference at this stage. So he just sat, not even talking, which she would have found an irritant. Later, when they were suckling, which did funny things to her insides, he came and looked at them more closely, nudging the smallest with his nose. O-ha snarled at him, baring her teeth savagely. He took the hint.

He backed off, saying sadly, "Looks like a runt." And indeed, before the day was over, that particular cub was dead. He took it out and put it somewhere well away from the earth. He carried out the last rites, scratching and scent-marking the ground as instructed by O-ha, and then left the rest to the fox-spirits.

The remaining three cubs looked strong enough, though, and weathered their first night without harm.

Camio spent most of his time outside the earth, ferrying food to her, and always announcing his arrival before entering cautiously. She was unpredictable in her present state. He placed the food within her reach and then retreated quickly. Her ways with him were sharp, but this was normal and did nothing to harm their relationship. He was obviously anticipating the time when this period would be over, when her maternal instincts would be softened and she would become less aggressive toward him. Dog foxes know that vixens are very tense, their nerves like taut wires, for a while after giving birth, and they take the treatment handed out to them in a subdued manner.

There were times when she realized he was a little jealous of the attention the cubs were receiving. There was little she could do about this. She was still very cautious when he was around, though she had no reason to be. He made no comment on her behavior, simply letting things ride for a while.

The cubs grew stronger by the day. After fourteen days the cubs could see and hear, though not well. Their eyes were bright blue sparks in their faces and they started at sharp sounds. They began crawling around inside the earth, very shakily. Occasionally O-ha got up and retrieved one before it fell outside the vehicle, but as time went on she fought a losing battle with them. They ignored her calls and came only when hungry.

During this time she talked to them, about their history, their religion, the topography of the land, and the waterholes and soaks (though many of the old parish watering places had disappeared and Camio had to tell her where the new ones were). She called the cubs

O-mitz, A-cam, and A-sac. A-cam had darker markings than O-mitz, who sported a thin white streak through her fur on the right side of her brow; A-sac was an albino, pure white with pink eyes. O-ha and Camio were both mystified by the coloring of A-sac. Though they had heard of such things, neither thought it would happen to them. It was upsetting, because A-sac was bound to have a life full of taunts, and problems with camouflage.

"He'll be all right in the snow," Camio kept saying to O-ha, as if this as yet unproven advantage outweighed all the disadvantages of having a white coat.

At first the youngsters just mewled and squeaked, but gradually picked up words from both parents. O-mitz seemed the brightest, but A-sac was a deep creature and it was difficult to decide whether he was extraordinarily stupid or incredibly intelligent. He was always the last to become aware of a worm that had broken the surface, and yet once when he was sitting and staring at a stormcloud moving across the sky, he said, "Dog. Dog."

Camio looked up, saw the fuzzy blackness, and replied, "No, A-sac. *Cloud.* Say cloud."

"Dog," A-sac repeated emphatically, shaking his white head.

And Camio glanced up at the black sky again to catch something in the shape, or movement, or even just the lowering impression of that particular cloud, and found himself shivering with apprehension.

He said to O-ha afterward, "For a moment I *did* see a hound in the sky—a dark thing, all jaws and teeth, with blood-red eyes. Why should I have see that?"

"Perhaps it was a dog-spirit?"

Camio shook his head.

"No, it wasn't like that. It was more like a thing of the imagination—something put there by A-sac's mind."

"That's silly," replied O-ha and refused to discuss it further. The idea frightened her, and she wanted her cubs to be normal creatures, whom she could understand.

Another time, after there had been no rain for several weeks, A-sac said, "Rain's coming, O-ha!" before he fell asleep that day.

She went outside and looked through the tangle of scrap at the sky, to see a clear, bright day. She sniffed the air and the scent of dryness and dust was in her nostrils. There was no smell of rain coming. She listened and the wind remained unhurried, calm.

"Ridiculous," she said to herself. "No rain coming."

Yet, by evening, the water was running beneath the scrap in brown rivulets. It came from the sky in torrents, creating a din on the metal and filling empty cans within minutes. How had her cub known about the rain? Was he merely extra perceptive and able to recognize signs not visible to less highly-strung foxes such as herself and Camio? Perhaps his senses were sharper than most? Or maybe— maybe there was something darker there, some divine or devilish power? She shuddered, not wanting to delve too deeply, for fear of finding something nasty.

The cubs gradually grew in strength and vocabulary. During this time, O-ha and Camio talked more than they had ever done and a mellow feeling grew between them, which was more than just wanting to be with a mate and sharing the business of life.

"This is a good thing we've done between us, Camio," she said one evening, while the cubs were gamboling just outside the earth. The faces of the little ones had changed from being stubby, with short rounded-tip ears, to becoming elongated, with pointed ears. Their tails had begun to bush.

"Yes, but they don't stay young for very long, do they?" he said.

O-ha shrugged. "We can't hold them back. I'd like to, of course, but it's not possible."

Outside, the cubs grew boisterous.

"You run away," shouted O-mitz, "and I'll chase you and jump on you! Wait until I can hide behind that thing there . . ."

There was a squeal from her a moment later, and she said, "Oh, that's not fair! You were sneaking up behind."

Then A-sac's haughty voice came to them.

"Surely that's what it's all about, O-mitz? Sneaking up— pouncing. Your prey isn't going to work out ways of being caught by you, unless it's to avoid you. You have to think the way the quarry thinks, and then do the opposite of what you planned in the first place."

"That's stupid, A-sac—isn't it, A-cam?"

"I don't know," said A-cam. "I wasn't watching. I caught this fly, see . . ."

O-mitz's voice: "Where?"

"Well, I let it out of my mouth when I opened it to talk."

A-sac: "And you call *me* stupid? The pair of you between you couldn't hunt down a slug, let alone a rabbit. Now watch this, the rudiments of stalking . . ."

They fought mock fights, they argued incessantly, they roughed and tumbled each other for hours on end. Once, A-cam fell down a shaft that was really an upended pipe. It took hours for Camio and O-ha to discover how to push the pipe over and release their cub. This close encounter with death—for A-cam would have starved if he had not been found and rescued—brought the two adults even closer together. It recalled to their minds the fact that though they hunted and killed prey every day, death was doing the same, stalking them.

Once, they lost A-sac for a whole day. They found him with a *rangfar*, outside the scrap-yard.

A-sac had awakened in the late morning, to find his parents and the other two cubs asleep. He went outside in search of a drink.

After he had slaked his thirst, he became curious and walked through a tunnel of thick, chewable cloth, to find himself outside the area of scrap. He sat and blinked at the outside world for a while, until a large dog fox came along.

The newcomer was not so much meaty as stringy and tough-looking. His coat was dry and coarse, and smelled smoky, as if it had been under the sun so long it had scorched. The stranger's eyes were deep in his head, but A-sac got the impression that he missed nothing, not the flicker of a gnat's nose nor the lifting of a bee's wing. He strode slowly along the concrete pavement, his claws making clicking sounds on the slabs. There were small bare patches here and there on his back, as if he had scrambled underneath many a barbed wire fence in haste. His nose had a deep scratch, which seemed to A-sac to serve as the badge for something.

The dog fox stopped by A-sac.

"What are you looking at, cub?" he said in a gravelly voice. "Why are you staring at A-gork?"

A-sac was afraid of this menacing creature.

"S-Sorry."

"Well?"

"Your scar. I was—I just looked at your scar."

The mean eyes narrowed.

"That scar was honorably bought."

"I'm sure it was," said A-sac, who was thinking that the one to be afraid of was not *this* fox, but the creature who gave him that scar. "Are you a *rangfar*?" he added, remembering his lessons.

"I might be. I might very well be. You have something against us rovers? How can you tell? Do I look seedy, *dirty*? What?"

"No—no—nothing like that. Your claws are rounded, worn at the ends, more than my parents' claws. I deduced that you must do a lot of walking. The only foxes who do that much walking are *travelers*."

The *rangfar* glanced down at his paws.

"Clever little white cub, aren't you? Where are your parents? It's nowhere near time for the dispersal. Have they disowned you because you're a whitey? What are you doing out alone?" the dog fox asked, looking around as if wondering whether anyone else was observing them. "Are you lost?"

"No," said A-sac, quickly. "I live in this yard. My parents are not far away. They're just snoozing. My father is a big fox." As he said this A-sac puffed himself up, lifting his shoulders. "He's very fond of me, actually," he continued to babble, "and he once fought A-magyr, the tyrant . . ."

The *rangfar* nodded.

"Warning me off, eh? Well, don't worry, little cub, I'm not interested in abducting you." He settled down full length on the pavement with A-sac. "I'm just interested, that's all. You're an unusual-looking creature, and you have a brain and a mouth that tells me you're going far. Let me tell you about a vixen I know, that lives in the marshes."

"Why?" asked A-sac guardedly.

"Why?" answered the rangy dog fox, "because you might want to hear about her, that's why. Don't interrupt while I'm talking—listen to your elders and betters. I've seen the world, cub, and I know things that would make your head spin. I could tell you stories to have your eyes swinging from your cheeks. Stories as would turn your ears inside-out. I could tell you tales that would make your sniffer twitch with the pungey smells of death's own earth. Listen . . ."

And the *rangfar* proceeded to talk about a vixen, a witch-fox called O-toltol, who lived away from the sight and sound of all creatures except her disciples. Those deep, small eyes of his were hypnotic, the voice mesmerizing.

After telling A-sac about O-toltol, the *rangfar* launched into parables and fables and all manner of tales that did indeed have A-sac listening intently, and wondering why his parents had not told him of the marvels of the world, and its weird wonders. Camio had told him about the Land of the Lions, and about elephants, but they seemed far away. This fox was telling about here, about now.

By the time the day was over, A-sac was almost a slave. "Well," said the *rangfar*, rising to his feet and stretching. "Are you coming?"

"Coming? Where?"

"To see the witch."

At that moment, O-ha appeared from out of the scrap. She took one look at the stranger and bared her teeth. Right behind her was Camio. The *rangfar* seemed to disappear into the dust at A-sac's feet. A-sac had looked around on scenting his parents, and when he looked back again, the fox in the ragged coat that smelled of dried grasses and the husks of seeds left too long in the sun, that fox called A-gork, had gone.

• • •

"Who were your parents?" asked O-mitz of her mother one day. The little chocolate-colored vixen cub had just begun to molt and patches of orange fur were visible on her face.

"My parents?" said O-ha. "Well, they were a pair who lived on the north of Trinity Wood—the place that is now a human parkland. In those days there was *hav* all around us, and the country was open and free."

"I like the town," said O-mitz. "Camio tells me all about the streets and houses and things."

Camio, who was listening, shrugged.

"This is where they have to live, at least to begin with," he said to O-ha. "Not much point in telling them what *was*—they need to know what *is*."

"I know," she said, but O-mitz cried, "Go on, O-ha—your parents."

"My mother was killed by a tractor which ran over her while she lay asleep. It was an accident. My father went away somewhere after that. Nothing much more to tell."

"*My* parents," said Camio, "were giants—"

"Don't tell them lies," said O-ha, shortly.

He looked contrite.

"My parents were *not* giants," continued Camio. "They were not as tall as oak trees, and my mother didn't have hair as red as the sunset we saw last night. My father did not wrestle with bears and win, and he didn't jump wide canyons where rivers flowed far below. . . ." He received a warning signal from O-ha again, as she realized what he was up to. "However, they *did* have silver hairs on their rumps, just as I do, and as you will probably have."

A-cam asked, "Why hasn't O-ha got silver hairs?"

"She has, only you can't see them so well on her because my coat is darker. My father was a black fox and you could see the silver hairs in his coat shining . . ."

"Camio!" said O-ha. "A *black* fox?"

"It's true," he said, indignantly. "True. My mother was a red fox

and my father was a black fox—that's why my coat is so dark. The trouble with you provincial vixens is that you think the world begins and ends with your own parish. There are all kinds of foxes out there: bat-eared foxes with lugs the size of my bib; Arctic foxes white as the snow—just like A-sac, though he isn't an Arctic fox, of course; desert foxes, fennec foxes—but red foxes are the best, I hasten to add."

"Really?" O-ha said in her haughty voice, but secretly impressed.

"Yes, really," he replied, either not catching, or simply ignoring, her tone. "There are still wolves in certain parts of the world too. Where I come from they still have the timber wolf. Man hasn't wiped them out entirely."

"You've met one of these wolves?" she said.

"No—not exactly, but they're talked about—and I've seen them in the zoo," he finished triumphantly, just as she was about to pour scorn on his claim.

"What's a zoo?" A-cam asked, at the same time trying to bite O-mitz's tail.

"A place where they lock animals up and leave them to die," he replied, brutally.

That night, when the cubs were asleep, O-ha snuggled up close to Camio and whispered: "It's all right now."

"What's all right?"

"We are," she said.

Somehow, without feeling any disloyalty toward A-ho, she had come to be glad it was Camio lying beside her, the father of her cubs. If she had ever thought badly of him, she had been wrong. He was a good mate and a dependable parent. She told him so.

When he did not reply, she changed the subject.

"I'm worried about A-sac," she said. "You don't think he'll be persecuted, because he's different?"

Camio shifted as though uncomfortable.

"Well, we mustn't fool ourselves. It's going to be difficult for him. His white coat is hardly good camouflage, and the other foxes are bound to tease him. We'll have to wait and see how we can help him. He seems to have a strong personality, though—he's not the shy,

retiring type—and sometimes differences can be turned to an advantage."

"How?"

"I'm not sure at the moment, but he's a survivor. He's got grit . . . and a certain—I don't know."

There was something in Camio's tone that made her say, "You *do* know. What is it?"

"Well, I don't want to upset you, but he reminds me of A-konkon a little. He's got that same depth of perception."

"Oh, no, I forbid it!" she cried. "I won't have it."

"You might not be able to prevent it—and let's face it, there was a lot of good in A-konkon. He was definitely weird, and had some strange ideas, but—anyway, we'll just have to wait and see."

After that she lay there, thinking about her young ones, wanting to protect them forever from all the terrible things in life, wanting to keep them as they were—innocent and happy—and never let them go out into a world of harsh reality.

The impossible dream of all mothers.

The skills of the cubs improved as Frashoon began to move Switter aside. They began bringing home small prey that they had managed to catch, beetles and woodlice, and were jealous over such tidbits. They learned to cache much of this extra food in places around the scrap-yard, which they visited when hungry.

O-ha and Camio grew more comfortable toward one another. It was difficult for O-ha to remember a time when Camio had not been there, with his dry witticisms, his soft drawl, and his warm body. There were a hundred ways in which she thought of him, and all of them good. Most of all she saw in him the one thing she had believed he lacked when they first met—reliability. She now knew that Camio stood as firm as an oak tree when it came to his family. He was fiercely loyal to her, and would not (like some dog foxes) mate with neighboring vixens; and he would stand in the way of mighty machines if they threatened her or his cubs. She knew that if she were ever lost, he would spend a lifetime looking for her. If they were ever parted he would cross mountains and seas to be with her again. She knew that if she were ever sick, he would stay by her side until death took her or she got well.

She realized how lucky she had been to have had two mates in her life, both of whom would have died for her.

The one cub neither of the adults worried about was A-cam. He seemed a little dense sometimes, but that had never been a great drawback to a fox. There are inventive foxes, who initiate new skills in hunting and new evasion techniques, but mostly these things are learned. A-cam, like the other two cubs, was taught all that his father and mother knew.

So A-cam was stolid and a little reckless at times, but he had none of the weirdness of A-sac, and little of the stubbornness of O-mitz. He was a playful, all-around fox, with no quirky corners to his character. When A-cam was not playing or hunting beetles, he would lay and sun himself on a warm piece of scrap metal, letting the world pass him by. Uncomplicated, he was his mother's favorite, though his father thought him a little too staid. He wanted to impress his father, and told the other two cubs that one day he was going on an adventure which would make him famous among foxes. *Then* Camio would have to take notice of him. O-ha heard this remark and was concerned about her cub for a while. Then she thought, *It's just young talk, not serious.* Nevertheless she determined to have a word with Camio, to see if he could not reassure A-cam that his father respected him as he was, without the need for any silly expeditions or adventures.

One day a cat wandered into the yard. It was a big bruiser, a black-and-white tom with a face like a flattened tin can. A-cam saw his chance for fame. The cat looked fat, old, and slow, and he thought he could run rings around this creature with his newly-acquired evasion tactics.

"I'm going to show Camio how much I've learned," he told the other two. "Watch me taunt this cat!"

A-sac shook his white head, sagely.

"You're going to get into trouble, A-cam."

O-mitz cried, "Don't do it, A-cam. A-sac, stop him."

"I can't stop him," said A-sac. "I've not been put into this world to watch over my brother. If he wants to get himself killed, let him go ahead."

"Killed?" said A-cam. "Me?"

Until that moment he had been half joking about the cat, but now he was determined to go through with it. He walked toward the beast, which was sunning itself on a patch of earth. It knew he was coming because the nose and whiskers twitched. As he got closer, A-cam could see just how big the tom was, and he began to quake inside. However, he was aware of O-mitz's round frightened eyes on him, and of A-sac's contemptuous stare.

A-cam stopped outside what he reckoned was the cat's pounce limit.

"Cat," he said, "you're a fat, lazy piece of mangy fur, not worth a second glance, but I challenge you to mortal combat."

The cat opened one eye. This organ looked as if it had seen battles galore and an eon of decadence. Cynicism ran deep in the animal's veins.

"*Pissenlit!*" said the monster.

A-cam gave the cat a withering stare.

"And what's *that* supposed to mean?"

To his horror and shock, for he was convinced that cats never learned any language but their own, he received a reply.

"It means," replied the cat softly, "that you are a fluffy bunch of seeds and I could blow you away with one puff. A dandelion of no account. Go away before I fill my lungs with air."

"You—you speak . . ." A-cam was trying to remember just what he had called the cat a few moments previously, so that he could work out some explanation.

"I speak with the tongues of dogs and of foxes. What? Did you think that cats and dogs who live under the same roof never talk to each other? Go away, ball of fluff, before your parents catch you. I should hate to have to move out of the sun to fight one of them."

A-cam suddenly saw himself through the cat's eyes. A tender little animal with fluffy fur, not yet formed into a fighter, still covered in cub fat.

"I'd—I'd better go then. I don't suppose you would care to just turn around and walk off, would you? My brother and sister are watching from that tangle of scrap over there."

"So that's what it's all about?" The tom yawned, revealing some very frightening teeth and a cavernous mouth. "No, I wouldn't."

"Oh, well . . ." said A-cam, a little dismayed.

He was about to turn away from the cat, when the beast suddenly yelled in that whine that felines employ, "Oh no, fox! I can't fight an animal as ferocious as you. Please leave me alone. I won't harm any of your family." The sound of the creature's voice made A-cam's fur stand on end.

Then in a much softer tone, the tom said, "How was that, *pissenlit*? Good enough to send you back a hero? Turn around now."

A-cam did as he was told, marching back to A-sac and O-mitz.

"What did you say to it?" whispered O-mitz.

"I just told him to watch himself, if he was coming into our yard," replied A-cam, his heart still beating fast after the cat's high yell.

A-sac nodded. "Sure you did," he said, and walked away.

TWENTY

Camio left the earth one day, after scrupulously observing the leaving-the-earth ritual, since now that the cubs were around O-ha had become stricter than ever about such things. He wanted to be out of the way when she lectured the young on "the right way" to mark, drink water, eat various kinds of food, enter and leave the earth, and observe the rites for the dead. True, he paid lip service to these observances, but he was becoming a little bored with the repetition of chants, rhymes, and songs—though he was secretly impressed, not to say amazed, at the number of euphemisms O-ha managed to find for the act of marking.

"Just a natural thing," he muttered to himself as he walked along the now-established fox highway through the *face*, which crossed seventeen back gardens, a factory yard, a bridge, three alleys, and two sets of garage rooftops, and ended up at the entrance to Trinity Parklands. "You mark your property—you mark your own. That's all there is to it. Nothing to get excited about. Can't see what the fuss is for. . . ."

He paused at the gates. Inside, there were human children playing on the apparatus, yipping away in shrill voices. He slipped into the shrubbery that ran around the edge, using it as a shield to travel to the wooded part and enjoying the soft feel and aroma of the peat-bark beneath his feet, which the park workers spread under the roses and rhododendrons. It was his intention to try to confirm some information that had come his way. He wanted to find out if Gar the badger was, indeed, still alive. O-ha had spoken of him often, during the time they were on the marshes, and he wanted to surprise her with the good news. Of course, if the old black-and-white grouch was dead, then Camio would keep it to himself for a while, until the cubs had left the earth.

O-lan and A-lon were both dead, he knew. They had been shot in the early hours of the morning that the *Unremembered Fear* was abroad. Many other animals had met their deaths that night, some of them mistaken for carriers when they were actually immune from the disease. A-magyr was missing and believed dead, though he could have gone on one of his famous walkabouts. Camio doubted that the old fox had escaped. There were now several new characters around and Camio was gradually getting to know some of them.

He traveled through the woodland, avoiding the human paths, sniffing for marks and trails, until he came upon a fox earth. There was litter all around the entrance, and he stood amongst this and cried out, "Anyone there?"

Shortly afterward a nose poked out.

It was another dog fox.

"What?" he said, brusquely. Camio guessed he had a mate inside the earth and was suspicious of another dog fox calling.

"You new around here?" asked Camio. "I mean, how many seasons have you seen in this parish?"

"What business is it of yours?"

"No need to be unfriendly, I've already got a mate if that's what you're worried about. I'm looking for a badger—big old gruff one by the name of Gar. You don't happen to know if he's still around these parts, do you?"

The dog fox emerged from the earth's entrance looking a little less aggressive.

"Don't know the names of any of the badgers—you're right, we are newcomers to the parish—but I think there's some of them living in the roots of an old blackthorn just south of here. Do you speak any *mustelidae?*"

"*Musta* . . . ? No, no I don't. I hadn't thought about that. The badger I'm after speaks some *canidae* so I didn't think . . ."

"You want me to come with you? I've lived with badgers. I can get by."

From being openly aggressive, the dog fox was now ready to become a bosom friend. Camio told the other that he would appreciate any help he could get, so long as it didn't put anyone out. No trouble at all, replied the dog fox, and gave his name as A-rythe.

"Camio."

"Funny name. You talk strangely too. You from up north somewhere? I once knew a *rangfar* from the high mountain country—always talking about the heather and pines. Used to call a lake, a *loch*—that sort of thing."

"I don't know where I'm from—that is, I *do*, but I couldn't tell you where it is in relation to here. I can tell you one thing, we didn't have any heather."

"Can't be the same place then," said A-rythe. "The way this *rangfar* talked, they had heather growing out of their ears up there. You new around here too? They had some nasty business here during Ransheen—almost wiped out the population. Genocide, just about. Massacred just about every living thing, apart from a few sparrows, and *Heff* knows there's enough of those in the world, they could do with a little culling—don't even make a decent meal—stick in your throat like a ball of fluff, and *chatter?* They never stop. You should hear them in here of a morning. Talk about a dawn chorus—worse than starlings—definitely worse than starlings. I was saying to O-rythe just before you called, O-rythe, I said . . ."

And so they walked on, with the dog fox battering the senses of Camio with his trivia, making him wish he had found some other animal to help him in his quest. They found the badgers' sett just as Camio was going down for the third time under the weight of nonsense the other fox was pouring out. A-rythe disappeared underground, announcing himself in that harsh guttural tone used by badgers, and was down there for what seemed an eternity. When he finally emerged, he informed Camio that there was an old badger of the description Camio had given him, living on his own. A-rythe said he would show Camio where he lived.

"If you could just give me the directions?" said Camio, weakly. "I'm sure I could find it and I don't want to trouble you . . ."

"No trouble at all," breezed the dog fox. "As I was saying to those badgers down there—do you know, despite the fact that I speak very little of the language, I get on quite well. A few signs here, a word or two there, and we can all understand one another, isn't that right? Communication. That's what it's all about. I have *no* problem in communicating. None at all. I could have talked to them all night, except . . . you know, they're not like us, even though we get on fairly well together, foxes and badgers, not like us really. They've got this habit of shuffling you toward the exit, and you have to pretend you don't notice. Funny lot . . . of course they talk too much, always did, but you have to allow them the license. As I say, I was . . ."

Camio sympathized with the badgers, wondering how they had managed to keep themselves from tearing this garrulous canid into little pieces and feeding him to the squirrels.

When they reached the sett, Camio had to be very forceful in pursuading the other fox to leave him to talk to the badger alone. A-rythe got a little huffy, but in the end bid Camio goodbye (an event that took almost as long as the walk itself) and then slipped away into the woodland. Camio heaved a sigh, shook himself, and then called down the sett.

"Is this the home of Gar?"

There was no answer.

He tried again. "Who lives here? I'm looking for Gar. Is that the name of the occupant?"

There was a rustling from behind him and a gruff voice said, "Ha, fox. *Hider*—come hither."

Camio turned to see an old grizzled badger standing under an ash tree. He looked annoyed. The fox did as he was asked.

"Are you Gar? I think you are, I saw you once when O-ha was living with you."

The darkness lifted from the badger's brow.

"O-ha? The little fox. You know her? What you do by my sett? Eh? Speak, fox."

"I am O-ha's mate, Camio."

A sparkle came into the badger's eyes.

"She's alive?"

Camio nodded. "We have cubs—three of them—down in the *face.*"

"Well, well," gargled the old badger. "Well, well—cubs too, eh? Ha! Is good. Come, come . . ." he said, and waddled toward his sett. "We talk together, fox."

Camio followed him down to a chamber where there were some rushes on the floor. When they had both settled, Gar motioned for him to proceed with his story and he told the badger all that had happened since he and O-ha had left the wood. The badger nodded approvingly in places, or clucked softly to himself when Camio touched on parts during which they were in danger. When he had finished, the big black-and-white head nodded, thoughtfully.

"So, she is well—is all turned out for good. And this Breaker?" He shook his head. "Hard to imagine this hound living from foxes. World is strange place, fox. *Wod* place. So, you get from here that night—me too, but alone. My sett-others, all killed."

"I'm sorry," said Camio. "That stupid fox . . ."

"Yes, I hear this and am very angry then, but now . . ." he shrugged. "I am *old* badger. Things get little dim in my head. Light grows little grey in my eyes."

"You've many got seasons yet," said Camio, politely. "But what *about* you? How did you escape that night?"

"Ha, that is good story. I think if I am younger it go to my head and this badger believe he is *the chosen one*. That night . . ." he said and paused for effect, settling down onto his haunches, which Camio had noticed were swollen with arthritis. "That night, Gar out hunting—out in cold snow. I hear guns go 'bang, bang, bang,' and think to myself, 'Gar, something happen down there.' Then I smell men coming, up hill from town. I smell the guns. I hear *guman* barking. I smell the *fear*.

"I feel the terror in this heart and I freeze, still, like rock. I think the foolish kitten—think, 'If Gar stays still, man pass by.' But then I see lights on snow—and gun fires in wood. Then I know I am to die. These men not play sport. Too many men. Too many guns. Too much fear.

"I run to edge of wood and there . . . there I see bright star—crossing the sky. It make a noise like this—" he growled softly in the back of his throat, "and flash on, flash off. On, off, on, off . . ." His voice drifted, but was pulled back again. "'Gar' I say to myself, 'this is sign. You follow this grumble star that makes brilliant on-off. It is holy sign, sent by *haelend, Fruma-ac-Geolca*.' So I go same direction, even though it lead me down into far side of town. Then I find this hole in ground—in street—where iron cover gone. Houses all dark. No people yet. I go under, into dark, and follow tunnels. Stay there for long, long time. This *syllicre* star save Gar's life. Show him safe hole. *Guman* not find Gar."

Gar went on to explain that he had lived in the sewers, which were not at that time in operation, until they began to complete the buildings. Then he thought it was time to get out, before the drains were put to use and he was drowned or "stinked to death." He poked his head out of the hole one morning and had a second mystical experience. There was a row of trees, not much more than saplings, which had been planted along the edge of the street. The weak winter sun had caught them and they shone like silver.

"You never see such trees," said Gar in a whisper. "They have bark that hurt your eyes to see. I think first they are made of shiny metal.

I think to myself, 'Gar, this is *second halig* sign. You go from this place *now* like *Fruma-ac-Geolca* tell you to.'"

Gar finished his story looking dreamily into space, and Camio had to make a noise to let the badger know he was still there.

"So," said Gar, "you are well, yes?"

"Me? Yes, I'm fine."

"I think you not from this place? You have strange tongue in your head. Ah—I remember something. You come from distant land. This is correct?"

"That's right, yes. I was captured and sent here. I don't know how I came—I was drugged at the time. I used to live in a country with wide streets and low houses. When I was a cub I thought the whole world was only as wide as a day's run."

Gar settled his large head onto his front paws. He sighed deeply, pear-shaped body heaving.

"Ah, when we were young . . . but the world has changed since then, Camio. The world has changed. We have lived through these changes. You think you live in strange land, but the land is strange to Gar too, and he was born in it. All the old ways are gone."

Camio slipped away after that, with a quiet farewell, and the badger fell asleep before the fox was even out of the sett. Camio suspected that the old badger did not have very long to live. His bones looked too heavy for him to carry around much longer, and his eyes were rheumy and distant. Still, he had had a long life, by all accounts—many seasons—and would probably not be sorry to go.

When Camio got back to the scrap-yard, he had to dodge the two men who worked there and were walking about, arranging their junk. Once before they had caught sight of him and were mildly excited, but he suspected that wild life was not an interest that held them for long. They must have heard the high-pitched squeals of the cubs from time to time, but either curiosity was not a strong motivator with them or the effort was not worth the reward, because they did not seem perturbed enough to go searching for the source amongst their rusting vehicles. In his short life, Camio had found that most humans were intrigued by foxes rather than disturbed by them. If indeed the men knew they had a fox earth full of cubs on their lot, it was more likely that they were proud of it than concerned by it. Camio had found that so long as he and his kind did not get in the way of human business, did not make threatening gestures toward human children, and generally kept a low profile, town dwellers were happy to leave them alone; they would even point them out to their friends as if to say, "Look at my strange neighbors—they chose my garden to have their family in!" Country people were inclined to look on foxes as vermin, but that was partly indoctrination and partly because of the domestic livestock.

He reached his little tunnel without being seen, and was fastidious about the procedures prior to entering the earth. When he got inside he saw that O-ha was looking weary. The cubs had no doubt had another boisterous day. Her tail was in a very sorry state where they had pulled out pieces of fur in their playfulness.

"You indulge those cubs too much," he said, looking down fondly on the sleeping bundles.

"Perhaps," she replied. "I'm hungry. Do we have a cache nearby?"

"Yes. Inside an old boiler. I'll get you something."

He slipped out again and returned with cold fried potatoes he had found a few days earlier in a side street. She wolfed them down greedily.

"Where have you been all day?" she asked.

"Ah. Now there's a thing. I heard that an old friend of yours was still living in Trinity. Went to visit him."

"An old friend?"

"Gar, the badger," he said.

Her eyes shone.

"Gar? Still alive? He escaped that dreadful time?"

"Had a 'mystical experience,'" said Camio. "Apparently his savior sent him a sign—a star to travel by—and then a row of glowing trees, to tell him when it was safe. He's a nice old thing, isn't he? I thought you said he was bad-tempered."

"Well, he can be. I expect you caught him on one of his rare good days."

"Anyway, he was delighted to hear about you. If you weren't so desperately attached to me, I might have been jealous. From the way he spoke about you, anyone listening would have thought you were responsible for the sun rising and setting each day. He thinks you're very special, doesn't he?"

This seemed to please her.

"We did get on rather well together. I suppose there are those who like to be needed—and he was there when I needed someone to talk to, someone strong."

"Oh, he's a strong old character, all right. A lot of authority there. Told me to look after you or I would answer to him. I found respect creeping into my voice when I spoke to him. Not many animals do that to me, I can tell you."

She lay with her head on her paws for a while, obviously musing over the news. Then she said, "Mystical experiences? Did you believe him? Or was he playing?"

Camio thought this was a strange remark coming from his mate, who not only believed in fox-spirits but claimed to have seen and been guided by one to her former mate's body. Perhaps, thought Camio, those things are facts to her, not mystical experiences?

"He didn't look or sound the sort to play games," replied Camio. "No, I think he believed what he was saying. However . . ."

"What?"

"Well, I can't explain his traveling star, but I'm sure the trees he mentioned were nothing but silver birches."

Her head came up sharply.

"You didn't tell him that."

"No—no, I didn't. Didn't want to spoil his illusion. I suppose he's never seen a silver birch before?"

"I doubt it. There were none around here before the town came. I hadn't seen one myself, until we came down here. Trinity Wood is an ancient covert—oaks, elms, blackthorns, alders, beeches—no silver birches. And with the sunlight on them . . ."

"They were, in his words, *halig* trees."

"Funny old Gar," she said. "I must try to get to see him one of these days, once the cubs are off our hands. . . ."

She had the dream. She dreamed she was in a bright place and struggling to walk. Suddenly, black bars fell across the ground. They were like the iron rods of a cage at the zoo, once described to her by Camio. Then she was being chased, and she sank to her shoulders in the snow, which hampered her escape. Finally, the shadow of . . .

PART FIVE

TERROR ON THE STREETS

TWENTY-ONE

Frashoon and the cubs were half grown. They played outside in the scrap-yard, when the men were not present, gamboling and fighting in the dust. They tracked spiders and pounced on them. They jumped for butterflies. They stalked each other and practiced their hunting skills. When they rested they did not go back into the metal shell of the car, the breeding earth, but found a hole somewhere under the junk and slept away from the adults. They had begun to forage for themselves, in the rubbish bags of the houses closest to the yard. There were narrow escapes, from dogs and people, but this was all part of the learning process. O-ha could no longer protect her young, even if she wanted to, because they now had individual wills and followed their own instincts. They remained close to their parents' earth, but were no longer part of it.

Of course, O-ha and Camio still talked with their three cubs, advised them, instructed them, and were anxious over their welfare.

O-mitz announced that she was dropping the O from her name.

"It's so old-fashioned," she said to her distressed mother. "Mitz sounds much better—I *feel* like a Mitz. All these silly distinctions between the sexes. Ask any of the foxes my age—they'll tell you they don't want all that labeling stuff. . . ."

O-ha asked Mitz's brothers how they felt about it.

A-cam said he had not thought about it and was quite happy with his name as it was.

"Don't see any point in changing it," he said. "That's just another one of O-mitz's silly affectations."

A-sac, the albino, said he was considering adding the repetitive syllable to his name; but that was traditional and so, to O-ha, acceptable.

"If I am to be a mystic, then I need to become A-sacsac—but that will not happen until the decision is made for me. I am waiting for the sign. It may never come." About his sister's decision, he said, "She's a foolish vixen. I feel sad for her. Her head's full of nonsense. Wait until she meets a partner and then see if she remains plain Mitz."

Mitz's reply concerning both her brothers was direct and blunt.

"A-cam is just too lazy to make *any* effort at individuality and A-sac is so lost in his own importance he can't see any further than his white nose."

So, personalities were developing—perhaps not in the way that O-ha might have wished, but then most mothers are slightly bewildered by the fact that their young do not follow paths imagined for them at birth. It was not that she wanted copies of herself, so much as shining versions of her ideal fox. Camio seemed quite happy with them and willing to accept their deviations from the standard model, but then (she told herself) he was a foreigner anyway and had some strange ideas about the role of foxes in the world. What she tolerated in her mate was not necessarily acceptable in her young. Her slightly rakish partner's quirky behavior was not her responsibility; and some of what she loved in him, she would have thoroughly disapproved of in another vixen's mate. She felt that if she were a less conventional fox herself and did not act as an anchor for him, he might get into all sorts of weird antisocial activities. No, she wanted her cubs to be like herself, not like her mate. She wanted them to be conventional.

One of O-ha's strongest warnings was to stay away from the manor house on the edge of town. She repeated this so often, and with such force, that the inevitable happened. The cubs were intrigued and two of them went there to find out what unspeakable horrors lay behind the wall that surrounded the gardens.

Late summer, and the dry, rustling grasses are alive with insects that hum, click, and crackle, and make amazing leaps between blades and stalks insect-miles apart. Toads squat patiently midway, ready to snatch them out of the air with whip-like tongues. Grass snakes bask on baked clay prior to seeking out the nests of hay where field mice are panting. Ground beetles, wings fused together in a coppery sheen, pounce on unwary caterpillars, tearing them to pieces with their powerful jaws. The small world below the level of the grasses, a hot and savage place, is working out the destinies of its many millions.

Life can be just as fleeting above the ground, where the green woodpecker drills into the bark of a tree, his head blurred with movement. The plump grub, being deep in the trunk, thinks it has escaped, until the sticky serrated tongue of the woodpecker comes snaking down its tunnel, elastically stretching to four times the length of the bird's beak.

Mitz and A-cam approached the wall of the manor house. Between the brickwork and the road was a greensward of uncut grass upon which stood a row of trees. The two foxes were able to slip through the grass, remaining hidden from the cars that flashed along the road. All along the wall, rooted at its base, was a cloak of ivy. The two foxes used this to scramble up and reach the top. Once there, they traveled along the wall's length, sniffing, listening, and occasionally peering down into the gardens with pattering hearts, to catch sight of the giant dog they had been threatened with as youngsters and warned off from more recently.

"I don't think there's such a dog," said A-cam. "I think O-ha made him up, just to scare us into doing as we were told."

The little vixen shook her head. "No, I heard Camio talk about him too, and anyway, O-ha doesn't tell lies—you know what she's like."

"Well, where is he then? Shall we just drop down inside and have a look around? There might be some juicy frogs in that pond over there."

Mitz tested the air for dog scent and listened hard, but could detect nothing unusual. Frashoon was veering off in a funny direction, though, due to the concave shape of the wall, and she was not sure which was up-wind and which was down-wind. To trust to her sight was not a fox's way, so she found herself relying on her hearing. There were plenty of sounds in the air, but none which might indicate the presence of a dog.

"No," said Mitz. "That's not a good idea at all. You stay up here."

Just as she said this, A-cam stepped out onto the branch of a tree growing on the garden side of the wall, and walked along it to its trunk. He dropped down to a lower bough. Then he called to Mitz, "See, I told you there was nothing to worry about—"

Just then a blur of brown caught Mitz's eye as something hurtled through the bushes, at the same time the scent of hound hit her nostrils.

"A-cam!" she screamed.

A-cam must already have caught the dog's smell, because he was in the act of jumping back up to the higher branch when the hound launched himself from the ground, his wide jaws slavering. There was a horrible smacking sound as the ridgeback's teeth cracked together. A-cam gave out a yell and his face registered pain. For a moment, Mitz was unsure of what was happening.

The dog fox's forepaws caught on the upper bough and he hung there precariously, as the hound crashed down into the bracken surrounding the bottom of the tree. There was blood pouring from A-cam's hindquarters and Mitz saw with horror that his tail was gone: bitten off at the base. The wound was awash with red.

"Hang on!" she cried, trying to keep the terror out of her voice. "Oh—get up, get up, A-cam!"

A-cam's face was twisted with the effort of regaining his safe perch, and with the agony of his injury. His back legs scratched at the air, trying to get a purchase on something to help him haul himself up. For a moment he dangled there, his front legs hooked over the branch and his body hanging.

Below, Sabre was back on his feet, the bloodied tail still in his mouth. He shook his prize as furiously as if it had been a dead rat, and then spat it out.

"My second fox this season," he said. "I chew them up and then throw them to the crows. You won't get away from me now."

He retreated, to give himself space to run and spring up from the ground again.

At last A-cam managed to get one of his back legs over the bough and Mitz ran out and gripped him by the ruff. The hound came thundering back, took a flying leap, and failed to reach the height of the second branch. The two foxes were now on top of the wall, though A-cam was still in a distressed state with blood gushing from his wound. He fell, rather than jumped, from the top of the wall to the greensward. There he lay on his side, when Mitz joined him. He was panting, tongue lolling out, the grass behind him stained scarlet.

"A-cam," said Mitz, "can you get up? What shall I do? Shall I go for O-ha and Camio?"

"I don't . . ." he managed to say, forcing himself up into a sitting position. From the other side of the wall came the sound of taunts and jibes. Sabre knew they were there, and in trouble.

"I've got your brush, fox," he called. "Going to give it to the chickens, to pick clean."

"Please, try to get up," begged Mitz.

A-cam did as he was asked, dragging himself to his feet. But then he staggered a few paces to the edge of the greensward, and walked dizzily into the road.

Mitz cried, "Come off there, you'll be hit!"

There were several cars going along the road. One of them swerved to avoid him, narrowly missing running him over. The vehicle behind that one, however, screeched to a halt.

Mitz crouched in the grass, hoping that she had not been seen, as a door came open and a human emerged, barking to someone else inside the vehicle. It was a male and he marched over to where A-cam lay panting on the tarmac. Hands reached down and A-cam snarled, "Don't—don't you touch me, you . . ."

But the almost-grown cub was too weak to move. The human went back to the car, put on thick gloves, and then quickly picked A-cam up from the ground and put him in the boot of the vehicle. The man got back into the car and then it drove off along the road. Soon it was gone.

"A-cam," whispered Mitz.

She was shocked at how quickly it had all happened. One moment they were playing a searching game—the next moment A-cam was mortally wounded and had been abducted by a human. Mitz knew that her brother was going to die. She had seen the size of the chunk that Sabre had taken from the cub's rear, and the amount of blood that had flowed. Now she had to go back to her parents and tell them that one of their cubs had gone, probably forever.

O-ha's grief at the loss of her cub was almost more than she could bear. Perhaps it was because she still retained a certain amount of those maternal instincts which have such a powerful hold over an animal following birth; perhaps this was why she missed the cub more than she had missed her mate A-ho. During the next few evenings she lay outside the earth, waiting for the fox-spirit to come and lead her to the body of her dog cub. One part of her hoped it would never appear, but since it seemed almost certain that he was dead, she desperately wanted to find his body and perform the last rites over it. Once again, the waves of hatred went out toward the hound at the manor house.

Camio too was devastated. Of the three cubs, although A-cam had been his mother's favorite, he had shared much with his father. Mitz was her father's cub, and A-sac belonged to some supreme being rather than to his parents. A-cam had been idle but lovable, and though there had been a restlessness in his nature, which meant that the time would have come when he would have left his parents for a life on the road, Camio felt that part of him would always have been with the cub, wherever he was.

Mitz wailed constantly at first, believing that it was her fault that her brother had been taken.

"It was me that persuaded him to go to the manor house," she whispered to Camio. "He wouldn't have gone if I hadn't suggested it. Why am I so stupid?"

"You're not stupid, Mitz. You're still a cub. It's not your fault, but mine," he said. "I should have kept a closer watch over you—explained more. You see, that dog at the manor has already been responsible for a lot of grief in your mother's life. He nearly caught the pair of us once, when we got our messages crossed and each of us went down there to save the other. . . ."

"You and O-ha?" said Mitz, wide-eyed.

"Oh, yes. We're quite capable of doing stupid things too, you know. Just because we're fully grown doesn't mean we know all there is to know, or follow our own good advice. Now, you have a life to lead. I want you to put this out of your mind as quickly as you can, because survival is tough enough, without bearing the weight of past mistakes on your shoulders. Look to the future, little one."

"I'll try," she said.

The summer moved on and the remaining cubs grew stronger. By the time Melloon was blowing across the land, the dispersal began in earnest in all the fox earths. It was time for A-sac to seek a mate, if he was so inclined, which he was not.

"I have heard of a great fox who lives in a mound that was not made by natural movements of the land," A-sac said to Camio one day. "It's a hill like a mole makes, only much smoother, much rounder, covered in turf. A giant molehill. Inside, I am told, there are chambers and passages, and in the center the ancient remains of a human who must have been very important at one time. O-toltol, the fox who lives in this hill, says the corpse must have been one of those who came up from the sea-of-chaos with the cats and dogs."

"O-toltol?" said Camio, thoughtfully. "A vixen?"

"A vixen, yes, but not a breeding one," said A-sac, "if that's what you're thinking—which you are. She, like myself, scorns the body's needs. For seventeen seasons she has lived inside the hill, and has not seen the light of day. She intends to die there without ever going out into the world again, or setting eyes on another two-legged beast—"

"On a human?"

"Yes. They have defiled our world, and she wishes never to hear or smell a living human again. The mound has been sealed for seasons out of time and there is no possibility that such creatures will enter it again."

Camio nodded.

"And you? You intend to lock yourself away in the dark for the rest of your life?"

"No," said the white fox, scornfully. "I am going there merely to consult with O-toltol, learn from her. The darkness and the silence have sharpened her mind, have concentrated her thoughts, and she has considered many things that normal foxes would not even contemplate. She has visions, and the depth of her understanding is beyond our ken."

"In that case, we shall expect to see you again."

"It's my belief," said A-sac, "that cubs should leave their parents' earth and never return. If we do meet again, it should be by accident and not design. I must find my own way to spiritual greatness, which means putting my origins behind me . . ."

"You're ashamed of us?"

"Not ashamed, but I have moved into a different sphere of light—you were merely the instruments of my happening into the world. Now that I am here, there is little to connect me with you."

"If I and your mother were priests of darkness, it would be different, I take it?"

A-sac shook his white head, and his pink eyes bore into Camio's.

"Now you're hurt," he said, "because you think I won't acknowledge you, once I leave the earth for good. You're wrong—you are my humble parents, who will be exalted with me, once I find my way along the path to truth and my name is used in praise. I expect you wish it were me that was gone, instead of A-cam. So do I. I think my spiritual rise would have been swifter, had I lost my tail to a hound of the Unplace and been wafted away by humans in one of their vehicles."

Camio shook his head.

"Well, A-sac, I hope you find what you're looking for out there. Whatever happens, your 'humble' parents will be happy to give you a roof over your head, should you ever feel gracious enough to pay us a visit once glory has descended on that great brow of yours."

"Yes, of course. I feel affection toward you, Camio, really. It's just that I must suppress such feelings once I have left the area of your earth."

After that encounter, Camio was pleased to chat with his little vixen, who was less happy about going away from them.

"I don't want to go out there," she said.

"But you've slept outside for months now," replied Camio.

"That's different. Once I leave here I'll be grown up. You won't bring me tidbits any more. I'll have to hunt for *all* my food, won't I?"

"That's true, but you're a good hunter and scavenger—you feed yourself already. I don't think you have any worries. Just make sure you cache your finds in a safe place, for the lean periods, and always get plenty of vegetables. You'll be all right—I have no worries about you. Tough as they come."

"I don't want a mate yet," she said, firmly.

"Well, that's up to you. Chase those dog foxes away, if you want to stay on your own. We're scared of you vixens, you know. All you have to do is bare your teeth and say no."

"I will—for the moment anyway."

"You'll always be welcome here, you know that."

"When must we go?" asked the little vixen.

"It would be proper to leave us quite soon now. I suggest you look around for a suitable earth within the next few days, then come back to us to say goodbye. I believe A-sac is doing the same thing, though he's warned us that he might not come back at all. If you really don't want to leave us, of course you must stay, but I'd like you to consider the outside world before you make up your mind. Lots of cubs do remain with their parents, but you can't know what's best for yourself unless you have a look and give things a try."

So, the lead up to the dispersal of the cubs had begun. They were about to make their own ways in the world. Both O-ha and Camio felt sad about that. Cubs often left home never to be seen again. They had been lucky, though, as half their litter had survived to reach the dispersal time. There were pairs left with only one cub, and many with none at all. The mortality rate of the young was high.

"It'll be quiet around here, won't it?" said O-ha.

"It'll be very different from what we've grown used to, that's for sure," replied Camio.

"I'll hate it, won't you?"

"Yes," he said, simply.

TWENTY-TWO

With the coming of the dispersal, Camio and O-ha talked about moving to another earth, away from the close proximity of men. Camio was concerned that the yard was growing too large and that they would soon have an Alsatian or a Doberman to guard the place. Already there was a night watchman in attendance. Apart from that, it was usual to move from the breeding earth once the dispersal of the cubs had taken place. The idea that the yard men might get a guard animal was of special concern to O-ha.

"Well, you know the *face* better than I do. Where shall we start looking?" she asked Camio one day.

"I've heard that the railway is coming to the town. We could make an earth on the embankment, in the *gerflan*."

She looked dubious.

"After that story you told me about the fox you met before you came here? Is it wise?"

Camio shook his head.

"That was different. It won't be anything like that. This will be new and clean, and there'll be wildflowers, bushes, tall grass—all the things you like. We won't be bothered because it'll be *gerflan*. The only thing is we'll have to get used to the noise of the trains, but I'm sure they won't come by *that* often. Anyway, you *do*, you know."

"Do what?"

"Get used to the trains. After a while you hardly notice them. You can sit there, watching the carriages full of humans go by, knowing they can't touch you, even if they wanted to. Glass boxes full of them. It can be quite fun. And you like the railway tracks, you told me so. You said they have nice clean lines, like the edges of the houses. You can sit and look at the strips of steel if you want to. Or you can laze around catching butterflies all day. Or even practice all those rituals you're so fond of."

She huffed at him.

"One doesn't *practice* rituals—not in the way you mean. Rituals are there to be observed. What would we eat?"

"We can still scavenge around the town. We can just make our caches on the bank, where only we can get at them. There'll be rats and mice too, and of course, worms."

"You make it sound all so idyllic."

"If that's the way it sounds, that's the way it is. I'm going out now, to scout around where the work is in progress. What do you want to do?"

"I think I'll wait here, in case O-mitz or A-sac comes back . . . or A-cam . . ." she said.

He left her then, and went out into the night streets. His heart felt heavy at the mention of their missing cub, and he knew she was still grieving over the loss, but there was nothing Camio could do about it. He could search—he *had* searched—but the world is a big

place. If A-cam was still alive, he could be many days' journey from the scrap-yard. Maybe even months! Humans could travel long distances fast and they could take a wild animal and place him in an area so far from his original home that it was impossible to find it again. Camio had experienced just that.

Camio padded down the empty main precinct of the town, a cobbled street lined with shops on both sides. Some nights, as he walked there, he paused to stare at the junk behind the glass screens: the variety of *things* that humans surrounded themselves with. But not tonight.

He passed another dog fox with barely a nod. Territories in the town were difficult to define and there were places, such as the food take-aways and restaurants, that were considered neutral ground and outside the patches that foxes defended as their "own." So chance encounters were reasonably common and unless there was a definite invasion of territory with an intent to steal a mate, or usurp an entrenched position, foxes were inclined to relax their parochial attitudes in the *face*—or at least more so than in the *hav*.

Camio passed through a pool of light, under a lamp, and slipped down an alley. There was a human asleep on some cardboard boxes at the bottom of the alley, exuding those fumes that made foxes gag. These creatures on the borderland of human society often made a lot of noise and shouted at foxes if they came too close; but in general they were harmless and seemed incapable of chase, so Camio did not pause in his stride. In any case, this one was snoring heavily and had obviously been imbibing deeply of the stuff that made their breath stink so foully.

He went up and over a fence at the end, into some gardens attached to houses behind the shops. He almost trod on a hedgehog which instantly rolled into a ball, its spines protecting it. There was a saucer of bread and milk nearby, which had been left out for the creature by the occupants of the house. Camio took a few laps of the milk and then continued on, down the side of the building and out into the next street. One or two cars were still humming along the tarmac, their blinding headlights sweeping the darkness away before them. Camio crossed the street quickly, keeping his head down. He knew too well that those bright beams could hypnotize an animal into rigidity, if you stared at them directly, and he had no wish to be squashed into *gubbins* on the asphalt.

There was a wind blowing up from the area beyond the marshes outside the town—from the sea—and the tangy smell reminded Camio of the months he and O-ha had spent in the old wreck. They had never encountered the hound, Breaker, since that time and he wondered whether the dog was now dead.

Suddenly, as the thought of "dog" entered his mind, he stopped and sniffed. There was something else caught up in Melloon besides the scent of salt, the smell of ripe fruit from the trees in the gardens—there was something sinister. It triggered the alarms that made up his nervous system. Had this happened before? What was so familiar yet at the same time strange and disturbing? His mind did a scan of all the scents and sounds that meant danger, and came up with—nothing. Nothing? Well, nothing definite.

He shrugged. Perhaps he was being overly cautious? It was best to keep his wits about him, fully, but it was also sensible not to get worked up about something that would probably turn out to be nothing in particular. There was the smell of dog, certainly, but in the *face* it was difficult to get away from such scents. There were many pet dogs around, leaving their marks on posts, in the corners of alleys, and, of course, in the gutter. It would have taken a hundred days of rain to wash away such odors.

He looked up, but it was not possible to see the night sky, which was obscured by the corners of buildings and the lights of the town. If he hoped to find a sign there, he thought to himself, he would wait all night. All he could see was a haze of half-light above him.

His instincts were probably tuned too sharply. It happened sometimes.

Just then, there was a cry from several streets away, followed by a chirruping sound. Two foxes were calling to one another. Was there anything sinister in that? Silence. He waited for a while, to see if anything further was said. Then came the word, full of fox-fear, that made his fur stand on end.

"*Dog!*"

240

"Dog"—but why such a call? There were several strays in the town—more than one hound was left out for the night. Town dogs were seldom dangerous. They hadn't the wit, nor the will, to catch a fox. So why . . .

The call came again, to be taken up by others: "*The dog is abroad!*"

"*The* dog?"

A long, chilling cry went out, over the rooftops, through the streets. It was the call of a hound: a hound in the full of the hunt. But there would be no horsemen—not in the *face*—so the dog would be hunting alone. What kind of dog would do that?

The call went out again, and then the shout of a fox.

"*Look out! Sabre is loose!*"

Sabre! The ridgeback was in the streets! It must have found a way out of the walled garden, and now it was hunting its favorite prey in the streets of the town.

O-ha, thought Camio. I must go back to her. The *beast* was abroad. Camio realized that he and his family were in great danger. Sabre was familiar with his and O-ha's scents. The dog would just have to catch a whiff of one of them, to be on their trail. All foxes were Sabre's prey, but those who had outwitted the beast would surely be at the top of his death list. And the most positive recognition signal amongst canids was the scent. The smell of an animal imprinted itself on the canid's brain. Camio might forget the physical appearance of the first dog he had ever scented, but he would recognize its odor in an instant. *Once smelled, never forgotten.* Sabre would be searching the highways and byways for a whiff of the two foxes who had make him look like a fool in front of his master. He would question other animals he caught, terrorizing them until he gained some information on the foxes' whereabouts. There was no question that O-ha especially was in terrible danger.

Camio began to retrace his steps, and all the while the fearful cries rose around him, filling the night air. Dogs in their houses began to take up the call too, some of them yelling, "Give it to them, Sabre!"—but others, perhaps confused by the general clamor, or possibly less partisan than most, shouted, "*Keep it quiet!*" or "*Go back home where you belong.*"

Lights began to go on in the houses and in the flats above the new shops, and humans started barking at their dogs, and then each other. Then suddenly there was a terrible scream from not far away and the whole town went quiet, listening. The sound of cracking bone followed, after which a voice full of triumph, in the rich timbre of the ridgeback, crooned out the words, "*A fox is dead!*"

Pandemonium in the houses.

Camio hurried on. Soon the main area of noise was behind him and he could concentrate on finding the shortest route back to the scrap-yard. He did not consider using the main highway. He followed his own instincts and cut a path over garages, sheds, and gardens, careless of any other known dogs in the area. He was moving too swiftly to be caught.

When he arrived back at the yard he went right through the tunnels in the metal junk and straight to the earth, where he found to his relief that O-ha was waiting.

"What's happened?" she said. "What's the matter? Is it the *Unremembered Fear?*"

Camio paused to get his breath.

"Nothing so pleasant," he said, once he was able. "Sabre's out. He's loose in the streets."

O-ha sank to her knees.

"Oh, my poor cubs!" she whispered.

A tingling sensation went down Camio's spine. Of course, A-sac and Mitz were out looking for earths! Camio remembered the horrible scream—the death scream of a fox having its neck broken—and tried to convince himself that the voice had not belonged to one of his own cubs.

I know my own. That was the voice of an adult. I would recognize my own cubs. But the doubt remained. Voices change when under the influence of fear. He said nothing to O-ha, however, about this incident. She would have been too far away to hear it, having caught only the general clamor rather than anything more specific.

"I must go back," he said to her, "and look for them."

"NO."

He was shocked by the violence in her voice.

"No," she said. "I don't want to lose you, too. We can have more cubs . . ."

"You don't mean that, I know," he replied, gently. "I realize you're afraid for me, but you needn't be. I've faced worse dangers than Sabre. I outwitted two Alsatians to escape from the zoo—"

"Sabre *eats* Alsatians."

"It's not the size—it's experience and intelligence that count. He won't get me, I can assure you of that. And I have to go out there, O-ha—they're my cubs too. With any luck A-sac will have gone to look for his mound on the *hav* just beyond the marshes. He'll be out of harm's way. It's Mitz I'm worried about."

"I'm coming too."

He did not reply for a few moments, while he stilled those thoughts that would have him argue her out of it. It was not that he considered himself more able than O-ha, but that Sabre would have only to catch a whiff of her scent and she would be in terrible danger. However, he realized that she was as much entitled to search for her cub as he was, and the big dog had not got her yet, despite two attempts. Had the situation been reversed and he, Camio, been the one in mortal danger, he knew he would not have allowed O-ha to talk him out of the quest to find Mitz.

"Fair enough. But we have to keep together unless we come up against him, in which case we immediately split up, the way we did in the manor garden. That was what confused him. All right?"

"You don't have to tell me."

"No, I don't. Just wanted to have things clear between us."

If Sabre was going to get one of them, Camio was going to make very sure it was him. However, he tried to think positively. There was no reason why the ridgeback should get either of them. They were two bright, fit foxes and they both knew tricks that would have most hounds chasing their own tails.

"Let's go then," said Camio.

"We'll try the area near the center of the *face* first. Keep your nose to the wind and your ears tuned, vixen. . . ."

With that, the pair of them left the earth. And for once, O-ha forgot to observe the rituals.

They traveled to the middle of the town swiftly, but cautiously. There was still an uproar in progress, but the barking humans were gradually winning their battle for silence. The two foxes came to a street that stank of Sabre residue. The body of a fox lay under the light from the lamps. It was twisted into an unnatural position and they could smell deadness about it, as they approached. It was a juvenile, but from a distance they knew it was not A-sac since it had a normal red coat, and when they got closer they were equally relieved to smell that it was not Mitz. They looked about them, nervously, wondering whether the hound from the Unplace was lurking in the shadows, waiting to pounce.

But then, thought Camio, that's not his way. He'll charge through the streets, looking for quarry, rather than sneak around like a fox.

"It's just a youngster," said O-ha, sadly, still sniffing the corpse.

"Let's get on," replied Camio.

They began a systematic search of the town—systematic by fox standards, of course, which meant a weaving, meandering course through streets and gardens, alleys and yards—but found no trace of either of their cubs. Always, somewhere around them, they sensed the presence of that great hound.

At one point O-ha stopped suddenly, stiff in her tracks.

"What's the matter?" whispered Camio, but even before the final word was out, he had caught the scent too.

"Quick, up on that roof!"

O-ha obviously needed no second warning. She leaped up onto the roof of a car parked outside a garage, then onto the roof of the garage itself. Camio was close behind her. The pair of them found the shadow where the garage roof joined the wall of the house, and they lay there. Camio could feel O-ha's heart pounding as they pressed against each other.

Down at the far end of the streets, in the light of a lamp, Sabre was standing. They could see him lifting his nose to the breeze, but they were up-wind of him. His scent came to them quite strongly, but theirs would hopefully not reach him.

The great hound stood for what seemed seasons out of time,

staring down the street. Then he began to walk along it, sniffing at the fence-posts and the bases of the garden walls. Camio held his breath. If Sabre reached the point where they had left the street, he would locate them for sure. Then it would be just a matter of time. The little fox was not so sure that the dog could not follow them, using the car as a launching platform.

Camio thought, *If he gets this far, I'll have a go. I'll have the advantage. The dog won't be able to keep his footing on the roof. Perhaps I'll be able to get to his throat, before he can get to mine?* The American fox was calm by this time. He knew that there was no other way out. He had to stand and fight. Once that decision had been made, the terror went out of him, to be replaced by that heightened feeling of controlled fear that is necessary to any animal about to fight— necessary to keep him honed to a sharp edge, to quicken his actions, to clear his brain.

The ridgeback got closer. Under the light of the street lamps, Camio and O-ha could see the ridged muscles on the great hound's back, the skin rippling like water over boulders in a stream. Closer. Closer. Until the foxes were sure he *must* have caught their scent.

The dog stopped. He looked up, turned his head.

They crouched closer to the wall in the black shadow. The wind was a friend to foxes that night, remaining constant in direction.

Suddenly something streaked across the end of the street, running for its life. Camio caught the strong scent of cat. It must have been hiding in the aromatic screen of an herb garden, because it trailed thyme and basil in its wake.

Sabre was off in pursuit, a thin growl at the back of his monstrous throat.

Once he was around the corner, the foxes leapt down from their hiding place and took the opposite direction. They carried on the search but they had had a bad fright and their attention was not completely on the task they had set themselves.

Eventually they felt they had covered all the ground they could, and with one area of the *face* still noisy with the yelling of dogs, they made their way back to their earth, hoping that the cubs would be there waiting for them.

They were not.

As the heron-grey dawn drifted into the yard, O-ha sat at the entrance to the earth, waiting. O-ha was good at waiting. She was the patient vixen with her nose to the wind and her ear tuned to the world. Around her the inane chatter of sparrows filled the hollows in the ironwork, the frames of cars, the old metal boilers, the cookers and stoves: sparrows, like fleas, got everywhere. Unlike fleas, however, they could not be scratched, and she suffered their irritating banalities in silence. In the earth, an exhausted Camio slept, his breathing sacred to her.

How long would that hound be loose? When such a dog got out it was often two or three days before they caught him, if he was indisposed toward going home himself. He might get hungry and return to the manor, but she doubted this. A dog such as that could forage for his own food. There was the fact that he was of an unusually large breed, and so, if he were seen by people, they would be curious as to why he was out on his own. But would they dare approach him?

She waited patiently, listening for the sounds of her cubs returning.

Later the men came to the yard, growling softly to one another in the way that they always did. A vehicle arrived and dropped its load and there was a lot of noise when the scrap was sorted. Dawn's light drifted away. Shadows began to harden.

At noon Camio rose and joined her, settling down beside her beneath their metal roof.

"No sign yet?" he asked, without hope in his voice.

"No—nothing."

"We mustn't lose hope. Remember, I told them both to take two or three days in searching for a new home, and A-sac said he might not come back at all."

"I haven't lost hope."

"Good."

A crow landed on the scrap, well out of their reach, and cried, "*Fuchs! Was fehlt Ihnen?*" but they ignored it. Crows always seemed to know when something was wrong, even when it was not clearly evident. Any response was usually met with mocking tones. Crows seemed to enjoy the misery of their fellow creatures. When this one was not chased away it began to get a little bolder, muttering to itself as it hopped from one piece of metal to another, almost within reach of their jaws. Finally it made a sound of disgust, and flew away.

That night O-ha had *the dream*, the recurring nightmare. She dreamed she was in a bright place and struggling to walk. Suddenly, black bars fell across the ground. They were like the iron rods of a cage at the zoo, once described to her by Camio. Then she was being chased, and she sank to her shoulders in the soil, which hampered her escape. Finally, the shadow of her pursuer fell across her path and she looked up to see . . .

The morning after he had killed the juvenile fox in a side street, Sabre found a resting place. It was in one of the newly built houses whose occupants had not yet arrived. He was feeling disappointed. Having got that fox, he had hoped it was one of the vixen's young, but her scent was nowhere on the creature. That was a shame. There were two reasons why it would have been a great victory to have snapped the spine of one of *her* cubs. The first was that Sabre would have considered the killing as partial repayment for his humiliation; and the second was that *she* might have come looking for her youngster.

Consequently, since her mark was not on the dead creature, he had gone off, roaming deeper into the town to see if he could pick up her scent. He had indeed caught a smell of her once or twice, but the odor had been too faint to give him direction. It was just a matter of time.

Having escaped through the hole he had been digging for such a long time, he was determined to stay out until he caught the vixen. She would not escape him now. He knew he would get a beating, once he was recaptured, but that did not bother him at all. Sabre had been in worse predicaments. When he was a puppy he had frequently been kicked and bullied by the owner's children, when the master was not around to prevent it. The children used the household pets to get rid of their own frustrations when their father went off hunting in the bush for weeks at a time.

Tomorrow he would take up the search again; then, let the vixen beware.

TWENTY-THREE

Unlike her father, Mitz was having a great deal of trouble staying out of other foxes' areas. Because she did not know the *face* as well as Camio, she found she was continually transgressing territorial rights in her search for an earth. She had been snarled, spat, and shouted at in the course of the night, and she was quickly learning that she should take serious note of "marked" areas and use her nose as a guide. The trouble was that the streets were full of stale scents, especially those of dogs, and the under-layers and over-layers of odors became confusing. It was a little disconcerting, to say the least, when you poked your nose into a hole in a fence, to be confronted by a head with flattened ears and bared teeth telling you to go and chase your tail elsewhere. She counted herself lucky that she had not been bitten on the occasions when she had quite innocently wandered into a likely-looking but inhabited hideaway. Even though much of the town was still under construction, there were foxes in almost every part of it; and though cats did not bother her a great deal, they too seemed to resent her presence. Being still a juvenile, she was wary of some of the big tomcats, with bellies that brushed the ground and faces like battered tin cans. They seldom ran away from her, once they saw she was not an adult; and their eyes would glint, their faces would contort into devilish features, and their fur would rise so that they looked twice as big as they actually were.

"*Peau-Rouge!*" they would hiss. "*Sauvage!*"

Although she did not understand these words, she guessed they were not complimentary.

Occasionally, she came across a cat that was so still she had not noticed it was there, until she smelled it. At one point she had felt hungry and was sniffing around a wastebin, only to see on looking up that a grey she-cat was sitting on the top. The feline seemed quite unconcerned by her presence and was viewing her activities with mild curiosity.

"Sorry," said Mitz. "Didn't see you there."

The cat shrugged.

"I—I don't suppose you could move, so that I could have a look in the bin?" Mitz asked.

The cat looked calmly firm and this time did not turn a hair. It merely regarded her with a disdainful stare as if she were a piece of garbage herself. However, the little grey creature looked so soft and vulnerable that Mitz decided it was time to make a stand and begin asserting herself. She could not allow herself to be pushed around forever. There came a point when one had to stop running.

Mitz bared her teeth and snarled.

The cat suddenly transformed herself into a monster: an arched grey fiend, covered in claws and teeth, and spitting incomprehensible obscenities.

Mitz left the scene hurriedly.

In the middle of the night there was a commotion in the town, but Mitz was too intent on finding a new home to take much notice of it. She thought she caught her father's scent on the breeze once or twice, and wondered whether he was out scavenging for food. It would have been nice to come across him, while she was looking so grown-up and purposeful, but somehow their paths never quite met.

She found a half-eaten package of fish and chips in the gutter and swallowed over three quarters of it before a human came along the street and she had to leave. Once, she was almost struck by a car that came sliding around a corner and caught her in the middle of the road. She remembered how A-cam had been abducted and a shiver went through her.

On the edge of town there were partially built houses that smelled of newness, and once or twice she was tempted to make an earth in one of these, but some instinct told her that such places would be alive with humans during the day, and she resisted the temptation. It was there that a mouse panicked and ran out, under her nose, from beneath a pile of bricks. It was only a length away from her, out on the churned mud, when from out of the night an owl swooped down suddenly and silently and snatched the creature from the ground in its talons. It happened so fast she hardly had time to blink, and the bird left a hoot in its wake, as if to say, "You're not quick enough, vixen! This is the big wide world and we're all out here competing with one another."

Didn't want the mouse anyway, she thought to herself. She wished she had had time to shout it, but the nightbird with the flat white face was long gone.

Finally, she came to a street where the houses had been occupied but the gardens were still unestablished. It was as she entered this long dark road that something came to her on the wind: the faint scent of dog. She stopped and stiffened. She had smelled that scent before! Where? The odor of the hound contained elements that disturbed her senses. There was an underlying whiff of chase-and-kill attached to the main odor, and though she had never been the quarry in a hunt, her racial memory sent needle-sharp warnings into her brain. There was a dog in the area that was specific in its intent. It

was out looking for creatures to kill, and Mitz had heard enough stories from her parents to know that foxes were high on the hunting list of any dog.

A large shadow crossed the bottom of the street and drifted into the blackness at the base of a wall. Luckily Mitz was down-wind and her scent was blowing away from the other creature, but she caught the full force of its smell and recognized it. She knew the owner of that huge shadowy form.

It was Sabre, the ridgeback.

All caution left her, and the fear that rippled through her small body took control. At that moment, a door opened in a house and she dashed forward into the blaze of light that seemed her only escape route from the terrible beast that was stalking the streets. There was a screech from a human as she ran through its pair of legs, but this was a minor consideration when the alternative was being ripped from throat to tail.

Blinded by the light, she ran around in circles for a while before finding some solid object under which to hide. There she crouched, her heart beating fast, and waited for death to descend.

Nothing happened, apart from some muted excited barking from the owners of the property she had invaded. The smells were overwhelming and if she had not been frozen into immobility Mitz might have gone berserk; but her body would not respond to any command at that time, reasonable or otherwise.

Someone came to the open doorway of the room she was in and bent down to look under the object that was sheltering her. Then the door was quietly shut and the human went away. There followed some whirring sounds and more growling noises from the humans. Then there was a long wait, during which Mitz got her breath back and began to consider her position.

At first she thought, *As soon as that door opens, I'm going through.* But then she remembered that Sabre might still be in the street and it did not seem like a good idea any more. The window was better! If they had only left a window open. She studied the walls around her. If there were any escape holes they were covered by cloth. So that was out.

Nothing to do, then, but wait and see.

After some while she heard a car stop right outside the house and then the sound of its door being slammed. Then the front door to the house was opened. There were barks and growls coming from the hallway. Finally, the door to the room was gently opened. A tall human male with black fur on his face entered the room and closed the door behind him.

For a moment the man stood still, allowing his scent to fill the room. When he moved again, Mitz noticed that he had something in his hand: a short pole with a loop at the end. She did not like the look of that pole and snarled at him.

All the while he was in the room he was growling softly at her, and surprisingly they were not menacing sounds. She sensed that he was trying to communicate with her. This was deeply suspicious. Why should he wish to talk at her if he was not trying to lull her into a false sense of security? Humans were out to get you, and that was that. All her learning directed her toward the thought that if a man got his claws on you, the end was near. Well, if this one so much as placed a toe within biting distance he was going to find it missing shortly afterward.

That did not happen. Ever so cautiously, the man came down to eye level with her and extended the pole with the loop, so that it was before her nose. She snapped at it, biting the loop of wire. It was hastily retrieved.

Next, the man barked and someone opened the door. Mitz's attention was distracted for a moment, and in that second the loop was round her neck. She tried to back off quickly, but the noose tightened until it was a collar.

O-ha had told Mitz about snares that were laid on fox highways and byways, and that strangled animals to death. Sometimes the choking was so agonizingly slow that it was better to commit *ranz-san* and cheat the snare of its ugly job. Mitz had now been snared and she thrashed around on the end of the pole, expecting the noose to begin it work of choking her.

It did not. There was some sort of catch on the loop which prevented it from closing any further than the approximate girth of her throat. Then strong hands were on her, lifting her up. She tried to snap at them, but they were gloved and out of reach. The noose was removed by the trembling hands of the householder, and a cage was brought forward. Mitz was thrust gently into this meshed metalwork and her exit locked. She knew then what was going to happen to her. Her father had told her enough tales about cages. . . .

She was going to the zoo.

As she was carried out of the house by the man with fur on his face, she felt thoroughly miserable. Oh yes, she had escaped from the killer, Sabre, but now she was going to spend the rest of her life locked up in a small room to be peered at by little humans with sticky faces, and poked and laughed at. The room she was destined for would have a few branches for her to play on, perhaps, and she would be fed and watered regularly, but it would indeed have been better to throw herself into the jaws of the ridgeback. Such an end was less distressing and certainly much quicker.

In the back of the vehicle she was bumped and jostled along, the movement making her spread her legs and flatten herself against the bottom of the cage. It sent a weird, insecure sensation through her body, and she wanted to urinate to relieve her tension. She did so, and the man, on hearing or smelling it turned briefly and showed her his even white teeth. He seemed to be aware of her distress and continually rumbled sounds at her in a deep, rich voice. This did nothing, however, to alleviate the strange sensation of floating through the air, and she continued to stare wildly at the interior of the vehicle and at the back of the human's head. The entire journey was stressful, but although she whined a couple of times, she did not disgrace herself by screaming for freedom. The thing to do, she had been told by Camio, was to watch and wait, and to take any opportunity that presented itself for escape, without causing too much fuss. "The quieter you stay," he had told his cubs, "the more they trust you. Pretty soon, they hardly notice you're there, and that's when they make mistakes."

So, having had a father who had been in a zoo for part of his life was proving useful to Mitz. At least it was not *all* incomprehensible to her. She knew what was happening, and why. It was just a matter of being patient. She would like to have told hairy-face what she thought of him—or even to have sunk her teeth into that nasty pair of hands—but discretion was wiser than revenge.

Eventually the vehicle drew to a halt and the back was opened. Sweet smells flowed into Mitz's nostrils, of apples, pears, and plums. She could see no buildings around, and could hear only the wind soughing through the branches of the trees. They were in the country somewhere. The cage was lifted out and Mitz was carried along a path to a house with a roof of dried reeds. The man barked at someone as they approached the door and it was opened to reveal a female human and—her heart skipped a beat—*a giant dog*! Despite her resolve to remain calm, she drew back in the cage and snarled at the hound. It gave her a mournful look.

"What are you getting so upset about?" it asked, not unkindly.

No dog had *ever* spoken to her in this way before—almost as an equal—and she was rather taken aback. All the stories her mother had told her about the slaves of men emphasized that they were foul creatures who would attack foxes without provocation, and who certainly had nothing civil to say.

Her cage was placed down on some paper, and the man left the room. The dog continued to regard her with a sad expression.

"I'm Betsy," said the hound. "I take it you have a name?"

"Why are you talking to me?" asked Mitz. "I don't understand what's happening here. Is this the zoo?"

"Zoo? Whatever gave you that idea? This is a cottage. Haven't you ever seen a cottage before?"

"I'm only young. I haven't even left my parents' earth yet—not properly. What kind of dog are you? You're not a ridgeback, are you?"

"Well, there you've got *me*. I've never heard of a ridgeback. They must be an unusual breed. I'm a St. Bernard," she said. "I have the reputation for saving humans in distress. Never done it myself, of course. No one seems to get lost around here. Still, I suppose one day . . ."

"Do you normally chat with foxes like this? The only dogs I know spend all their time chasing us."

"Ah, well, that's because this is an unusual household. Lots of foxes get brought here. Him, my master, he brings them."

Mitz was almost afraid to ask what for. She had visions of being killed, roasted, and eaten. It was her understanding that when men trapped wild animals like herself, it was either to kill them because they were considered pests—which would probably have been done to her before now—or because they wanted them for food. Then she recalled an even more chilling reason. Sometimes, especially with furry animals like foxes, they skinned them and turned their coats into human clothes. She imagined what the knife would feel like, slitting her belly and along each leg. Then the skin being peeled off her body and raw, bloody flesh appearing. Did they kill you first? She hoped so.

"Disgusting practice," she snapped.

"What?" asked Betsy mildly, at the same time pausing in the act of scratching her ear with her hind leg, no doubt thinking that she had broken protocol in front of this little fox.

"Skinning foxes," replied Mitz.

Betsy shuddered and resumed her scratching, now that it was obvious that her manners were not at fault.

"I should say so," she replied.

"Isn't that what your master brings us here for?"

"Not usually," said Betsy. "In fact I can't think of one single fox that he's skinned."

"Then what am I here for?"

"To look at."

"To look at? Then this is a zoo."

"Not it isn't, it's a cottage. Look," said Betsy patiently. "For some reason—Lord knows why—this man of mine likes to catch foxes and look at them. I think it must be the result of some kind of brain damage when he was a puppy, because I don't know any other humans that do this and his own friends think he's crackers. Anyway, little fox, you can rest assured that no harm will come to you while you're here. He treats you creatures as if you were fragile. You might get pulled about a bit, but not too roughly. All he wants to do is look at you. Spends hours doing it. Almost every day we go out somewhere and look at foxes and we follow them wherever they lead us. Crazy, I know, but there it is. One can choose one's friends, but not one's master or mistress. These two are as bad as each other. *She's* always stroking your lot, as if you were dogs. Both mad, but I wouldn't change them, you know. Oh Lord, no. They're nice people in a peculiar way. . . ."

"So they won't harm me?"

"Not at all. You're as safe here as you would be in your own earth."

"And you? You won't hurt me?"

Betsy looked offended.

"Of course not. What do you take me for? I shan't want to *look* at you, the way he does all the time, but there's no need to be rude. I've never hurt anyone in my life. Why, only the other day we had an intruder in here and I was the first one under the bed."

The man re-entered the room, while the woman stood behind him in the doorway with her arms folded across her chest. There was a perfumed odor wafting over from her, and Mitz wondered whether she had rubbed herself all over in wildflower blossoms to get such a smell.

"Ah, look," said Betsy, "he's brought you a dish of water. Trying to make friends with you. Take my advice and play hard to get at first—it pleases them more when they have to work to get you to trust them. I know that sounds silly, but it's true."

The man barked at Betsy, and she got up and lumbered over to the other side of the room.

"Thinks I'm upsetting you," she said, over her shoulder.

The front of the cage was lifted gingerly and the water dish pushed inside.

Mitz eyed it for a moment, and then said the ritual chant:

"*Water, preserver of life, body of A-O the first fox of Firstdark, cleanse my spirit as well as my limbs, my torso, my head. Water, clarify my soul, my sensations, my senses. All.*"

The man got very excited at this reaction from her and barked at

the woman, who nodded and showed her teeth the way he had done in the vehicle on the journey to the cottage.

"That's it," said Betsy, before the man could shut her up. "Play hard to get. Do a bit more of that rigmarole. It gets them going—it really does."

But the ritual was over, and Mitz was thirsty. She drank the liquid gratefully.

TWENTY-FOUR

Later, Mitz was taken out to the garden at the back of the house and into a much larger cage, which was similar, she imagined, to those Camio had described as being part of the zoo. There she underwent a rather undignified inspection. The man who had captured her checked every inch of her and found the small cut on her paw that she had received in the scrap-yard. He called to the woman who brought him a pot of paste, some of which he smeared on the cut. Then she was left there for the rest of the night, with a plate of meat mixed with some sort of vegetable. The first thing she did was lick as much of the paste away from her wound as possible, though it tasted horrible. After that, she ate the food they had left her.

There was hay on the bottom of the cage and she lay on this, feeling quite miserable. The dog had told her that she was not destined to be sent to a zoo, but how much could she trust the St. Bernard? Betsy was, after all, one of the minions of the oldest enemies of foxes. Perhaps the hound had been trained to put foxes at their ease, so that they caused the least trouble possible? Humans were devious creatures that spent a great deal of time making things easy for themselves. No, she could not trust either the dog or the man.

She settled down with her head on her front paws, to spend the rest of the night morosely imagining the worst. She could hear a brook gurgling somewhere at the bottom of the man's garden and when she listened very hard she could hear sounds of activity coming from that direction. There was some creature making noises down there. She wondered if she should call to it and perhaps obtain some reliable information, if it were able to speak *Canidae*. She began to bemoan her fate loudly, to anyone who might be listening.

The sounds that Mitz could hear were in fact coming from the vicinity of an otter's holt in the bank of the brook. There a bitch and a dog otter were feeding their cubs on a rock, worn smooth by generations of use, known as an *altar*. Scattered around the *altar* were the otters' droppings, or *spraints*, which served to mark their territory and warn away intruders. The dog otter, whose name was Stigand, was familiar with and to the pair of humans that lived in the house. Over the course of a year the otters and the humans had reached an understanding of one another. Stigand and his partner, Sona, would often accept fish from the humans since this act seemed to please them. Stigand was all for maintaining good relations with any creature living close to his holt; and unlike foxes, his kind had no reason to hate the two-legged beasts that took little notice of territorial markings. Otters are members of the *Mustelidae* family, which includes badgers, and he often spoke to his black-and-white cousins, some of whom had a sett out in the field close to the brook. There was a pair of foxes living in the same sett, and though Stigand and Sona steered clear of these red-coated cohabitants of their cousins, the badgers would often slip *Canidae* into their conversation to impress visitors. Consequently, Stigand had picked up a certain amount of the foxes' tongue, which in any case had originally derived from his own ancient language. These vocabulary gleanings he had augmented and, he believed, perfected in discussions with the dog Betsy on the cottage lawn.

When he heard the fox cub calling plaintively, he said to Sona, "Sounds like they've grabbed another fox—a young one. We shan't get any rest if the cub keeps that up."

"Poor creature's probably frightened. How would you like to be locked up in a cage?"

"Well, of course I wouldn't," replied Stigand, "but Betsy must have told her that there's nothing to worry about. She usually does, you know."

"Perhaps Betsy wasn't around when the cub arrived? Sometimes they lock her away, thinking she's going to frighten any fox they bring in."

"True. True." Stigand began to play with one of his own cubs, knocking her off the *altar* into the water. The cub squeaked in delight. The fox in the cage became louder in her complaints. Stigand sighed.

Sona said, "Well, if you're going to reassure the cub you might as well do it now, before the sun comes up. You know how irritable you get when your coat dries up."

"Of course I get testy—it's uncomfortable. So do you, as a matter of fact. All right, I'll go and have a word with her, if you think it'll do any good."

He slipped from the *altar* into the cool waters of the stream and swam to the bank. Once on dry land, he waddled the length of the garden to where the cage stood, and peered through the wire at the little fox that was whining in the corner. He cleared his mind of the *Mustelidae* in which he had been conversing with Sona, and gathered together his command of *Canidae*. He prided himself on being fairly adept at languages, and refused to punctuate his speech now with words of his own tongue. What came out was rather stilted, rather precise, but perfectly correct. He was quite sure of this because his badger cousins often remarked on how fluently he spoke *Canidae*, and swore they could recognize no difference between his use of the language and that of a fox.

"Hello, smallish fox," he said. "You make quite a clamorous noise for one such as your dimensions."

Mitz had never seen an otter before, but her education had been good and her mother had provided her with descriptions of every animal she might ever encounter within her own land. (Camio had provided the cubs with many that were not indigenous, despite O-ha's warnings that they might get overloaded with information; and so, alongside pictures in their minds of otters, deer, stoats, weasels and the like, were exotic creatures called elephants, tigers, and boa constrictors.)

Mitz stopped yelling and regarded the chocolate-brown creature for a moment, thinking how smooth and sleek it looked in the moonlight.

"Better," said the otter. "Better indeed that you should fall to quietness on this wonderfully still night, with the stars like stipple on a silver-sided trout. . . ."

The otter seemed to be something of a poet, which was appreciated by one who loved chants and songs as she did, though the otter's syntax seemed to lack a certain discipline.

"Who are you?" she asked.

"Fine question. Quite logical, if I may say so. My name is Stigand. *Stig-and*." He pronounced it very precisely, in order that there should be no mistakes. "I have my holt not far from this region and your complaints have been borne by the wind to my sensitive ears. It is a peaceful night, a tranquil hour—almost holy in its silence—and what a pity it is to spoil such a beautified night with wailings, unless they be wassails, if you view what I intend. Might I comprehend your own title?"

Mitz struggled with the sense of this speech which seemed to become more convoluted with each sentence. It was not that the

words were strange to her, but they seemed to turn in on each other and the overall effect was a little bewildering.

"My title? Oh, my name. Mitz."

"And you are almost young, I think?"

"Almost, yes. I'm just about to leave the earth. At least," she sighed, "I was before this human abducted me."

"Ah, this is one of the motives why my confederate, Sona, alluded that I speak with you. I have undertaken my journey from the crystal waters of my brook to inform you that there is no requirement for you to be unhappy. This human is not dangerous. I think the dog might have said something?"

"Yes, she did, but you can't trust dogs. At least, I can't trust them. . . ."

"Not in the typical course of history, that is true," replied Stigand, "but here the dog is like the pair with which it cohabits— soft as summer mud to the very medium of its soul. One considers vaguely how such sentimental creatures survive in the mainstream of human activity, but one must judge from the rich supplies of food that they do, rather."

"So, you think I can trust them all?"

"Without dubiety. The dog can be trusted. The humans can be trusted. Is it certain that we shall now entertain silence?"

"I suppose so," said Mitz.

"Good," said the otter, and turned to go; but then, seemingly as an afterthought, it asked, "My fox talk. You find it well founded in excellence?"

"You speak it very well," replied Mitz, "only . . ."

"Only?" There was a stiffness in the word.

"Only—*if only* all creatures were as good."

The otter nodded.

"This is how I think of things myself, but then otters have this precise gift. Goodbye, smallish fox."

"Goodbye, Stigand."

So Mitz spent the rest of the night in quiet contemplation of the world beyond the cage. She heard the hooting of an owl, and the rustlings of the small creatures of the grasslands. With the early morning came a mist that wound itself around the fruit trees in the garden and clung to the branches of the bushes. The day drifted in and spiders' webs trembled at its coming, the prismatic dew sparkling as the sun shone through the drops. Melloon increased in strength and dandelion seeds began to detach themselves from their hosts, floating over ground covered with windfalls. As the sun warmed some of the more violent balsams—the jumping jacks and touch-me-nots—there were minor explosions and seeds went flying through the air like pellets from a shotgun. Finches arrived to breakfast on these and other small kernels.

Mitz fell asleep just as the household began to stir, and she dreamed of her home, of her mother and father, and the dream was full of anxiety.

She was awakened by the man when he came to give her water and food. Then he sat with her for a long time, after having edged himself gradually inside the cage. He made crooning noises the whole time and slowly reached out and touched her once or twice. She watched the hand warily, but did not snap or bite. Eventually he took her up in his arms and stroked her, though she remained stiff and unyielding. It was true that his touch was sure and firm, and if she had to be handled she preferred such a grip. The man knew what he was doing.

Betsy came out into the garden a little later and when the man saw that the two animals were not going to attack each other, he allowed the dog to go up to the cage.

"How did you spend your night?" said Betsy.

"How do you think? Would you like to be locked up in a strange place?"

"No, I wouldn't, but you couldn't be in better hands. He'll probably let you go today or tomorrow."

This was the best news Mitz could have heard. She sat up immediately and said, "Are you sure? I mean, how do you know?"

"Oh, he never keeps you foxes for very long."

Mitz was relieved.

"I think I believe you," she said. "There was an otter here last night . . ."

"Oh, Sona? Or was it Stigand?"

"Stigand. Rather pompous, but friendly. He said I should trust you. Since he had nothing to gain by telling me that, except a peaceful night, I decided he was right. My parents will never believe this—me, making friends with a *dog*. They're a little prejudiced, you know. I suppose most of the older generation are. . . ."

Betsy said, "Well, you can't blame them. We've been at each other's throats for centuries—ever since men started using us for hunting foxes. Fortunately all that is changing. Some humans find the idea of hunting abominable and try to disrupt it when they see it happening. There will always be some dogs that will never accept you—but that's the way of the world."

"I think the hunts stopped in our area only because the town was built and they couldn't go charging through the streets on horseback any more."

"That may be right, but I know *they* have friends that want it all stopped. I've spoken to the dogs of these people. They go out on some days to spray things on the ground to mess up the scent."

At that point Betsy was pulled away, since they had been talking to each other for several minutes and the man never seemed sure whether or not their conversations were friendly.

There were continued efforts on the part of the humans to gain Mitz's friendship, and she finally found out the reason. As she was being fondled and stroked, a collar was slipped over her head and fastened. She was angry. What were they trying to do to her? Dogs wore collars—and, very occasionally, cats—but these were domestic beasts and the collar was to foxes the mark of a slave. She tried to get it off with her hind legs, but it was quite secure. Unlike those leather collars she had seen on dogs, the one she was wearing was quite thick in places, and had a little strip of steel poking out of the side. Betsy came over to look at her.

"Very smart," said the dog. "Such a nice shape, too."

"What are they trying to do to me?" growled Mitz. "Turn me into a dog? If they try to put a leash on this thing . . ."

"They won't," said Betsy. "It's not that kind of collar. He has a device—you know how fond humans are of their devices—that somehow connects with the collar you're wearing. When he sets you loose, he wants to be able to track you—find out where you go each day. And night."

"Spies!" Mitz snapped. "You mean they want me to lead them to my family, so they can annihilate us all in one go! Gas us, like they do the badgers sometimes. Genocide. Well, they won't get that out of me. I shall walk in the opposite direction. Lead them to the nearest dog pound . . ."

Betsy shook her head.

"No, no. You don't understand. All he wants to do is *look* at you. It's this business he's been up to all the time. He watches, scratches marks on a piece of paper, or growls into another of his devices, and just watches—nothing else. I can't explain it, but he certainly won't harm your family. He wants to find out all about foxes. My guess is, once he knows what you're all about, he'll inform his pack leaders— they're like us dogs in that respect—and there will be a greater understanding between humans and foxes. That can't be bad, can it?"

Once again, Mitz suspected Betsy of being an agent of the man and his tricks. But then, what about the otter? Why had he bothered to soothe away her qualms? The man fed the otters, of course, but she doubted they needed such handouts. They were perfectly capable of catching their own fish. In fact O-ha had told her that they were better at it than men themselves. The otters could probably feed the humans, if that was the way of things.

So, what was she to think? The collar was uncomfortable, but not unbearable. It was merely an irritant. And she was not being treated like a dog. The man, according to that great floppy beast with the sad brown eyes, merely wished to find out what foxes were doing when they were out of the sight of men. It did make a *little* sense. If she could just be sure that this was not a trick to discover where the fox hideouts were situated. Men had wiped out the wolves because they had known where to find the creatures. Men knew foxes well enough to realize that following one of them would not lead them to a whole colony, or they would have found out some way to do that before now. They knew well enough that foxes lived in family cells and that the most, the very most, you could get at one time was eight or nine. From a fox point of view, that was enough, but it certainly did not spell the destruction of the whole fox race.

"How will he get his collar back, if he lets me go?" she asked Betsy.

"Don't suppose he'll want it back. If he does, he'll just find you and take it, without any fuss. You worry too much. What you should do now is just accept it, forget about it, and once you're free and you see him sneaking around out of the corner of your eye, or catch a whiff of his scent, then just ignore him. Once he lets you go, he won't bother you much."

"There's not much privacy in this world, is there?" grumbled Mitz.

"Lord, no," said Betsy, "not where humans are concerned. They say cats are curious, but to my mind they don't come anywhere near humans in that respect. Some humans want to know anything and everything. They're the best kind, though—the kind that don't seem to fill their time destroying things. Well, it's nearly time for my meal. My advice to you is, *don't worry*. You can spend your life worrying and it's not worth it."

With that the big hound lumbered off toward the house. Mitz was left to an autumnal afternoon, full of wasps feeding from the ripe fruit and the sound of crows out in the *havnot* beyond the stream. She listened to the "Oh *ja*, oh *ja*," of the latter until she was sick of them. Captivity was getting on her nerves and she wanted to be back with her own kind.

TWENTY-FIVE

Mitz fussed over the collar for a long time, scratching at it with her hind legs and trying to force it over her head. The exercise was useless. The collar was fastened very firmly, and in the end she gave up and decided to accept it for the time being. She realized that if she took if off now, the man would only replace it anyway.

In the early part of the evening the man came out of the cottage carrying a box with a metal rod sticking out of the top. From the way he played with it and kept staring in her direction, she guessed this was the device that Betsy had told her about, for tracking her after she had been set free.

When the man had finished experimenting, the woman came out of the house and they went together down to the brook. Mitz could hear Stigand splashing about in the water with his family and she guessed the humans had gone to "look" at them. These two people were certainly very keen on watching the private lives of other animals. Later the couple collected windfalls from the orchard, and the acidy odor of fermenting fruit was in the air. Melloon was a plum time, with richly adorned skies of an evening, and full-blown smells drifting just above the ground. Even a fox looking for her first earth could spare the time to appreciate the opulence with which nature decked the world at this time. Swollen yellow pears hung succulent in the evening air, and the trees were blotched red with apples. Mitz's thoughts soon turned to hunger.

She was given another meal at which Betsy was allowed to be present. The dog chatted with her while she ate.

"He's going to let you go, now."

Mitz said, "But I don't know where I am. I feel I'm a long way from home and I'm not sure if I can find my way back again."

Betsy scratched her ear and shook her mournful head.

"Oh, he won't do that to you. He knows what's what. He'll take you to the spot where he found you and let you go there."

"Not back to the humans' house?"

"I shouldn't think so. I imagine the reason he was called to get you was because you worried them by being there. He'll let you go somewhere outside that house, but nearby. I've seen it all before."

Once it was dark, Mitz was encouraged to go into the small carrying cage again. She resisted this, not because she did not trust the man but because she hated being confined to a small space. The thought made her heart thump in her breast and she knew that as soon as she was in it she would feel like screaming. However, she eventually entered it and tried to keep calm as she was carried to the vehicle. The woman was there too, still smelling of wildflowers and honey, and she stroked Mitz's back with her fingers through the cage. The woman did not come on the journey, but Betsy did, clambering into the seat next to the man and sitting up like a human to stare out of the front window.

"Doesn't this frighten you?" said Mitz, as the vehicle roared and that funny sensation began again in her stomach.

Betsy said, "No, I like it. I suppose when you've been driven around since a puppy, you get to enjoy it. I find it quite exhilarating."

"Oh, I find it exhilarating all right," said Mitz. "It's just that I think my stomach has difficulty in keeping up with the rest of my body. It keeps dropping behind a little. You sure we're safe?"

"No, he's a terrible driver, but I wouldn't worry about it. If he ever does have an accident, we won't know anything about it. He drives so fast. If we hit anything we'll be—what do you foxes call it?—*gubbins?*—*gubbins* on the highway. We won't feel a thing. Just try to relax and enjoy the ride. You won't get many of these in your life, I can tell you."

"That's the best news I've heard today," replied Mitz, firmly.

Lights flowed on the outside of the vehicle and Mitz crouched in the bottom of the cage until the ordeal was over and everything stopped spinning. She was taken out of the back and saw that she was in the street where she had been shadowed by the ridgeback. A shudder went through her, as she remembered that he might still be around.

She called to Betsy, "There's a huge dog loose—a hound called Sabre. He'll kill me if he catches me."

"Don't worry," shouted Betsy. "We'll be following you on foot. I won't let him touch you."

"You'd protect me? Against one of your own kind?"

"Listen, don't put me in the same category as that creature. I know him. The manor dog. He's despised by everyone that knows him. Arrogant slob. Thinks he's king of the neighborhood, but I could give him a walloping."

Mitz doubted that, but she was relieved that she would have some company. Then the man barked at Betsy and the bitch told Mitz that she had been ordered to keep quiet.

"I suggest we do as he says," she added.

Mitz was then released and she immediately began walking along the street. She glanced back once, to see the man and his dog

following at a distance. At each corner she paused and studied the dark shadows thrown by the street lamps. Out of any one of these a giant beast might hurtle and fall upon her with terrible jaws.

She took the shortest route back to the scrap-yard, her heart pattering all the time, and finally reached it without being attacked. She slipped through the hole in the fence, looking back one last time, to see that the man and his dog were some distance behind. They had stopped: two dark figures in the night. She gave a farewell call to Betsy, and then traversed the tunnels through the jagged metal to her parents' earth.

After performing the rituals, she entered, to find O-ha and Camio.

They had obviously smelled her scent before she confronted them, and she was surprised to see the relief and joy in her mother's features. O-ha leapt forward and licked her daughter's face with such enthusiasm that Mitz felt she wouldn't need a wash for another season.

"You missed me then?" she said.

"Missed you?" cried Camio. "Of course we missed you. What in the world did you think?"

Mitz shrugged.

"Oh, I don't know. I thought . . . well, you were both kind to me as a cub, but . . ."

"But nothing," said O-ha. "You're our *daughter*. Where have you been? Tell us all about it."

She told them her story and they listened, fascinated.

"They let you go again?" said Camio. "That's amazing. I've never heard of that before in my life."

"Yes," she said, simply.

O-ha said, "And you have to wear that slave ring around your neck? Shall we try to gnaw it off for you?"

"Earlier on today, I would have jumped at the chance of getting rid of it," said Mitz, "but I think I owe it to Betsy to keep it on for a while. I'm certain no harm will come to us because of it. She's quite a creature, Betsy. She told me she would defend me against Sabre, if he tried anything."

"Well, that *is* a little far-fetched," said Camio. "I wonder if it's true?"

"I think it is. I'm sure it is."

Her parents looked at each other, and Mitz could see that they were doubtful, but *she* knew and that was all that mattered. Now that the welcome was over, Mitz studied the ambience of the earth and came up with the conclusion that fear was still in the air.

She asked, "Is Sabre still at large?"

Camio nodded. "We think so. It's best to remain here for a while. There are a few caches of food in the yard, so we don't need to worry about eating. Water might be a problem, but I can smell rain coming. We're more worried about your brother, A-sac. He hasn't been seen since the night you disappeared. It would be too much to hope for that he had been picked up by kindly humans. If he doesn't return soon, I suppose we shall have to suspect the worst."

So the foxes settled down for another night of waiting. During the small hours, there came the sound of raindrops hitting the metal above their heads, which grew to a thunderous drumming as the skies opened up and let fall a heavy load. Water swilled around underneath the earth, which was raised slightly on the scrap metal. Camio went out in the downpour and returned with some food, which the three of them ate in silence.

Toward dawn the rain stopped, and the ground smelled musty and dank. Camio and O-ha talked of various matters—one of which was, again, the possibility of abandoning their earth. Foxes knew their territories intimately, and very rarely (except in the case of *rangfars*) consider leaving it, but the home was a different matter. The home could be abandoned on the slightest provocation, pro-vided a new home presented no difficulty. It was unimportant because there was nothing there. Except for the rubbish in and around their earths, foxes collect nothing, not even bedding, so the home is literally a hidey-hole from the world.

They discussed various places where they might search for a new earth, and also made some suggestions to Mitz as to where she might look. Camio was still in favor of the new railway embankment.

"We'll be among the first there," he said. "We can mark any posts

in the area, to warn off others . . ." It was the same sort of discussion that would be going on in many fox homes at that time, as the parents were preparing to leave the breeding earth.

"So," said Camio to Mitz, "you'll be setting up your own home at last. I remember when you were a little fluffy brown thing with a short pointy tail . . ."

"Oh, Camio," she said, "not 'I remember when' again!"

Camio took no notice of this.

". . . you used to play with an old bone, outside in the scrap—you and A-cam. A-sac was never one much for play. I used to sit and watch you all, and wonder, was I ever like that."

"Of course you were," said O-ha. "We all were."

Camio continued. "I would watch you chasing beetles, or even bits of paper floating by in the wind. You would sneak up on one another—and on *me*—using every little bump in the ground as a vantage point. Clever little cubs, you were. I was so proud of you. Still am, of course, only you're not cubs any longer."

"Were you?" said Mitz. "Were you proud of us? You didn't seem to be. You were forever telling us off."

"Oh, I know I was a bit hard on you, when it came to discipline, but your mother let you get away with murder. I remember when her teats were sore and bleeding because you cubs wouldn't leave her alone, and she would indulge you. You were *always* hungry. I don't remember a moment when you weren't hungry. Still, those days are gone—the stalking and pouncing are for real now. You have to feed yourselves, thank goodness."

O-ha said, "You sound really *old*. I'm glad I'm not as old as you think you are."

"I don't think I'm old—I'm just a family fox reminiscing. What's the point of having all these memories if you can't talk about them once in a while?"

"Those aren't memories, Camio," said Mitz. "They're pictures you make in your head. I know there's *some* truth there, but you embellish everything. When you told us about your fight with A-magyr, you said it was over O-ha—that it was a battle to the death,

the winner take all, the prize being the favors of our mother. But when mother told us about it, it sounded very different."

Camio shifted his position, seemingly uncomfortable under O-ha's intense gaze.

"Quite right, too. What's the point of having a memory if you can't make a decent story out of it? Anyone can *remember* things. It takes a special talent to make that memory interesting to others. Why, I recall the time your mother and I . . ."

In this way they passed the night, each one of them waiting, each one hoping that the dark hours would not be interrupted by some terrible event. They knew the danger they were in, with the ridgeback still abroad. The hound was specifically out to get O-ha and her family. Every small noise outside made them start with fear. Sabre had only to get within a short distance of the scrap-yard to scent O-ha, and unless he was caught he would reach that point eventually by the process of elimination.

When the sun was well up, O-ha went out for a look around just outside the yard, but within short reach of the hole in the fence. She sniffed the air for a scent of Sabre, but could not make a decision as to whether it was clean or not. The strong scent of iron and steel was in her nostrils, a result of having spent so long in the scrap-yard, and it was difficult to get rid of that within a few moments. There was no scent, either, of her albino cub.

Sadly, she returned to the earth.

"We'll wait one more day," she said to Camio. "They *must* have caught Sabre by then. He can't roam the streets forever. Then we have to look for A-sac. He might be miles away, but we can't be sure of that. Once I know he's safe, I shan't worry any more."

"Fair enough," replied her mate. "That sounds like a sensible course of action to me."

It turned out that the decision was a timely one. The men in the scrap-yard had brought in a machine and were now busy crushing down the metal objects into small cubes. They were working slowly

through the scrap and would reach the foxes' breeding earth in two or three days' time.

The noise made by the machine was at first a little frightening to the foxes, but after a while—as with all things—they got used to it, when they realized it was not going to eat its way toward them in a hurry and that they still had a little time left.

The sun came out and dried the rain, sending clouds of steam into the pockets of scrap and along the tunnels. The foxes spent their time cleaning each other, fastidious as ever about their personal hygiene, if not their home. The time passed slowly for them.

Just as a hunter's moon was rising, however, they heard scrabbling sounds outside, in the metal tunnels. Something, someone, was out there. Suddenly a strong, familiar scent invaded the earth.

Camio sat up with a jerk.

"Oh, Menxito!" he said quietly. "It can't be . . ."

TWENTY-SIX

A-sac had left the *face* long before Sabre began terrorizing the streets, and was on his way north, toward the other side of the river. Deep in the marshes, there was an island. On this dry area there stood a mound in which the vixen mystic O-toltol lived. A-sac had been told that she had not left this place for many seasons, but remained there in the chamber-tomb of some long-dead human from which her words of wisdom traveled far and wide. He was informed that *rangfars* visited this elderly *stoad* and carried her words to *ords* who were afraid to leave their parishes, and that until recently she had had an assistant who visited the sick and lame, carrying her cures with him. Like A-konkon, O-toltol was supposed to be an herbalist and therefore able to cure many injuries and illnesses by prescribing the use of various plants. However, according to the *rangfar* from whom A-sac had gathered all this information, the assistant had recently met with a fatal accident out on the wetlands. It was A-sac's intention to offer his services to O-toltol and thus become her new assistant.

A-sac made his way to the river and then west, along the dike, until he reached the first bridge upstream from the estuary. On the way he spied a partridge in the long grasses, tracked it and killed it with his scissor jaws. He ate most of the unlucky bird on the spot, and then cached the rest under a large log before resuming his journey.

The bridge was busy with traffic, so he waited until nightfall before attempting the crossing. He hid in the deep grasses of the dike under the shadow of a huge disused river mill, its clinkered weatherboarding painted black and its gantry idle. Alongside the mill was moored a seagoing barge with rust-colored sails and a webwork of rigging, masts, and stays. The boat was also now out of use and firmly embedded in the mud, though it looked as if it might lift itself up at any moment and shake the sludge from its keel before setting sail once more.

The mill had a smell of fermented hops, mixed with the smell of ancient grain pressed into the clay floors by a million leather soles. During the evening several men came and went, some of them leaving the mill on boneless legs. A-sac waited hopefully for one of them to fall into the sludge at the edge of the river and join the barge in an endless sleep.

When all was finally still and quiet, A-sac crossed the bridge by the stone parapet, rather than using the actual roadway. By that time the tide had gone out and the river was a dribble in the center of the mud.

Now the young dog fox struck east, along the opposite dike, passing a rubbish tip which was the home of two fox families and hundreds of seagulls. As he passed the groups of seagulls, the stench of the tip in his nostrils, the birds rose and began clamoring in the

air around him. Most of the birds were juveniles, their markings still indistinct, but they were strong in flight.

"I'm not interested in you," he shouted. "Go away!"

But they refused to leave him alone. He tried to explain to them that he never attacked white creatures like themselves, because he himself was the same color: that it would be like eating his own flesh. They did not understand—or chose not to listen—and dived low over him, screeching obscenities in their own language. It was not until he was well away from the rubbish site that the last of them left him to continue his journey in peace. He traveled along the dike until morning and then struck out across the marsh, where it took him some time to acclimatize himself to the effluvia.

Out on the mud there were many wading birds, mostly dunlin, but among them were one or two avocets. A-sac stopped to study them for a while, but they glared at him and made it plain that he should be on his way. O-ha had told him a great deal about the creatures with whom he shared his world. Obviously, the idea behind mothers teaching their young about the habits of other animals and birds was to enable their cubs to hunt more efficiently. *Know your prey* was a byword amongst foxes. But A-sac found the actual knowledge stimulating from a *thinker's* point of view. He was interested in the creatures themselves and found the facts about them exciting. Each individual animal and bird had a life-style that was different enough from the others to be worth investigating as a subject in itself. For instance the wren, one of the smallest birds, ate mostly spiders and sometimes starved to death in the winter when there were few arachnids available. That was fascinating to A-sac. That such specialized feeders should exist was to him a remarkable thing. He also knew that the cock wren built several nests and showed his prospective hen all of them and let her choose her favorite, which she lined herself. In areas where there were more female than male birds, the cock wren would have several mates, setting them all up in their own nests and helping with the feeding of the young when they arrived.

It was this kind of knowledge that captivated A-sac, and he found it hard to reconcile his urge to hunt with his interest in the quarry.

The partridge he had killed had a life-style behind it that fascinated him, but this did not prevent his instincts from switching to the hunting mode when he scented or heard one and was hungry. This, too, was an aspect of himself that occupied his mind a great deal. He hoped that O-toltol would be able to discuss these matters with him in great depth, so that he could better understand the world in which he lived and the creatures who were his neighbors. Even more important, he wanted to understand himself.

A-gork, the *rangfar* who had told him about O-toltol, was an itinerant storyteller who traded what he called the Baffles of A-sop (a long-dead but very wise fox) for food. There were supposedly hundreds of these baffles, or tales, but though A-sac had been thoroughly captivated by them he had been able to get only enough spare food to purchase three. (Even so, he had had to steal the food from Camio's caches and his father had been quite angry with him for 'wasting' the stores.) The tales that A-gork had told him were now firmly embedded in his mind. These are the tales, which presuppose that humans are able to talk:

THE FOXCUB AND THE MANCHILD

A foxcub often visited an orchard at the same time as a child and after eating windfalls they would wrestle with one another in the tall grasses. During these times the foxcub would say to his playmate, When we are grown you will come hunting for me, and kill me. Never, said the manchild, for you are my friend. Many seasons later they came across each other in a field and the grown fox remained at a safe distance. The man had a gun, which he immediately pointed at the fox. Don't you recognize me? said the fox. Your old playmate? I remember you used to steal my father's apples, said the man. Ah, said the fox, if your aim is as true as your words then I am safe from harm—and he sped away without being hit.

"The moral of this story," A-gork had said, "which will cost you nothing extra, is: Never trust a man, despite childhood friendships and promises."

One hot summer's day, when Frashoon breathed down long, rocky valleys, a vixen went to drink in a beck. At that moment a hunter arrived and began drinking upstream from the fox. The vixen was too thirsty to leave, but suddenly the hunter looked up, demanding to know why the vixen was muddying the water. He began unslinging his rifle. The vixen said, How can that be, when I am drinking downstream from you? Be that as it may, said the hunter, I'm told you called me names five seasons ago, behind my back. All the while he spoke, the hunter was loading his rifle. That is impossible, said the vixen, since I am only three seasons old. In that case, it was your mother, said the hunter, and shot the poor vixen dead.

"The moral of this story is that foxes should never stay to argue with hunters, no matter what the injustice or bodily needs."

THE FOX AND THE FARMER

A farmer with a gun had found a fox earth and was waiting for the owner to emerge from or return to it. To while away the time the farmer began to sing, and the fox, who was indeed at home, devised a clever scheme to snatch the farmer's gun. The fox called from the earth, commenting on the beauty of the man's voice. Really? said the farmer, who had found out what he wished to know concerning the fox's whereabouts. No one ever told me that before. Perhaps foxes have a more musical ear than most? Undoubtedly, said the fox, but might I suggest that since you have a voice like a bird, you climb a tree and sing out over the evening hills, for the benefit of all? The man proceeded to shin up the tree, and since he had to use his hands, he left the gun on the ground. Once the man had reached a suitably high branch, the fox dashed out of the earth only to catch his neck in a snare that had been set by the farmer.

"The moral of this story is that man is too devious a creature to outwit by direct confrontation. A fox should remain silent and unseen, and rely on stealth."

These stories had greatly impressed A-sac, and the albino foxcub wanted to go out and immediately tell them to others, but he had promised A-gork that he would keep them to himself because the *rangfar*'s livelihood depended upon being able to retell his tales.

"Can't you hunt for your food?" asked A-sac.

"Ah, well that's where I'm vulnerable. I made a vow as a young fox that I would never kill another creature, so now I have to either tell my stories or starve."

This statement, too, impressed A-sac. It was a revelation to him at the time that a fox could actually make a choice between hunting and not hunting. Until then he had thought that the instinct to hunt could not be overridden, no matter what the feelings of the fox. He wondered if he himself could ever attain the strength to reject hunting.

Afterward, when he considered the matter a little more deeply, he realized that in fact the moral standpoint of A-gork was no better than that of others, since he still ate the creatures all foxes ate. He just let others do his hunting for him.

Before the *rangfar* left him, however, A-sac asked, "So you think I stand a chance of becoming O-toltol's assistant?"

The *rangfar* nodded. "Most assuredly. She asked me to be on the lookout for a young healthy fox to fetch-and-carry messages for her over the marshlands. One that was not afraid to be alone with an old vixen in a strange earth. I should think you'd be fine for the task."

"Why 'young'?" asked A-sac.

The *rangfar* looked at him strangely, and then said, "I suppose you need a bit of youth in you, to traverse those wetlands. There's not a great deal to eat out there. You need something to live on. She doesn't want a skinny old fox on his last legs—she needs a strong one."

"I expect you're right," said A-sac.

Once he was in the marshes, A-sac discovered that his search was

going to be more difficult than he had previously imagined. He had hoped that the chamber-tomb island would be visible above all other landmarks, that it would stand high on the skyline. This was not so, and on the saltings there were no highways to follow. He found himself utterly lost, and floundering in deep pits of mud. The tide began coming in and the water swirled around the creeks; before long he was marooned on a piece of ground no larger than the spread of a mature oak's roots. He tried calling, but apart from being mocked by unseen birds that navigated the waterways, he received no answer. He settled down amongst the saltwort to spend an uncomfortable night in the open.

Being out in the wetlands was eerie and frightening to a foxcub who had spent most of his life in a scrap-yard, surrounded by the *face*. He listened to Melloon winding through the reeds, and the very night sky itself seemed to have a voice that spoke to him of the vastness of the world around him. Hundreds of new kinds of scents came to his nostrils, many of them unrecognizable, and he did not know danger from safety. There was not a great deal he could do about it anyway. If some terrible fate was lurking out there amongst the creeks, it would find him unable to run. He was trapped there with his overactive imagination. His mother had told him that fox-spirits were kindly beings who would not harm him, but that did not prevent him from feeling afraid of them. And what of all the other kinds of spirits? If there were ghosts of foxes, then there were ghosts of dogs. What if one of them were to rise up out of the mud, dripping slime and gore? What if one were to crawl up from the creek now, its eyes blazing with supernatural fire and its mouth full of metal-sharp teeth? He would be helpless before it.

He lay there and shivered, his white coat visible to any creature, whether mortal or otherwise, for miles around. In the distance he could hear an irregular roaring, which was not the wind. He knew this to be the ocean, beyond the salt marshes, but since he had never seen this great expanse of water he had no real picture of it in his head and it became a frightening thing, a monster with high white jaws. Its foaming mouth stretched the whole expanse of the land, and sucked at the edge of the solid world, dragging in dirt and stones with every slavering swallow.

With morning came a kind of relief. At first he thought the ocean really was rolling across the land, but it turned out to be a dense white mist that swept over him, leaving him dripping wet. Then the sun came up and the vapor retreated, falling heavily into the now waterless creeks and swilling away.

Once again A-sac continued his journey, battling through the mud bogs. He stopped and crunched on shellfish when he grew hungry, hating the sliminess and the salty taste of the molluscs within the shells, but having no choice if he wanted to appease his hunger.

His thirst was another thing. The water was far too brackish to drink and he was almost on his last legs when he came to one of the many rotten hulls of sunken boats, which had retained rainwater in its hollows. He drank the liquid gratefully. Once he trod on a mud-skipper and swallowed the fish whole without even pausing in the shank-high sludge. The gulls often flew overhead and then dived down low, possibly hoping that he was exhausted to the point of dropping; but he snarled at them and they left, shrieking harshly at him.

Once, when crossing an island, a shadow crossed his soul and he realized he was on a *sowander*—the deathplace of another fox—and he left the spirit-stained holy ground with a shiver. It did nothing to help his sense of insecurity and vulnerability to realize that some other fox had met death on this forsaken area of land.

Around noon A-sac caught the musty scent of an old fox's marks and his heart began to lift a little. The urine marks were on gobbets of dried mud that had been piled into cairns. Some of these cairns had been partially washed away by the tides, but others, on higher ground, remained intact. He was disappointed, though, since it meant that the stories about O-toltol were not *entirely* true. She must have left her earth-grave recently in order to freshen the marking posts. Still, no doubt she did this at night and went straight back into the tomb. He entered the area with a great feeling of having accomplished his mission—thus far, at least—and followed his nose to the huge mound that was his destination.

Apart from the cairns, the island was humped in the middle with an eerie-looking dolmen, which, if it had not been for the tufted

grasses, would have been as smooth as an egg. This was no natural mound.

A-sac paused before going up to the earth-grave. The wind lifted his white fur as he studied his surroundings. It was a lonely place, isolated by the creeks full of dark sludge and inlets incised by tidal currents. Around him the somber cairns testified to an occupation of a kind, but what struck him most of all was the lack of birdlife. Not a living thing moved or sounded. Only an occasional bubble of fetid gas, belched by the mud, interrupted Melloon's sighs.

At first he could see no opening to the earth, and even when he found it, he wondered if it really was the place he had been searching for, since it looked deserted. There was no rubbish, no old bones or shells, no feathers or skins of mammals, outside the forbidding-looking entrance. If she was indeed inside, O-toltol left none of the usual foxy signs outside her strange earth.

He stuck his head inside and sniffed. Rank smells assailed his nostrils. The murk within was dismaying. He was used to the dark, of course, and his fox eyes were aware of shapes in the poorest light, but the black interior of that mound was quite frightening. Anything could be lurking inside, from ghosts to men. It was large enough to hold a man, though there was no scent of human on the stale air within.

For a while he was almost tempted to turn back. He stared over his shoulder at the hazy wastelands behind him, wondering if he would ever see his home again. For the first time since leaving he wanted to be with his parents, safe in their earth, with their comforting scents giving him a sense of security. The wetlands seemed to go on forever. The return journey would be just as bad as the walk out there, if not worse, and he was tempted to simply sit down and wail.

Then he gathered his spiritual strength together.

"This is silly," he told himself. "I came out here to do something, and I shall do it."

He put his mouth to the entrance and yelled.

"Hello! Anyone here?"

Silence.

He called again. This time there was an answer from deep within the bowels of the hummock. Still he could not enter that seemingly impenetrable darkness. He waited for a long time. Then a scent began to get stronger—the smell of a *stoad*—and finally a narrow head appeared at the hole. The eyes were small but bright. The muzzle was almost devoid of hair. The breath coming from the mouth was vile and he could see that the teeth were worn and cracked.

"What do you want?" asked the old fox.

The grating voice alarmed him a little. He took a step back.

"Are you O-toltol, the mystic vixen?" said A-sac, finally gathering up all his courage and finding his voice.

"So they tell me," came the answer, "though I've never been sure."

"What—that you are a mystic?"

"No, that I'm a vixen. I've forgotten what I am. It doesn't matter, does it?" The words were sharp and meant to intimidate.

A-sac quaked. "No, I suppose not, but your name's O-toltol—"

"Bah! Stupid cub. I could call myself Gogamagog, but that wouldn't make me a human, would it? Then again, it might . . . I shall try it some day."

"You just did," said A-sac, getting a little braver.

Her eyes narrowed even more, until they were slits.

"Smart little whitey-fur, aren't we? Where did you get the coat? Who was your mother? A seagull? Who was your father? A duck? *Cark* for me, whitey. Or *quack*. One or the other."

"I don't think . . ." he began, indignantly, but she cut him short with, "Come on in. You'll want to rest, I suppose. Lost your way, eh whitey? Bring those nasty pink eyes into my earth."

"I haven't lost my way. I came looking for you. I heard you needed an assistant. A-gork, a *rangfar* . . ."

"That old charlatan? Come on in, then. We'll talk about it inside."

She made way for him and he entered, not without some misgivings. The darkness was just as dense inside as it had looked from the daylight end of the tunnel.

TWENTY-SEVEN

Once A-sac had entered O-toltol's earth, his senses of touch and smell became stronger and he gradually became able to orientate himself. He had never been in an earth under the ground before. His home with his parents had always had light and air coming in through the holes in the scrap. This vixen's earth, dark and enclosed, was very daunting. A-sac took a pause in the first tunnel, in order to throw off the oppressive feeling of being surrounded by damp-smelling earth and stone. Even the darkness seemed moist and heavy. After a while he found he could sense his surroundings despite the blackness. He did not need his sight to be able to place his position in the earth. A certain amount of confidence returned to him.

The actual narrow tunnel into the chamber-tomb was quite short, and opened out into a stone-lined passage. This, in turn, widened into an antechamber made of solid slabs and finally into the chamber itself. He had the feeling of being pressed on all sides, and from above, by a weight of stone, this was mentally stifling, especially in the musty atmosphere of the chamber. Water dripped from the ceiling and walls, and when he brushed against a stone, it felt soft and thick with algae.

He made a coughing sound, and it echoed and caused him to jump, nervously.

"What's the matter?" snapped O-toltol.

"Nothing," replied A-sac.

There were many smells in the earth. There were the underlying scents of ancient stone, cold to the touch, and of damp lichen. Over this was an odor of old animal bones, the remains of O-toltol's hunts, no doubt, which were probably scattered over the floor. Then there was the deep, dusty smell of something within the stone casket that lay in the middle of the chamber. Finally, overpowering almost every other scent, was the stink of O-toltol herself. Her molted fur was everywhere and got into A-sac's nostrils, making him want to sneeze. For the first time in his life he became acutely aware of his own fleas, and began to scratch himself vigorously. They had been taking advantage of his nervousness and begun to assert themselves; their increased activity made A-sac realize just how low he was feeling.

There was also another smell in the chamber-tomb—a smell that aroused some primal fear: an instinctive revulsion for something he could not name, but one that triggered alarms in his subconscious. A less perceptive fox than A-sac might have suppressed these prickings after a few minutes, when it was apparent that nothing terrible was going to happen immediately, but he kept these signals alive in the back of his brain. He knew he was out of his depth. He was a young, inexperienced dog fox—a juvenile—far from home and in a strange earth. He knew there were many things in the world about which he was totally ignorant, and that some of these unseen faces of life were unpleasant, even horrific. The fact that he was in the earth of an old vixen, and should thus have little to fear, did nothing to alleviate his tension. He felt it was to his credit that he *was* aware of his innocence and inexperience, and that he did not mentally swagger through these subliminal thorns. And so he allowed what was intrinsic to keep pricking his awareness.

"Well, pinky?" said O-toltol. "What do you think of my earth?"

"Don't call me *pinky* or *whitey* or any other name like that," he said assertively. "My name is A-sac."

The vixen's breath hit him full in the face. She had moved very close and was invading his body space. He stayed where he was, however, thinking that she was trying to intimidate him and that he was not going to react.

"So, your name is A-sac? A little dog fox from the edge of the marshes. And A-gork sent you?"

"He said you needed an assistant, to carry messages. I'm quite strong and I'll grow even stronger. I know my coloring is against me—I can be seen quite easily—but that should not concern you. There are no humans out here, on the marshes. If I'm seen and chased, it will be in the *havnot* or *face*, not out here."

Her fusty breath was almost overwhelming.

"Isn't it just a *little* early for dispersal?" she said.

"No one knows I'm here. My parents sent me out to find my own earth. I'm to go back to them when I've found a place to live." That was not quite true: he had told Camio where he was coming. It would have sounded very adolescent, however, had he told her his parents knew of his whereabouts.

"Ah . . ." she said, in a dreamy kind of voice. She moved back a little, then added, "So—you came to me. You must forgive my brusqueness when you first arrived. I have to be careful. It was a kind of . . . test. I have my enemies, you see. There are those who call me witch, and many other names. They hate me because I'm different from ordinary foxes. Have you heard anything about me? That would cause you to find me—unlikeable?"

"No. I've heard you cure diseases with your knowledge of herbs. I think that's a good thing. They say you have visions, too, that have helped to avoid disasters. They say you have the welfare of all foxes at heart and that your philosophies give foxes hope, when they are in distress. . . ."

They. He had carefully said *they,* but in fact all he knew about her had come from A-gork.

"True," she said. "All true. But we mystics are too often misunderstood. We frighten other foxes—you must admit I frighten you a little—and what they don't understand, they condemn. Well, so you're here. I like that kind of faith. It shows promise. I think you might well make me a good assistant. Perhaps you might prove your worth, by going out and getting us something good to eat? Did you bring any presents with you, for your future mistress? Food isn't easy to find out here—you should have brought some with you."

"Not with me. But I will go out . . ." he said too eagerly. He had already decided that he did not wish to stay. It was not at all like he had imagined it would be. In his daydreams he had seen the vixen's earth as a dry, warm place, slightly dusty, with an atmosphere of stored knowledge about it. He had seen her as an old but gently-spoken female, willing to teach him all she knew about the mysteries of life and death; as a benign vixen with the welfare of the foxworld at heart. But he could not think that this harsh-voiced witch, carrying the faint stink of something evil about her, could teach him anything he wanted to know.

"Hmmm," she said. "Yes, you would go. . . . Later. Later. For the moment, let's just lie here and talk. I want to hear all about you. Then perhaps we'll have a little sleep and then you can hunt. Are you thirsty?"

"Yes, I am—a little."

"If you go over to the corner of the chamber, over there, you'll find a small pool of water in the hollow of the stone. It runs from the walls and collects there. Don't drink it all. Just slake your thirst. Water is very precious out here."

He did as he was told. The water tasted stagnant, but he was in no mood to argue. In any case, he had little choice if he wanted to drink. The coldness of the chamber-tomb was penetrating his bones, making him feel very tired. He realized the journey had taken a lot out of him, leaving him exhausted in body and spirit.

When he had finished he returned to the middle of the chamber, beside the long stone casket.

"What exactly is this place?" he asked her, feeling her eyes on him though he could not see them.

"This? This is a human *sowander*. In that stone box is the body of a human pack leader, but so ancient . . . seasons out of time."

"How—how do you know the corpse was a pack leader?"

"Because humans don't build elaborate graves like this for ordinary people. She, or he, must have been very important. Perhaps a magician or a priestess? A mystic, like myself? Makes an appropriate earth, don't you think?" Her voice went into its dreamy tone again. "You see, I feel the power of that corpse. Its waves flow into my own body, my own spirit. I have inherited many of its secrets. I know the dark ways of the human soul. If you think you know evil, and you have not tasted of human ghosts, sipped at the deep waters of their bloodstained history, then you are foolishly ignorant. Those early men were closer to foxes than humans are today. Their instincts, their senses, were almost as sharply primed as our own. They ran the forests under a hunter's moon, naked, strong—and their gods were the sun, the trees, the stones, the owl, the fox . . ."

He stared into the blackness and sensed the aroma of something gone beyond the stage of decay, drifting from the cracks and crevices in the stones. Around him the hewn rock, worn smooth by constantly running water, closed in, grew tighter around him. Was he already in his own grave?

"We were gods?"

"Oh yes. They prayed to us to lend them our cunning, our savage instinct for survival, our ability to make ourselves invisible."

"But," protested A-sac, "we were never allies with men. They hunted us from the very beginning—"

"That's true, little fox, but therein lies the secret of man's success. He studies his foe, borrows the traits of his enemies. Just because we were gods did not stop them from killing us. It is precisely *because* we have qualities that they admire, which makes us a prime quarry. They

have to outwit us, you see. They prayed to us, drew magic pictures of foxes on walls of rock, hunted us, killed us, dressed themselves in our skins, used our skulls for totems . . . do you see? *They tried to become foxes.* We were not the only animals that were both gods and prey, all in one. The wolf, the bear, the wildcat . . . there were many. Man is not satisfied with being just *man.* He wants to be everything, all creatures, and still remain himself. Man has unfathomable depths to his goodness and his evil, his intelligence and his ignorance—he is a dark region of wells and wishes to drink at them all."

She paused a moment and then added, "I have imbibed much of this, soaked up the spirit of what lies there in that stone box. Sometimes I think I am human."

A-sac shivered on hearing this last sentence, thinking *This fox is mad.* But then O-toltol took the ground out from under him by saying, "You will think me mad, but that is a prejudice. It is because I have insight and forbidden knowledge that I am able to speak thus."

A-sac scratched at his fleas and thought miserably of home. Why had he come to this place? To this crazy vixen, who festered in a place without light and who stank of grave-earth and the fetid fumes of tainted bones? The first chance he got, he promised himself, he would run away across the marshes and would never return. A fox that thought herself human? There was something utterly revolting about such a statement.

"Are you feeling tired? Do you wish to sleep?" asked O-toltol, softly.

"Not—not just yet. I wondered—will you teach me something about herbs? I should like to learn."

"Now?" she snapped. "Impossible. I have none around at the moment, for you to smell."

"Well, we could *talk* about them. For instance, I've heard that feverfew can cure a headache. Is that true?"

"Yes, of course it is."

A-sac asked, "Well, what does it look like? I've lived in the *face* for most of my life. I've no idea what to look for."

The vixen was quiet for a moment, and then she said, "It's a daisy, with little green leaves."

"How many petals does it have?"

"How many . . . Six, of course. Six petals. Now . . ."

"And what color are henbane flowers?—I've always wanted to know that."

"Henbane? White. The flowers are white."

A-sac nodded, thoughtfully.

"Well, there you are, you see. I've learned something already."

He had indeed learned something. He had discovered that O-toltol knew very little about herbs. O-ha—and he trusted his mother's knowledge far more than that of a scraggy vixen of the marshes—had given him a thorough education regarding herbs and their uses. He knew that the feverfew flowers had far more than six petals and that henbane had yellow blooms, not white. For some reason this vixen was lying to him.

He got up and started to walk around, feeling his way through the darkness of the chamber-tomb.

"What are you doing?" asked the vixen.

"Oh, just feeling around. It's all right, isn't it?"

"I—I suppose so. Don't touch anything. I keep some old bones in that corner over there. You mustn't touch them. . . ."

That was strange. A *tidy* fox? A-sac had never heard of such a thing. He went to the corner in question and pushed his snout close to the heap without actually disturbing it, so that she could not tell what he was doing. He sniffed. The pricking alarms he had experienced on first entering the earth began jabbing him again, much more forcefully. He touched the bones gently with his nose, running it over their contours.

They were large—too large to be the bones of any birds she might have caught on the saltings. There was a skull there, almost as large, if not the same size, as A-sac's own head . . . and a chilling thought ran through his head. Perhaps O-toltol had had more than one "assistant" in the past? Perhaps she had had many—had gone through such assistants quite quickly, in fact?

"How did your last . . . assistant die?" he asked her.

"An accident," she answered, brusquely. "The tides out here are dangerous. If you intend staying, you must be aware that these things can happen. The mud sucks things to their deaths. The water drowns them. Unpredictable currents, neap tides in the spring after an eclipse. I have heard of times when the whole marshes were beneath water."

The implication was that the young fox had drowned: that this was a common cause of death in the saltings. If so, and if these *were* the bones of a fox (or foxes), why were the bones in the tomb? The body would have been swept away, taken by the currents downstream, or back to the sea on the tide. He remembered what she had said earlier: *Food is not easy to find on the marshland.*

"I suggest we get some sleep now," she called. "You can use this patch here, by the corner of the stone box. I'll sleep over there, by the door. I like the draft. Come on."

He did as he was told.

She was guarding the door, of that there was no doubt. What he was still unsure of was *why*. There was a dreadful thought running through his mind. The only thing to do now was try to stay awake and wait for her to make the next move.

It seemed a season. His eyelids drooped and the closeness of the atmosphere worked on his exhaustion. To stop himself from sleeping he bit his lip, using the pain to keep from falling into a state from which he might never recover. All he could hear was the steady breathing of the vixen by the exit. He began to regulate his own breathing, as if he had indeed dropped off.

Nothing happened for a very long time. He could hear the water dripping from stone to stone, the beetles scrabbling in the cracks, the whisper of dainty spiders running over the slabs. He fought to stay awake, though he desperately wanted to sleep. His mind was spinning with thoughts, racing with wild ideas. Around him the stale currents of air moved lethargically, leaving any dust unmoved. The marshland earth tightened around him: he could hear the slow pressure of the stone, the force of peat. His eyelids were like heavy weights.

After what seemed like an age, he heard her stir. He heard her sliding, creeping slowly across the stone floor to where he lay. His heart began to palpitate. There was the acrid scent of his own fear in his nostrils. He pressed his throat against his paws, so that it was not exposed. If she tried to turn him over, he would know.

For a while she lay in front of him, breathing softly, that fetid breath going up his own nostrils. Then she went around to his side, pushed her nose gently under his chin, and tried to nudge him over without waking him. His heart raced and his mind spun wildly as he realized what he must do. But he was a young fox, unaccustomed to fighting, except in fun with his brother and sister. His courage almost failed him. Then an idea came to him. He had to think of his adversary as a rabbit, or a bird, rather than another fox.

He turned suddenly and gripped O-toltol by the throat with his teeth. She screamed, lashing her body, and then thrashed around heavily to get him to release his hold, but he hung on. The pair of them rolled about on the stone floor as she got her hind legs up and began raking his stomach with her claws. Still he maintained his hold, knowing that if he let go she would be on him in an instant. He brought his own hind legs into play, as the pain began to sear through him.

Hold on, he told himself. *I must hold on!*

She began to snake herself toward the exit, her voice still at high pitch. His own claws scraped against the stonework as he fought to anchor himself. Her mouth began snapping against air.

"Let—me—go," she gargled.

He ignored the plea.

Then she went quite still, as if dead, but he knew this was a trick. Nevertheless he used her inertia to get a firmer grip and with his scissor jaws he buried his teeth deeper into her throat, searching for the jugular. Her breath was coming out in short gasps now and as he tore at the flesh, without releasing his grip, he could smell the blood. It dripped from her mouth onto the floor.

She made a last desperate effort to flip herself over onto her feet again, but the young fox was determined that she would not get away. He swung her around so that she swept the floor, and her back struck the corner of the sarcophagus. Though the blow was not hard

enough to break her back, it must have pained her considerably and she ceased her struggles at last.

When he was sure she was finished, he let go and sprang onto the top of the stone coffin. There was blood everywhere now: on his coat, in small pools on the stone floor, and over the sarcophagus. He waited, in case she still had some fight left in her, but all he could hear were bubbling breaths. He could smell the warm sweetness of life draining from her body.

He remained on the top of the coffin, waiting.

Despite the darkness, he could see her eyes staring up at him accusingly. That was strange, because he could see no other part of her nor could he see anything else in the tomb. The eyes were glowing like charcoal embers.

The eyes said: *Why did you do that?*

"You were going to kill me," he replied aloud to the whispers he heard in his head. "I know you were going to kill me. Those are the bones of young foxes in the corner. You kill and eat your own kind. You, you're a *cannibal*. I think you get *rangfars* like A-gork to send you young foxes. You tasted the blood of your own kind, and found you liked it—don't try to deny it. Somehow your twisted mind has become addicted to foxblood."

You don't know that, the eyes said, *you're just guessing. What if you're wrong? You've murdered a vixen, simply because you were afraid of this place, these strange odors. They all went to your head. You're a wicked fox. You must breathe life back into my body.*

"I can't help you any more, even if I wanted to. You're a disgusting creature. Those bones in the corner—they're from youngsters like me, aren't they?"

You foolish creature. You have too much imagination. Those bones are ancient—from animals killed by the foxclan hunter who is buried in this tomb. They are foxes from just after the Firstdark. Nothing to do with me. They are the remains of man's quarry.

He heard her shudder: a convulsion. She was nearing her end. How many young foxes she had killed would remain a mystery to A-sac, but he was sure, absolutely certain, that she had intended to kill *him*. That was justification enough for what he had done to her.

A horrible thing, to be sure, but he was not to blame. If it had not been her lying on the floor, kicking out the last few wisps of mortality, it would have been him.

"You're lying about the bones. You have only yourself to blame," he said, trying to convince them both with the same argument.

You will go to the Unplace, said the eyes.

"No, why should I? I was just protecting myself. But I'll try to ensure you don't either, though you deserve it. I'll perform the last rites. . . ."

There was a long, withering sigh from the floor, and then all was quiet. He descended from his perch and nudged the body. It was still. He licked the blood from his own coat and then went to the corner, where the bones were piled. Sifting through them with his muzzle, he found lots of smaller bones now that he had not detected before when he was only able to touch them gently. So she had eaten birds. But that was no proof of anything, since she could not possibly have lived on small foxes the *whole* time. The larger bones—he was *sure* they were not ancient. They were new bones.

"She was lying," he shouted, the sound echoing through the chamber tomb. "I know she was lying. She *ate* foxes."

He went to the body and performed the rituals around it. Then he went back to the heap of bones and lifted up one of the skulls between his jaws. He dragged it through the antechamber, along the passage, and out into the open air. It was night now. He studied the skull under the light of the moon. It was of a fox, or a small dog. It looked old, smelled old, certainly—but not *ancient*. At the most—he said to himself—at the most it was only a few seasons old. Those hunters, they had lived seasons out of time ago—she had said so. It was definitely not that old. . . .

Anyway, he thought, what was done was done. He could not bring her back to life again. What had she been doing anyway, nudging him over? And why didn't she know about the herbs he had mentioned? Of course, if she had guessed he was testing her, then she might have been contrary enough to give the wrong answers on purpose, out of spite. She was that sort of fox. But—no, no, that was . . .

A-sac was very unhappy. He wanted to be home. He could not think why he had ever left it in the first place. To become a mystic? How stupid of him. That was the last thing he wanted now. To have to live in some damp human tomb out on the marshes, living on molluscs and fish, drinking stagnant water? No. Never.

He went back into the tomb and drank some more of the water. Then he stood over the body of the vixen again. Had it moved? Surely it had not been in that position when he left it? Perhaps he was going mad? The act of killing one of his own kind had turned his brain. That, and the loneliness of the wasteland, where even the birds had voices like ghouls.

Suddenly, he wrenched at her tail with his jaws, the fur coming out and getting between his teeth.

"You couldn't even admit it when you died!" he shrieked. "You couldn't even do *that*. Now I'll never know. All my life I'll be haunted by you, thinking—thinking that just perhaps you were telling the truth, even though I know you weren't. You—" He could not think of a word terrible enough for her, and stale hotness entered his mouth, almost choking him.

In the end, she had won.

TWENTY-EIGHT

Not wishing to leave O-toltol's mortal remains entombed with a human hunter, A-sac dragged the body out through the passage and into the open air. There, he had to perform the death rituals all over again, and found it difficult to mark the spongy turf in the way that was required. When he had finished, he filled in the entrance to the earth-tomb. He was not sure why he did this, but it seemed appropriate. Then he set out into the night, his head buzzing with bloodflies.

At first he tried following the firmer ground and avoiding the deep gullies full of sucking mud that slowed him down so much. He found some soft-shelled crabs, which he ate whole, to sustain him on his journey. However, though he traveled all night he seemed to get no nearer to the edge of the marshes. In fact he had the feeling that he was going deeper into the saltings, and indeed when the morning came he found himself on a high, grassy sea wall.

He smelled the strong salty spray of the ocean and watched the rollers crashing against the land's defenses that kept this mighty body of water at bay. Spume the color of his own fur frothed at the base of the dike. Here, at least, was something stronger than humans. They had made attempts at containing the ocean, but A-sac realized—looking at the vast expanse of thundering water, this seascape that built mountains out of itself and threw them relentlessly at the land—that there must be times when the sea broke through and engulfed all in its path.

A-sac was still in a somewhat mesmerized state. Part of this was due to hunger, but much of it had its origins in the act he had committed the previous night. He still had the taste of blood in his mouth, which would not be washed away, even by drinking salt water. His head swam with sounds, and strange scents assailed his nostrils. He seemed to be viewing the world through a red mist; and once or twice during the night, frightening hallucinations had swept by at the borders of his vision. He knew these were not real, but they filled him with terror just the same. The daylight had brought no relief.

Now, seeing this immense watery giant before him, which wanted no borders, he suddenly felt a profound love for his ancestor, the firstfox A-O. This was A-O, kissing the base of the sky with liquid lips. These towering waves with the white foaming crests were A-O's muscles rippling. This thunderous roar was A-O's voice.

"A-O!" he screamed into the crashing wind. "A-O! I am your servant! I am your fox! Command me!"

His head was a whirlpool, a maelstrom of love for his ancient parent. And A-O thundered to him from out of the storm-rolled ocean. The voice was distorted, but he understood the words. They said that A-sac had killed another fox—a *bad* fox. A-sac was A-O's chosen assassin, to do his-her bidding and rid the world of evil. A beginning had been made. A-sac had been *commanded* by A-O in his dreams, and the white fox had executed the witch. Now there were more tasks to perform. Greater deeds.

"What must I do, A-O?" he shouted. "How can I serve?"

And the wind brought the name to him. And the name was one feared by all the Trinity foxes. It was the name of a giant. A-sac was instructed by the waves to destroy this giant.

"I am your servant, A-O," cried the white fox. "I must do your bidding. I am not afraid. You will protect me." After watching the white-topped waves for some time, he turned and traveled south along the sea wall. He was aware that the air was full of birds, but he had not the strength of mind to concentrate on anything but where his next paw would fall. The grasses on the top of the sea wall curled over the pathway, and he was effectively traveling through an endless tunnel, hidden from the outside world.

At one point he heard the voice of a dog and the sound of a human barking somewhere ahead, and he hid in a concrete hut set into the sea wall, which had slits for windows. The place smelled of human excrement, having been used as a toilet since it had been abandoned, and when he left A-sac vomited the soft-shelled crabs he had eaten earlier. His head spun again after this and he had to stop and rest, lying in the grass and chewing at a few blades, to get his strength back. The gulls came down and peered at him from a safe distance, but did not jeer the way those on the rubbish tip had done. They walked around him, cocking their heads on one side, as if studying his attitude and sympathizing.

When he felt able, he got back onto his feet and continued through the curved-grass tunnel. He finally emerged on the north bank of the river, in an area of land that was clearly *havnot*, but that did not have the appearance of farmland. It was a tufted, grassy area where huge concrete blocks stood like single walls here and there, and great sheets of metal were propped up by posts. Some of the concrete blocks were pitted, as if they had been struck by a giant iron fist. The metal sheets had jagged holes punched through them. The whole area was fenced off and had a gate guarded by men all wearing clothes of the same cut. They had flat black hats on their heads and carried guns. Apart from these men, the large expanse of land seemed deserted.

A-sac was desperately in need of sleep and decided to slip behind one of the metal sheets, out of the way of Melloon, and get a proper rest. He found a comfortable spot and almost immediately dropped off.

He was awakened by a noise like the world exploding, and his head rang hideously in tune with the strong vibrations of the metal sheet. Just above his head, a new hole had appeared in the steel plate, frayed outward along its edge. The hole was quite round.

Shaken, his head clanging, he staggered away from the place, unable to orientate himself properly. There was a second, distant explosion a few moments later and the metal plate rang again, this time not so loud. Another hole was visible. From somewhere on the *havnot*, on the back of Melloon, came the acrid smell that normally followed gunfire. It was an odor the knowledge of which is deeply buried in the racial consciousness of all foxes, and though A-sac had not experienced it before, he knew instinctively that this was the smell his father had warned him about. He knew that there were men in the region who must be avoided at all costs. Judging by the denseness of the odor, A-sac realized that it had come from a very large weapon. A-sac could have pushed his head through one of the holes in the metal sheet without touching the sides. Who on earth, he wondered, would they hunt with such a giant gun? Were there creatures in the world with skins as thick as metal planks? If so, they must be the size of houses.

He walked to the fence around the perimeter of the area and just as he found a hole in it, the giant gun boomed again. The ground shook and the chain-link fence rattled. A-sac slipped through the hole, skipped under some unrolled barbed wire, and found himself on a road. For a while he traveled on the tarmac, but when a vehicle whipped by him, missing him by a hair, he took to the ditch. He had no idea where he was going, but guessed that it was in the direction of the *face* since he was traveling west. He was still on the wrong side of the river, but that was not so important as getting away from the thunderous gunfire.

To the south of the road lay the river itself, and to the north, the marshes, and soon the road swept round and over a hard on the river mud with a ford in the middle.

The tide was coming in and A-sac knew that if he did not get across soon, he would either have to walk to the bridge or wait many hours for the ebb again. The bridge, he guessed, was a long way off and there were few places nearby to hide for a nap. He felt ragged and worn, his head still buzzing and his stomach churning. He had one thought in mind now: to destroy the giant hound. After that he could return to his parents in the scrap-yard.

He walked over the hard, splashed through the cold water and up onto the other side. The road sloped up to a gap in the dike, but A-sac ignored this, to travel along the edge of the river. The tide kept pace with him, swirling in and filling the deeper indentations in the mud first of all, then assuming a more placid face but still steadily moving and rising.

When he reached a certain point, he cut inland, crossing a short stretch of *havnot* to the edge of town. It was here that a rabbit panicked and ran through the corn stubble; A-sac gave chase, and despite his feeling of ill health he overtook the rabbit and was soon appeasing his hunger. After that his legs felt more steady and he was able to continue the journey without feeling as if he was about to keel over at any time.

There was a long row of sweet chestnut trees, just before the *face*, and A-sac climbed one of these to the consternation of a squirrel who jumped from branch to branch squeaking, *"Posso fare qualcosa per Lei? Posso fare qualcosa per Lei? Torni fra uno giorni, eh?"*

A-sac took no notice of the grey squirrel, but lay on a large bough until the meal of rabbit had settled a little in his stomach.

Just when he was ready to move, some human children came to play around the base of the trees. The squirrel was able to skip from one chestnut tree to the other, since the top branches were almost touching, but A-sac was trapped until the children went away. Then he climbed down and entered the *face* through an alley. He found himself in a quiet residential area where only one or two houses had been occupied, and the rest were still being built though they were almost finished. The street was still caked with builder's mud, and there were empty cement bags lying in the gutter. The front gardens of the houses, even the inhabited ones, were like badly plowed fields.

A-sac followed the crescent-shaped street around to a better road, hoping to find a familiar landmark. He stayed close to the buildings, as his mother had taught him, and tried to blend in with his surroundings. Eventually he came to the center of the new town, which though not yet completely inhabited was better established than the fringes. More than half the shops in the main square were now open for business, and there were quite a few people hurrying through the precincts.

A-sac dropped back and went down an unfamiliar alley. It was only when he reached the end that he could see it was blocked by a high wall: he was in a cul-de-sac. He turned, to brave the peopled streets once again, only to find the other end of the alley also blocked. This time the barrier was animate: a huge dog.

The monstrous creature moved forward, crouching low, fangs bared to the gums.

A voice in A-sac's head cried, *"This is the one!"*

A-sac waited, and when the giant beast was within attack distance, the little fox said, "I've been looking for you."

The dog paused and looked confused.

A-sac sprang for the throat of his enemy. The ferociousness of the attack took his opponent completely by surprise. . . .

Since they had heard nothing for several days, Camio decided to reconnoiter the area. Mitz and O-ha were asleep so he left the earth quietly and worked his way through the elaborate system of tunnels that the foxes had discovered under the mountain of scrap. Here and there were open pockets, like caverns, but for the most part the channels were narrow enough to allow passage only to creatures no bigger than cats or foxes. On reaching the edge, Camio spent a long time just waiting and listening, sniffing the air, making absolutely certain that no danger lay behind the immediate surrounds of the scrap-yard. One or two pigeons fluttered down onto the rooftops beyond the scrap-yard, and of course there were sparrows bickering and battling everywhere, but not much other movement. There were few humans about, since it was early morning and not many had risen from their beds.

He went cautiously out into the *face* and found the streets remarkably clear of other animals. That could have meant that Sabre had been caught by his owners, but quietly and without any fuss, so that no one knew he had gone. Or it could have meant that he was still out there somewhere and all the other creatures were still in hiding. There were one or two cats around, but it was no use asking them. Even if they spoke fox they would not necessarily tell him the truth. They were great ones for posing enigmas too, giving convoluted or ambiguous answers and leaving the recipient to try to work it out.

Camio did try one dog, a nervous terrier smaller than himself, and received the answer, "O horror! O horror!" before the dog ran away; this left him more puzzled than he had been before. He guessed that the ridgeback was just as terrible to smaller dogs as he was to foxes, and that the question had stirred fear in the terrier's heart.

Someone had left a black rubbish bag by a door and Camio tore this open to find some scraps inside. If he could feed himself out here, there would be more for the other two back at the yard.

When the sun was beginning to climb the wall of the sky and more people were in the streets, Camio felt it was time either to return to the earth or to find another way of searching the area. He was crouched by a rosebush in a garden when he heard a sound with which he was reasonably familiar. It was the deliberate ringing of a bell, accompanied by a gruff barking. A vehicle was moving slowly along the road: an open truck with junk in the back.

Camio waited until the truck was alongside the garden in which he was hiding and then he ran out and jumped into the back. There he found some old coats which he crept underneath. There were many smells wafting from the junk that he knew would mask his own scent, so that he could travel the streets in safety. However, it meant that he himself could not use his nose but had to rely on his poor eyesight to scan the streets for signs of the ridgeback.

From time to time the vehicle stopped and something was tossed into the back. The swarthy human in charge of the truck only dropped the tailgate and began moving the junk around when someone had given him a large item. By the time Camio had toured several streets he realized that he was getting nowhere. He left the pile of rags and jumped down into the street. A human mouth dropped open and some barking ensued but Camio knew he would not be attacked by the man. He trotted off, down an alley.

After a fruitless period of time, Camio began to make his way back to the earth. He was naturally still very cautious and as he got closer to home, he was aware of a figure at the end of a street. He recognized her scent instantly. It was Mitz. He walked up to her.

"What are you doing out?" he cried.

"I was worried about you. I woke up from being asleep and O-ha had gone too. I got lonely."

"Your mother's probably still in the scrap-yard, looking for a cache of food. Come on, let's get back. That dog . . ." suddenly, as if his words had conjured his enemy into being, he caught the whiff of a scent. He saw Mitz stiffen and realized that she had too.

"He's around here somewhere," she whispered.

The two foxes moved off the street and melted away into the shadows. They were about two roads from the scrap-yard. Camio led the way behind an old fence, by some vegetable allotments. They worked their way through the grasses to a hole in the fence, some thirty yards from where they had first met. Camio peered out through the hole, sniffing the air. It still had that faint scent of the ridgehound.

"We'd better make a dash for it," he told Mitz. "You go first. Head for that narrow street over there, and follow it through to the scrap-yard. You have two corners to pass. *Don't* look down the side streets. Don't worry about what's behind the corners. Just run for all you're worth. I'll be right behind you."

She did as she was told, streaking over the main road. Camio was right behind her. They reached the first corner without incident. It was when they passed the second that they knew he was behind them.

A car came around the corner and passed between the two foxes. *Hit the dog!* thought Camio. *Please hit the dog!*

But his prayers went unanswered, because a moment later a yell came from just behind him.

"I know you foxes. I know both of you." His strong body odor was in the air. "You're dead! I'm going to gut you, one at a time—rip open your bellies and let the insides out."

"Keep running!" shouted Camio.

The dog was trying to frighten them. A scared animal will often freeze in its tracks. Camio's body was tingling with fear. He could almost feel the hot breath of the beast on his hindquarters. His head was jangling with the terror of being torn limb from limb.

"You—know—you're dead, fox. You can—feel my teeth at your—throat. Blood spurting—over the ground. Windpipe bubbling, gasping—gasping for that—that *final* breath—"

The sound of feet on the road. An elderly human stood like a statue, shopping bag in hand, gawking. Two human children on wheeled boards, unaware of the drama, had their eyes on their task. Mitz almost bowled one over as she ran between them. There were squeals in the foxes' wake.

None of this had slowed the ridgeback.

"This—is—it—fox. Time. Time to die."

The dog was right. A few more steps and he would have one of them. It was obvious to Camio that they were not going to make the scrap-yard in time. One of them would be caught. He wondered whether to turn and face the dog now, but as always there was a faint hope in his chest that something might turn up, something might . . .

Suddenly, a blur of brown and white flashed behind the running fox. Out of the corner of his eye he caught sight of a huge mound of hair; his nose snatched at the smell of a strange dog; his ears captured the sounds of heavy breathing. What was this?

Camio heard the angry shout, "Out of the way! Out of the way you stupid . . ."

The foxes kept going, but just before the yard Camio glanced over his shoulder. What he saw pulled him up short. Mitz had stopped to get her breath too. Both foxes' nerves were taut, their muscles like tight springs ready for instant release, for the leap into the junk and the safety of its labyrinth of tunnels.

Standing in the middle of the street, barring the ridgeback's path, was another giant dog. This second dog was slightly smaller than the hound from the Unplace, but more solid-looking.

"It's Betsy," said Mitz in excitement. "You know, that dog I told you about? And there's the man!"

"You stupid bitch!" screamed the ridgehound, his anger making the hair on his back bristle. "They'll get away. What are you? A fox-lover? Fox-lover bitch?"

A human stepped onto the street. He moved toward the ridgeback who was still screaming at Betsy. The St. Bernard stayed where she was, looking bulky and immovable. The foxes heard her say, "I'm waiting for an insult. I *am* a bitch, though I suppose you've seen so few of us in your time you don't recognize one. Never been with one of us, I suppose? Can't imagine any of us wanting you."

"So that's it," snarled Sabre, "a frustrated bitch in season. I'll gut you . . ."

Betsy glanced behind at Camio and Mitz, and then, turning back, nodded.

"I see. I *am* sorry to hear that."

"You will be. You will be."

But by this time the man was closing in on the ridgeback. He held a stick in front of him like a bar, one hand on each end of it. He held it horizontally, as if offering the middle of it for the hound to bite. Camio had seen this method of keeping a dog at bay back home and it always worked. Humans familiar with animal ways, like this man, knew that using a stick like a club does not work on a dog. Dogs can avoid the swings, and duck underneath. However, a dog has certain predictable ways, especially in an attack mode. They go for the part of their victim that is closest to them, in this case the stick extended like a bar. They see the figure as a whole, not as individual parts, and to them the stick is as much part of the man as his arm or leg. In savaging the stick the dog believes he is biting the man.

Sabre leapt forward and gripped the thick pole in his massive jaws, tearing at it. Bits of chewed wood fell to the ground.

The man barked: a firm clear bark. Camio could hear the confidence, the absolute lack of fear in that voice. It was a stern command and a warning. The command was repeated. Sabre stopped attacking the pole.

No doubt he was coming to his senses and realizing his crime: that if he actually inflicted a serious wound on this human, he was in danger of taking a one-way trip to the man in the white coat. The sentence would be death.

The ridgeback ran off, away from the scene.

Betsy scratched behind her ear with her hind leg, a sure sign to Camio that she had been scared. Dogs were like foxes in that their nervousness about an event came out in some casual activity afterward, like fussing over their fleas. He wanted to go up and thank the bitch for helping them escape, but it would have been an unnatural action, and instead he nosed Mitz toward the scrap-yard and followed her in.

She said, "Good old Betsy. Did you see that? She's got courage, that dog."

"She's very brave," agreed Camio.

"They were following *me*," said Mitz proudly. "They were tracking me by my collar. Now you see why I didn't want you to gnaw it off?"

"Indeed I do," said Camio, gravely.

O-ha was waiting for them back in the earth, frantic about the fact that Mitz was missing. She gave her daughter a scolding, after which there was a cooling-off period for all concerned. Then they recounted the story to her.

Reports came to them later of another fox killed in the *face* just a few hours earlier, though the newsbearers were not certain whether the big dog had been responsible for this, or whether it was just another road death. It was true that many more foxes lost their lives to traffic on the roads than were killed by dogs—even by dedicated fox murderers like Sabre—but somehow the thought of a giant beast systematically hunting them down in their own parish was much more terrible. It seemed that nowhere was safe, not even one's own earth. And while the hound was running loose, the foxes could do no real hunting, nor any gathering of discarded human fodder outside restaurants. It was too dangerous to be out on the streets at *any* hour of the day or night. So caches close to their earth were used, and then marked when empty. But these stored food supplies were beginning to run out.

"We'll give them one more day to catch him," said Camio, "and then I have to go out again, to hunt. I'm sick of being trapped in this place. Today was a bad experience, but we've got to learn to live again. To evade danger, rather than sit here, hiding from it."

O-ha said, "Hasn't today taught you anything?"

"Yes," he replied, "today has taught me to be more cautious. Today I ran when I should have sneaked, over the rooftops, under the fences. I'll be more careful in the future."

She nodded. "You're right, I suppose. We can't stay in here forever."

Mitz said nothing.

Later that day she had a strange experience, which she recognized because of her mother's tales. A fox came to the earth, standing off from it, and remained there for some time, waiting. Mitz first thought of waking her mother, who was asleep at the time, but then she changed her mind. O-ha would have wanted to go with the fox-spirit. Mitz knew that her brother was dead and that the creature with the pure white flame over its head was waiting to lead someone to the corpse. She also knew that her mother would want to see her cub have his last rites, and would be likely to die in the attempt to make that possible.

The streets were still being patrolled by a killer. Hunting for food was an essential task, and Mitz saw the need for them to do that. But seeing that the dead were sent peacefully onward, toward their destination, was to her mind a luxury that could be foregone in times of emergency.

She did not want to lose one of her parents now. They were all she had left, especially since that insubstantial-looking creature out there had brought a message that needed no words.

The fox-spirit stayed for some time, and all the while its shape was gradually diminishing, pieces drifting from it like smoke from a dampened fire on a still day. After a while, and before Camio or O-ha awakened, there were nothing but threads of mist hanging in the air. Then these too were gone.

Then Mitz herself fell asleep.

All three foxes were awakened by a sound outside the earth. Since the wind in the tunnels of scrap could not be trusted for an instant scent, they had to wait in trepidation until some recognizable signal was given to them. Mitz's heart was pounding. Then the smell was with them. It was a fox, and it was coming through the scrap-metal tunnel. Camio whispered the name of a legendary giant.

Mitz sniffed the scent of this creature and was overjoyed: her brother had returned. Although she had not got on well with her siblings while they had all been living together, she now felt a great fondness for them both. Her brother was back! The thought made her want to race around in circles, chasing her tail. However, she had to wait patiently, in the back of the earth, confined as she was to a small area.

She saw Camio and O-ha exchange glances. There was happiness in their eyes too. Another of their cubs had managed to get back to them safely.

There was a scrabbling at the door—the rituals—and then a red-muzzled face poked through. The lost one had returned from the dead.

A-cam said, "I'm *home* . . ."

He looked extremely healthy. They covered him with licks and nips, and groaned at the stump where his tail used to be, though he assured them he was getting used to balancing himself without it. He then informed them all, quite proudly, that he had set up his own home north of the river, beyond the marshes.

"I live with my mate and her sister—but I'll tell you all about them in a moment. Let me just say that my name is A-salla now, but I expect it'll take a bit of time getting used to that. We'd better keep to my old name for the time being, otherwise we'll all get confused. Mitz! Why are you wearing a collar?"

"Later," said Mitz. "Let's hear your story first."

"Where's A-sac?"

Camio said, "Still out, looking for his earth somewhere."

"Oh," said A-cam, and Mitz could see by his expression that he had caught the undercurrent of concern in Camio's reply. He said nothing more on the subject.

"So, you won't be living with us any more?" said O-ha. "You'll be staying with these—vixens?"

There was a faint note of jealousy in O-ha's tone, which Mitz knew her mother had tried to conceal. She wondered at this, since it was inevitable that her cubs, especially the males, would leave the earth. In fact her mother had encouraged them to look for their own homes. Now that the dispersal was fact, and not just something to be talked about, Mitz saw that O-ha was desperately unhappy about losing them. And the thought that A-cam had already found himself a vixen—perhaps *two* vixens—obviously cut deeply into some maternal emotion that Mitz had yet to experience. However, A-cam had not noticed the edge to his mother's voice, and continued to babble about "reaching adulthood at last."

He then told them the story of his adventures, from the point where the car driver had picked him up off the road outside the manor, and had driven him away from his sister.

PART SIX

THE TIME OF THE OF THE DISPERSAL

TWENTY-NINE

Inside the boot of the car it was dark. Although he was lying on something soft, A-cam felt himself being bumped and tossed, and his tail-stub was extremely painful. There was still blood leaking from it. He reflected miserably on his present state. He was a captive, he was probably bleeding to death, and he was alone. It was extremely distressing for a young fox to whom a little earlier the world had seemed a bright, promising place, but he was determined that he would not go down easily. Camio had always taught him to fight until the last ebb of his strength, and O-ha had more grit than a dozen other animals. His parents would not approve of him whining about his condition while doing nothing to improve it.

He set to work trying to gnaw his way out of the boot, starting with the fabric liner.

He was just starting to make good progress when the feeling of motion ceased abruptly; and then, after some bangs that rocked the car, the prison door was flung open. The man with the thick gloves reached inside and grabbed him, and again A-cam tried to bite his attacker.

He was then carried through a door and into a room full of humans holding other animals, mostly dogs and cats. Pandemonium ensued. Humans started barking at the tops of their voices; dogs were shouting and straining at leashes; cats were crying and spitting, their fur on end. One small terrier was the most vocal, yelling, "Let me get at him! It's a fox. Let me just . . ." The rest of the words were choked off by an alarmed owner who jerked at his head. A white rabbit, its eyes bugging out of its head, had shrunk to the back of its box and was trying to bury itself in the plywood paneling. An elderly budgerigar fell off its perch and lay still on the sandpaper, either feigning a heart attack, or genuinely scared to death. A boxer dog, whose owner had immediately turned its face to a corner and was holding it there, was crying, "What is it? I can't see. Who is it?" A-cam was hurried out again and around to the rear of the building. Then the man opened another door and took A-cam into a room where another human was waiting: a woman wearing a white coat. Without any regard for his dignity, he was stretched out on a table and his rear end inspected and prodded.

"Let me bleed to death in peace," he yelled.

They growled back at him in strangely sympathetic voices.

The smells in the room were appalling. A-cam had never in his life experienced such sharp unpleasant odors and he began to wonder whether he was indeed already dead, and in the Unplace. He was trembling from nose to tail—or to where his tail used to be—and to his consternation they began to run their hands through his fur, the growls softer and even less alarming. Surely they were trying to lull him into a state of complacency before blowing his brains out? He could think of no other explanation for their bizarre behavior.

White fluff was applied to his wound, followed swiftly by a stinging sensation. The soothing tones from his captors continued the whole while. Finally, some sweet-smelling paste was applied to the injury and then he was held tightly while the two humans barked at each other.

A little while later he found himself in the back of the car again and the sense of motion returned. This time the journey was a much longer one. The pain in his rear had dulled somewhat and he was able to fall asleep. When he woke, the vehicle was still moving and he felt sick. He urinated quietly into the bedding and then concentrated on his sickness. Once he had vomited, he felt much better. He was able to gnaw away a bit more of the boot lining after that.

The car stopped, the boot was flung open again.

The daylight hurt his eyes, but he sat up and sniffed. Country smells hit his nostrils, overpowering the petrol and oil. The human staggered back, holding his nose. Then he returned and gingerly lifted A-cam out and placed him on some grass. The blanket and the remains of the boot lining were then removed and flung into a ditch. As A-cam staggered away, the car door slammed again and the vehicle roared away.

He was alone again.

Still very unsteady on his feet, the little fox made his way across some *havnot* to a spinney on the far side of a field of shire horses. There he lay down in the fallen leaves to recover his strength, allowing other leaves to float down upon him. In the meantime, he chewed grass.

Night came and the leaves continued to cover his body. He could smell chestnuts all about him and only had to nose around a little to find some. He crunched them and swallowed. They tasted good. He staggered to his feet and searched the ground, finding many more. Soon he had taken the edge off his hunger.

A-cam inspected his tail-stub as well as he was able. He licked at the ointment the woman in white had smeared on it. It tasted good, and the pain was now bearable. He was going to live. But as he tried to walk around, he found that his balance had been impaired. His tail had obviously had a use that he had not considered until its loss. The best he could manage was a lopsided stagger for a while. He hoped it would not take long to adapt.

The next thing was to find some water. He sniffed the air and then followed his nose around the copse, licking puddles from root hollows and the bowls in malformed trunks. The area was one of those overgrown deciduous woodland remnants that foxes often talked about but few had seen. It was a delightfully dark and dank-smelling place, with rotten logs, balls of ants, and thousands of woodlice. There were tree fungi low enough to gobble while still standing on the ground, and edible toadstools around the base of the trees. Pigeons made a racket in the treetops, when he passed beneath a roosting bough, but apart from that it was a quiet place—not *silent* like the new conifer forests—quiet, soft, mossy, with a spongy humus for a floor and lots of small holes that probably held interesting meals.

He had absolutely no idea where he was.

The humans, though they had been kind to him (he could see that now), had dumped him far from home. No doubt their intentions had been good. They had found a wild creature and naturally thought it had come from the wilds. Therefore they had returned it to the wilderness, not realizing that he was a town fox, born and bred.

So where did he go from here?

The thing to do first was rest, and concentrate on becoming used to having no tail.

He spent the whole of the next day in the wood. The owners of the horses came, took them away for the day (allowing A-cam to drink at their field trough in comfort), and then brought them back in the evening. A party of human walkers went through the copse. They caught a glimpse of him lying amongst the leaves and stopped to twitter to each other, pointing at him as if he was not aware of their presence. Then they tiptoed away.

Evening came and he was back on his feet. He took a quick drink at the trough while the horses munched in the far corner of their field, and then set off. At the corner of the wood a partridge whirred out of hiding, its wings almost swiveling in their sockets. A-cam was too slow to catch this bird, but at the bottom of the hill on which the copse stood, there was a dairy farm. He crept under a fence and found an area where chickens roamed. The hen's scattered at his approach and he was just about to chase them, wondering which one looked the fattest, when he discovered some eggs in the grass. Still feeling weak, he settled for the eggs, which was just as well because a human came out not long after and A-cam only just managed to slip back under the fence before a dog was released.

He struck out across the countryside, often faltering because of his dizziness and lack of balance. Eventually he reached a river. There he drank, and ate some watercress. He realized that he had become a *rangfar* through circumstance, and he wondered if it happened to many foxes that way. Perhaps few of them started out on the road from choice; but once they had, many may have developed a taste for travel and been unable to give it up. He could see why it was attractive. Each hour brought a different perspective to the land. There were plowed, empty fields, and fields of stubble; there were coverts and woods, rolling pastureland and hilly steeps. It was all very exciting and addictive. He felt as if he were seeing something of life: the world had opened up before him. Also, apart from the farmer, he had not run into any humans so far. He felt it possible that one could walk and walk and still find plenty of *hav* or *havnot*, both more delightful than the *face*, though not as easy to live in.

Once, he caught the smell of another dog fox and paused to sniff the breeze, wondering where the creature was hiding. A voice from a bramble bush said, "Keep walking," in a casual but firm tone, and it brought home to him that he was probably crossing parishes already marked and with established hunting rights for local foxes. They did not mind him passing through, so long as he was out of the area quickly. When he concentrated, of course, he could smell their marks on posts around the area, and so he knew that—apart from snapping up the odd fieldmouse or shrew—he was not going to be allowed to hunt.

That morning he reached a rise from beyond which came a

constant rumble, like deep, rolling thunder, muffled by a land embankment. He went to the top and looked down in wonder on a roadway that was thick with fast vehicles; two roadways, in fact, running parallel, each with three lanes of traffic. He wanted none of that. He could see the crows taking advantage of *gubbins* there, but it looked like an extremely dangerous business, dashing out and grabbing the remains of some creature that had refused to acknowledge that its ancient highway was now severed by an impassable river of traffic. Some animals were just too stubborn to change their habits. If their old paths went *that way*, then *that way* they were going, instant death or not.

Those birds that were not feeding on *gubbins* were finding worms in the short grass of the verges, where, incidentally, it was easy for the kestrels to see mammals intent on traveling across country that way. Once or twice A-cam saw a kestrel swoop down and rise with a meal in its talons.

He turned from this madness on wheels and retraced his steps for some distance before striking out southward.

He spent that day by a large lake, which looked too uniform to be natural. Though there were no obvious signs of man-made banks, there were leafless trees sticking up from the water like skeletal hands grasping at clouds. It was an eerie lake: too quiet, too lifeless. The still waters went beyond calmness and tranquility into a state of deadness that made A-cam think of the Unplace. Such a stagnant atmosphere, he had been told, was to be expected in the Unplace, where the trees and grass were like stone and the waters were dark, with no tides, currents, or eddies. Only the blind mists drifting by islands of black mud provided any movement.

He drank the water, but its taste was like dust and it increased rather than slaked his thirst.

When night came back again, he continued his journey.

He found a road and traveled along the verge, ignoring the cars that flashed past him occasionally, their lights stabbing away the darkness for a few moments. When he eventually reached a village he passed through it and beyond without encountering any other foxes, or indeed even dogs. Some instinct told him he was moving in the right direction. When he felt he was close to home he would seek out a fox and ask it for directions, though he had no idea what to ask for. He had some idea that if he mentioned names—Camio, O-ha, others—the listener would then say, "Oh, yes, just over the next rise you'll find the marshes. Once you get across those, you'll know where you are."

As the sun laid its first rays across the countryside, he came to a wayside cottage with a small shed in its garden. The roof of the shed looked warm and inviting and he jumped up onto the wall, and thence to the top of the shed. There he fell asleep in the soft warmth of the autumn sun, with Melloon gently ruffling his fur.

He was awakened abruptly by the rain, which fell in torrents. It was around noon, and he shook himself and climbed down from the shed, back to the edge of the roadway. There was a deep ditch running alongside the road and he slipped down into this gully and walked along it, snapping up beetles and whatever else came into his path. With the wet came the cold, and he shivered constantly as he walked, a fever coming over him that made him giddy. At one point he felt that he had to stop and rest, and he lay under a hawthorn bush by the ditch and tried to sleep.

Perhaps the rain was responsible for blanketing the scent and sound of the human, but the first A-cam knew of his presence was when hands gripped him and he was lifted from the ground. He turned and bit the fingers, causing the man to bark loudly and drop him. A-cam walked away, feeling very aggrieved, looking back once to see the man sucking his fingers and appearing puzzled. Then the vision blurred as the human remained standing still, melting into the scenery.

It occurred to A-cam a little later that the human had probably been out for a walk when he saw a fox lying on the ground in the pouring rain, and had thought him dead.

The downpour became torrential and hampered A-cam's progress as it splashed up from the ground, constantly spraying his face, getting in his eyes and nostrils. He found himself wading through deep puddles, and getting his paws clogged with sodden clay. The only recognizable smells were those of musty, churned earth and wet grass. Visibility was down to the distance of a nose.

A-cam decided to leave the highway for the woodlands, where the rain that fell in large gobbets was immediately sucked into the humus. He found such a wood in the middle of some *havnot* and spent the rest of the day there.

That night, when he woke, he found that the rain had stopped. The soft sweet scents of autumn were back in play. There was the smell of rotting crabapples nearby, and he made for these, but overriding this odor was the scent of foxes. Not just one or two foxes, but hundreds, perhaps thousands of them. This was both alarming and puzzling. He could not think why so many of his kind would have gathered together in one place. Was it a meeting of some sort? If so, it was unprecedented. Foxes prided themselves on the fact that they were not pack or herd creatures. They might live in small groups of four or five, but more than one of these groups never gathered in one spot. It was too dangerous. They would be vulnerable not only because of their numbers, but also because the humans would become alarmed. They would ask themselves what it meant, all these foxes who *never* gathered in large numbers, now collecting in one place. They would put the worst possible reasons to each other for such an unnatural phenomenon, and deal with it the way they did with other things that were not understood. They would gather together themselves; there would be a lot of barking, and many cross-country vehicles roaring over the fields, and then the guns would begin to cut down the foxes.

So A-cam ate his fill of crabapples, and then walked to the edge of the wood. He looked down the slope. At the bottom was a large piece of land surrounded by a high chain-link fence. Beyond this were some long wooden huts. They looked ominously dark—the kind of darkness that prickles the senses—and A-cam felt a chill of apprehension go through him. The place below stank of evil.

This was where the scent of the foxes was coming from.

So, what was this place? A zoo, like the one his father had told him about? But zoos were not full of foxes. The whole idea of a zoo was to have lots of different animals and birds for the humans to come and stare at. They would get bored looking at a thousand foxes. Perhaps it was a kind of prison, where they took foxes prior to killing them? That too seemed unlikely, though. Men were more fond of shooting foxes or running them down with dogs in their own environment. There seemed to be more excitement from the chase and kill that way. Perhaps it was a home for foxes, provided by *kindly* humans who were unaware that wild creatures did not like to live in huts like themselves? That seemed the *least* likely idea.

A-cam gave up on his speculations, and was about to turn away and head out in the opposite direction, when he saw a chain of lights moving across the distant landscape. After a while he knew what it was and he became excited. It was a train, racing along a track. He knew that a railway track passed quite close to his own home, and though his father had told him that there were more than one of these steel roadways running across the land, he considered it a strong possibility that this was his way home. After all, the vehicle could not have taken him *that* far from his own *face*. The human that had helped him would have wanted to get rid of him as soon as possible, and no doubt had done so in the first piece of real countryside.

So here was the first landmark that might help him get back to his parents again.

However, to reach the railway, he had to cross through that fenced-in piece of *havnot*, which was not a comforting thought. He did not want to end up in one of those huts with all the other inmates, whatever the reason they were being held.

He decided to spend the night in the wood and then go down there at daybreak, to inspect the fence. He would be able to find a way through, he had no doubt. Foxes, when they have to, can squeeze through a pinhole.

THIRTY

A-cam's fever took a stronger hold on him during the night, and by the time dawn came he no longer felt able to go down to the fence. His nose was dry and he felt overheated and lethargic. Besides, a group of travelers had arrived with the coming of the sun and their caravan encampment was between him and his goal. He watched through narrowed eyes as lurcher dogs strolled around the camp below, sniffing at anything they came across. These were very dangerous animals to a fox: they had the savagery of an Alsatian and the speed of a greyhound. They were lean whippet-like crossbreeds, trained to hunt hares and rabbits, but they would undoubtedly settle for a fox if one broke cover. A-cam hoped the travelers would not stay long.

During that day, he watched the activity below. There was much coming and going: humans carrying water from one place to another, children running and screaming in play; hissing, rattling old vehicles arriving and leaving, covered in rust, their doors hanging off; lurchers nipping each other to get at scraps of food; dusty, swarthy men banging away at old metal; dark women stringing up lines of wet, grey clothes; a dozen radios on different stations, blaring out on full volume. Then some men in flat hats arrived in their black-and-white car. The hard, dusty men began barking with the soft-cheeked ones in hats, who stood with their hands on their hips and looked everywhere but into the flashing eyes before them. Finally, the black-and-white car drove away and the camp returned to its normal activities.

That evening there was music, which A-cam enjoyed. He listened to the wailing, dancing sounds that came from the stringed device that one traveler had tucked under his chin. When birds made sounds like that, it was usually to warn others away from their territory. A-cam wondered if these humans were sending signals to the flat-capped ones, saying, *Keep away, this is our hunting ground.*

Light from an open bonfire caught the children's faces, and the swirling clothes of the women, as they sat or moved around the camp. Later, overriding the odor of mansweat and diesel fumes, came the smell of cooked food. A-cam's saliva flowed and his stomach churned. His fever was easing now and he felt able to get back on his feet. His nose was once more wet and sensitive, and a useful tool. Without it, he had been like a blind hawk.

He toured the wood, looking for places to dig for worms and beetles. There were fungi to be had, and crabapples, and sloes. A-cam ate his fill and then settled back down to sleep again.

When morning came, the travelers had moved on. Where they had been was a sea of rubbish. Paper stuck to the chain-link fence, and there were cans, bottles, and plastic cartons littering the ground. It seemed that those people with their hot, narrow eyes and mean hunting dogs could conjure rubbish from beneath the turf, for surely they could not have produced such an amount of waste all on their own, in just one day?

A-cam went down the hill and inspected the fence. Moving along it he found a place where he could dig, and there he burrowed underneath the wire. Once he was on the other side he became a little more wary. There might be dogs guarding the place. It all depended on what was in the huts. Camio had told him about guard dogs, usually Alsatians or Dobermans, which often ran loose inside chain-link fences.

"Keep your wits about you," Camio had said, "at all times, especially if you see a wooden board fastened to the wire, or on a pole near to it. It's well accepted that these are warning totems that define well-protected land. These human 'marking posts' are not associated with scent or smell, the way ours are, but with sight. Humans look at them and *know* that the territory within the fence will be guarded. Since we don't know what to look for on these totems, and our sight is not as good as that of humans anyway, we must be generally wary about entering such places."

A-cam had indeed seen two boards affixed to the wire, though of course when he stared at them they went fuzzy after a while. He wondered what it was that humans could see, when they looked at such things. Certainly more than a fox could see, and there were scratches on the boards like the ritual marks that foxes made in the dust sometimes.

He trotted quickly across the flat, empty ground beyond the fence to the first long hut. Since the dwellings were raised off the ground, he intended to go underneath them all the way to the other side, walking quickly from hut to hut. He would not run. He had been trained by his parents not to run except in a dire emergency. Running creatures, like deer, only attracted attention with their swift movement. If you were a deer in a forest it was all right to run, as deer could outrun their pursuers. Foxes, however, were not fleet of foot. At top speed a fox did not stand a chance against greyhounds, lurchers, and many other breeds of dog.

Once under the huts, A-cam was sure they contained foxes. Also there was a chilling sense of being close to a thousand *sowanders*.

Many foxes had died in this place and the atmosphere was one of terror that had been overtaken finally by hopelessness and despair. In places like this, animals shuffled their way to a death as certain as tomorrow follows today.

The scents were overpowering. Under the third hut he found a small knothole, and, curious about the inhabitants of these forbidding dark places, he whispered, "Who's there? Can anybody hear me?" Then he put his ear to the hole through which bits of dirty straw were poking.

He could hear breathing from above, and a shuffling. Then a faltering voice, which sounded like that of a vixen, spoke: "Is—is that a fox-spirit?"

"No," he said, "I'm a real fox. I was just passing by. Who are you? What's your name?"

"O-sollo," came the reply. Then, "What are you doing out there? Have you escaped? How did you get out?"

"I didn't get out—I've never been in. What is this place?"

There was a long silence; then, "This is a place where they keep foxes." The answer was delivered in a puzzled tone of voice, as if the speaker were not sure of the answer herself.

"What for?" he asked.

"What for? The disappeared ones could tell you better than I, except that they're likely never to come back."

The "disappeared ones"? What did that mean? He was about to leave when the voice said, "Listen, can you help us escape? My sister and I are in a cage above your head. Only this wooden floor stands between us and freedom."

A-cam paused. He knew he was in great danger. If foxes were being kept caged in long dark huts, it meant that humans would go to enormous lengths to keep them there. What did it all mean? He was in a quandary. His instinct told him to get away from the place as fast as he could, but the voice above had aroused something within him which he might have recognized had he the time to think about it.

Then he remembered something his father had told him. There were places called fox farms, where foxes were bred and then taken

away and . . . nobody knew what happened to them, but it was easy to guess. Foxes are not stupid. They had seen their skins used as clothes: wrapped around ladies who smelled as if they had an overdose of violets. The "disappeared ones"—they were taken away, killed, and skinned.

He studied the planks above his head. They looked very formidable. He knew that what he should be doing was trotting on to the next hut and getting to the railway line.

"O-sollo," he said. "I would like to help you, but I don't see how . . ."

"One of the boards is rotten," she whispered. "We've been wetting on it ever since we've been here—always in the same place. If you could gnaw from your side . . ."

He sniffed around the area and found the plank that smelled. He pushed his nose against it. The wood was soft. The two vixens must have been urinating on that plank several times a day for more than a season to get it in that state. But how to get his teeth to it? The planks were flat. There was nowhere to get a grip.

Then he thought of something quite extraordinary. Such an idea came only once—if ever—to a dog fox, even one born of clever parents like his own, and it had come now out of an emergency situation. The pressure of the moment had pried something from the depths of his foxy brain, something that was—relatively—equal to any human invention. It remained to see whether an achievement could be produced.

"I've got an idea," he said, proudly. "Give me a few moments."

"You won't be sorry," she whispered back. "I'm a vixen of rare beauty." Then she added, modestly, "We all are in here. It's only among common foxes that I'm rare. But you'll . . . you'll have a mate to treasure . . . if you want one."

He turned around and began digging with his hind legs, until he had piled earth up under the softened plank. When he had got it high enough, he squeezed his body between the mound and the plank, and then arched his back, pressing down with his four legs. To his intense delight the plank began to move, bending upward. It was indeed rotten. The wood was like sodden cardboard.

"All right," came a voice from above, "we can get at it now."

Above him, the two vixens tore at the pulpy wood, pulling it away in great chunks until there was a hole half the size of a man's head. In the meantime, A-cam slipped to the edge of the hut and sniffed at Melloon. There were no dangerous scents abroad. He could see no movement either. He went back as the second vixen was forcing her way out through the hole.

When both were safely out, A-cam said, "We must make for the railway. It's *gerflan*, and they'll have difficulty following us. Also, I need it to guide me home. Which one of you is O-sollo?" he added, staring at the twins.

"I am," said the one with the darker ears. "This is O-fall."

"Right. Let's go then. Move from hut to hut until we come to the last one, then I'll go out, dig us a hole under the fence, and we'll be free."

"Free," breathed O-fall, speaking for the first time.

They did as instructed, slipping from one hut to another, but just as they came to the last hut the sound of a human's barking was heard. The foxes in the huts, who until now had been lying in placid, sorry silence just awaiting the next meal, took up the human's cry and began shouting to one another.

"What's wrong? What's up?" and "Someone's escaped! Someone's out! Dog's spit, why isn't it me? Why always someone else?"

The noise was appalling. A-cam realized they had been discovered and his heart began hammering a little. What to do? Remain where they were? He put the suggestion to the other two.

"No," said O-fall, firmly. "The first thing they'll do is search the grounds. There'll be a vehicle full of them here in a moment and they'll start inside the compound. We have to get out."

"Will they use dogs?" asked A-cam.

"And ruin these beautiful furs?" replied O-sollo. "That's one advantage we *have* got. We're valuable. No dogs."

A-cam heaved a sigh of relief.

"Good. Very good. Now for that fence . . ."

Without waiting to think about it, he trotted over to the fence and found some soft earth. He dug like fury and then shouted to the two vixens, "Come on!" At that moment, he saw a man running from behind the huts. He had a gun in his hands.

"Come on, come on."

O-sollo was through to the other side and O-fall had her head through when the first bullet zinged off the wire, just above her head.

"Keep going!" yelled A-cam.

She was through in an instant. A-cam then scrambled under the wire. Another shot raised some turf an inch from his nose. The two vixens were already running into the shrubbery beyond the fence. He followed them, zigzagging. He heard the sound of the last shot, but did not know where it had hit.

Maybe he got me, thought A-cam, *and I won't feel it until I stop?*

He scrambled under a bush and waited until he got his breath back; then he called, "Are you two all right?"

"Yes," called O-sollo.

"Lets go again. Make for the railway and get down on the other side of the tracks."

The three of them slunk quickly through the shrubs, using the cover to hide their progress. At the last minute they trotted up the railway bank, and down the other side. A-cam kept them on the move for a mile, before he let them stop and rest. Then they sat down beside the track, to get their breath back.

Suddenly, O-sollo cried out.

"What is it?" asked A-cam, alarmed. "Were you hit?"

"No," she cried. "It's *you!*"

"Me?" he hastily inspected himself all over. "Where? I can't see where I've been hit. *Tell* me."

But O-sollo seemed too upset to answer.

Instead, in a much calmer, softer voice, O-fall said, "Oh dear. It's your tail. The man shot your tail off."

A-cam sank to the ground in relief.

"Oh, *that*. Don't worry about that. I lost my tail a few days ago—to a dog the size of one of your huts. That's no exaggeration either. He's a monster. Why are you staring at me like that, O-sollo?"

"You've lost your tail," she said, sadly.

"If you don't want him, I'll have him," said O-fall, quickly.

"Don't be silly," said her sister, "of course I want him. He's my rescuer. I just think it's sad, that's all. Anyway, there's nothing to stop us from all living together, in one earth. Is there?"

"I've always wanted to live in an earth," sighed O-fall. "They spoke about these things in the compound, but none of us had ever seen one. We were born there, you see. And we would have died there. What . . . what's an earth look like?"

"Look like?" A-cam scratched his haunch against a bush. "I suppose it looks like whatever you want it to. Depends where it is. The only one I know—my parents' breeding earth—was in an old car hulk in the middle of a scrap-yard. Traditionally, I suppose, they're dug out of the ground, under the root of some tree. But I've heard of foxes who live under the floorboards of houses . . ."

"No boards," said O-sollo, firmly. "Ever."

"I would really like a *traditional* earth," mused O-fall.

"And you?" asked A-cam of O-sollo.

"Me too."

"In that case we'll dig ourselves an earth, just as soon as we find a suitable place."

They walked on for some miles along the railway embankment, until they came to a wooded area that spilled down close to the track. A-cam spent a long time sniffing around the area, checking for other foxes' marker posts. When he found none, he concluded that they could make their home in that place. All three foxes were exhausted by this time, so they went up into the wood and found a place to rest for the night. The two vixens, although they had never hunted, were willing to learn from A-cam. He talked to them about it first, saying that he was not an expert, yet—not like his mother, who could track anything over the poorest ground, and bring it down when she found it—but that he would pass on to them what he had learned from her. He would also teach them about berries, roots, worms, plants, spiders, insects, beetles, dragonflies, woodlice, fungi, and all things edible, just as his mother had taught him.

"Did your father teach you nothing?" asked O-fall.

"Camio? Yes, but about town living. He's not such a good hunter as O-ha, but he's a better scavenger. He once told me he had taken a meal out of a man's hand on the run—he's very good at that sort of thing. He's good at storytelling, too. . . ."

"Sounds like it," said O-fall, wryly.

A-cam glared at her.

"My father is still alive after being snatched from his home territory, which is far from this land, and placed in a zoo just like your fox farm. He escaped, even though there were Alsatians patrolling the zoo, and survived in a foreign place—*alone*. He's a wonderful fox."

"I'm sorry," whispered O-fall, but she gave her sister a significant look, which O-sollo ignored.

"So," said O-sollo, "your parents are Camio and O-ha? They sound like good foxes. But now we are on our own. I think we're a few seasons older than you, A-cam, but because we've been locked up since birth we're going to be a bit of a burden for a while. You'll probably have to feed us all. But we'll learn quickly, don't you worry. I don't want to be dependent on a dog fox for my food, even if he is my mate . . ."

"Your mate," A-cam said, remembering. It sounded good. How proud of him his parents would be. He had found himself a mate—a very *pretty* mate. One of rare beauty, when detached from the thousand or so other rare beauties.

"At least," said O-fall, dropping off to sleep, "we shall never become one of the disappeared. . . ."

A-cam lay awake long after the vixens were asleep, thinking about what he had said to them. He had been bragging a little and was not as confident as he pretended. Yes, O-ha had taught him a great deal about living off the countryside, and he had to admit he had been a good pupil. He had stored all her descriptions of edible fruit, nuts, fungi, roots, and leaves in the back of his brain, and had no problem with bringing them forward. But that was all theory, and he had been lucky so far. Crabapples, sloes, acorns, and chestnuts were easy to recognize, and the two types of fungi he had eaten, chanterelle and grisette, had also not been difficult to identify. But what about when food got scarce, in midwinter, and they had to take anything they could find? During autumn there was a wide choice, and anything dubious could be ignored. But there would be times when he would have only two choices—eat it or go hungry. Then, he would have to *know*.

And what if he turned out to be a bad hunter, unable to catch rabbits or birds? What if all three of them were useless at living off the countryside?

These questions turned around in his brain, as he lay awake. He decided that, once he had set up some caches around the place, he would leave the vixens and visit his parents, one last time. They would be able to advise him further.

PART SEVEN

THE PALACE OF THE WINDS

PART SEVEN

THE
PALACE
OF THE
WINDS

THIRTY-ONE

"A vixen of rare beauty?" repeated O-ha, as A-cam neared the end of his tale. She regarded her son with questioning eyes. He seemed to have landed on his feet, albeit without a tail. She was very pleased for him.

"Well, no more beautiful than yourself . . . or Mitz . . ." stumbled A-cam in an attempt at diplomacy.

"Now you're spoiling it," said Mitz. "You shouldn't be so eager to please us all. I have this vision of a vixen with a soft, velvety coat that shines in the sun—a light frame and a high, pert head, with deep brown eyes . . . a fox to put a hunter's moon to shame."

"Yes, yes, that's her exactly," said A-cam, excitedly.

"Well then, don't try to ruin my pictures. I shall always think of you as this dashing creature rescuing a vixen of rare beauty from the clutches of certain death."

Camio interrupted.

"You were telling us, A-cam, about your inability to put into practice your mother's teaching."

A-cam looked at his father with a hurt expression.

"No, Camio. I was saying that I *thought* we might not manage. As it turned out, we got along very well. Of course, there's Ransheen to contend with yet—the time of scarcity—but I know now that we'll manage. We've learned an awful lot in just a short time. And though I'm not as good at hunting as the other two—O-fall is the best—I can catch most things. O-fall will probably not be with us for long, anyway. There's a dog fox in the area interested in her."

"I was wondering about that," said Camio. "I mean, *two* mates. It doesn't work, you know. No reason why foxes can't live together as a small group, but you need to decide who is with whom."

"Oh, don't be boring, Camio," said Mitz. "A-cam knows what he's doing. He's your cub, after all."

A-cam said, "I never intended to have two mates. That's not how we manage things at all. O-fall's staying because she has nowhere else to go at the moment. We'll survive, don't you worry."

"I'm sure you will," said O-ha. "I'm very proud of you."

A-cam nodded and looked down. Then he cried, "Sister! What about this collar you're wearing? Were you caught? What's it for? You look like a dog."

"I don't need to be told that, thank you. I had an adventure too, just like you—well, quite different, actually. I was captured by a human and taken to a house, met a friendly bitch called Betsy, had a conversation with an otter, and then this collar was put on my neck. The man who captured me uses it to track me, wherever I go."

"Don't you mind that?" said the wide-eyed dog fox.

"Not really. The human doesn't intend me any harm, and it's a good thing to be tracked at the moment, with that killer dog loose. We've been rescued once already!"

"Yes, I heard rumors about Sabre as I came across the *face*. I must

admit it put a bit of zip in my feet. Having lost my tail to that beast, I have no wish to offer him the other end. Can't something be done?"

Camio replied, "He'll be caught soon. He can't survive without raiding dustbins and he's no slinking fox, to do such things silently. I expect he makes a terrible racket and he's not exactly invisible. They'll get him soon."

"I hope so," said A-cam. "I have to get back to my mate. I need to reach the railway track, so that I can follow it along to my earth. You must come and visit me one day, all of you."

They all nodded, knowing that it would never happen. They had their own busy lives to lead. It was right that A-cam had returned to the breeding earth to inform his parents of his success in finding a mate and establishing his own home, but foxes are not humans, to make regular visits. It was possible that they might run across each other again, sometime—all things are possible—but it was doubtful that such a dangerous journey, outside their respective parishes, would be undertaken simply for reasons of filial relationships. A-cam had left the earth. He was now a fox with his own responsibilities. He would soon have his own young to feed.

They continued to exchange news for some time, when suddenly there was a barking from beyond the yard. Some humans were getting upset about something. The noise of a chase came to the foxes' ears: the panting of an animal, the sound of running feet.

The men from the scrap-yard began barking then.

O-ha was the first to catch the scent.

"Sabre! He's in the yard!" she whispered.

The two cubs crouched instinctively and began backing into the rear of the earth. Camio bristled, baring his teeth.

Next came the sounds of a creature forcing its way along the tunnel to their earth. The tunnel was wider at its opening and became narrower toward the center of the heap of scrap, where the car body was situated.

"I can smell you in there!" called the dog. "One, two, three, four—I can smell you. This time! This time!"

O-ha's blood went cold at the sound of the voice. She felt as if her stomach was in her mouth. She was sick, sick of running from this

deviant hound that would never let them rest. Fear was there, but also a bitter hatred for one who would never let her or her family alone, never let them live their lives. If only she were larger, more powerful! She would give anything for just a *chance* to win.

Scrap metal was being moved around the car's shell. The dog seemed determined to reach the foxes before the men caught him, and as he shouldered his way through the piles of scrap they shifted, some pieces clattered down the hill of junk. They could hear his exertions as he squirmed and pushed his way onward, toward them.

Halfway along, there was a pause in the activity, and then the ridgeback's voice came to them again.

"I can smell you, vixen. This time I've got you—all of you. No St. Bernard bitches to protect you now. No do-gooder humans in here. Just us. My teeth ache to sink into your skull. I'll crush it like a rotten apple. I'll spread your brains from here to Trinity."

The foxes said nothing to each other. There was no other way out of the place. The two adults positioned themselves at the entrance to the earth.

O-ha's whole body was tense with apprehension. She could sense the wild terror in her cubs and tried to remain outwardly calm. Camio was scratching himself. His eyes were vacant, expressionless. Thank O-A for a dog fox that did not panic! Oh O-A, she thought, why? Why are we plagued by this beast? Will we all die, one by one, in this dog's bloody jaws? Already the *face* was stained in many parts with his kills.

There were further sounds coming from Sabre now, grunting and swearing as he continued to heave his bulk into the narrow passage through the scrap. The whole heap moved as if an earthquake were in progress, cooking stoves grinding against rusty bedframes, empty oil drums rolling across the mountain of scrap, freezers grating and sliding. Sabre's immense strength might have been a source of wonder to the foxes, were they not the dog's target. Even the hulk in which they were waiting shifted a few inches as the hound pressed his way closer.

"My head," gasped the hound, the exertion evident in his voice, "my head swims with the sweet taste of blood. I am near—I am *so* near. I can smell the blood in my nostrils—sweet, sweeter than the sweetest blood of a baby deer. Fox blood. Drinking fox blood. Sucking out the brains from a crushed skull. I'll have you twitching, this way, that way. I'll have you . . ."

At one point, when he came into sight of the foxes, Sabre got so excited that in his frenzy to reach them he caught his thick leather collar on a jagged piece of metal sheeting. Notwithstanding, he pulled against this, half-dragging the heavy piece of scrap with him. Finally it sawed through the collar, releasing him and tearing a gash along the edge of his throat. Blood began to run down his right foreleg. He did not stop his efforts for a moment.

They could see his eyes now, blazing in triumph. Demented eyes. The jaws were opened wide, revealing the red, cavernous throat. There was foam around the lips of his mouth. The veins on his neck stood out like thick cords as he forced himself, inch by inch, closer to the little foxes.

"Heady—smell—of—death—" he grunted, his nostrils dilating, his red-veined eyes narrowing.

The crazed beast was only a few feet away from the entrance. At the rear of the earth the two terrified juveniles were scratching at the walls.

Men were on top of the scrap-heap now, burrowing to get at the hound, probably unaware that the dog's interest was in a family of foxes.

Sabre gave one last heave and brought himself within a nose of Camio and O-ha.

This last thrust loosened a bale of barbed wire, which had been balanced on top of the scrap. It fell on the dog, who was stretching his whole frame in order to get at the foxes. His continued efforts to cross those last few inches between him and his hated enemies served only to entangle him in the wire. His forelegs were caught in the mesh and were being ripped open by the barbs. His head and throat were scissored by two strands that closed every time he tried to move forward.

A bellow of frustration came from his mouth.

"I—*will*—get . . ."

With a supreme effort he launched himself forward, only to bring the roof of scrap metal crashing down on him. Junk metal fell all around. The whole heap of scrap heaved and swayed, began rolling like a rockslide, a landslip of jagged, battered objects that shifted, rolled, knitted together. A hole opened above the earth, through which the blue sky was visible. An enamel bowl rolled away, over the springs of rusted bedframes. A bucket bounced onto the head of the dog. Everything was moving, twisting, turning. Nothing had stability. The world was made of loosely fitting scrap metal that shifted and collapsed.

"Once—more—"

The hole in the scrap-heap widened. The four foxes left the earth by this new exit, one by one, avoiding the men balanced precariously on top of the heaving scrap, and trying to keep their footing.

The foxes skipped around obstacles and made their escape with the hound's muffled words in their ears:

"I'll—get— . . . !"

As they raced for the street, a man with fur on his face and a box on his back waved them on and gave out encouraging barks. When one of the humans from the manor appeared and gave chase to the foxes, Betsy's master barred the way, allowing them time to escape.

They gathered on the edge of town.

"Well," O-ha said, "that's that—until he gets out the next time. I'm sick of him. Surely we'll get rid of him one day?"

She said this in the knowledge that her dreams of confrontation with the beast were becoming more frequent and more intense. These were dark yet startling dreams of confused chases and combat, which were nothing like the incidents they had already gone through. What her dreams seemed to be telling her was *Keep running and don't look back*. And always, the black bars worried her.

"Well," said A-cam to his parents, "I'll be on my way then."

They said their goodbyes in the way that foxes do, very formally, with little outward show of emotion. Inside, however, O-ha was awash with sentiment. She knew she would not see her cub again and it saddened her. She felt as though a piece of herself had come adrift and was floating away from her. Camio too, despite that casual expression, would be feeling something.

A-cam left, and Camio suggested that they find a temporary earth until they set up their permanent one on the embankment.

Mitz said to her mother, "If it's all right with you two, I shan't look for an earth yet. I'll stay with you for a while. It's not that I'm not ready to leave home, but I want a year without cubs. If I set up an earth with a dog fox, I know I shan't be able to resist having cubs, in spite of my feelings now. Although it's never happened to me I can imagine that when the time comes to mate, despite whatever promises you've made to yourself beforehand, something inside takes over and you find yourself saying *who cares* . . ."

"Something like that," replied O-ha. "It's one of those times when the body rules the mind."

"Just as I thought," said Mitz. "Well, I'm not going to give mine the chance. If I deny myself a mate, I remove the temptation to succumb to his charms and my feelings. I can wait. There'll be other seasons. What's it like, O-ha?"

"What?"

"Mating with Camio. Or that first one, what was he called, A-ho?"

"I don't want to talk about Camio, that wouldn't be right, but I don't mind telling you about A-ho. He was a fine fox, physically different from your father—not so dark, and smaller—but in character, very similar: presumptuous, good-humored, and a little dreamy. He was not much more than a cub when I met him, so we entered adulthood together, learning things side by side the way A-cam—sorry, A-*salla*—is with O-sollo. . . ."

"You still haven't told me what it's like—mating."

"I *am* telling you about it, only you have preconceived ideas about what it actually is. Mating isn't just the physical union of two foxes—there's much more to it. You have to *like* each other, for a start, and then there's the meeting of spirits . . . no, I was wrong. I *can't* explain it. You'll have to wait and find out for yourself."

Mitz nodded.

"From what you've told me, it isn't just finding a dog fox and that's it."

"No, there are other considerations."

"But A-cam just found O-sollo."

"He was lucky."

Mitz said, "But mostly foxes just find a mate and move in together. They don't spend a lifetime choosing, do they?"

O-ha had to acknowledge that this was true, but she wanted her daughter to stop and think before rushing down the nearest hole and having cubs. Of course, Mitz had no intention of doing that: in fact she had stated that she was going to remain with O-ha and Camio for a few seasons at least. So what was worrying her?

Nothing. Nothing's worrying me, she thought.

Melloon began to blow herself out, and Ransheen sharpened her teeth, ready to savage the landscape. Those animals that wished to sleep the winter away, like the hedgehog, went into hibernation. It is a dangerous state. The creature is physically vulnerable and its body mechanisms fall to such a slow rate, that they sometimes come to a stop altogether. Animals in hibernation are so close to death, they can look over the edge and see what it's like on the other side. Camio always said that if you want to know about death, ask a hedgehog.

Most of the plants followed suit, all except those like shepherd's purse, groundsel, and chickweed, which are prepared to battle through the winter as individuals. The frogs buried themselves in mud and changed their breathing habits, taking all their oxygen from the water, since they need very little while they are dozing the winter away. The owls sharpened their claws, honed their beaks, and like most carnivores prepared themselves for a hard time.

A-sac never returned and eventually O-ha and Camio realized that he was not going to come home. Camio said that the white fox had probably found a vixen and settled down with her. O-ha agreed, saying that there were plenty of peculiar females around who would want a potential mystic for a mate.

They moved, with Mitz, to an earth on the embankment of the railway loop that was in the process of being built to accommodate the town. At first there were quite a few humans around, working on the rails, but they had no time to bother foxes—and, like the builders in the *face*, they were even quite pleased to see them. Mitz became friendly with a group of young foxes living just along the track, and Camio said that it would not be long before she moved in with them. Mitz denied this, but the signs were definitely there.

The frost crackled across the land, covering tree-stumps with hard white crystals, turning them into gravestones. Brambles became thick wire with metal hooks that caught the fur. Ice crept across the world at night, in thin layers that formed thicker wedges, until water was scarce.

The town continued to expand and food became easier to find, in the bins, outside homes and restaurants. Foxes and kestrels ate well, though if not on the waste food itself, then on the rats and mice that appeared out of nowhere to cohabit with the humans. Of course, the people did not realize that the rodents had arrived, since they kept a low profile, but the foxes did. So did the kestrels. In fact, it was the exceptional human that even noticed the hawks and foxes, let alone mice and rats.

O-ha was more at home in the embankment than she had been in the scrap-yard. An earth was an earth to her—it should be fashioned out of the material that made its name. She was still a rural fox at heart (a rustic, Camio called her playfully) and disliked and distrusted the town. The *gerflan* on which she lived now was a compromise: something between *face* and *hav*. She did not like eating worms out of the gutters in the street; she preferred to dig them out of the ground. They seemed to taste different straight from the soil. Slugs and snails, too, were somehow more tasty from a leaf than they were from a wall.

She wondered how she would feel once the trains began to thunder along the line. Camio had told her that one got used to the vibration and the sound, but she wondered how much he actually knew and how much he only believed he knew. There was a difference. Camio often repeated what other foxes had told him as if he had experienced the thing himself.

"I've seen down the new sewers, they're quite wide," she had heard a fox tell Camio. Later she heard Camio use exactly the same words when mentioning the sewers to Mitz. When she challenged him, saying, "You *haven't* seen the new sewers yourself. You haven't been near them yet," he replied, "Oh, it's too complicated to start explaining that so-and-so told whatsisname, who passed it on to him, who carried the tale to her—much easier to repeat what you've heard." "But that's dishonest," she said. "Oh, is it?" he answered, unperturbed.

Yet she still thought more of Camio than of any other fox alive. And it was not as if such aberrations were harmful. They meant very little, in real terms.

From her hole in the long grass at the top of the bank, she watched the bright steel rails being laid. They looked magnificent. She admired their clean, straight dimensions. There was great beauty in a strip of steel, she decided. It looked cold, hard, and efficient, just like a fox should be. The soul of a living fox, she decided, should be modeled on a steel rail. It should shine, but it should be immune from injury, devoid of anything but stark, capable toughness. This was the ascetic fox coming out in her. She enjoyed the austere life, enjoyed living in a hole in the ground—just the bare earth without any embellishments. In fact, she was a warm creature, inside, and confused her distaste for material comforts with a desire to own a severe spirit. She felt the two were one and the same. Camio frequently told her that she was a *caring* creature, and that her dislike for soft beds did not mean she had a hard soul. O-ha grieved over this. Some deep teaching from somewhere, perhaps her parents, had left her feeling it was wrong to be emotional.

Over the next month the high, dark winds without names rushed heavy clouds over the land. Shadows swept across the wastelands and over the *face*. The mating period came around, but a sudden fall of snow trapped Camio on the far side of town. He struggled to reach home but though he fought his way through drifts, it was three days before he reached the earth on the *gerflan*. By that time,

O-ha's desire was waning. She was irritable with Camio for not being around at the right time, and when she finally accepted that it was not his fault, and the mating took place, her oestrus was over. There would be no cubs. Mitz was not slow to state that she thought this was a good thing. She did not entirely approve of O-ha having litter after litter of cubs.

The men finished work on the railway and the trains began to use the loop. At first O-ha thought she would never get used to the noise, but gradually the trains seemed to become quieter until she had to concentrate to hear them at all. Of an evening she liked to lie side by side with Camio, staring down at the trains going by, all lit up. She wondered what the fox-spirits of the *Firstdark* thought about these modern times, when humans hurtled from one place to another inside glass boxes. She thought of the fox-spirits as being rather conventional, slow to change. After all, they had known the earth when it was young. When there were no machines at all, and men were running naked through the forests, killing things with sticks and stones instead of guns. The fox-spirits had seen a lot of changes, and would probably see more. No doubt they would be there to witness the end of the world when it came.

Fox mythology said that one day all the waters would rise up and reshape themselves into O-A's ancient foxform, which was like an ordinary fox only a thousand times larger and with eyes so full of severe compassion that no mortal could look directly into them. O-A would then begin swallowing the sun, moon, and earth, in that order. In this way, the ghosts of all dead foxes would become part of O-A.

So, contemplating her immortal state, O-ha daydreamed. It was only when she slept that the nightmares came, of black bars falling across a wide bright field of snow, and then the chase, and then . . . finally, the shadow of her pursuer fell across her path. She had seen that shadow seasons ago, when A-ho had still been alive. She had gone to the duck pond at the farm in the middle of a Ransheen night. She had crossed the frozen pond to get at the coop, but halfway over had looked down and seen a dark shadow under the ice. Now, in her dream, she looked up to see the shape that cast the shadow—or was it the shadow that cast the shape? She was confused. Was the thing above her head, or below her feet?

She woke, whining pitifully in her distress.

THIRTY-TWO

It was Ransheen and the world had turned to bone. The sky had moved down onto the land. Shapes were lost to the sight, even in open spaces, and scents and sounds were whisked away by blizzards, carried upward to be buried in the grey above. Creatures became statues, freezing in their tracks, their eyes like flints.

Life had become hard for the creatures of the *face*, since heavy snowfalls had brought the town to a standstill. Restaurants had closed temporarily, there were no rubbish collections, few people ventured out at all. The foxes who relied on waste food to live found the sources had disappeared. Starvation moved into the homes of the animals and took up residence. O-ha, Camio, and Mitz became thin and wasted creatures. Their bellies pinched tight beneath their fur and their eyes burned dimly from the depths of hollow sockets. In desperation they ate snow, trying to fill the pits of pain inside them. Any scrap that had even the appearance of food was hastily devoured. Camio ate some unidentifiable piece of trash and it made him ill. He lay close to death on the floor of their earth on a day when Ransheen gnawed at the bare-boned land with fine sharp teeth.

On such a day, O-ha decided to raid the farmhouse on the edge of the *face*, for anything that was available. It was during such weather that farmers forgot to lock up the chicken coop, or failed to shut the barn door on stored vegetables. The three foxes were so desperately hungry that she knew she had to risk the journey, even in such appalling conditions. Camio was not fit for the enterprise, so she decided to brave the blizzard alone. The townspeople remained in their houses, heading out only when they had to replenish their own supplies. There was still no throwaway food to be had in the streets.

Camio, from his sickbed, tried to dissuade her from the trip.

"Why don't you wait a little while longer? Perhaps the blizzard will clear up soon?"

"Perhaps it *won't*," she said, emphatically. "It's no good—I'm going, and that's that. If we don't get something to eat, we'll die anyway."

"It's a bad time," was all he added.

"Mitz will look after you," said O-ha. "She's outside now, getting some ice for you to lick. You need water. I wish we could find you some grass, but it's buried deep under the snow. Perhaps soon, once it begins to thaw . . ."

"I shall be all right. Don't you worry about me." He did not look all right. He lay full length on his side, panting, his ribs sticking through his ragged fur like small wire hoops. O-ha was frightened to nuzzle him since the skin was so taut it seemed as if it would split open at the slightest pressure.

Mitz came in then, with an icicle in her mouth. She dropped it in

front of Camio, then flopped down beside him. It seemed an effort for her to keep her head upright.

"There," she said, breathlessly. "That's as clear a piece of ice as you'll ever see. Outside in the light, you can see right through it—and it sparkles. Where are you going, O-ha?"

O-ha had been edging toward the exit, mumbling her orisons.

"Out. I have to look for food. You see to Camio. I won't be long."

She knew that Mitz thought she was going to search locally, so she hurried out of the earth before the vixen discovered that her mother was going on a much longer journey, to the farm. She would have insisted on going with her.

O-ha struggled through the shoulder-high snow, plowing forward with effort. It got into her mouth and nostrils, and the going was hard, but she was determined not to rest until she made it to the point where the streets sloped upward to Trinity Parklands.

The snow had fallen in soft lumps at first, putting down that crisp underlayer that crunched beneath the paws. At that time the air had had the sort of stillness, the deadened effect, that tells all creatures even before they leave their homes that there has been a fall of snow. The world had looked pure for a day. Then there had followed three days of a different kind of snow, one that came in on the back of an angry Ransheen, driving in hard with small, gritty flakes. This was the snowstorm that was still raging now as O-ha battled against the drifts, her eyes stinging in the flailing wind and ice.

Her legs quickly became tired, but she forced them to carry on. When she fell into the deeper drifts, she burrowed her way through. There was a terrible pain in her stomach which she knew was being echoed inside Camio and Mitz. Her head felt light, however, and not quite part of her. She forced herself to think of things other than her own agony, her own situation.

Mitz! She had started calling her daughter *Mitz* at long last, finally giving in and dropping the prefix. How is she ever going to get a mate? thought O-ha. She'll meet a dog fox, tell him her name, and he'll think . . . well, there was no reasoning what he would think. Still, the vixen was grown now. There was nothing more O-ha could do about it. At least the collar had gone, had slipped off when Mitz lost weight and her face got pared down by lack of food. That collar had been enough in itself to turn any dog fox's thoughts away from her daughter.

She forced herself to think these thoughts, in order to keep her mind from her hunger and waning strength. There were pictures at the back of her brain of foxes lying dead in the snow, their bodies frozen solid. They too had set out in search of food, but they had eked out their last few wisps of energy, had fallen and never risen again. Well, if it was to be like that, it was as good a death as any. She had had a good life—some tragedy, admittedly, but what vixen gets through as many seasons as she had seen without tragedy of some kind?

She found herself in a tunnel of snow and followed it to the end, emerging at the foot of the slope that lead to Trinity. So far, so good. There were very few people abroad, which gave her one less thing to think about. In any case, humans relied on their eyes, and the visibility was so poor they would have to be on top of her to see her.

She began climbing the slippery street, her paws skidding on the ice that cars had made by riding over packed snow. Her stomach pulled, once or twice, as if it were on a line with someone yanking the other end. She fought back the pain and continued the slow climb. The blizzard increased in strength, and Ransheen threatened to throw O-ha back down the slope like a rag. Sleet whipped along O-ha's right flank and she closed the eye on that side. If there were scents in the air, she could not smell them, and any sounds were lost in a banshee-like howling. These were dangerous conditions for a wild creature.

She reached the gates to the parklands and wearily settled down for a rest. It would have been easy, so easy, to let that last little ember of warmth inside her go out. Just to sleep where she lay, and never wake up. Such a tempting . . . But there were others relying on her. Perhaps they didn't want to go to the Perfect Here? She had to force herself back up onto her legs, and to continue. The thing to do was keep the farm in mind.

O-ha entered the woods, and once among the trees the going was a little easier. The woodlands kept out a lot of the blizzard. There were one or two people about, walking their dogs or each other, but she kept to the edge, away from the main paths. She passed a small depression at the bottom of a tree. Gar's sett. But though she had not seen the badger for a long while, this was no time to go visiting. Even in the wood the snow was past her haunches, impeding her progress.

In the summer, when Frashoon came back, she promised herself. Then she would visit Gar.

There was a hole in the snowscape ahead of her. Almost immediately she caught the scent of ermine and nosed it out. The creature was lying still, white on white, having given up its life to the winter. No doubt it had been on a desperate hunt for rabbits, who were wisely dying somewhere else—in the relative warmth of their burrows, while in the company of others. She made a swift meal of the small ermine, the meat giving her the energy she needed to make that long trek down through the edge of the *face* to the farm on the far side. She felt guilty, but there was little enough for one, let alone three. O-ha needed the strength to return.

Just as she finished her meal, the blizzard drifted away and the skies began to clear. So startling was the effect that two hunched, heavy-coated humans, walking their dogs, emerged from their collars and stared at the heavens. O-ha too was stunned at how quickly the blueness took over from the grey. It was as if the sky were covered in sheets and someone had pulled away the bottom one to reveal a complete contrast.

A few moments later, the sun came out and the shadows of the trees fell in black bars across the now glinting snow.

Familiar scene: black bars on white.

A chill went through her that had nothing to do with the cold.

O-ha's eyes took in the strange uniform pattern of the shadows: they played across her mind like a tune. She was mesmerized by them. The scene was quite familiar. The trees, the clear day, the white world, and the black shadows like bars . . . something ran through her mind, a dark shape tripping between the bars, in the sunlight, in the shadows, running fearful as if in a dream. Over and over played the tune, and she recognized the form. She knew it so well because she had seen it night after night in her restless sleep . . . running like a dream, through a dream, and it was *she* and she was the dream.

She looked around quickly, as a scent came to her from the direction of the parklands. There were two silhouettes there: a man in a heavy coat and hat, and a dog. The hound was tall and red in the light of the sun. His big-boned skull was full of brute strength.

Then the image blurred as she failed to focus on the still scene. It had been enough, that one glimpse, accompanied by the odor. O-ha knew who that couple was. *Sabre and his master*!

Had he seen her? She waited, crouched in the snow, her heart beating fast. She was aware of her own red coat against the white landscape. The figures were up-wind, but if the man had even mediocre eyesight he would see her. It was doubtful that he would encourage Sabre to chase her, but could he keep the hound back, if it caught its master's interest in a distant object?

Then the wind changed direction, and though it did not blow directly toward O-ha's enemy, it swirled around the trees, carrying her scent with it. Ransheen, she thought, you traitor!

She looked toward the man and the dog. The hound stood almost as high as the man's chest, and its head jerked up quickly and then swiveled, scanning the countryside. Then the head stopped moving.

"Fox!"

She heard Sabre shout, the word muffled by the snow.

Was it her? Had he seen *her*? Perhaps there was another fox? Better to freeze, remain still, just in case, just to be sure.

Sabre began pulling on the leash. The man jerked the dog's head back, snarling at him. The dog began straining, pulling his master toward the edge of the wood. He was heading straight for the spot where O-ha crouched. It *was* her he had seen.

She broke cover and began to run, wading through the belly-high snow. The dog, now sure of his quarry, began running too. The man was jerked off his feet, dragged for a while, his body cutting a furrow through the snow. Then the lead was released, a harsh scream of anger coming from the man's open red mouth. A hat went blowing away, across the field.

O-ha knew the situation was desperate. She was afraid, it was true, but not terror-stricken, the way she had been in her dream. She had a job to do, which was to escape. She went through the snow in a series of leaps, as if she were jumping hurdles. It was a slow business. The snow dragged her down, hindered any nimble progress. She could sense the long-legged hound gaining on her, relatively unhampered by the deep drifts. Where he could not remain clear he would force his way through. Sabre was well fed and immensely strong.

Once she reached the road, she ran, skidding a little on the hard-packed snow. A slow vehicle came toward her, shunting its way amid clouds of steam, in the same channel between walls of piled-up snow. She was not going to give way and at the last moment the driver saw her and swerved instinctively, burying the front of his car in a side drift.

She ran on, a quick glance behind her telling her that the dog was closing in.

He began the traditional taunting that hounds are so fond of doing during a chase.

"Skinny vixen! I'm going to break every bone in your body, suck out the marrow and spit it in your face. You'll live long enough to feel me cracking open your skull. I'll color the snow with your blood and brains."

A young human came around a corner, bent low against the wind, and Sabre struck him, sending the youth flying into the road. The boy went sliding along the ice, too shocked to scream. He struck his shoulder hard against the curbstone.

The glassy surface took the dog's legs away from him too, but he soon regained control and continued the chase, ignoring the shrieking of the human he had hurt.

The streets ended and the lane leading to the farm came in sight. Why she was running toward this place, O-ha had no idea. It just seemed right. It was the way it had happened in her dream. She knew that a head-to-head confrontation was going to take place soon.

It seemed likely that Sabre would catch her before she got through the gate. He was inches behind her now, his teeth snapping at her hind legs as he tried to bring her down.

She skipped sideways, but rolled over onto her back. The dog followed her movements, his savage jaws going for her now exposed belly. She waited for the pain of the strike.

"Gagggaaah!" The dog's head was pulled up short just a fraction from its target. She saw his legs go out from under him as if he'd been shot in mid-run. He crashed down heavily on his back. O-ha was up in a second and continued to run. Had he been shot? There had been no sound.

No. A quick glance behind her told her he was back on his feet. His flailing leash had caught on a post and had jerked him off his legs, but he was back up now and straining to move forward. The post cracked at the bottom, where it was undoubtedly rotten. Sabre dragged it along with him for several yards before the lead fell free of it.

O-ha had gained about twenty yards, but she knew the dog would soon recover this distance. Much of the snow had been cleared from around the farm and while she found it easier to run, so did Sabre.

"Thought you had me, eh?" he shouted. "Deathday is here. You have no hope of escape. Nothing will stop me from killing you now. Not walls, not people, nothing. I *will* kill. I'll kill anything and anyone who gets in the way."

She ran down the long driveway to the farmhouse, and past the whitewashed building, her breath laboring in her chest. There were sparrows on the snow. They scattered with cries of terror frozen in their throats as she ran between them. Sabre was very close again. One quick glance told her he would be on her within a few moments. He too was breathing heavily, his exhalations filling the air around his head with sprigs of steam. She could smell his scent now, the odor heavy in her nostrils. His great paws drummed on the snowpacked earth just a few yards behind her.

She ran between the barn and the house, thinking to head across open fields again. If they had been plowed up and left fallow, ready for spring planting, then the hard-edged furrows might slow the dog up. If there were a tree out there! But there were only low hedgerows.

There was a snapping at her heels and she half-twisted in her run, to bite back. Death was only a second away. He was almost on her. One more yard . . .

Something flashed between her and the hound and Sabre went tumbling, somersaulting onto his back. He had tripped over a taut chain, attached to a kennel. Blood came from deep jagged gashes on the big dog's forelegs. He screamed an oath. On the end of the chain was Breaker, the old foxhound. Breaker yelled something at O-ha and then threw himself on top of the ridgeback.

It was no match. Despite Sabre's agony, he was soon back on his feet. There was a very brief struggle, which gave O-ha a few more yards, before Breaker was thrown aside. The foxhound struck the side of his kennel and lay still. One of his legs was bent at a sharp angle.

"Stupid traitor!" screamed the ridgeback.

Sabre was immediately back on O-ha's trail again.

This time the dog was limping, though his wounds did not seem to slow him any. His determination was evident in his whole demeanor.

"Not this time," he was saying. "Not this time, fox. I will have your throat. I can taste it—taste it . . ."

She ran around behind the back of the barn, looking for a shed to climb. There was nothing suitable. All the buildings were too high. She ran inside the barn and in and out of the machinery, hoping Sabre might be skewered on one of the blades; but he stayed by the door, getting his breath back, knowing this was the only way out.

"I've got you, fox—the vixen that's given me so much trouble, all these seasons . . ."

She crouched behind a tractor.

"And you . . ." she gasped, gulping for air, "you've never let me or my family rest. You killed my firstborn litter. You hurt my cub . . ."

"Yes?"

"Yes. You bit off his tail."

"I did more than that, vixen. Give me credit. I'm told that the white one was yours, too—"

"A-sac?" Her heart turned over.

"I broke his neck. Snapped it like a twig."

"You—you're lying. The fox-spirit never came."

"I don't know about any spirits, but I know I killed that white thing you spawned. Went down hard. You'd have thought he was full of demons the way he fought. Said he had come looking for *me*. Went at me like a demented beast. Still got a scar on my neck. Said he'd been ordained by some god and was on a holy mission to destroy evil."

Yes, that was A-sac.

"And now you're going to kill me."

For an answer the hound began to move toward her. She waited until he was almost up to the tractor and then dashed around to the other side. He followed and his jaws clashed together, caught her ear, held on.

O-ha thrashed around, twisting, turning, trying to loosen the dog's hold on her ear. She clawed at his eyes with her back legs, scratching deep grooves in his snout. Still he held onto her. She could feel him trying to quell her frantic movements, trying to get a firmer grip on her head. If those jaws closed on her skull, she knew they would crush it instantly, as Sabre had so often promised. Her blood mingled with his.

Finally her ear tore away from her head and she found herself running again, out into the open. Her strength was all but gone now. The dog was still on her tail, despite his damaged legs, his wounded face. He would not be deterred.

She raced across the yard, toward the pond. She had some idea that if she could reach the railway she could lead him down the tracks and let a train hit him, squash him to pulp. It was a foolish plan and in her heart she knew how futile it was, but she had nothing else. The savage ridgeback would run her down long before she reached the railway and his brute strength would overwhelm the last vestiges of energy that kept her legs moving.

She was fading fast and the ridgeback would soon be on her. He tripped a couple of times, where the tractor had churned up the mud and it had frozen beneath the snow, but this was just a minor hindrance to the dog. He knew he had her now. She was staggering, dripping blood from her torn ear.

When she reached the pond, she was down to a tottering walk. The mist of imminent death had fallen over her eyes. She was numb from head to tail. No hunger pangs, no ghastly fear, no tortured heart—merely a regret that she had failed Camio. If she did not return to the earth with food, he would surely die too. Sabre had managed to destroy both of them just as he had always promised he would.

She staggered onto the ice, aware that her walk was as unsteady as that of a poisoned rat. Sabre followed, sure of his quarry.

This was the final confrontation.

The ridgeback cried, "At *last*—"

Then she heard the *crack* of the ice breaking.

She turned, instinctively glancing back, and saw him go through.

The huge dog disappeared into a jagged hole, the black water sucking him down. For a few moments there was just a swirling. Then his head came up and his forelegs found the edge of the ice. They began scratching and scraping, trying to find a purchase. Another plate of ice broke away and the demonic hound flailed forward, his head still above the water that must have been freezing his muscles to a standstill. There was a determined look in his eyes as he found the edge with his forepaws yet again.

Suddenly O-ha came to her senses. Sabre was getting closer! His front legs were snapping a path through the frozen water, forcing a channel through the ice. She began to run, but her movements were frantic and her claws skidded on the slippery surface. She fell over, several times. Her heart was on the point of bursting. She kept regaining her feet, only to lose them again. They skittered and scrabbled on the ice as she worked them in her frenzied desire to escape, getting nowhere, racing on the spot.

"Fox . . ." grunted the dog, his face rigid.

Snap, snap, snap, the ice cracked and split under the hound's weight. His eyes were glazed now, fixed on her. The jaws were open, ready to spring shut. His whole body looked stiff, as if the blood were already frozen to red ice in his veins. The big-boned head came toward her, slowly, determinedly. The front legs broke away at the sheets of ice.

Still her claws would not grip. They skidded and slid, her legs whipping away uselessly beneath her.

He was close. His breath on her rump.

"*Now!*"

She felt the teeth on her rear, gripping her haunch firmly. There was only a vestige of strength in them. She turned her head to see the triumph in his eyes, a final burning from within, as Sabre began slipping under the deadly water. He was pulling her with him, determined that they should drown together.

One of her legs entered the water, froze. It roused her to anger.

"NO!" she shouted.

She wrenched herself free from those clamped jaws, now frozen solid, leaving rump fur behind. Sabre's body went down alone.

O-ha lay on the edge of the hole, panting. Even at the last, as his head sank out of sight, Sabre's eyes were still on hers, full of cold hatred.

She waited a long time, hardly daring to believe what had happened. Her heart was still thumping in her breast. Her legs were still taut, ready to run, in case the hound emerged roaring from that black hole and fell on her like the devil he was.

Nothing happened.

When she eventually gathered enough strength and courage to investigate she went as close to the hole as she dared. His body was floating gently under the ice. It was some yards from the hole. She could still see the eyes, the *dead* eyes, staring up at her. They had lost their look of hatred. Then the body rolled over, slowly, and she caught a last glimpse of the dark ridge of hair running down its back before it sank out of sight.

She walked back, around the barn, to where Breaker lay. He lifted his head as she approached.

"He's dead," she said simply.

Breaker coughed. "So am I, I think."

"Thank you—Breaker."

"How did he die? You tear his throat out?"

"Me? No, he fell through the ice. He drowned."

Breaker coughed again, then said, "Serve him right. Arrogant swine. You'd better get out of here, vixen. . . ."

"But you're bleeding."

His left flank was seeping blood.

"Someone will come out of the farmhouse soon. They'll find me, and then it'll just be a visit to the vet—"

It looked like a death wound to her.

"Goodbye, Breaker. We were enemies once. . . ."

"We still are," he gasped. "I just repaid a favor. Now get out of here, you red devil, before I break your back."

"Oh Breaker, you poor proud old dog. Don't you know you've made friends with the very creatures you profess to hate? It happens, you know. It's not your fault that a fox has grown to like you, or that you saved a fox's life and she's indebted to you."

"You're right," he murmured, "about me being old. Fifty-six seasons have passed. Fifty-six. And now I'm tired. I want to close my eyes and die in peace.

And he did. His eyes closed. And he was dead.

She left him then, turning the snow red, and went out into the fields. There she found some rotting turnips. She ate her fill, then took one in her teeth, carrying it on the long journey back to her earth. When she got there she found that Mitz had been out, during the sunshine period after the storm. A kitchen door had been open and she ran in and snatched some bacon. Mitz was good at that: better than her mother. Mitz had been in houses, knew that kind of fear and how to cope with it in an emergency.

Camio looked as if he were recovering already.

He coughed. "You brought a turnip—well done," he said. "Any trouble out there?"

"No," she lied, snuggling up next to his warm, furry body. "It's a white, peaceful world, with hardly anyone out."

Mitz cried, "O-ha! Your ear!"

Camio rolled over, looked up.

"Oh, that? A little tussle with an ermine."

"But your ear . . ."

"Be quiet, Mitz," said O-ha. "Camio's not well."

Mitz did as she was told.

That storm was the worst of the winter. Once it had blown itself out, they were well on their way to Scresheen. There were no cubs to look forward to this time, but it gave O-ha time to appreciate the change in the seasons without being preoccupied. It was a good time.

THIRTY-THREE

O-ha's wound healed. She was of too advanced an age for other foxes to give her some silly nickname, like "one-ear," but she found herself cocking her head to the side in order to listen to the world. Camio, fully recovered, said it made her look endearing.

That winter had aged both foxes. O-ha and Camio discovered in themselves certain small weaknesses that had not been there before. Nothing that was serious. Nothing that would impair their skills as hunters, or cause them to come to grief. Still, they recognized that the flush of youth had gone from them. They were no longer regarded as a young pair. They were mature foxes who knew the tricks, who knew the old ways and the new.

Camio learned of Sabre's death, but said nothing to O-ha. He guessed she wanted it out of her head forever. They had many long talks about the past, but it concerned the good times they had shared, not the terrors. There were still plenty of those around, even with the giant hound gone to the Unplace.

Season drifted into season and the town expanded. O-ha and Camio had two more litters: some of the cubs survived, some did not. Those that did grow to adulthood had their own litters, which dispersed and carried the blood of the original pair into new regions.

O-ha and Camio remained on the embankment of the railway, changing their earth at the appropriate times. The days of harassment were over for the old pair and they came to know the kind of contentment that is rare but golden. They had their sad memories too.

Mitz lived close by and they saw her occasionally. She had found a mate and had her own cubs whom the older pair recognized from their markings; but were not themselves known to the cubs. They were town foxes, of course, and their education had been appropriate to their environment. Knowledge of the ancient highways and waterholes, passed on to O-ha through many generations, had no significance to the new foxes: the land had changed its surface, and they were foxes of the *face*. There were new maps in the minds of new foxes and the world was a different place—no better or worse than when O-ha was a cub, just different. She did not necessarily like the changes, of course, because she had pleasant pictures in her head of the times when she was a cub herself, chasing the butterflies over the *hav* and wrestling with her brothers and sisters in the tall grasses of the slopes below Trinity Wood.

A-salla sent word from time to time, the news easy to verify since all they had to ask was, "Did this fox have anything unusual about him?" and wait for the reply, "Yes, he had no tail."

The time was Ransheen and the cold hard streets were thick

with snow and ice. O-ha remembered when she had first encountered snow. She had been with A-ho then and had been halfway through the leaving-the-earth ritual, her nose poking outside, when something fluffy and cold had landed on the tip. She had jerked her head inside, only to find a droplet of water where the white spider had landed. Then she had remembered what her mother had told her about the winter white, and gathering her courage together, she went outside. She had been astounded at the change in the world. The whole landscape was covered in a blinding, soft fur. Each footstep she took was an adventure, and all ways were hidden beneath the albino coat that had descended from the sky.

There was no magic in snow now, of course. It was merely a nuisance, since it hid any *gubbins* on the roads, or food that had been tossed away by humans the night before.

"Did you ever have snow where you came from?" she asked Camio one day, as she was braving herself to leave the earth. A train rumbled by below them, making the earth vibrate a little. She had grown so used to the giant metal snakes that she would be lost without them now. There was a certain comfort, a security to be had in the regular passing by of trains. The noise was reassuring somehow, as if it meant that the world was still working properly.

"Snow? If we did, I don't remember it. But then it seems seasons out of time since I was in that land. Things get a little fuzzy. I don't think my life began until I met you."

She did not know whether or not he was saying this to please her, but she liked it. She knew she was very special to him: that she was his vixen; but she also knew that he had memories of another fox, as she did of A-ho. If they were warm memories, then so much the better, but the fact that he did not parade them before her proved him a caring old dog fox who spared her comparisons that meant nothing anyway.

"I think I'll go out soon," she said.

She was feeling peculiar. A little tired. She suddenly had the urge to go up to Trinity Parklands and see if Gar was still around. She would like to have seen Gar one last time, before either of them . . . before something happened. Just a little weariness in her bones, that was all. It would pass off, once she started walking.

"I might go to the top of town," she said. "I want to see the trees."

"As you wish. I think I'll rest a little longer. My leg is worse today." He had trapped his paw in a drain a few seasons previously, and on wrenching it out, had dislocated a bone. The dislocation had clicked back into place, but it had left some torn ligaments inside which had never completely healed.

O-ha carried out the rituals and then walked swiftly to the top of the embankment, under the fence, and onto the path. Ransheen swirled top-snow around her. It really was bitterly cold, with a sheet of ice under the snow. Most of the humans remained within their houses and the streets were almost empty. A dog passed by on the other side, giving her only the slightest of glances. Most of the town dogs were now used to foxes—it was only the excitable breeds like setters or boxers that bothered to chase them. They never caught her, of course. In the *face* there were many places to hide, many fences and walls to leap which could not be jumped by dogs. They would not know what to do with her if they caught her anyway. She had given more than one dog a nipped ear or nose. Gone were those terrible days of pack hounds and thundering hooves.

As she walked along the street, close to the redbrick walls, the sun came out and icicles hanging from the eves of the houses began to sparkle with frostfire—

—and then,
        strangely,
            they began
                to
        jingle.

She stopped and listened as the sound tinkled along the gutters, increasing in volume, until the whole *face* was alive with their music. It was as if Ransheen were running her fingers along the lines of ice

cones, sounding their individual notes for O-ha's benefit. She
wondered what it meant.

Then,
>   just as suddenly,
>   the music
>   stopped.

She stood there, by the window of a shop that was just a sheen
of light, bemused by the experience. She could not have been more
surprised had the world suddenly tilted and turned on its edge. The
dog she had passed went around a corner without pausing in his
stride. Clearly he had not heard the phenomenon. Thus, she
deduced, it had to be a mystical happening, relevant perhaps only to
herself.

A kestrel dropped from a building, stooping low over her path.
Then it rose toward the sun, to spiral upward and out of sight.

She crossed an empty cobbled square and pigeons rose in a flock,
scattering before her.

Strange that there were no humans abroad.

The tired feeling she had had on waking that morning increased
in intensity, until her eyelids drooped and her step began to falter.
There was a pain in her breast now, like a dull ache, which seemed
both near and far to her. She tried to reach the pain with her mind,
but it was elusive. She thought it had something to say to her, if only
she could make contact with it.

The sparrows that normally decorated the pavements suddenly
disappeared. She looked about her, alarmed, to see if they had taken
to the air. There was no noise, no sound now. Even Ransheen had
stopped screaming at the corners. Everywhere, there was a deathly
stillness, a silence that hurt her ears. The street before her had
opened up into a wide avenue, with snow-covered trees and tall
houses on either side. The avenue seemed to dip at the far end and
then slope upward, disappearing into the grey clouds. She felt
terribly cold.

She stopped and lay down full length in the snow. It melted

beneath her and the thaw miraculously spread, moving outward from her body. As the snow disappeared from the *face*, so the warmth returned to her body and the pain began to disappear. Soon the world was a summer place and she felt no reason to move.

She waited, patiently.

She waited, and time passed without passing. She waited through moments that no longer followed, but overlaid each other. She waited for a long time that was not time at all.

While she lay there in her warmth, the streets melted like the snow and the buildings dribbled away to nothing. Grasslands replaced the concrete. Coverts of blackthorn sprang up around her. The land became full and sweet-smelling.

She was at the head of a wide valley that she had never seen before, but that was familiar to her. In the distance there was movement. A fox came through the bracken: a fox with a pure white flame hovering over its head. It walked toward her slowly.

When the fox-spirit reached her it told her to rise up onto her feet and follow it down the valley.

"What is it?" she asked. "Who is it? Has Camio died? Are you taking me to his body, so that I can send him to you?"

"I am not the fox who leads the living to the dead. I am the fox who leads the dead to the Perfect There." There was a pause, then. "Your living mate has been here. He found you in the snow. He has done what you would have wished him to do."

"Oh," she said, realizing now what had happened. "He gave me my last rites."

"Yes."

She began to follow the fox-spirit down the long valley, thinking, the Perfect *There*? But of course, since she had now crossed over.

"Would it," she asked, looking into the vacant eyes of her guide, "have made any difference if no one had found my body?"

"You might have had to wait longer, that is all. I would have had to search for you, over the timeless wastes between life and death, but I would have found you, eventually."

O-ha was surprised rather than annoyed.

"So all the rituals—they weren't of any real use?"

The fox-spirit replied, "They were of use to *you*."

She acknowledged this.

"That's true. I needed them, once."

Finally they came to Trinity Wood, with all its old scents and sounds, all its old highways and paths, its soaks and waterholes. Down at the end of the valley, shining like polished redwood, stood a tall, wide structure made of hollow tree-trunks. It was magnificent. The trunks were of varying girths and heights and were joined together to form a concave wall that spanned the whole width of the valley. In each trunk was a series of holes, all of different sizes, and from these orifices came the notes of many winds and breezes. The giant pipes were blowing now.

"The Palace of the Winds," explained the fox-spirit.

"So that's where *Heff* is—and so close to my covert. It's very beautiful. I wonder why I never saw it before?"

"Because you weren't looking for it."

At that moment Gar came out of the trees, ambling down to meet her. She gave a shout of delight.

"I was coming to see you," she said, "and here you are."

"Oh, ya. Here I am, here I am," he rumbled.

"But," she said, confused, "why are you here? With the foxes?"

"I am here and I am somewhere else," he said. "You are here, and you are somewhere else. What place must the soul stay? No one place. It is everywhere. I knew it all along. I spoke about this thing. Here you are and here am I. So, and others . . ."

And the others came out of the covert to meet her, among them the ones she had most hoped to see.

Camio went sadly back to the earth after carrying out the ritual for the dead around the body of his O-ha. He had been a skeptic for most of his life, in regard to life after death, but now he had seen a creature with a flame over its head and things were not the same. More importantly, he now found it impossible to believe that he would never find O-ha again. Her scent was still strong in his nostrils, and he knew that it would linger there for the rest of his life.

They had done so much together. They had a history that went back so many seasons. Surely that couldn't be wiped out by something so negative as *not life*? The flesh had gone cold and still, but the rest still existed, somewhere.

So perhaps he could believe that she was in the place she called the Perfect Here? If that was so, A-ho, her former mate, would be there to greet her. Camio wondered if he ought to feel jealous, but he could only be glad that she would not be lonely in the valley of death. He and A-ho might even like each other. Camio could not imagine that such necessary but worldly feelings as jealousy still survived in the spirit pure.

Later that day he went to find his daughter Mitz's earth on another section of the embankment, and called to her from outside so that the other occupants would not feel he was invading the family home.

Mitz came out and said, "Camio?"

"I thought you ought to know—your mother is dead."

Mitz stood there for a while, and then nodded.

"You'd better go back, Camio. Get out of the snow. It's a very cold day."

"I hadn't noticed," he said. "I suppose you're right."

He started to walk away when she called, "Father!"

He turned. Foxes seldom used titles for each other and Mitz had called him Camio for as long as she had been his cub.

"Yes?"

"I'll miss her too, you know. You're not alone in the way that you feel. She's gone to a good place."

"I hope so," he said. "I keep telling myself the same thing."

He left her then. She was too much like her mother and it hurt him to look at her. Walking along the embankment, he wondered how he was going to spend the hours. He glanced up at the white, swirling skies, not finding an answer.

When he entered the earth—*their* earth—he was amazed at how large and empty it appeared to be. He wondered about that. When she was alive it had seemed there was hardly room to move in there without touching each other. Now, every sound he made echoed in the stillness. He would surely have to move, make himself a new home. Someplace smaller, where he could closet his memories.

Mitz was wrong, of course. He *was* alone in his feelings. Mitz would miss a mother, but the seasons would still turn for his daughter.

As far as Camio was concerned, O-ha had taken the seasons with her.

DATE DUE